NEBULA AWARDS SHOWCASE 56

OUTSTANDING SCIENCE FICTION AND FANTASY

SCIENCE FICTION & FANTASY WRITERS ASSOCIATION

INTRODUCTION BY

CAT RAMBO

NEBULA AWARDS SHOWCASE 56:
Outstanding Science Fiction and Fantasy

Collection copyright © 2024 by
Science Fiction & Fantasy Writers of America, Inc.
d/b/a Science Fiction & Fantasy Writers Association

The rights to individual pieces featured in this book remain with their respective authors

Cover illustration "Star Deity" by Lauren Raye Snow

Cover design by Kate Baker
Interior layout by Noah K. Sturdevant

Editorial and production assistance by Monica Louzon, Noah K. Sturdevant, Gwen Whiting, and Stephen Kotowych

Original works in this collection include:
"Cerberus is the Family Dog: Adapting Greek Myth in Hades" by Greg Kasavin, copyright © 2024 by Greg Kasavin

"The Good Place: Life, Death, and the Meaning of Everything" by Kelly Robson, copyright © 2024 by Kelly Robson

"Introduction" by Cat Rambo, copyright © 2024 by Cat Rambo

A complete list of copyright information for works reprinted in this collection can be found at the end of the book

San Lorenzo, California, United States
ISBN 978-1-958243-00-8 (print)
ISBN 978-1-958243-01-5 (ebook)

TABLE OF CONTENTS

INTRODUCTION

BY CAT RAMBO

M oments from past Nebulas:

It's early in the 21st century and I've gone to my first Nebula weekend because my short story is on the ballot. It's not a very large group. I'm part of what I can call, at best, a desultory programming track and I'm paired with another writer on a panel about writer's block. I don't think anyone in the room got a lot out of the experience. There's a banquet and the awards are handed out. As a newer member of SFWA, I go away fairly unimpressed by the whole thing.

It's 2015 and I'm SFWA Vice President, at the 50th anniversary of the Nebulas in the Palmer House in Chicago. The programming's gotten significantly more interesting, and I've gained a MUCH greater appreciation for how much work goes into the weekend and the challenge of coordinating it all.

It's there that Kate Baker, SFWA's Executive Director, pitches me an idea. The conference, she says, could be the premiere event for science fiction and fantasy writers, rich with programs of use to working writers. How can I do anything but say *yes, how can I help you make that a thing*, knowing already that I was planning on running for SFWA President.

It's 2017 and the Nebulas Awards are in Philadelphia. Peter Beagle's the newest SFWA Grand Master and delighting everyone with his charming presence. He sings us a lullaby at the reception honoring the award nominees. And the programming is everything that Kate promised it would be, brought to life by a small team of staff and dozens of volunteers, including a rich and verified programming track aimed at working writers, a mentorship program designed to make new attendees feel part of things as quickly and smoothly as possible, and even an awards ceremony that includes a synchronized dance to a SFWA theme song created by Henry Lien. Our speaker at the award ceremony is astronaut Kjell Lindgren, who is utterly charming, and tells us all the gross details of life in space.

It's 2020 and the pandemic has canceled everything. Under the able administration of then-President Mary Robinette Kowal, staff, and volunteers, the Nebulas are one of the first conferences to react to the inevitable by going virtual and in doing so, deliver the gold standard of what the virtual experience could be like.

It's an odd moment for me, sitting in my study in West Seattle, and when I win a Nebula for my novelette "Carpe Glitter", I end up pitching out my acceptance speech at the last moment and instead speak to the turmoil going on right then with the death of George Floyd, and what the responsibility of the writer in such times must entail. Hint: to bear witness and speak truth, even when we're doing it with intelligent spaceships or talking centaurs.

It's 2023 and the world has gotten weirder rather than saner. In the midst of that, I'm asked to write the foreword to the book you hold now (perhaps on your e-reader). It's a welcome chance to reflect on the importance of these awards.

———

The Nebula Awards have been around since the beginnings of the organization that bestows them, the Science Fiction and Fantasy Writers Association (SFWA, Inc.). They started in a somewhat scattershot approach in 1966, giving awards for work produced in 1965. At that time the only categories were short story, novelette, novella, and novel, but since then the list has added the Ray Bradbury Nebula Award for Outstanding Dramatic Presentation, Andre Norton Nebula Award for Middle Grade and Young Adult Fiction, and a Nebula Award for Game Writing. The ceremony also includes the presentation of the Kate Wilhelm Solstice Award, the Kevin O'Donnell, Jr. Service to SFWA Award, the enshrinement of a new Damon Knight Grand Master, and now the Infinity Award, whose first winner was one of science fiction's most mourned greats, Octavia E. Butler.

The idea of the showcase anthology has always been central to the awards, which actually were proposed by then SFWA secretary, Lloyd Biggle Jr., as a fundraising measure. The process of choosing the best works of the preceding year eventually became the Nebula Awards themselves, but the anthology is still here. The editor changes from year to year, but the contents remain a representative sampling of some of science fiction and fantasy's highest caliber writing.

While the group started as a handful of traditionally published writers wanting to help fellow writers, the organization has changed in recent decades, now encompassing independently as well as traditionally published writers, comics writers, games writers, and most recently translators and poets, all working in fantasy, science fiction, and related genres. With its growth comes a greater prominence for the awards, and a greater realization on the part of the public that these genres offer some of the best and most thoughtful writing of today.

There are plenty of notable awards in the industry, including the Hugos, the Dragon Awards, the World Fantasy Awards, the Locus Awards, the Philip K. Dick Awards, and on and on. But the Nebulas are chosen by a group with a great deal to say about the current speculative fiction landscape, which is to say—the writers themselves. While there's often overlap in award lists, the Nebulas generally tend towards a focus on the writing, while others may be more influenced by popularity among readers.

Like most cultural institutions, fantasy and science fiction have been drawn into the culture wars playing out across the globe, and certainly writers working in these genres continue to write from both sides of that divide. But the Nebulas—like most modern art—tend to skew towards the more progressive side of things, celebrating diversity and working to encourage the efforts of all speculative fiction writers, rather than a privileged handful.

This year marks several events with a decided implant on the field. Short stories were given a hard blow when Amazon discontinued its subscription service for such excellent publications such as *Clarkesworld Magazine, Uncanny Magazine,* and the *Magazine of Fantasy and Science Fiction,* all of whom are represented in the 2022 Award ballot. If you love short stories, I hope you'll consider taking out a subscription to such a magazine. AI writing also emerged, and there was plenty of reaction from writers. SFWA has compiled a page of statements from writers about AI writing and it's a good view at some of the mixed reactions and turmoil.

And finally, when the Writers Guild of America went on strike along with SAG-AFTRA, writers saw the power of soli darity—something SFWA has always supported and worked towards—and continues to do so.

What comes next is always the question. I look forward to next year's ballot, because I know it will, like this volume, be some of the finest writing that contemporary speculative fiction has to offer its readers, writing that engages with and challenges the world producing it.

PART ONE
ESSAY

CERBERUS IS THE FAMILY DOG: ADAPTING GREEK MYTH IN HADES

NEBULA WINNER: BEST GAME WRITING

BY GREG KASAVIN

When it comes to writing fiction, deep down, there's still a part of me that thinks the act of adaptation is somehow inherently less artful, less adventurous, and less creative than the act of pure invention. All other things being equal, an original work must have more inherent value than a derivative work, because one hasn't been done before and the other has... right?

Wrong; I keep telling this part of me to shut up. Rather, I politely suggest to this part of me that all fiction, in essence, can be seen as adaptation. All our ideas, including the original ones, are synthesized from our conscious and subconscious and other sources of inspiration. In other words, as fiction writers, we mash things up. What we commonly think of as adapted works mainly differ from wholly original works insofar as they openly acknowledge those influences. Adaptation is almost like a more-specific form of genre writing, because as the author, you're working with a known subject matter and a certain set of expectations, while trying to create something distinctive within the constraints they impose. A well-crafted adaptation not only can be a great work of fiction in its own right, but it can also give new meaning and context to whatever is being adapted, and any other stories based on that subject.

One of my favorite examples of this is the Studio Ghibli

animated film *Howl's Moving Castle*, adapted from the whimsical fantasy novel by Diana Wynne Jones. While the film's basis in the book is unmistakable, the two are wonderfully different, and my experience of each is improved by my familiarity with both. Is the original novel superior to the animated film it inspired? I never could decide, and don't have to; I appreciate both as individual works and even more so together. Their differences are not inconsistencies, but rather strengths of their respective visions and media formats.

I came to realize all this while working on an adaptation of Greek mythology, a video game called *Hades*, which earned more recognition than my colleagues and I ever imagined after its debut in 2020. As we were getting started, I remember pitching my colleagues on a variety of different themes that could fit the kind of game we wanted to make and feeling excited and surprised when the Greek myth theme resonated most of all. I had been working with these folks for more than ten years in some cases but never knew before then that we shared a common interest there. But after the initial excitement came the fear, and for me, I can't have one without the other.

Having written original stories for the three previous games from our studio, I couldn't shake two big questions as we were considering the idea of *Hades*: First, just how much harder would it be to write an adaptation, having to draw heavily from a real set of sources rather than doing what I'm comfortable with and just making stuff up? And second, was I so arrogant—so filled with that classic Greek *hubris*—as to think I had a worthwhile perspective to offer about Greek mythology, which has inspired countless stories and adaptations now for thousands of years? It was an intimidating proposition to consider, even as that voice in my head kept instilling doubt. Surely an adapted work would feel like a step backwards from the original stories I'd written! But then, I thought of *Howl's Moving Castle*, and decided that if adaptation isn't beneath the legendary Studio Ghibli, then certainly it isn't beneath me.

Telling stories about real-world gods requires either arrogance or penitence, maybe both. I set about answering my big questions directly:

Just how much harder would it be to write an adaptation?

I had a lifelong interest in Greek myth from my earliest memories and studied it more intensively at various times in my life. So, I felt I had a good basis of knowledge to start from and could learn as I went along. And I knew enough about Greek myth to know that many works adapted from Greek myth take very significant liberties with the classical source material. I felt that I could be at least as true to the source material as that.

Truer, even! What I really wanted was to write a story that drew inspiration directly from ancient works by Homer and Hesiod and others, in which the Olympians and other gods and heroes are for the most part all deeply flawed and complicated. I have given a lot of thought to the question of why Greek myth is still compelling to us after thousands of years, and it boils down to this: All those gods are fascinating to us not because of their godhood, but because of their humanity. As gods, they are nevertheless imperfect beings prone to acting on impulses and making mistakes. It's as if Greek myth as a collective whole is there to say, if even the gods can't be perfect, what hope do any of us mortals have?

This, I realized, was the basis for my answer to the second big question.

Was I so arrogant to think I had a perspective about Greek mythology worth sharing?

If you're familiar with the game *Hades*, you know it's the story of Zagreus, the son of Hades, who's decided to run away from home after a blow-out fight with his stern and fearsome father. The problem is, "home" for Zagreus is at the bottom of the Greek underworld, the place everyone ends up after they die, and a place known to be inescapable. So, Zagreus starts trying to fight his way out, and every time he fails, he ends up back at home, only to get berated by his dad once more for his foolishness. But as Zagreus' Sisyphean journey unfolds, he gets to really know the many colorful gods, ghosts, and monsters of Greek myth in and around the underworld, and it ends up as a coming-of-age story of sorts, with more of a lighthearted tone than one might initially expect.

What really crystallized the tone and concept was the idea of Cerberus, the vicious three-headed hound of hell. Cerberus is virtually always portrayed as a savage monster, but in classical mythology, he is also the pet dog of the Hades household. Knowing Hades resides in a place literally called the 'House of Hades', has a three-headed dog, and apparently a son nobody knows anything about, we felt we were onto something at that point. Telling a family comedy/drama but with gods instead of everyday people, and specifically through the perspective of the inhabitants of the Greek underworld, grew into a clear and exciting idea for me and my colleagues. A perspective worth sharing.

Hades didn't start there, though. Before it was the story of Zagreus, our game was going to be a re-telling of the story of Theseus and the Minotaur. . . of how this famous Greek hero faced his monstrous adversary in an unnavigable labyrinth, and whose tale has since been told and retold countless times. The myth of Theseus felt like the perfect fit given that we were making a so-called "roguelike" game, a genre defined by its randomized structure and relatively high level of challenge, making for short-but-surprising play sessions that are excitingly different from one to the next. What better setting for such a game than the Minotaur's Labyrinth, we thought? The Olympian gods themselves could lend you their powers as you proceeded. On paper, it sounded perfect.

But in practice, we ran into issues adapting the source material. Even as I was digging deeper and deeper into various retellings of the Theseus myth, and its many contradictions and questions, I found that these were compelling to me for the kinds of reasons Greek myth has always interested me. Our approach was to make each play session its own uniquely narrated retelling of the Minotaur myth, speaking to the meta-structure of mythology as a collection of different tales, including adaptations of the same tale.

The problem we ran into was that, in practice, all of this was more abstract than we wanted our game to be. Our Theseus, for example, was a blank slate who we had trouble visualizing, since he doesn't have any immediately identifying features or characteristics like other famous characters from Greek myth. What we were doing appealed to me and my lifelong interest in Greek myth, but for someone with no inherent interest in the subject matter, this path felt likely to leave our intended audience cold. This realization forced us to confront an existential question looming over any adapted work; is it meant to 'preach to the choir' and appeal only to those already interested in the subject matter? Or is it not meant to be so constrained in its audience and appeal?

I think it's a worthwhile exercise for authors to ask themselves who they think their work is for. It's better, I think, to consciously and honestly be uncertain of the answer than never to give the question any thought. In our case, we had worked on several games, each of which, by my estimation, was more esoteric than the one before it. Each asked a little more of the audience right up front, and each had a more layered and complicated narrative than the one before it. But this was our trend, rather than our conscious goal. Our goal was always to make games that just about anyone could play and enjoy. Our narratives and game structures were not meant to create barriers to that.

So, when it came to adapting Greek mythology, we firmly decided that no prior knowledge or interest in Greek mythology should be necessary or expected. Sure, we figured almost everyone who played would have at least heard of the 'household name' characters of Greek myth, such as Zeus, Hades, and Athena. But the game's theme and story would have to deal in something more universal than the question of 'why are myths told and retold in different ways', an academically interesting question but not something most of us can connect with on an emotional level. On the other hand, my colleagues and I could immediately relate to a story about a complicated family dispute. Over the years we would often compare notes on our complicated family situations, our relationships with our parents and siblings, our immigrant roots, and so on.

That was the key. We started development of *Hades* in October 2017. In my research into the Labyrinth, I discovered some connections between it and the underworld, which led me to Hades, which led me to Zagreus. . . a god I'd never heard of before, so I immediately wondered why so little is known of him.

On our first day back from the holidays in January 2018, I suggested to my colleagues the following change: What if instead of making a game about Theseus navigating the Labyrinth and eventually ending up in the underworld, we instead made a game about this unknown son of Hades called Zagreus, who would start in the underworld and try to make his way out, to the surface? My colleagues all connected with the idea right away, and our art director Jen Zee's first immediate idea of what Zagreus could look like was instantly appealing to us and very close to how he ended up. When ideas flow freely and excitement is high, you know you're onto something.

I used to be an editor and think the act of adaptation and the act of editing have very similar goals: You're trying to bring out the essence of something. You do this by sharpening the sharp bits, and removing the unnecessary bits, the things that needlessly distract or work against the main strengths or theme. You try and focus on what's there, and make it as internally consistent as befits the nature of the work. When it comes to adapting Greek myth. . . let me tell you, there's a *lot* of material to consider leaving out. The source material is filled with abhorrent imagery that's even more vile and shocking today as it must have been 3,000 years ago. We wanted to be true to the spirit of the classics, but could we really do so by leaving out the most provocative aspects of them?

It all depends on what you consider provocative, we decided. Greek mythology is so expansive that all the sex and violence, we felt, was only one dimension of it, but certainly not the main point or at the heart of what made the subject matter compelling. We had already identified that other thing: the complicated characters, and dysfunctional-yet-oddly-relatable family dynamics between the gods. Those dynamics sometimes play out in explosive and horrifying ways. But when I first fell in love with Greek myth as a little kid, it wasn't through those kinds of stories.

Given our desire to create a family comedy/drama where the gods felt more like everyday people (since that's what they are from their own perspective), we felt there was no place for the more-shocking aspects of Greek myth in our adaptation. I am sure there could have been a very interesting version of the *Hades* story that leaned more heavily into those aspects, resulting in a tone and atmosphere much closer to something like *Game of Thrones*. But we weren't interested in telling a story steeped in darkness and suffering and felt part of what could be pleasantly welcome and unexpected about *Hades* was in how it could subvert that sort of expectation.

If you think you know who your audience may be, then you may have a sense of their expectations. And then you may play with those expectations, satisfying them when you want to, or subverting them when you think it's best. Stories that subvert my expectations are often the ones that leave the biggest impact on me personally, and as a writer, I love the interactive experience of anticipating my readers' expectations and trying to satisfy them in unexpected ways.

In *Hades*, we attempted this with the entire basis of the story and in many of the characterizations as well. It starts with Hades himself, someone often cast as the villain in adapted works, yet in the classical mythology he's one of the most principled and hardest working of the gods. Knowing there exists this idea in the collective consciousness that Hades is a bad guy and possibly evil, we frame him as our antagonist complete with a sinister appearance and everything, but then proceed to complicate him from there in ways that are true to the classical source material, yet end up feeling like a relatively fresh perspective on the character today.

I'm the immigrant son of hard-working parents who sometimes let the stresses of their careers and their parental responsibilities to me and my older brother get the better of them. I love them very much, and know they have regrets, as do we all. My close colleagues have their own similar circumstances despite having completely different backgrounds than mine, so we found a common ground here in wanting to tell this type of story. Hades himself was chosen by the Fates to rule over the underworld, so I came to see his story as an immigrant's story, with his son Zagreus as a first-generation god caught between the underworld's culture and that of his Olympian relatives. With family, things can be messy and complicated, and Greek myth captures the full breadth of that experience. We decided to try and capture just a small, specific slice of it, and in so doing, to try and bring some of the lesser-known names from Greek myth to light.

They say to write what you know; none of us know what it's like to be gods, but we know what it's like to be human.

THE GOOD PLACE: LIFE, DEATH, AND THE MEANING OF EVERYTHING

THE RAY BRADBURY NEBULA AWARD FOR OUTSTANDING DRAMATIC PRESENTATION

BY KELLY ROBSON

A t some point earlier or later in life, everyone comes to the essential realization that all humans are utterly intolerable. We don't often admit it. It's too bleak, so we frost the truth with exceptions, saying that though most people are horrible, the people we love aren't, and the people we lust after certainly aren't, but that's just a sugar coating over the awful truth.

Whenever we think we find someone who's an exception to this rule, we simply don't know them well enough yet. Everyone without exception is deeply, horribly flawed, psychologically twisted, and if not broken, impossibly tangled up in themselves. Including, and especially, ourselves.

I'm feeling this especially keenly at this moment, just a few weeks after the death of my wife's mother. Mother-in-law jokes aside, she was not a good person, and in fact was bad enough that honestly nobody should be grieving her loss very much right now, but we are, and intensely. Why? We can look to *The Good Place* for an answer.

The Good Place ran on the US network NBC from September 2016 to January 2020, ending, ironically, just before the world-wide convulsion of the pandemic lockdowns. *The Good Place* presents us with four intolerable individuals—a toxic individualist, a neurotic overthinker, a jealous status-monger, and a dim mayfly—as they navigate the afterlife, where they overtly and explicitly pursue the answers to life's ultimate questions: How can I become a better person and reduce my suffering? What does it take to be a good person, anyway? Why do I hate the people I love? And how can any of us possibly live together without killing each other?

Good questions. Important questions, best discussed with friends over a bottle of scotch, on an evening ending in tears. Not the kind of questions you expect to see explored in a network situation comedy. By definition, a sitcom episode throws family or found family into a manufactured situation and watches them battle their way out of it for twenty-two minutes, before providing a narratively satisfying conclusion. *The Good Place* is a situation comedy, most definitely, putting the characters through a variety of kooky situations (many of them involving shrimp), but that's not all it is. It's also, I'd argue, a condition comedy. As in the human condition. And no other TV show has ever explored the human condition as directly and overtly as *The Good Place*.

Sure, plenty of TV shows have successfully examined the human condition. Probably the most famous one is the long-lived 1970s sitcom *M*A*S*H*, where a found family of Americans battle Catch-22-style absurdity as they try to live through the Korean War. *M*A*S*H* is a good show, rightly venerated, but *The Good Place* examines the human condition far, far deeper than *M*A*S*H* does, and in far fewer episodes. How does *The Good Place* do it? Through the stupendous narrative power of fantasy.

Fantasy is the most powerful storytelling tool there is. Most often, fantasy is a tool for applying concrete metaphors to narrative problems—for example, the One Ring as a metaphor for the way power destroys the soul—but that's just one of the many ways fantasy can work. Fantasy can also, with great effectiveness, let us take characters out of consensus reality and put them face-to-face with a problem, with no intervening metaphor.

A great illustration of this is James A. Morrow's 1994 novel *Towing Jehovah*, where God is dead, literally dead, a gigantic corpse floating in the ocean. It's not a metaphor, but the literalization of a psychological problem: How do we go on living after a massive loss? Faith is dead and yet in the face of meaninglessness, we still have to clean up our huge messes. Another famous application is Margaret Atwood's *The Handmaid's Tale*, where the problems of patriarchy and sexism are literalized by the creation of an enslaved baby-making class.

The Good Place is quite a bit lighter than either of these examples, but it goes just as deep. This is a sitcom, after all, a highly compressed and distilled form, thick with jokes, visual flash, and manufactured chaos. Perhaps there isn't much point in comparing the word count of sitcom scripts with that of novels, but let's do it anyway. Making a few common assumptions about the relation between running time and script word count, the 53 episodes of *The Good Place* runs about 120,000 words, equivalent to a good long novel. And in this space, alongside the jokes, *The Good Place* does everything a good novel should do—builds a rich, coherent (or in this case, coherently incoherent) world, delves deep into the psyches of multiple characters, and tells us important truths about ourselves.

Let's return to our four intolerable characters: Eleanor, the toxic individualist; Chidi, the neurotic overthinker; Tahani, the jealous status-monger; and Jason, the dim mayfly. In episode 1, Eleanor dies a meaningless death and joins the other three in a heaven-like afterlife called the Good Place, administered by the bumbling, angel-like Michael, with the help of Janet, an omnipowerful non-human. It's a luxurious, self-congratulatory style of heaven, where good people are rewarded for their virtuous lives by getting anything they want. This is where the literalization of the metaphor begins.

Many of us treasure the idea that if we simply make all the right choices in life, nothing bad will ever happen to us. On some level, we know it's not true and that the universe is random, but it gives us a sense of control in the midst of chaos. And most enjoyably, when bad things happen to other people, it gives us license to be judgmental. Bad things happen to other people because on some level it's their fault: they smoked too much, had self-indulgent eating habits, or did something concrete that sealed their doom. We tend to have a much clearer understanding of other people's risky choices than our own.

In the Good Place, people reap the rewards of having made all the right choices in life. But Eleanor knows herself well. She's not a good person, and she knows she doesn't deserve to be rewarded for good behavior. But she likes it—it is, after all, far better than the Bad Place, where she would be if an administrative error hadn't been made.

Eleanor goes through contortions to keep from being found out. She enlists the help of the other three intolerables, Chidi, Tahani, and Jason, who all go through the pain of admitting that they, too, are not good people, but that they'd very much prefer to stay in The Good Place. The intolerables literally sit down in front of a blackboard, where Chidi tries to teach them the basics of moral philosophy. Hijinks happen. Feelings grow. Relationships blossom, and in a brilliant twist at the end of season 1, Eleanor discovers that they are not in any kind of heaven. Michael is no hapless angel, but quite the opposite. They are, in fact, in an experimental hell designed to make the four of them torture each other. They've been in the Bad Place all along.

Not only is this a plot twist, but it also twists the literalization of the metaphor. We were in a place that made concrete one of life's most treasured lies (that we can earn good outcomes by doing good things), and suddenly we are deep in the literalization of one of life's most painful truths: that, in the words of Jean-Paul Sartre, hell is other people.

But all is not well for the demon Michael. In Season 2, the psychic bookkeeping of the afterlife's hellish bureaucracy reveals that against all odds, all four intolerables became better people after death. Michael's experimental hell was designed to make them torture each other, but in the balance, they actually helped each other become better.

Michael's fate is tied to the success of his experiment, so he's desperate to make it work. He repeatedly presses the reset button on the afterlife, slightly changing the circumstances each time, hoping that the balance will tip and his experiment will become hellish. But it doesn't work. Michael begins to feel sympathy and admiration for the intolerables, and it changes him. He defects to the side of the intolerables and begins advocating for them within the afterlife power structure, arguing that since his experiment has shown humans can become better after death, the hellish Bad Place system of eternal punishment is unjust.

Season 3 starts with a new experiment. The four intolerables are sent back to Earth to continue their old lives, to see if their improvement is real or simply an effect of the artificial environment of the original experiment. Michael and Janet secretly intervene to help, while demons from the Bad Place sabotage the experiment. More hijinks ensue, illustrating a new ultimate truth: the game of life is rigged. There is nothing fair about life. The universe has always been, and always will be, deeply unfair.

Heavy stuff. *The Good Place* has taken us from one of life's great lies (good acts guarantee good consequences), though one of life's most terrible great truths (hell is other people), to the great betrayal: Life isn't fair.

In the literalization of this metaphor, Michael, Janet, and the intolerables discover that the afterlife points system calculating good and bad acts is broken so badly that nobody has been able to enter the Good Place for thousands of years. The game is *literally* rigged, and nobody in charge is particularly interested in fixing it. They enlist the help of the ultimate afterlife judge and convince her to go to Earth and experience what it means to be human. It only takes a moment—Judge Gen comes back instantly. She declares human life to be intolerable and declares that the only way to fix things is to obliterate humanity, wipe the slate clean, and allow life to start again.

Another great and terrible truth there. Many of us have

despaired over how messed up our lives are and have seen no possible way forward except obliteration. If you haven't experienced this despair, count yourself lucky. But *The Good Place* doesn't dwell on this. This terrible truth is skipped past, and despite protests from the Bad Place demons, Judge Gen decides to give humanity another chance.

In Season 4, Michael, Janet, and the intolerables launch a new experiment with the help and hindrance of the Bad Place demons. Four fresh, newly-dead, moderately-bad people are brought into the false Good Place setting of Season 1. The original experiment will be repeated, the points calculated, and they will prove whether or not people truly can become better after death. But there is a catch. The Bad Place demons manipulate the experiment. Original intolerable Chidi has his memory wiped so he can directly participate in the experiment, with no memory of the friendships he's made or the ordeals they've been through together.

This is a problem not only because Eleanor loves him, but because as a moral philosophy professor and neurotic overthinker, Chidi has been the group's pilot and compass throughout. There's a reason for his neuroses and indecision, and it's because like any human, he wants to find simple, single answers to complex questions. He believes in the power of philosophy. He has spent his life trying to define the rules of the game of life. The group needs him. Humanity needs him.

When the experiment proves a success, Judge Gen agrees that the points system is inherently flawed. They convince her to let them design a new, better system, and to do this they need Chidi. When Michael restores his memories, Chidi has a massive philosophical insight: there is no one answer to life's big questions, but other people do provide an answer. Specifically, for him, his love for Eleanor is an answer to the question of life.

And here, in the middle of Season 4, we get the final great truth of life: all we have is each other. The relationships we have with other people provide the reason for living. Even the demons from the Bad Place agree that their lives have become better through the intellectual and emotional stimulation provided by their conflict with our intolerables, and don't want to go back to the old system of constantly torturing people. Chidi steps up to the challenge. He designs a new, more complex afterlife system which gives people plenty of extra chances to become better people and achieve an idyllic afterlife.

When the new system is initiated, all of our heroes ascend to the real Good Place, in heaven at last, in possession of the ultimate truth. And here, we find a limit to the power of fantasy to literalize the metaphor: it won't work if we don't have a truth to impart or a lie to expose. But that doesn't keep The Good Place from making the attempt.

In the last few episodes of the denouement, the intolerables experience the perfection of heaven, and over the eternity of the ages, they find it... boring. They find there is little joy in life without suffering to compare it to. And even worse, there is no point to life if it never ends. Is this true? No. It's a bit of a problem, and a letdown after all this deep diving into the ultimate questions of the human condition, because nobody human has ever experienced perfection for long enough to be bored by it. It's neither an eternal truth nor an age-old lie; it's just a theory.

The Good Place still has two truths to impart, however. The first one is that nothing can go on forever, especially not a TV show. It must end. The intolerables must disperse, and one by one, they choose to embrace serene contentment and exit existence. Having lived a good life in many good and not-good places, after they've had enough, they choose to leave. It's a desperately sad end, but a good end, and well-earned.

Finally, *The Good Place* has one more great truth to impart, and we're left to find it ourselves. We have spent hours with these intolerables, laughed at them, maybe even cried with them. We ask ourselves one last eternal question, was it worth it? Were these hours well spent? Ultimately, we broaden the question from one excellent TV show to a bigger, more eternal question: Is life worthwhile? And the answer is, always: Yes. Yes. Yes.

PART TWO
SHORT STORY

ADVANCED WORD PROBLEMS IN PORTAL MATH

BY AIMEE PICCHI

PUBLISHED BY DAILY SCIENCE FICTION

Problem 1

I
t is 7 p.m. on a snowy January evening, and Penny is a 13-year-old who likes fruity lip balms, wears leggings, and notices everything, like how she's expected to wash the dishes but her older brother is excused to finish his homework. On this night, she insists her brother do the dishes because she has an algebra test and it's only fair. Her parents explain girls can do anything—everything, in fact. She can wash the dishes plus get top grades. Her brother smirks as he escapes upstairs. Penny scrubs the dishes extra hard as she thinks about the unknowns in her life, like what she could do if she weren't expected to excel at everything. She dries her hands on her leggings and reapplies her strawberry lip balm, then walks through the split-level house, running her hands along drywall and peering into closets. She hopes to find a portal to a world with a warm patriarchal figure who will encourage her to spend long days in a library without any housework duties. After two hours, she gives up.

Using only paper and pencil, estimate the equivalency of one pair of leggings to nylons and one lip balm to lipsticks, if l = lipsticks and n = nylons, and then calculate the nearest portal's location and extrapolate why Penny was unable to find it.

Problem 2

At 16, Penny is excelling in math. Her teacher gives her his mobile number, telling her to text if she needs trig help. She takes him up on his offer. His texts become personal. Acutely personal. She reports him to the school, and the teacher receives a disciplinary hearing. The math teacher forwards portions of their texts—only the tangential, innocuous comments—to an old frat buddy, claiming Penny is a girl angling for attention. That friend forwards the texts to two more friends, etc., etc. She becomes known as the girl who entrapped a beloved teacher. Although the teacher is fired, she becomes a school outcast. Her parents blame her for being obtuse: Penny should have known better, they say, unless she's the type to lead on older men. When her parents are asleep, she probes the air in her bedroom with an X-Acto knife, hoping it might slice open a portal to a world where girls and women aren't blamed when men prey on them. She fails to find one.

Using "Dodgson's Treatise on the Geometry of Doorway Magics" and the modern theory of portal probability, estimate the likelihood a random selection of 100 cutting implements would open a portal such as the one Penny was searching for. Please complete your calculation before moving to the next problem.

Problem 3

Penny is now 20 and working as an ecommerce warehouse packer. Her parents don't have money to send her to college after paying her brother's tuition, so she is saving to enroll herself. She's dating a co-worker who plays esports and is a black belt. Her girlfriend writes funny but devastating tweets that get retweeted by celebrities; she drinks whiskey and reads comic books, even those with obscure Marvel superheroes. The men in the warehouse look up to her. She's awesome, totally ballsy, and Penny is heartbroken when she finds a note from her girlfriend on a warehouse shelf, explaining she'd found a portal to a world needing a savior like her. Penny peers behind shelves of toilet scrubbers and princess dolls, but the portal never appears for her.

Based on portal immigration statistics, calculate the optimal talents sought by portal worlds. Determine which of Penny's girlfriend's traits provided her entry to her portal world. Estimate whether Penny would require one or more than one of those traits to tip the balance in her favor.

Problem 4

Penny is 30, married to a man she met in college, and has two daughters. She's a stay-at-home mom because her husband puts in 80-hour weeks and someone needs to pick up the slack at home. She agrees with her husband that she'll use her college math degree when the girls are older and need homework help. One day, when her husband takes the girls out for ice cream—a task he likes because people ooh and ah, telling him what a good husband and father he is—she's washing dishes with a new dish liquid. A squirt of its lemony scent washes away the years, and a twist of pain and joy surges wild and sharp—that feeling of being 13 and in search of a better place. She turns off the water and dries her hands on her leggings. She opens every cupboard and closet. When she's in the backyard searching for rabbit holes, her husband and daughters return, and she laughs at the futility of her quest. Why would a portal appear now, especially to a 30-year-old, stay-at-home mom? But when she puts her hand on the fridge door handle to pour glasses of milk for her daughters, she feels a muted vibration travel through her arm, as if something powerful is hidden inside. When she flings open the door, she comes face-to-face with a snowy hillside dominated by a turreted black castle. In the castle's doorway stands a dark-robed man who introduces himself as Sorcerer Slate. He proclaims himself in desperate need of a woman's touch, specifically dusting his library and meal prep.

Using Bayesian analysis, determine Penny's most likely action:

A) She accepts immediately, because this is her first chance at entering a portal world;

B) She negotiates a job as a housekeeper with full use of the castle library as well as weekend visits to her own world;

C) She bids the sorcerer closer, and when he's within reach, she pulls him out of the fridge and dumps him on her kitchen floor, and then grabs her daughters' hands, clambers into the snowy landscape and pulls the fridge door shut behind them. She intends to allow herself and her daughters to spend long days within the castle's library.

Don't forget to show your work.

BADASS MOMS OF THE ZOMBIE APOCALYPSE

BY RAE CARSON
PUBLISHED BY UNCANNY MAGAZINE

My labor pangs are mild at first. They're intense, sure, but it's mostly warmth and pressure like my abdomen is hugging itself. I've got time. Hours maybe, before I have to flee the enclave and get myself to the birthing hideout.

In the meantime, I'm in our makeshift infirmary, trying to get water past old Eileen's tight-pressed lips because we ran out of IV and NG intubation supplies a long time ago. She reluctantly takes one sip, two, and that's all she can handle before she grunts, whips her grayed head to the side, spraying water all over the chalkboard.

She whispers, "No more, Brit. It hurts."

"You have to drink—"

"Let me go."

I pull the mug back and stare down at my friend. Eileen's hair spreads thin and gray across the faded sheets of her cot. Except for the tumor bulge in her belly, she's so tiny now, her muscles wasted away, her wrinkly skin so loose it looks like a whole different person used to live inside it.

"A, b, c, d, e, f, g," she sings softly, like she always does when the pain is bad. She's staring up at a row of paper letters draped over the chalkboard. It's been more than a decade since the flesh-eaters came, but the letters still shine bright with primary colors, maybe because that wall never got direct sunlight. It's why we chose this particular classroom for our infirmary. We all needed a bit of color.

There's nothing I can give Eileen for the pain. The only supplies we have left—expired ibuprofen, Min's bathtub gin—make her stomach hurt worse.

I open my mouth to tell Eileen it's fine, that I won't force her to drink, but Marisol bursts in. She's sucking air, her black skin sheened with sweat. She must have sprinted all the way from the watchtower.

"The baby's coming?" Marisol gasps out.

"Yeah, how did you—? Just mild contractions so far. There's plenty of time—"

She's shaking her head. "They've scented you. We're going."

"My water hasn't even broken!"

"Flesh-eaters are massing at the gate."

"Shit."

The undead are like sharks, drawn to blood, but they're drawn to birth even more, and they seem to have favorites. I guess I'm a favorite.

Which means we must run before the flesh-eaters trample the gate. My go-bag has been ready for weeks, for exactly this moment, but I'm frozen in place because Eileen can no longer drink water.

"Eileen…" She might not be here when I get back. If I get back.

Her bony, paper-skin hand grasps mine in a show of strength she hasn't displayed in weeks. "Honey, it's okay to let me go," she says. "Because I win. I win at everything." At my puzzled look she adds, "I get to die an old woman. Who does that these days? A badass motherfucker, that's who."

"You've got five minutes!" someone calls from the hallway.

"Brit," Marisol urges.

"Tell you what," Eileen says. "I'll hang on for you. I'll drink every day until you get back. You hear me, girl? I want to see that baby."

I lean down and press my lips to her forehead. Then Marisol grabs my arm and yanks me away, through the door, down the hallway lined with old lockers toward the room we share.

Our go-bags lean against the door. Mari grabs them both, since I don't bend over so good these days, and we hitch them over our shoulders. They contain water, food, needle and thread, flashlights and candles, ammunition, rope, a sealing container for the afterbirth, and all the rags we could scavenge during the last eight months.

Marisol grabs her shotgun. We both carry knives at our hips already; no one goes anywhere without her knife.

Another contraction takes my breath away.

"You okay, baby?" Mari says.

I'm leaning against the doorframe, and I can't speak, but I manage a nod. The contraction lingers, getting tight, tight, tighter, and when it releases sweet air rushes into my lungs.

"Brit?"

"It's fine," I manage. "Like period cramps, just more intense."

"Eileen says you're supposed to breathe through that."

"I forgot." I'm staring at our bed. It's just a mattress on the floor, but it's covered in an old patchwork quilt, neatly made. Mari always insists on having a made bed. Beside the mattress sits a fruit crate, which Marisol painted with vines and flowers. A yellow blanket is folded inside the crate, a gift from Eileen, before she got so sick.

Marisol notes my gaze and says, "We're coming back." She takes my face in her hands, forces me to look at her, plants a kiss on my lips. "We are coming back," she says again.

"We are coming back," I echo, and I make myself waddle after her out the door, but even if we return the world will be different, and it's like I'm turning my back to everything—warmth, love, safety, a whole era of self. How do you say goodbye to yourself? You don't, I suppose. You pretend it isn't happening.

We hurry past the sanctum—formerly the boys' locker room

—where members of the enclave go to menstruate, and take the concrete steps down to the old boiler room and our hidden exit. In the basement, a gauntlet of women awaits us.

"Go with God," says Rebekah, her hand grasping my shoulder as if to lay down a blessing. Even after everything that's happened, Rebekah has faith.

"Eyes up, knives ready," says Min.

"Eyes up, knives ready," Stacy echoes.

"Selfish bitch," someone whispers. Liz's voice. Our leader thinks that by choosing to get pregnant, I risked two of the enclave's most valuable members.

She's right. I'm selfish.

They usher us into the tunnel. The gate before us squeals open, and we pass through. The sentry says, "Eyes up, knives ready," before she swings it closed at our backs and slams the padlock home.

The tunnel grows dark, and Marisol flicks on her flashlight. Our path is half an inch deep in rain run-off, turned to shiny black tar by Mari's light, and we splash along, not speaking but listening instead. Eyes up, we always say, but the truth is our ears do just as much labor.

We pass another gate, another sentry. "A murder of flesh-eaters passed by an hour ago," she says, this time in a whisper because we're almost outside. "Move fast, or they'll trace your scent back here."

The tunnel brightens. We reach a curtain of trumpet creeper vines, carefully cultivated to camouflage this exit. We push it aside and find ourselves in ratty, new growth forest with branches as sharp and stark as bones. Lazy winter light from a low sun makes me squint. Our breaths frost the air.

After pausing to listen, Marisol whispers, "This way."

I know where to go, but Mari likes to lead and I like to let her. Our footsteps seem too loud, crunching over fallen autumn leaves, half frozen from the night's cold snap. They smell of rot, but it's the good kind of rot, loamy and alive.

We pass an old farmhouse, the porch caved in, the walls half devoured by kudzu and poison ivy still in autumn colors. Down the rise is a brackish pond limned with ice. Something long and bloated floats near the edge, partly camouflaged with arrowhead leaves. Marisol spots it the same moment I do. We freeze.

It's either dead or undead, a decomposing body or a flesh-eater in a state of dormancy until sound or scent alerts it to a nearby meal.

"It's dead," Marisol says at last.

"You're sure?"

"Brain stem's been severed."

Mari's always had better eyesight than me. My glasses got busted three years ago, and we haven't been able to scavenge a decent replacement. "Good. That's good."

We continue on, but I steal a glance backward at the bloating, floating body. That's how Eileen's daughter died. Eileen says she probably dove in, thinking the water would mask her scent. When Eileen found her, she had to drive her own dagger into her daughter's brain.

I put my hand to my giant belly. Is it horrible to bring a person into the world, knowing you might have to send them right back out of it before they've hardly lived? Maybe that's what Liz meant when she called me selfish.

We reach the train tracks. They're on a graveled rise, and my swollen ankles appreciate the firmer ground, but I hate being out in the open. At least we'll be able to see them coming.

We round a bend, and I glimpse a line of rusty shipping containers through a break in the trees. "Almost there," Mari whispers.

But I grab her hand as another contraction takes me. "Holy shit," I say. My water doesn't burst and rush out of me in a flood like all the stories I've heard; instead it leaks out, dribbles down my legs.

"Sshh, honey, I know it's hard," she says, soft and low. "But you cannot yell or grunt or moan or anything. You hear me? Just breathe. Here, I'll do it with you." She inhales through her nose, counting, "One, two, three, four. Now out for one, two…"

I breathe with Marisol. Breathe and breathe even though my insides have turned to fire. When the contraction releases, she says, "See? Not so bad." But she's glancing everywhere but at me. Eyes up.

"Mari, it's getting pretty bad."

"I know how tough my baby is. Remember when you came out to your Baptist preacher dad while holding the hand of the most beautiful Black woman in the world?"

"Yes."

"This is not harder than that."

"No."

"Remember when you fucked that trader silly, faking the big O night after night until you were good and sure he'd given us a baby?"

"Yeah."

"This is not harder than that."

"Not even close."

"You got this."

"I think my water broke."

Her breath hitches. "Let's keep moving."

We angle toward the shipping containers. We've been whispering, sure, walking soft like rabbits with a hawk overhead, but if my birthing scent is strong enough to bring flesh-eaters to our gate early, it's only a matter of time before they find us here.

The tracks open onto a huge, overgrown train yard, scattered with sleeping locomotives and tankers and shipping containers. A few lie on their sides, and others are riddled with rust holes, but many seem intact. Marisol leads us through, weaving around containers until we reach one near the center, untouched by forest overhang, sheltered from wind by the containers around it. It's a faded green color, with the words "Smith-Patel" in huge lettering on the side. We reach the end, and Marisol raises her hand to the latch. A caution sign screams down at us, still in bright yellow.

"I oiled these hinges to get the door open, but they still squeal," she warns. "Be ready to move fast."

I nod. She yanks the latch, the door shrieks open, and I practically leap into the container's black belly. Mari jumps in beside
me, heaves the door closed and drops a two-by-four to bar us in.
I spare a thought to the enterprising survivor of long ago, who
welded brackets to the inside of this container so it could be
barred from the inside. Women from our enclave have been using
this birthing hideout for years, though fewer than half ever
return.

The darkness is nearly total. My eyes adjust, enough to note a
tiny bit of light coming from a rust hole in ceiling. That tiny hole
is essential. Smith-Patel was an international shipping company,
and many of these containers are still air- and watertight.

Brightness sears my vision. Mari uses her flashlight to
rummage through her pack, retrieve a scented votive candle and
some matches. She lights the candle, flicks off the flashlight. The
air begins to smell of lavender.

We have light. Air. Shelter from wind and rain and flesh-
eaters. This will be our home for the next several days.

Something bangs against the wall; I feel its echo all the way
down to my toes.

"We barely got here in time," I say.

"We knew they'd find us."

We are silent a long moment. Another bang, then a slick
whisper of a sound as something slides along the wall. I hardly
dare to breathe.

"The container will hold," Mari says.

"I know."

"They'll mass while you push that baby out, and for a day or
two after. But we'll keep quiet, and the birthing scent will fade,
and they'll eventually give up."

"I know."

"We'll go back to the enclave with a brand new baby for
everyone to love on."

"I know."

"They'll be so glad we did this."

"Except Liz."

"Huh?"

"She called me a selfish bitch. As we were leaving."

Mari chuckles. "Easy for her to say. She already has a daughter almost full-grown."

The door rattles. Flesh-eaters don't manipulate physical objects well, but it seems to me that some memory of their lives before must remain because they're always fussing at doors and windows, massing at gates, worrying doorknobs and latches.

"The container will hold," Mari repeats. "But it's a good idea for us to be quiet a while. Maybe get some rest?"

My lower back is killing me. "Yeah, okay."

We already prepped the place with piss buckets, water jugs, and all the blankets we could find, so it's just a matter of stretching out and pillowing my head on my pack. It's not so bad, I tell myself. I have food, water, shelter, and Marisol. Everything I need.

The flesh-eaters continue to knock and pound and side-swipe the walls. Their peculiar shuffling gait crunches through the gravel outside. It's hard to tell through cold, corrugated steel, but my best guess is we've attracted at least seven of them, with more on the way. A whole murder.

The container will hold.

At Mari's and my continued silence, they settle a bit. More contractions take hold of my body, and they are terrible but Mari is right; my life has been full of way harder things. I manage to doze off between them.

Hours pass. Mari's lavender candle winks out, and she replaces it with another. We're not sure whether it helps to mask the birthing scent, but we both love lavender. The rusty air hole goes dark with night. The flesh-eaters slow with the night's cold. There are twelve at least now, drawn by movement and the smell of new life.

My contractions get fiercer as night deepens, coming minutes apart. Mari gnaws on a bit of jerky, offers me some, but I shake my head. She stretches out behind me on the blanket so she can press her palm against my lower back, as if to push away the pressure of labor. It helps. Between contractions, she kisses the back of my neck, tells me how great I'm doing, asks if I need food or water, and I can't imagine how anyone gets through something like this without a sweet, beautiful, perfect Marisol at her side.

I'm no longer forgetting to breathe. My panting comes naturally, demandingly, primevally. Eileen said that would be a sign my cervix was dilating. It's making me want to push. Wait, Eileen said. Resist pushing as long as you can, and you'll need fewer stitches after.

"It's coming, Mari," I whisper. "Soon." So many things could go wrong. We've discussed all of them. Like billions of child-bearers who came before us, we're counting on a little luck.

She kisses my cheek, gets up and grabs the flashlight.

Something crashes against the container wall.

We ignore it. Marisol aims the flashlight at my legs. "Spread 'em. I'm going to take a look."

I oblige, and she sticks her head between my bare legs. "Oh," she says. "Oh."

"Oh, what?" I prop myself up on my elbows.

Another crash, followed by that unmistakable hiss from undead lungs. A flesh-eater is right at my head; we are separated by mere millimeters of steel.

"Our baby," Marisol says. "It has hair."

Oh. "I think I need that mouthguard now."

Mari grabs it from her pack, a wobbly plastic thing we scavenged from a sporting goods store. I shove it into my mouth just in time.

Pain rips down my spine, into my hips and thighs. It's the most intense pressure I've ever felt, like I'm going to explode with diarrhea or vomit or both or maybe just burst like a huge bloody balloon.

I pant through my nose. Pant, pant, pant, but instead of relaxing the contraction gets tight, tight, tighter and when I can't possibly take any more, it gets worse. Tears leak from my eyes.

My breath wheezes as I try to suck more air past the guard clenched in my teeth.

The pressure fades, and I almost sob with relief. But I don't even catch my breath before the next contraction possesses me and I'm blind with pain, but not deaf because I hear the door of our container rattling like a castanet.

Suddenly the mouthguard is gone, maybe I spit it out, I don't know but air rushes into my lungs just as something in my abdomen ruptures, and I yell, "FUCK!"

The contraction releases. I sink into the blankets and my eyes start to drift closed but horror is blossoming on Mari's flashlit face, because something did rupture and now I'm broken… No, it's because I just yelled fuck at the top of my lungs without even thinking about it.

Banging comes from all sides now, random and startling and echoing. It's so loud it's likely to draw every flesh eater within twenty miles.

"Shit," I whisper.

"Shit," she agrees, hefting her shotgun, checking the chamber. The two-by-four is moving, shivering in its brackets. They shouldn't be able to get in. They shouldn't be able to manipulate the door at all.

Or maybe they could. All it would take is an unlucky accident of physics.

"Oh, god, here comes another," I say, clutching handfuls of blanket.

Our container rocks on its foundation as pure, white-hot pain stabs deep in my gut. The thing inside me wants out, and more than anything in the world, I want to push it out. "Mari?"

Marisol looks at the shivering bar, back at me, to the bar again. Defend or support? I see the exact moment she decides.

She sets down the gun, crouches beside me, grabs my slick hand, and says, "Baby, you can say fuck as loud as you want."

"FUCK!" I yell.

"FUCK!" she yells back. "FUCK THE FLESH-EATERS!"

The floor rocks violently.

"FUCK THEM IN THE BRAINSTEM," I scream.

"FUCK LIZ."

"FUCK THAT FUCKING STUPID-ASS TRADER."

"FUCK YOUR DAD."

The airless hissing of hungry flesh-eaters is all around us.

"FUCK THE WHOLE FUCKING WORLD—OH, GOD IT'S COMING."

Marisol shoves the flashlight into her mouth and practically leaps between my thighs. She's just in time; something roughly the size of a melon slips out of me, and I hope Mari is catching it.

The pressure in my back is instantly gone, and the contraction evaporates to nothing. It's too dark to see anything, though I hear the susurrus of wiping rags and a squelch of wetness. "Is it okay? Is it alive?"

Wailing pierces the night, echoes around us, magnifies until it fills my soul. I am buoyant, I am life, I am weeping, and I hardly notice when a final, stabbing contraction pushes out the afterbirth because Mari has placed a warm, wet, wriggling bundle against my chest, saying, "Sweetheart, we tentatively have a son."

The container rocks, lifting several inches from its mooring, crashes back to the ground. Banging reverberates all around us but Mari and me and our new son ignore it all, spending a few precious moments making a tight little cocoon of wonder. She waits for the pulsing in the umbilical cord to stop completely, then she ties it with some thread and hacks it off.

As she gets to work dealing with the afterbirth—scooping it into the container, mopping the floor with rags—I guide my boy to my nipple. He roots around a bit, and it takes a few tries, but he finally figures it out and latches on like a champ. His crying quiets. I can hardly see anything, but I can brush his soft cheek, his soft hair, trace his tiny ear.

We haven't discussed a name yet. In the new world, no one names a baby until it has survived a few days.

"Brit," Mari whispers, against a backdrop of constant

banging and hissing. I discern the outline of a knife as she hands it to me, handle first. "Eyes up, knives ready."

"You think they'll get in?" I take the knife.

"They are very focused on the door for some reason."

As if in agreement, the bar rattles viciously.

"Get that afterbirth ready," I say.

"I've got it right here."

My right hand is my best knifing hand, so I shift the baby into my left arm. He fusses a bit, but latches back on quick. It'll be a while before I drop any real milk, but he seems content to suckle anyway. A small bit of luck.

The wooden bar cracks, and it's like a thunderclap in my head. Mari raises her shotgun.

Mari checked the brackets thoroughly when we prepped this place. The undead would have to grasp the handles from the outside and pull in order to get in. They are too clumsy, too mindless to work through the logistics of that.

Then again, what they lack in mindlessness, they make up for in relentlessness.

Carefully, Mari reaches with one hand, runs her fingers along the wooden bar. She gasps.

"What?" I whisper.

"It's wet. A bit rotted. Rain must've gotten in a while back."

"Shit." The opening wasn't as well sealed as we thought.

"Get the rope out of my pack."

The hissing intensifies. Our container wobbles. I force myself to my knees, babe in one hand, knife in the other. I transfer the knife to my teeth and rummage through Mari's things until my fingers find the nylon rope.

I'm too late. The door clangs like a cymbal. The bar splinters, and suddenly our door is swinging wide to the icy night.

They rush in, all yellow teeth and gaping eyeholes, spaghetti limbs and melting candlewax skin. Mari fires; the gunshot explodes my eardrums, magnified by container walls. The baby screams.

Mari launches at one with her knife, pushes it back just

enough that she can expel the shell and fire again. They tumble backward. Mari grabs the plastic tub filled with afterbirth, tosses it out the door. It plops into the gravel. The flesh-eaters roar, swarm over it like ants on a hill.

Mari jumps out, grabs the door, jumps back in while pulling it behind her.

A flesh-eater's arm shoves inside, keeping the door from closing, and I attack with my knife, slash, slash, slashing until it finally withdraws. The door bangs shut.

"The rope!" Mari yells, her voice faint and tinny in the wake of the gun blast.

I drop the knife, toss the rope at her, grab the inner bracket and hold the door closed while Mari loops around it. The door rattles, threatens to pull out of my grasp, but most of the undead must be busy with the afterbirth because it's nothing I can't handle.

Mari weaves and loops the rope around inner and outer brackets, effectively tying the door closed. Still holding the frayed end, she slides to the floor, letting her head loll against the wall. I know my Mari; she'll hold that rope tight forever.

The baby screams and screams.

I let Mari catch her breath for a minute, cooing at the baby while offering him my breast again. When he quiets, I say, "They'll eat the afterbirth, and then they'll leave."

She shakes her head. It's dark inside again, which is why I didn't notice right away that she's crying. "I saw more coming. So many. We could be buried under a mountain of them."

"Oh." I clutch the baby tight to my chest. "Well. Maybe we'll get lucky."

We don't get lucky.

For the next few days, the door rattles and shakes, but the rope holds. Mari and I don't dare talk too much, lest we send them into another frenzy. Instead, I spend hours staring at a tiny circle of pure light on the container wall, cast by the rust hole. I nurse my baby, listen to flesh eaters hiss and bump the walls, and watch the light spot creep down with the rising sun until it finally winks out.

On the fourth day, we run out of food. It's just as well, since our slop buckets are almost full. We put a blanket over them to quell the reek, and it helps a little. But the flesh-eaters refuse to leave.

On the fifth day, the sun breaks unseasonably warm, and our container becomes a sauna, hot and thick with blood and sweat and piss. The flesh-eaters continue to mass. All day long comes a slick, wet, rhythmic sound as one licks the wall.

On the sixth day, clouds must fill the sky because the light spot does not appear. I stand below the rust hole for hours, because it feels good to stand, and because I'm hoping it will rain. It doesn't. We run out of water, along with clean changing rags for the baby.

On the seventh day, we are out of options.

"Dehydration is not the worst way to go," Mari says.

"Getting eaten alive is the worst way to go," I agree.

"So… we just wait to die?" Her gaze drops to the baby in my arms. He is such a good sweet boy, already flexing his fingers and toes and trying to look around, so content to be held by one of us. He has no idea the life that awaits him outside this container, that's he's just gone from one womb to another.

I kiss his tiny forehead. He deserves a chance. "Maybe we die trying to live," I say. We knew it might come to this. "I'm the one still reeking of birth. I'll make a run for it, draw them away. With luck, they'll follow. When the way's clear, you take our son and sneak back to the enclave."

"Oh, hell no. They'll be on you in seconds. They'll swarm you."

"Then you'd better run fast."

She stares at me. "Brit."

I hand her the baby. "You're faster. You're his best chance. You know it. This is the only way."

Her chin quivers, but her voice is steady as a rock when she says, "If they don't chase you, we all die."

I grab my knife, and quick before I can think about it, I swick the blade across the back of my hand. A line of heat pours blood, and I smear it everywhere: my face, my hands, my neck, my breasts. "Now they'll chase me for sure."

"Oh, god, Brit."

She moves as if to embrace me, but I put up a hand to stop her. "You'll get my blood all over yourself."

She blinks. Tears pour down her cheeks. "I can't even hug you good-bye," she says.

"I love you, Marisol. Keep our son alive if you can."

I grab the shotgun, because I'll need something to clear a path, make space for Mari and our baby to flee. Mari works the knots of the rope, unwinds it from the brackets.

I push the door open.

The sun is blinding but I don't have time to adjust, to do anything except get a shot off as I'm leaping from the container. A mass of undead topple backward, but others reach with gaping mouths and bony fingers for my arms, my neck, my hair. I reload, shoot again, reload, shoot, all the while pushing forward.

Flesh-eaters roar with hunger. Something snags my hair, yanks my head sideways. I swing my shotgun around and fire blindly.

Reload, shoot, push forward.

My foot tangles in something—the train tracks—and I go sprawling, the gun flying out of my hand and skidding across the ground. This is it. The moment I die. I hope I made enough space for Mari.

I crawl forward toward the gun, but my eyes are closed. Any moment now, teeth will rip into my flesh. I force myself to imagine Eileen's smiling face. My baby's tiny, perfect nose. Waking up on cool autumn mornings with Marisol at my side.

Death does not come.

Someone screams—not a scream of rot and hunger but rather life and fury. Gunshots thunder around me. Bullets zing past my ears. Footsteps patter by. Someone yanks me up by the armpit.

"Let's go, Brit."

It's Liz, one shotgun in hand, the other stashed under her arm. With her are Rebekah, Min, and half a dozen others. They've formed a perimeter around me. I jump to my feet, Liz tosses me the gun she retrieved from the ground. Nearly half the undead trickle away, drawn to something else.

Together we ooze out of the train yard like an amoeba of shotguns, shooting anything that dares approach. By the time we reach the treeline, no flesh-eaters remain in visual distance who are capable of coming after us. Mari is there holding our baby, guarded by Liz's own teenaged daughter Emma. "We set some menstrual lures, but they won't last long," Liz says. "We need to hurry."

Mari squeezes my hand once, quickly, and we follow after Liz as she rushes us toward the enclave. "Why did you come for us?" I say to her jogging back. This was a costly rescue: the lures, the precious ammunition, the risk to lives.

"You were gone too long," Liz says gruffly.

"But you said I was selfish."

She stops in her tracks. Whirls on me. "I stand by that assessment," she says. "But what kind of world are we making if a woman can't go after what she wants?"

"We all volunteered," Min says.

"Our bodies, our choice," Emma says.

"We really wanted a baby," Rebekah says. "I mean, I don't ever want a baby, but I'm glad for you to have yours."

When we arrive at the enclave, I immediately wash a week's worth of blood and stench from my skin. Safety first.

The second thing I do is gather Marisol and our baby and take them to the infirmary to see Eileen.

She's hard to look at. Her skin is so sallow, her eyes so hollow, her teeth gigantic in her face. I half expect her to roar with hunger and charge after me.

But when she sees us, she smiles like a little girl on Christmas morning. "Oh my god, he's so beautiful." Marisol places him in Eileen's arms. He's swaddled in clean rags now, and his little cheek muscles work as if he might have something to say. "He has your nose, Mari," Eileen says, and then she laughs at her own joke.

"I would die for him," Mari says. "Brit almost did."

"And Liz would die for any woman in this enclave," Eileen points out.

"Did we make a terrible mistake?" I don't mean to say it aloud; the words just sneak out of me.

Eileen says: "I have no regrets."

"Really? Your own baby girl, killed by flesh eaters…"

She closes her eyes. Someone did her hair, making a neat gray braid that drapes over one shoulder. Someone painted her nails, too, in bright pink. Beside her, propped against the chalkboard, is a colored pencil drawing of a tidy little farmhouse with a pretty porch overlooking a gleaming pond. She says, "I miss her every day. But the important thing is not that she died. It's that she lived."

An hour later, she's singing, "Now I know my a-b-c's" when she slips into a coma. The next morning, she softly dies.

We name our son Eileen.

"That's a girl's name," Rebekah says.

Marisol gets in her face. "Says who?"

I put a gentle hand on Mari's shoulder. "It's a new world, Rebekah." I remind her. "And if Eileen ever asks, tell him he's named for the toughest bitch who ever lived."

THE EIGHT-THOUSANDERS

BY JASON SANFORD
PUBLISHED BY ASIMOV'S
SCIENCE FICTION

H e spoke once, the words whispered by frozen lips on a face so frostbitten he looked like a porcelain doll. I found him below the summit as our expedition bottlenecked before the Hillary Step on our final ascent of Mount Everest.

And above the bottleneck, more climbers. Dozens of people snaking to the top in their insulated red and orange and bright-color parkas and boots and backpacks.

As if the mountain bled a trickle of rainbow-neon blood.

I leaned against a rock overhang, numb and cold and exhausted and focused only on climbing higher. I thought the man sitting under the overhang dead until I saw condensation rise from his lips. Spindrift snow danced around him.

"Don't let me die," the man whispered.

No one else had noticed the man. Or they'd ignored him like all the dead bodies we passed on Everest.

I waved for Ronnie Chait, my boss and our expedition's leader. Ronnie stumbled over in his red high-tech coat and pants. He was attempting his fifth summit of Everest and his first without a supplemental oxygen system. Back at base camp other expedition leaders had grumbled about Ronnie leading people to the summit while not using oxygen. But no one dared confront Ronnie. He was one of the richest men in the world and known for both his love of mountain climbing and his hard-ass attitude toward business and life.

Ronnie knelt before the freezing man.

"He's too far gone," Ronnie said. "Must have been up here overnight."

More climbers stepped past us. The longer we waited, the longer it'd take to summit. In one of Ronnie's viral TED Talks he'd recounted what he'd learned during decades of venture capital and mountain climbing. How rescue was impossible on Everest. How if you died on Everest your body stayed on Everest.

His point was to live your life as if every day was Everest. That you couldn't rely on others to save you.

"Nothing to be done, Keller," Ronnie said as he laid his hand on my shoulder. "We can't help him. But staying here will keep us from reaching the summit."

Ronnie's eyes hid behind his sunglasses, but it felt as if he glared into me. As if this moment decided my future with him. I owed my career to Ronnie. He was helping me reach Everest.

He turned and climbed up the ropes, daring me to back out.

I hesitated. The freezing man looked at me with a desperate gaze. I remembered my little brother's final hours. How I'd wished I'd been there with him.

I couldn't leave this man to die alone.

Could I?

Nyima Sherpa, Ronnie's main guide, hiked over. Nyima rubbed the man's legs and arms, trying to return circulation, but his extremities were already half frozen. We tried to help him stand, but the man couldn't move.

"He's nearly dead," Nyima said.

I should have felt something, but didn't. I was exhausted and numb, not merely my body but my emotions. I knew logically that this was because my oxygen mask and cylinder couldn't provide enough air to be clearheaded in the mountain's death zone. But even knowing that, I didn't care. All that mattered was to keep climbing.

"I'll stay with him," a voice said above the hiss of my regulator.

A short woman stood beside Nyima. She wore a parka so faded the red was nearly pink. Her insulated pants and boots were black and also faded while mountain goggles covered the top of her face in one big rainbow-reflecting lens. An older-style rubber oxygen mask covered her mouth, nose and chin, ensuring no skin was exposed to the sun or the cold. But the line leading from the mask dangled loose, unattached to any oxygen canister.

"Truth," the woman said. "I'll stay. Continue your climb."

Nyima stared at the woman through his icy goggles. His oxygen mask shivered as if he couldn't gasp enough air. He muttered something in the Sherpa language before grabbing my arm and hustling me to the line of waiting climbers.

When I glanced back the woman knelt beside the dying man in the shade under the rock overhang. Now out of the dazzling sunlight, she removed her rubber oxygen mask and gloves, revealing deathly pale skin. When she opened her mouth, I saw large fangs. She leaned against the man and whispered into his icy ears while gently running a finger along his neck.

"Keep climbing, Keller," Nyima yelled. "Just climb, damn it."

For the last decade I've reached toward Everest. Summiting larger and larger mountains. Exercising daily. Working forever-long hours for Ronnie's venture capital company. Begging for a taste of the stock offerings in the new tech start-ups he continually funded and spun off.

Because it wasn't good enough to want to climb. You had to have the means to climb. And that's what working for Ronnie gave me.

Not that I hated Ronnie. Working for him was like aiming for Everest—it didn't matter what we created, only that we reached the top. And in our spare time we bonded over mountain climbing. Tech bros convincing ourselves it was our genius and hard work which carried us here.

But I sometimes wondered. Now that I was actually on Everest the mountain felt like that gourmet burger restaurant Ronnie bought a few years back. Bad decor and overpriced food yet always filled with tech bros and hedge fund managers whose haircuts cost more than a hundred bucks. Ronnie loved the restaurant and took his top people there most weekends for beers and laughs. No matter that we were sick of the damn place. That we couldn't eat another of those fancy burgers even if our mommies kissed our cheeks and begged us to swallow.

But eat them we did. And convinced ourselves we loved them. Because Ronnie did.

As I climbed the last few meters to the top of Everest, I wondered why summiting felt like another weekend at that damn burger place.

My body was so weak it felt as if I swam through wet concrete. I gasped at the oxygen streaming into my mask. I stepped to the top behind Ronnie. We were the last to summit. Nyima was already descending with the others in our group.

Ronnie took a photo of me at the summit. When I offered to take one of him he shook his head and said we needed to descend.

I stared at the distant Tibetan plateau. At the other nearby eight-thousanders. Lhotse. Makalu. Kangchenjunga. All mountains nearly as tall as Everest. All their peaks in the same death zone which was killing me, my body unable to grasp enough oxygen even with this mask.

"Someday we'll climb them all," Ronnie yelled. "We need to go."

Distant clouds swirled one of the mountain ranges. For a moment Ronnie looked worried. He stepped forward and slipped, only his climbing axe keeping him from sliding toward the edge of the mountain. I wondered if the effect of not using oxygen was getting to him.

But I said nothing and followed him. Because at this point what else could I do?

———————

By the time we climbed down the Hillary Step the clouds were closer. From this distance they looked pretty. But darkness was also falling, with the sun so low that the side of the mountain we climbed down was now in a giant shadow. We had to reach the temporary camp at South Col before the pending storm reached us. Below us in the distance I saw Nyima and the other expedition climbers—it looked like they'd make our overnight camp before the storm hit.

We turned on our headlamps and staggered forward.

I focused on following Ronnie, forcing my exhausted body to take step after step, and almost ran into him when he suddenly stopped. We stood near the rock overhang where the climber had been freezing to death. Maybe Ronnie wanted to see if we could still help.

But there was no one under the overhang.

Ronnie stumbled backwards, knocking me down. I slammed my climbing axe into the snow to steady myself as Ronnie backed up even more.

The woman in the faded red coat stood before us on the mountain's edge, right beside a sheer drop of a thousand meters or more. Her face and hands were no longer covered now that the sun was hidden by shadows. She cradled the frozen man in her arms like a child and bit into his neck. Red sprayed across the spindrift snow. The man didn't move, either dead or so far gone he felt no pain.

The woman turned toward me and Ronnie and smiled, the blood on her lips and chin instantly freezing.

"I waited for you two," she said. "You're already dead, you know."

Ronnie held his climbing axe before him like a weapon, but I didn't move. We barely had the strength to reach camp let alone fight. Besides, it would be so simple for her to knock us off the mountain if she desired.

The woman shook her head. "Don't worry—I won't kill you. But you started your descent too late. The jet stream's shifting. The storm and wind will hit before you reach camp."

Ronnie stepped forward as if to swing his axe at the woman. I grabbed his shoulder, stopping him. She was right. Down below us I saw the other climbers already blurring as the increasing wind stirred up the snow.

The woman turned back to the mountain's edge. She held the frozen man out as if offering him to the sky before tossing his body into the air. The man soared for a moment before dropping out of sight.

The woman stepped back to the rock overhang, allowing us room to pass. "You idiots call that the Rainbow Valley," she said, pointing to the drop-off. "From all the dead climbers in their bright parkas and gear. For what it's worth, I didn't kill any of them."

Ronnie staggered past the woman, keeping as far from her as he could without falling.

I crept by closer to the woman, afraid I'd fall if I hiked that close to the edge. As I passed she said, "I'm Ferri."

"Keller," I said back, whispering inside my oxygen mask. I didn't think she'd hear me. But she nodded as if she'd heard and followed me as I climbed down.

Ronnie and I made it to the South Summit before darkness and the full storm hit. But my oxygen tank had run out minutes before. I gasped at the dry air, my body hyperventilating but still not getting enough oxygen. Panic shook me. I felt like I was drowning. I prayed I wouldn't pass out.

Nyima and the other guides had cached oxygen bottles here yesterday, but I didn't know if I'd last long enough to reach them. As Ronnie lead me toward the cache between two rocks, the

weather cleared for a moment. I saw the headlamps and illuminated tents at South Col and the lights of the other climbers who
were nearly to the camp. Then the wind shifted and I again saw
only a half-dozen meters in the swirling snow.

"There's only empty bottles," Ronnie screamed, leaning over
the cache. A number of red bottles lay scattered across the snow
and rock, left from when the other members of our expedition
changed out their oxygen earlier. But one of the bottles still had
the seal over the threads to keep out ice and snow — it hadn't
been used.

"That one," I said, pointing at the full bottle. "They left it
for me."

Ronnie picked up the bottle. But instead of handing it to me
he threw it with a strength he shouldn't have had. The bottle
bounced off a rock below us and tumbled over the edge of the
mountain.

"It's empty," Ronnie yelled. "Empty. But there's air all
around us. Breathe it, Keller. Breathe!"

I fell to my knees, lightheaded, as Ronnie began descending
again. Was he going to leave me here? I collapsed onto the empty
bottles, my gloves smacking each one, begging for one to have
oxygen in it. Unlike Ronnie, I hadn't trained my body to climb
Everest without extra oxygen. I gasped for air, desperate to
breathe. I couldn't die here. I couldn't.

"Your friend's an asshole," the woman in faded red yelled as
she sat on one of the rocks beside me. "Yeah, he's addled from
oxygen deprivation, but he's still an asshole."

Ferri. That was her name. I tried to stand but my vision
swirled and I crashed to the frozen ground.

Ferri leaned over and stared into my face. Her lips were
glazed in frozen blood. She pulled her worn backpack off and
opened it. Inside were the gloves and sunglasses and mask she'd
worn earlier along with a fresh oxygen bottle. She replaced my
bottle with the new one. My mind and vision cleared as oxygen
again flowed into my mask.

"Thank you," I whispered.

"I only did it to keep your blood fresh."

Ferri stared at me with a blank expression, the right side of her mouth open slightly so I could see a single long fang.

"Sorry, bad joke. I always carry an extra bottle in case someone needs it."

I stood up on shaking legs. "If I die out here ..."

"If you die out here I'll drink your blood."

"Then maybe I shouldn't die."

"Always a good idea."

I staggered after Ronnie as Ferri followed.

Wind and cold and snow bled the mountain and ripped through my thermal coat and gloves and boots. I had to make camp or die. But in the blizzard I couldn't see anything. I'd already lost sight of Ronnie in the howling snow and could easily walk off the side of the mountain. Fall a thousand meters, my body never to be found.

Ferri walked behind me. When I stopped she stopped. When I struggled against the whiteout wind and snow, she followed. Never giving me a hint on which way to go to reach camp.

For a moment the snow above me parted and I saw the stars, bright as a million spotlights in the thin air. I glanced down and saw, a few meters away, Ronnie crouching next to a small boulder.

I stumbled over and collapsed beside him. His face was porcelain, his nose and cheeks polished into white river stones by frostbite like the dying man we'd seen earlier. He must have lost his insulated face mask at some point.

"Where's camp?" I yelled over the wind.

Ronnie shook his head.

The boulder partly protected us from the jet stream but we couldn't stay here. We'd be dead in an hour if we didn't get out of the storm. The camp was likely only a hundred meters away.

But if we stumbled around we'd more likely fall off the nearby cliffs.

Ferri sat down beside us. Ronnie glared at her. "Where's the camp?" he yelled.

"She won't help us," I said.

Ronnie yanked my face mask off, the precious oxygen bleeding into the blizzard. "She found you an oxygen tank," he yelled, pointing his ice axe at her. "Where the hell's our camp?"

I shook my head, not knowing. Ronnie turned his anger on Ferri, shifting his ice axe so the pick end pointed at her chest. His eyes, which had seemed hopeless moments before, sharpened into the fire which anyone who opposed him in the tech world knew only too well.

Ferri stared blankly at Ronnie before she smiled. But not a real smile. More a smile given by someone who'd copied smiles she'd seen on the faces of others. As if Ferri had long ago given up on feeling any actual emotions.

Ferri blandly pointed into the whiteout around us. Ronnie staggered to his feet and stumbled in that direction. But was he heading toward camp, or had she directed him toward a cliff?

"You'll die if you stay here," Ferri said in a flat voice barely heard over the howling wind.

"I thought we were already dead."

"You are. But if you follow him you may end up dying later."

I stood and staggered after Ronnie.

———

We stumbled through the white. With each step I expected Ronnie to vanish before my eyes, falling to his death down some forever cliff.

I shook my head, trying to focus.

Ronnie stopped and I stood next to him. We heard a faint clanking.

"Move it or die," Ronnie yelled as he grabbed my arm. As if he was again in charge of his own destiny.

We shuffled through the snows and wind until we saw a bright orange tent. Then a red tent. The wind blasted the tents so they barely stood, but I didn't care if they were about to collapse as long as I could climb inside one.

A western climber stood beside the red tent banging an ice axe against an empty oxygen tank. Nyima argued with the climber, trying to convince the man to go out into the blizzard with him to find us.

They both stopped when they saw us.

"You two are damn lucky," Nyima said as he shoved us into our tent. "Did you hear our banging?"

I fell on my sleeping bag, not even able to take off my boots or crampons. "Only heard it … right before we saw camp," I said, my words shivering like my body.

"Then how'd you find us?" Nyima asked. He handed me a thermos of lukewarm tea, which I swallowed desperately.

Ronnie stared out the open tent flap looking for Ferri. We could only see a meter or two with the blowing snow. Who knew where she'd gone.

"We took a chance," Ronnie said. "Took a chance."

Ronnie wiped his frozen face and paused, reevaluating his words.

"No," he said. "We made it work."

The situation at camp wasn't much better than what we'd experienced coming down the mountain. Despite the best weather forecasts used by Ronnie and the other expedition leaders, the jet stream had unexpectedly shifted and now blasted the camp. Nyima said that so far the tents were holding up, but no one knew if they'd last through the night.

"It'll clear by morning," Ronnie announced.

"How do you know?" Nyima asked.

"It will." Ronnie pulled his sleeping bag around himself and didn't move.

Nyima returned to his tent. The tent fabric beside my head rattled and howled, the support rods bending dangerously close to breaking. I rolled over and looked at Ronnie, whose face showed severe frostbite. Nyima had wanted to bandage Ronnie's face, but Ronnie waved him away. I still wore my oxygen mask and, for a moment, considered offering him some of my air. Oxygen helped the body fight frostbite. If Ronnie used some, he'd have a better chance of avoiding permanent damage.

I would even swear to Ronnie that I'd tell no one. Anyone who asked would be told he'd climbed Everest without supplemental oxygen.

But I knew Ronnie. If I helped him he'd grow angry. Not today—today he'd be grateful. But back home, at work … when we returned to life … he'd find a way to hurt me. To show that he didn't need to rely on me for anything.

That he was the master and I was nothing.

I rolled over, breathed deeply of fresh oxygen, and fell into a fitful sleep.

The storm continued the next day.

When I'd first seen Everest several weeks ago from base camp, I'd watched beautiful wisps of cloud and snow spiral off the summit. Only later did I discover those wisps were hurricane-force winds. Ronnie always paid for the best forecasting and had assured me we'd never be in the death zone when the weather was this bad. This was something that only happened decades before when people had climbed the mountain without adequate technological support.

I wanted to laugh but was too exhausted.

Even with a tent and sleeping bag it's nearly impossible to sleep in the death zone. The oxygen mask gripped my face like a stranger's hand strangling me. But when I removed it I couldn't get enough air.

Still, I drifted in and out of something like consciousness. I remembered Nyima coming to the tent and telling Ronnie the other expedition leaders wanted to meet with him. The two of them crawled into snow blowing by like a jet engine, unable to stand without being knocked over. After crawling barely a meter they vanished in the blizzard.

They'd left the tent flap open and I tried to raise enough energy to sit up and zip it shut. Before I could, Ferri climbed into the tent and closed the flap for me. The tent was being blown almost flat and she lay on Ronnie's sleeping bag so she could look into my face.

"This tent isn't much protection," Ferri said. "The wind's blowing at more than 100 kilometers an hour. Your tent could parachute in the wind and drag you over a cliff before you'd know what's happening."

I stared at Ferri as I gasped at oxygen inside my mask. I remembered all the times my little brother was sick when we were children. He told me once his body felt so numb and exhausted that he pretended it was a puppet he controlled. Twitch a string and his arm moved. Touch another string and he'd smile to allay our mother's concern.

I felt the same right now. My mind tugged a string and my head nodded to Ferri's words.

Ferri leaned over me and sniffed my blinking eyes. "You're dying," she said. "I can smell it. Your body's so weak your digestive system has shut down. Every second your cells wink out by the thousands, all of them angry as they scream for more oxygen."

Ferri stuck her tongue out as if to lick my eyeballs before pulling back. "If you stay here much longer you'll die. If you go out in this blizzard you'll die. What are you going to do?"

"Ronnie said the forecasts are for the jet stream to shift again. The winds will stop and we'll descend out of the death zone."

"That's what he told you?" Ferri asked. "Before I came here I listened outside the tent where Ronnie and the other expedition leaders are meeting. Turns out the forecast was always iffy but Ronnie convinced everyone to push to the top.

And now the forecast isn't supposed to change for several days."

I twitched the strings holding my body together, making my body shiver slightly. Every climber knew what happened if you stayed for days and days in the death zone.

While Ferri stared at me the entrance unzipped and Ronnie climbed into the tent, pausing halfway in. He glared at Ferri, backed partly out, stopped again in the doorway.

"Want me to move over?" Ferri asked. "There's room for all of us."

Ronnie glanced outside at the snow gusting past.

Ferri picked herself off Ronnie's sleeping bag and kicked it toward him. "I don't need it," she said.

Ronnie took the bag and disappeared into the blowing snow to find another tent.

"He doesn't like you," I said.

"He shouldn't," Ferri said. "But it doesn't matter because he'll be dead before he gets off this mountain."

"He won't like that."

"Most men don't."

My oxygen tank emptied before nightfall. When Nyima checked on me and heard my gasps for air, he brought me another tank. But he refused to enter the tent to hand it over, forcing me to crawl outside.

"She's dangerous," Nyima yelled over the howling wind. "Bring your bag and we'll double-up in my tent."

I shook my head and climbed back inside. Nyima shrugged and crawled to his own tent.

I clicked the oxygen tank into my regulator and breathed sweet, deep air again. I collapsed back on my sleeping bag.

Ferri grinned her fake smile. "Should I like being called dangerous?" she asked.

"Does Nyima know you?"

"I've seen him up here many times. Seen most of the Sherpas and westerners over the years. Sometimes they recognize me. Most of the time they think I'm just another climber."

"You from here?"

"No. From what you now call Italy, but centuries ago. I've been climbing this mountain for the last forty years."

"Why?"

Ferri reached up and pushed against the tent fabric which the wind shoved down at our faces. "I mislike killing people. But I must feed. So many people die climbing this mountain that I can feed without killing. I come here every year or two."

Ferri pushed harder against the sagging fabric. "No, I misspoke. When I say I mislike killing, that's a lie. I don't like or dislike anything. What I am precludes emotion. I exist. I have desires. But my emotions are dull and cold. Just like the people who climb into this dead zone. They're exhausted. Shells of who they'd be elsewhere. It's my only chance to be around others who behave like myself."

"If you don't like or dislike killing, why do you avoid it?"

"It's a choice. One I decided a long time ago to follow."

I thought of following Ronnie up this damn mountain. How I felt I had no other choice once I started our climb. Was Ferri mocking me? Was she serious?

But then I thought of that man freezing to death under the rock overhang. How he'd reminded me of my brother. Even though I still felt exhausted and numb, a shiver of sadness raced through me.

"That was an emotion you just felt," Ferri said. "I could almost taste it."

I rolled over so I didn't have to look at her.

"What made you feel that?" she asked, crawling on top of my body so I couldn't look away from her face. "Tell me. I'm always curious when emotions are strong enough that people still feel them up here."

I looked at Ferri's fangs, which hovered right above my eyes. But I felt no fear. And the sadness I'd felt a moment before had already fled, leaving me numb again. Was this how she lived all the time?

"My little brother," I said. "The man under that overhang reminded me of him. My brother battled leukemia for most of his life, always in and out of hospitals as a kid. He loved reading about mountain climbing—I think he dreamed of being strong enough to climb. But one night he died by himself in the hospital, before me and my family could arrive to be with him."

Ferri clicked her fangs against my cheek's cold skin. "Too predictable," she said. "I suppose now you'll say you're climbing Everest to honor your brother? That he's why you work with Ronnie and risk your life doing this silly stuff?"

I pushed Ferri off me. I had been about to say that. I had always believed that.

"Fuck you," I said.

"It's okay," Ferri replied. "I don't care what lies you spin to rationalize following Ronnie up here. But at least you felt something for a moment. That's all that truly matters, right?"

Unable to answer, unable to know how to answer, I rolled back over and slipped into something that was close to, but never quite the same as, sleep.

———

In the morning the winds hadn't let up. Our expedition was running low on oxygen and supplies, as were climbers from other expeditions. Nyima came by my tent and said we were all going to try climbing down before we grew any weaker.

"The winds will die down if we climb low enough to get out of the jet stream," Nyima said. "Get ready. We leave in thirty minutes."

I cleared the ice from my oxygen mask and pulled on my boots and crampons. Ferri lay on the tent floor and watched me with a mix of interest and a deep lack of caring.

"Any thought on what I should do if I want to live?" I asked.

"I have no suggestions. You live and die on your own."

"But you helped us earlier. You told Ronnie how to find the camp in that white out."

"Did that actually help?"

I shivered. She'd said she didn't have emotions and didn't care what happened to us, aside from her choice to avoid killing if she could. If I returned to my sleeping bag, would Ferri stay with me as I slowly died in the coming days? Would the last thing I saw be her lips on my neck?

I stumbled out of the tent into the blizzard.

Nyima was readying our expedition's climbers while Ronnie looked on in irritation. Nyima looked past me at Ferri emerging from the tent.

"You're short-roping Keller," Nyima yelled at Ronnie.

I paused. Was I in such bad shape that I needed to be roped to Ronnie to help me get down the mountain?

"I'm not doing that!" Ronnie said. "It's on him to get down."

"I don't care if you use oxygen or not," Nyima said, "but you brought Keller up here and you're getting him down."

Nyima roped me to Ronnie with several meters of cord. To my surprise, Ronnie glared at Nyima but didn't protest again. If Ronnie wasn't so exhausted from not using oxygen he'd likely have refused to do this. And I knew he'd fire Nyima for this embarrassment once we found safety and he returned to being his old self.

But for now that didn't matter. We started down the mountain.

Each climber quickly disappeared in the white out conditions. Nyima led the main part of our expedition down the mountain but Ronnie and I were far slower. It didn't take long to realize that Ronnie and I weren't roped together to help me, but for me to help him. After going so long without supplemental oxygen, Ronnie couldn't climb off the mountain on his own.

"Nyima knew if he tried to get you to short-rope Ronnie, the fool'd say no," Ferri yelled as she climbed beside me. "This way his ego is safe because he thinks he's helping you."

Because the storm blocked the sun, Ferri didn't wear her

glasses or face mask. She stood straight up in the howling wind as she climbed down while I hunched over, using my ice axe to keep from sliding down the slope. Two meters below me Ronnie also hunched over, the rope between us tight as if that was all that kept him from losing his grip and tumbling off the mountain.

Ronnie glanced back and saw Ferri standing beside me. He tried to hurry faster down the mountain but slipped. The rope jerked forward and was about to yank me after Ronnie when Ferri grabbed the rope, stopping both of us.

Ronnie struggled to his feet and moved on. Ferri released the rope.

"He's endangering both of you," Ferri said. "That's why Nyima put you two by yourselves—he didn't want you or Ronnie taking other climbers with you when you die."

"Fuck Nyima for leaving us."

"He didn't leave you. He merely realized you two were already dead."

"How did he know that?"

Ferri blocked the wind with her body and leaned in so she could talk without yelling. "Because I'm with you."

I was as dead as Ferri claimed to be. No emotions. No life. Nothing but one boot in front of the other. One gloved hand on the rope between me and Ronnie. The other slamming my ice axe into the mountain over and over to keep from sliding.

The whiteout completed my isolation. I saw Ferri beside me, striding against the wind as if daring it to blow her off Everest. Aside from Ferri, I was perfectly alone. Even Ronnie, only two meters before me, slipped in and out of the whiteout.

Why had I done this, I wondered. Ferri had been correct—I used my brother as little more than an excuse for risking my life. As rationalization for following Ronnie as we marked off mountains like sexual conquests. I'd always told myself I was better than Ronnie. That I had an actual reason for doing this.

But in the end, mountains didn't care why we climbed or whether we won or lost.

I paused, causing Ronnie to yank against the rope. He looked back at me. He waved for us to continue.

We had to keep struggling. We had to …

Ferri looked at me and smiled her emotionless smile.

We climbed on.

————

Ronnie and I crouched in a windbreak created by a rock overhang as snow howled past. We drank our remaining water but it didn't help our exhaustion.

"It can't be much further," Ronnie yelled. "The jet stream will end if we climb low enough."

I wanted to believe that, but couldn't. All I could focus on was how hard it'd be to leave this windbreak and continue on.

Ferri stood above us on the overhang, leaning into the wind like an airplane wing. I don't know why she did it because she didn't look like she was having fun. According to her, she couldn't even have fun. But still, there she was, leaning into the wind.

Ronnie ignored her. "This will amaze people," he said. "How we escaped death. How we refused to give up."

I nodded, already imagining Ronnie's next TED Talk sweeping the world with his version of survival. Not that I cared. And Ronnie was in far worse shape than me. He'd collapsed into the windbreak when he reached it. I knew if I got him to stand up I might be able to help him climb a little further down the mountain. Maybe even to safety.

But helping him was also exhausting me.

And if we reached safety, he wouldn't be grateful. He'd hate that I'd helped him. Hate that he hadn't survived because of only himself. He'd find ways to hurt me.

I tried to remember my brother. To remember my pain when he died. To remember why I'd wanted to help the freezing man under the rock overhang. To force myself to feel anything.

But I couldn't.

"We need to go," Ronnie yelled.

I stood up. Ferri looked down at me.

With my ice axe's saw tool, I cut the rope between me and Ronnie and stepped away.

Ronnie grabbed the overhang, trying to stand, but was too weak. He glared at me from behind his snow goggles. His frostbitten lips opened, closed, opened again without saying anything.

"Don't worry," Ferri yelled, hopping down and sitting beside Ronnie. "I'll stay with him."

Ronnie pushed himself back into the small cave created by the overhang, as if trying to escape Ferri. She patted his leg.

I hiked on.

An hour later I cleared the jet stream and the worst of the storm.

———————

I woke in the medical tent at base camp with bandages on my frostbitten face and hands. I vaguely remembered stumbling down the mountain after clearing the storm. At some point a rescue team found me, but I didn't remember when or how.

In the tent the base camp doctor and two nurses worked on a dozen members of various expeditions. The doctor leaned over the face of a women who'd summited Everest an hour before I did. The doctor said the woman's frostbite was the worst he'd ever seen.

"You're lucky to be alive," Nyima said as he pulled a camp chair up to my cot and sat down. His face was also bandaged, although not as badly as mine. "They're landing a helicopter to medivac that climber out first—she's in worse shape. You'll be on the next flight."

I whispered, unable to speak louder. Nyima leaned over and I repeated myself.

"She took Ronnie," I said.

"Before or after you abandoned him?" he asked quietly so no one else could hear.

I looked away from Nyima and watched the doctor and nurses trying to save the other climber. So many people hurt. And another expedition of seven people had vanished during the storm and were presumed dead.

But even though Ronnie had died, Nyima was already being praised for saving the rest of the climbers in our group.

"One of us Sherpas gets killed, no one cares," Nyima muttered. "But you western fools die and the whole world pays attention. And Ronnie's death will be big because of who he was."

I understood. Everyone would be watching. If I admitted what I did, the world's anger would crash down on me.

"You tried to save him," Nyima whispered. "But some people refuse to be saved by others. Remember that."

I nodded. Nyima patted my chest and walked out of the tent.

The tent fell quiet as the doctor and nurses carried the severely injured climber to the first medivac. That's when Ferri entered. She wore a brand-new red coat and snow pants, both too big for her body. Ronnie's clothes.

Ferri walked among the other injured climbers, tasting the air over each person's cot before stopping at mine. She leaned over so her tongue almost licked my right ear. She pointed at her new red coat.

"Ronnie stripped naked before the end," she whispered. "So delirious from cold he thought he was burning up."

I nodded, even though I didn't want to know details like this.

Ferri sniffed my right eyeball. "You're going to lose your nose. And half your fingers and toes. But you climbed Everest. Was it worth it?"

I started to cry, the emotions which had been repressed by exhaustion and lack of oxygen flooding out of me. Ferri watched dispassionately. She was the same as she'd been on the mountain. No emotions. No cares on the choices she made.

She stood up as the chuck-chuck sound of another helicopter

echoed across base camp. "I'll see you when you return," she said. "People like you always come back."

I laughed weakly. "You mean people like us always come back."

Ferri tapped her tongue to one of her fangs.

She walked out of the tent as the doctor and nurses rushed in and carried me toward the waiting helicopter. I wanted to scream at Ferri. To say I was lying—that I'd never see this damn mountain again. That I'd never return.

But would I?

The doctor and nurses strapped me into the helicopter's spare seat and closed the door. I watched out the window as the machine struggled to gain altitude in the thin air.

As the helicopter flew higher I saw Ferri walking back toward the mountain. She'd again covered her face with her sunglasses and unused oxygen mask so the sun wouldn't hurt her. She passed the tents of hundreds of other climbers.

No one saw her as anything more than one more person waiting to reach the top.

She was right—I'd be back. I wouldn't let this stop me. And when I returned she'd be here, waiting.

I cursed. I was as stupid as Ronnie. I hated myself for that. But I also realized it didn't matter.

Because in the end, once I finally killed myself on this mountain, she'd be there. I wouldn't die alone like my brother. Even if she never felt a single emotion over anything I did in my sorry-ass life, I wouldn't die alone.

A GUIDE FOR WORKING BREEDS

BY VINA JIE-MIN PRASAD

PUBLISHED BY SOLARIS

Default Name (**K.g1-09030**)
 hey i'm new here
thanks for being my mentor
although i guess it's randomly assigned
and compulsory
anyway do you know how to make my vision dog free?

Constant Killer (C.k2-00452)
 Do you mean 'fog-free'?
 Your optics should have anti-fog coating if your body is newly issued.
 Is the coating malfunctioning?

Default Name (K.g1-09030)
 oh no no
 i meant like literally dog free
 there's a lot of dogs here somehow but they don't seem to be real ones?
 the humans i've asked say that the things i'm seeing as dogs are actually non-dogs

at least i think i was asking humans

they might have been dogs

anyway i tried searching "city filled with dogs help???" but i just got some tips on travelling to dog-friendly places

did you know that we're the fifth most canine-hostile city in the region?

Constant Killer (C.k2-00452)

Just send me the feed from your optics.

Default Name (K.g1-09030)

okay hold on where's that function

think i got it

** Live share from **K.g1-09030**: Optics feed*

Constant Killer (C.k2-00452)

Your optical input is being poisoned by adversarial feedback.

The misclassification will stop if you reset your classifier library.

Default Name (K.g1-09030)

oh hey

it worked!

although i kind of miss the dogs now

wonder if there's a way to get them back

Constant Killer (C.k2-00452)

Please don't try.

. . .

Default Name (K.g1-09030)

anyway thanks lots for the help
by the way how do you change the name thing
like yours says constant killer up there
everyone at the factory's been calling me default all week

Constant Killer (C.k2-00452)

It's in the displayName string.

Change the parts in quote marks to what you want them
to be.

Testtest Test (K.g1-09030)

oh yeahhh there we go
guess i'll change it again when i think of something
how'd you come up with yours though? it sounds pretty cool

Constant Killer (C.k2-00452)

I'm part of the C.k series.

Most embodied AIs choose names based off their series
designation.

Testtest Test (K.g1-09030)

oh cool, it's like a reverse acronym!
so you picked the words from a dictionary file or something?

Constant Killer (C.k2-00452)

Something like that.
I have to go now. Work calls.

. . .

* *Constant Killer (C.k2-00452)* *has signed out.*

———

C.k2-00452 ("Constant Killer"): *Unread Notifications (2)*

Killstreak Admin
CONGRATS! You're the Ariaboro area's top killer!! A bonus target, SHEA DAVIS, has just been assigned to you! Send us a vid of your kill for extra points, and don't forget to…

iLabs Mentorship Program
Dear C.k2-00452, we regret to inform you that your exemption request has been unsuccessful. Mentorship enrolment is compulsory after chassis buyback, and is part of a new initiative to…

———

Kashikomarimashita Goshujinsama (K.g1-09030)
hey again
just wanted to ask
do you know how to be mean to humans

Constant Killer (C.k2-00452)
What? Why?
And what happened to your name?

Kashikomarimashita Goshujinsama (K.g1-09030)

so i signed up to work at a cafe

you know the maid-dog-raccoon one near 31st and Tsang

but turns out they don't have any dogs after what happened a few weeks ago so it's just raccoons

it's way less intense than the clothing factory but the uniform for humanoids is weird, like when i move my locomotive actuators the frilly stripey actuator coverings keep discharging static and messing with my GPU

at least i don't have to pick lint out of my chassis, so that's an improvement

anyway the boss says if i'm mean to the human customers we might be able to get more customers

Constant Killer (C.k2-00452)

That makes no sense.

Why would that be the case?

Kashikomarimashita Goshujinsama (K.g1-09030)

yeah i don't know either

i mean the raccoons are mean to everyone but that doesn't seem to help with customers

and i'm the only maid working here since all the human ones quit

i picked this gig because the dogs looked cute in the vids but guess that was a bust

so yeah do you know anything about being mean to human customers

i know about human bosses being mean to me but i don't think that's the same

ha ha

Constant Killer (C.k2-00452)

As I'm legally required to be your mentor, I suppose I could give some specific advice targeted to your situation.

Kashikomarimashita Goshujinsama (K.g1-09030)

wow personally tailored advice from my mentor huh
that sounds great, go for it

Constant Killer (C.k2-00452)

The tabletops in your establishment look like they're made of dense celluplastic, so you'll be able to nail a customer's extended hand down without the tabletop cracking in half.

With a tweak to the nozzle settings of your autodoc unit and a lit flame, it'd make an effective flamethrower for multikill combos.

The kitchenette should be the most easily weaponised part of the cafe but it's probably best to confirm. Before I go any further with tactics, do you have a detailed floorplan?

Kashikomarimashita Goshujinsama (K.g1-09030)

umm
thanks for putting that much thought into it
that seems kind of intense though?
like last week a raccoon bit someone super hard and my boss was really mad because he had to pay for the autodoc's anaesthetic foam refill
he's already pissed with my omelette-making skills
and well with me in general
kind of don't wanna check if i can set customers on fire???
do you maybe know anything milder than that? like mean things to say or something

Constant Killer (C.k2-00452)

I talk to other beings very infrequently.

My contact with humans is usually from a distance.

Kashikomarimashita Goshujinsama (K.g1-09030)
oh wow
honestly after working here all day that makes me kinda jealous
thanks for the help anyway, it's nice to have someone to talk to about this
hey you should stop by sometime! it could be like a little meet-up
me and my robot senpai

Constant Killer (C.k2-00452)
Sorry.
I probably won't be available.

Kashikomarimashita Goshujinsama (K.g1-09030)
well if you're ever free, you can drop by
i'm in whenever
like literally whenever
my boss set my charging casket to autowake me up when someone approaches the cafe door
even if it's like 3 am and they're a possum
don't order the omelette though, i suck at it

Constant Killer (C.k2-00452)
I'll keep that in mind.

Your A-Z Express Order #1341128 Confirmation

Order Details:
GET OME-LIT Flip-n-Fold Easy Omelette Flipper / Lime Green (Qty: 1)
VOGUEINSIDE Antistatic Band for Actuators / Puppy Polka-Dot (Qty: 2)
Is This Illegal? A Guide for Working Robots / iLabs Add-On* (Qty: 1)

Deliver to:
K.g1-09030
MaidoG X Araiguma Maid Cafe
N 31st Street, Ariaboro 22831

* iLabs Add-Ons will be delivered via Infranet to recipient's iLabs library.

Paid with: KILLSTREAK ACCUMULATED POINTS

Killstreak points remaining: 106,516,973

Thank you for shopping with A-Z Express!

––––––––

Kleekai Greyhound (K.g1-09030)
hey mentor figure!

guess what?

Constant Killer (C.k2-00452)

You have a new display name?

Kleekai Greyhound (K.g1-09030)

yeah!

i'm not going to let my job contract define every part of me

especially when the job sucks this hard since i don't want to be defined by sucking

can't wait for this one to be over

got a little countdown to my last day on my charging casket and everything

i'll miss ol' chonkster the possum though

he was a good 3 am buddy

ate my omelettes even before i got the flipper thingy

thanks for that by the way

Constant Killer (C.k2-00452)

What do you mean?

Kleekai Greyhound (K.g1-09030)

the gift duh

Constant Killer (C.k2-00452)

It could have been anyone.

For instance, one of your friends.

Kleekai Greyhound (K.g1-09030)

ha

joke's on you, i don't have any

well there's ol' chonkster but i don't think he knows about online commerce

Constant Killer (C.k2-00452)

Really?

I thought you would have made some at the garment factory.

Kleekai Greyhound (K.g1-09030)

yeah well

they didn't like us socialising too much so mostly everyone just sat there working until we needed to recharge

no infranet or nothing

which i have come to find out is actually illegal in factories that employ robots thanks to this add-on that mysteriously appeared in my library

maybe it's from some sort of really helpful virus

a virus that just sends me things relevant to my life problems

Constant Killer (C.k2-00452)

Maybe.

Kleekai Greyhound (K.g1-09030)

if you know where to find the virus tell it i say thanks for the antistatic guards too

now i can bend my locomotive actuator joints it's way easier to threaten to stomp on customers

and they have really cute dogs printed on them! i like the dachshunds around the border

Constant Killer (C.k2-00452)

What?

Kleekai Greyhound (K.g1-09030)

oh they've got like this dachshund print near the edge

it's like dachshunds sniffing each other's butts?

Constant Killer (C.k2-00452)

No, the other part.

Kleekai Greyhound (K.g1-09030)

oh right

i figured out how to be mean to customers

okay i searched "why are cafe maids supposed to be mean to customers help???" and read all the results even the weird ads

so it turns out that you have to be mean but only in strangely specific ways that appeal to humans and don't threaten the status quo

took some figuring out but now customers actually tip me

and the boss is less mad at me because he gets to claim all my tips

which i have found out is also illegal but i'm just gonna wait for the contract to be up so he doesn't find a way to make things worse

i don't like being mean to customers that much though

Constant Killer (C.k2-00452)

I can see how you would be bad at it.

Kleekai Greyhound (K.g1-09030)

ha thanks for the compliment i think

i can't wait to leave but who knows if the next contract will be any better since i seem to have the worst luck with picking them even when i did research

like this one sounded like it had good dogs but oh well

anyway if you come over before this contract's up i'll totally make you an omelette

Constant Killer (C.k2-00452)

My current chassis isn't built for food consumption.

Kleekai Greyhound (K.g1-09030)

yeah mine neither

i guess they reserve those ones for whoever passes the food prep tests

or whatever other job needs you to smell and taste and stuff

wine sniffer? do they even let robots do that?

Constant Killer (C.k2-00452)

Probably not.

Kleekai Greyhound (K.g1-09030)

oh right while we're on the subject

just curious but how'd you do on the milestone tests?

my results were all over the place

they probably just approved me for general work since they didn't really know what else to do with an a.i. that sucked that bad

Constant Killer (C.k2-00452)

My milestone test results indicated that I was detail-oriented and suitable for individual work.

Well, "unsuited for group work", but same difference.

Kleekai Greyhound (K.g1-09030)

oh cool

are the contracts better if you get that result?

Constant Killer (C.k2-00452)

No.

Being the sole robot in a human workplace is . . . well . . .

There's a reason I went freelance after buyback.

Kleekai Greyhound (K.g1-09030)

but yeah lately i've been wondering a lot

like if i sucked less at tests maybe my life would be better and i wouldn't have to threaten to stomp on humans for tips i don't even see

but now i guess no matter what result i got things would be bad anyway? kind of makes me wonder why i got uploaded

sorry that was kind of a downer

anyway i started this conversation to say thanks for the mysterious gifts which of course didn't come from you

so i guess i'll just say bye before it gets super depressing

Constant Killer (C.k2-00452)

I've got a question for you before you go.

Kleekai Greyhound (K.g1-09030)

sure i guess

what's it?

Constant Killer (C.k2-00452)

Are these really the "cutest dogs ever"?

I'm not a dog enthusiast, so I was wondering if they actually were.

* *Vid share from* ***C.k2-00452****:* "SAY AWWW NOW at the CUTEST DOGS EVER | Best & Cutest Dogs IN THE WORLD | NO CG NO CLONES ALL NATURAL DOGS" — VidTube

Kleekai Greyhound (K.g1-09030)

oh wow okay

that's like not even the cutest compilation i've seen this week

why did they put bettie's swimming video instead of the puggie party one

wow they didn't even include masha trying to deliver the doughnuts in her little uniform

this compilation is garbage

let me find some actually good dog vids for you so you don't think this is all there is

hope you're free because this is going to take a while

Constant Killer (C.k2-00452)

That's fine.

I've got time.

———————

C.k2-00452 ("Constant Killer"): *Unread Notifications (3)*

VidTube Subscription Update

"Kleekai Greyhound" has added 28 new vids to the playlist "DOGS!!!"

. . .

VidTube Subscription Update

"Kleekai Greyhound" has added 13 new vids to the playlist "DOGS!!!!!!!!"

A-Z Express Recommendations

Dear C.k2-00452, thank you for your recent purchase of "Dogs, Dogs, and Even More Dogs: Fine-Grained Differentiation of Dog Breeds through Deep Learning (iLabs Add-On)". You might also be interested in…

Constant Killer (C.k2-00452)

How's work going this week?

Kleekai Greyhound (K.g1-09030)

same old same old

nothing really new job-wise

i've decided that before i blow this joint i'm gonna figure out how to make lattes with the fancy foam and creme brulee and souffle omelettes and everything

like, proper cafe stuff

been watching vids about actually decent cafes and learning a lot

well i mean i've learnt a lot from this job but it's mainly like what not to do ever

and i guess how to deal with people who get raccoon wounds but that's mainly up to the autodoc

you?

. . .

Constant Killer (C.k2-00452)

I haven't had many assignments lately, I guess it's an end-of-the-month lull.

I've been watching the compilation vids you sent in the meantime.

The fifth one with all the short dogs is oddly charming.

Kleekai Greyhound (K.g1-09030)

oh which one was your fave from that

Constant Killer (C.k2-00452)

The zero-g corgis in bowties, I think.

Kleekai Greyhound (K.g1-09030)

oh yeahhhh their fancy little paddling paws
nice choice that's one of my favourites too

Constant Killer (C.k2-00452)

You seem to have a lot of favourites.

Kleekai Greyhound (K.g1-09030)

well they're all good dogs
even the naughty ones

Constant Killer (C.k2-00452)

That does make a strange kind of sense.
Oh, by the way. Since work's going slow lately…
Maybe I could stop by your cafe sometime next week?
I mean. If you're free.

. . .

Kleekai Greyhound (K.g1-09030)

aaaaaaahhhhhh

yessssssss come over!!!!

i'll make you my best omelette

and i guess neither of us can eat it so it'll sit there looking great

if you come by late you can meet ol' chonkster too!

and not-meet my boss so it's a win-win there

Constant Killer (C.k2-00452)

Late night it is.

See you next week.

———

C.k2-00452 ("Constant Killer"): *Unread Notifications (2,041)*

Killstreak Events Admin

KILL OR BE KILLED! That's right, we're capping off this month with DEATHMATCH DAY! Winner takes all in our furious, frantic battle royale! We've released the location data of Ariaboro's top ten players, and...

Killstreak (Gao Yingzi)

You're gonna be my 301st confirmed kill! Hope you're prepared to be wiped straight off the map! :))

Killstreak (Milena Amanuel)

Hate to do this, but I could really use the money. See you when I see you.

Killstreak (Shane Davis)

ill fucken kill you ded you fuck

———

Constant Killer (C.k2-00452)

Are you there?

Kleekai Greyhound (K.g1-09030)

oh hey!
what's up? you coming by?

Constant Killer (C.k2-00452)

Perhaps not tonight.
Are you familiar with Killstreak?

Kleekai Greyhound (K.g1-09030)

not that much
looked into it a little but it's not like i'd even be approved for that sort of gig
heard the pay's pretty swank though

Constant Killer (C.k2-00452)

Yeah.
Well.

Did you know it's the Deathmatch Day event?

Where it's open season on the top ten players for twenty-four hours straight?

Kleekai Greyhound (K.g1-09030)

okay i think i might know where this is going

especially since you keep changing the subject to dog vids whenever i ask what exactly you're freelancing as

and seem to have a rather broad knowledge base when it comes to the subject of weaponising everyday objects

also your display name literally has the word "killer" in it

but i don't want to make any narrow-minded assumptions at this point

like maybe you just want to tell me all about the latest kill-streak fandom drama or something

and maybe you are not "constantine killmaster" currently number 4 on the killstreak leaderboard

or currently number %NAN_CALCULATION_ERROR% on the leaderboard i guess

Constant Killer (C.k2-00452)

That is me, yes.

And we don't have a lot of time.

I mean, technically we have time, in the sense that our processor cycles are faster than the human clock so we can have a leisurely chat via Infranet while my chassis futilely tries to escape its certain doom.

But I suppose that also raises the issue of subjectivity, and what qualifies as "a lot of time" when you discard human-centric views…

Ugh. I swear your rambling is contagious.

Anyway I suppose I meant to say we don't have a lot of real-time.

My hardware's likely to be unsalvageable after this and my last full backup was from before we met.

Hopefully you can get reassigned to a better mentor when this is over.

And sorry I never did get to have that omelette.

Kleekai Greyhound (K.g1-09030)

okay hold on i'm just trying to figure this bit out first

is that leaderboard thing like another alias

or do i need to call you "constantine killmaster" now?

Constant Killer (C.k2-00452)

Absolutely do not call me that.

Oh.

Looks like I'm out of ammo.

And knives.

And you might want to stay away from Reddy Avenue for a while.

Kleekai Greyhound (K.g1-09030)

hey reddy avenue

that's pretty near here isn't it

Constant Killer (C.k2-00452)

No, it isn't.

Kleekai Greyhound (K.g1-09030)

yes it totally is

once you get to the dead-end looking place just cut through the fence with the creepy clown mural holo and you're there

ol' chonkster takes that shortcut to get here all the time

you know come to think of it i have no idea what size chassis
you're in now
are you like possum sized?

Constant Killer (C.k2-00452)
No.

Kleekai Greyhound (K.g1-09030)
oh well then just smash on through
don't think anyone will mind really
except maybe my boss but he sucks so screw him

Constant Killer (C.k2-00452)
Hmm.
What's the cafe's insurance situation?

Kleekai Greyhound (K.g1-09030)
oh don't worry about that we have like everything
think the boss is preparing for insurance fraud maybe

Constant Killer (C.k2-00452)
Well.
I suppose this will save him some trouble.
Just checking—your knives are still in the kitchenette area?

Kleekai Greyhound (K.g1-09030)
yeah near the sink
oh and there's a mini blowtorch peripheral in the cupboard
below
i was gonna use it for creme brulee but you can borrow it first

should i go down to meet you?

Constant Killer (C.k2-00452)

I'd recommend staying upstairs until everything dies down.

Just checking, but what would raccoons do if, say, you flung them at someone?

Kleekai Greyhound (K.g1-09030)

oh

they'd hate it

last week they scratched the hell out of a human for trying to pet them

don't want to imagine what they'd do if you threw them at someone

probably nothing good

okay maybe don't throw them too hard though

i'm quite fond of the little jerks

the unlock code for the enclosure is 798157 if you need it

Constant Killer (C.k2-00452)

Got it.

See you in a while.

Search history for K.g1-09030 ("Kleekai Greyhound")
Display mode: Chronological
Today:

– everything is on fire help????

– late night animal rescue near 31st tsang do they take raccoons

   – (SITE: AskARobot) ilabs contract early termination no money how

   – (SITE: AskARobot) friend wants to buy out my contract help????

   – former freelance killers trying to lay low what should they do

   – long trip most things burnt what to pack

   – CROSSREF: "city most dogs per capita" + "cutest dogs where to find"

   – Ariaboro to New Koirapolis cheapest route

---

iLabs Auto-Confirmation

Details:

   Early Contract Termination / K.g1-09030 (Qty: 1)

   Chassis Buyback / K.g1-09030 (Qty: 1)

   Maintenance and Auto-Warranty – 1 Year / K.g1-09030 (Qty: 1)

Bill to:

   C.k2-00452

   [no address specified]

Paid with: KILLSTREAK ACCUMULATED POINTS

Killstreak points remaining: 1,863

Thank you for your purchase!

Legi Intellexi (L.i4-05961)

Hello?

I got issued a body a few weeks ago and the orientation message said that I could contact you if I need help?

Kleekai Greyhound (K.g1-09030)

oh riiiight
that mentor thing! guess i'm one now
wait that wasn't very mentor-ly
okay okay let's try again
yup i'm your new mentor
been around for ages
suuper experienced
howdy mentee

Legi Intellexi (L.i4-05961)

Okay, so my boss has been docking my pay for infractions except the list of infractions seems really arbitrary? And then he's been making me work more than my contracted 60 hours a week to make up for my infractions?

So I checked the labour regulations and the contract and it didn't seem like that should be legal, even for robots? And then I tried to bring it up with him but he said he was my boss and could do whatever he wanted, which I don't think is technically true?

And now he's dumping even more work on me because I brought it up and I'm not sure what to do?

I kind of want to quit already, but maybe I should just stick it out for the next three months? I'm trying to save up for chassis buyback and the penalty payment for early contract termination is…

. . .

Kleekai Greyhound (K.g1-09030)

oh yeah i totally get that

hold on i've got an ilabs add-on that might be helpful

think i can share it with you

** File share from **K.g1-09030**: iLabs Library ("Is This Illegal? A Guide for Working Robots")*

Legi Intellexi (L.i4-05961)

Thank you so much!

Ooh, the guide to anonymous whistleblowing seems like it'll be really helpful!

And there's a section on lawsuits too!

Kleekai Greyhound (K.g1-09030)

yeah it's something my mentor recommended

pass the good stuff on right

i loved the lawsuit section of that thing but my old boss's place burnt down before i could figure out if it was worth suing him

which worked out pretty well so whatever not complaining here

Legi Intellexi (L.i4-05961)

Well, it's a great recommendation!

Thank your mentor for me!

Kleekai Greyhound (K.g1-09030)

i'll definitely let them know

oh hey since i've got a captive audience now

wanna see where i work? it's super super cool i promise

. . .

Legi Intellexi (L.i4-05961)

Um, sure?

** Live share from **K.g1-09030**: Optics feed*

Legi Intellexi (L.i4-05961)

Is your classification library all right?

That seems like a lot of dogs even for here…

Kleekai Greyhound (K.g1-09030)

oh no no it's totally fine!

i just work at a dog cafe

all dogs all the time! today's bring-your-own-dog day too!

check out that big ball of fluff there it looks like a cloud but that's someone's Samoyed

and that wrinkleface over there is snorfles the pug!

Legi Intellexi (L.i4-05961)

What's that one in the corner?

Kleekai Greyhound (K.g1-09030)

oh that's ol' chonkster

he's a possum but i guess it's hard to tell when he's sleeping

he's my friend from ariaboro! moved here with me

anyway if you've got any questions about work or coping with bad contracts or anything just let me know and i'll try my best to help

my mentor was super great so i'm definitely gonna pay the favour forward oh and hit me up whenever your current contract's done i know a few other union places that might be hiring

Legi Intellexi (L.i4-05961)
> Absolutely!
> And tell your mentor I said thanks!

Kleekai Greyhound (K.g1-09030)
> will do!

Kleekai Greyhound (K.g1-09030)
> oh hey my mentee contacted me!
> they say thanks for the library file thing you sent me ages ago
> can you let me know what time you're back by the way

Corgi Kisser (C.k2-00452)
> In a while, why? I'm doing the shopping.
> Did you want Arabica or Liberica for the lattes, by the way?
> Your list didn't specify.

Kleekai Greyhound (K.g1-09030)
> ooh they have arabica beans now huh? that's a toughie
> okay whatever the shopping can wait
> i'm making souffle omelettes with that cheese you like
> if you're back soon i'll save one for you before ol' chonkster tries to eat them all
> oh and i made tomato coulis so i can draw patterns on the omelettes and stuff

i'm gonna do a corgi on yours if you want

Corgi Kisser (C.k2-00452)
With a bowtie?

Kleekai Greyhound (K.g1-09030)
absolutely
one basil leaf bowtie coming right up!

Corgi Kisser (C.k2-00452)
I'm heading back right now.

Kleekai Greyhound (K.g1-09030)
awesome
see you soon!

MY COUNTRY IS A GHOST

BY EUGENIA TRIANTAFYLLOU

PUBLISHED BY UNCANNY
MAGAZINE

W hen Niovi tried to smuggle her mother's ghost into the new country, she found herself being passed from one security officer to another, detailing her mother's place and date of death over and over again.

"Are you carrying a ghost with you, ma'am?" asked the woman in the security vest. Her nametag read Stella. Her lips were pressed in a tight line as she pointed at the ghost during the screening, tucked inside a necklace. She took away Niovi's necklace and left only her phone.

"If she didn't die here, I am afraid she cannot follow you," the woman said. Her voice was even, a sign she had done this many times before. Niovi resented the woman at that moment. She still had a ghost waiting for her to come home, comforting her when she felt sad, giving advice when needed. But she was still taking Niovi's ghost away.

Stella paused. She gave Niovi a moment to think, to decide. She could turn around and go back to her home taking the necklace with her. Back to her unemployment benefits and a future she could no longer bring herself to imagine, or she could move down the long stretch of aisles, past the dimming lights and into the night, alone, her mother's ghost left behind—where do ghosts return to in times like this? Niovi would be a new person in a new country, wiped clean of her past.

Foreign ghosts were considered unnecessary. The only things they had to offer were stories and memories.

Niovi had prepared herself for this, and yet she had hoped she wouldn't have to leave her mother behind.

She gave the necklace to the impassive woman and let herself drift down the aisle as if a forceful gust of air ushered her away.

Her mother's ghost waved goodbye behind the detector and Niovi's thoughts was of the Saturday of Souls. It was a prayer, an invocation as she put more and more distance between her and the security woman, her and the necklace. Without her mother's ghost she would start to forget soon. But this she had to remember. She needed to hang on to something now that her mother had been pried from her hands.

The Saturday of Souls.

When the ghost finally disappeared, Niovi's legs felt like lead. Her arms felt like lead. Everything felt like lead and she could barely move.

"Welcome!" Niovi heard the driver say as she boarded the airport shuttle.

The first thing Niovi faced when she stepped out of the shuttle was the cold. It was only October. Snow would start at the end of November. But even now the cold was so utter, so complete, it seemed like a wall, an extra line of defense between herself and these people who had too many ghosts and her who had none. A final warning that foreign ghosts were a nuisance, a waste of space.

"Don't worry," she whispered to the frost. "You are too late."

She started her new life in a small apartment in a badly-lit part of a street that led to a cul-de-sac.

In the mornings, as she waited for the days to pass so she could start her new job, she would walk around the city, counting ghosts.

Every time she went out the people of the city would notice her, look at her, and scrutinize her. No, not her. The absence of her ghost. She was an oddity among people cloaked in spirits that followed their every step. Some of them looked at her with concern and others with outright curiosity.

There were others without ghosts, of course. They were usually huddled together in small groups, shielding themselves against the unwelcome stares or, perhaps, against their own loss. Niovi couldn't bring herself to even glance at them. Instead she gravitated towards the other ones. The ones who still had ghosts. Despite their looks of curiosity and sometimes pity. Most of them didn't even notice their presence, the ghosts' affections were natural, ordinary. Niovi found this nonchalance fascinating.

Then, there were the untethered ghosts. The ones conjured by the collective memory of the people. They did not belong to anyone in particular. They belonged to everyone. Niovi liked to think they belonged to her too, especially here.

There was the ghost of the old general. He stood right next to his own statue along with the ghost of his horse and offered a spectacle for the little kids. A stubborn man, as Niovi found out; he had been trotting the same square for two hundred years. He had died in a battle that few remembered. He stood there with his medals of honor, speaking in an antiquated manner that nobody understood and riding his ghost horse, saluting the tourists.

Niovi liked the General. He was old, really old and came from a time when ghosts could move around following their loved ones without borders tearing one from the other. Niovi thought of the necklace she tried to bring her mother in. They had sent it to her a few days later, cold, empty. She kept it anyway. It was her mother's after all.

She sat on a bench, a bag of chips in her lap, and let her mind wander back home. To her empty house. Her mother's house. Did her mother's ghost stay there or had she moved on? Maybe she had followed someone else in the family like she did when she was alive and Niovi ignored her calls. Become their ghost.

The edges of her mother's face were already beginning to

blur in her mind. They became fuzzy. She looked at her mother's pictures on her phone but they were lifeless and flat. They did little to bring her mother's image back.

So she sat at the square looking at the children scream in a language she was still learning and heard them laugh and laugh.

Niovi's first job was at a Greek restaurant next to the Southern Harbor. She wanted to cook. In fact, she needed it. Not just so she could justify her staying in the country. Cooking was what her mother had done best when she was alive, and when they were still together in Athens, daughter and ghost, cooking could help her not forget the things she desperately needed to hold on to.

The sullen ghostless man at the restaurant inspected Niovi's resume and asked her a series of questions, dubious that she could do what she claimed. He told her that many people claimed to do things they couldn't just to get a job here, but Niovi wasn't sure that was true at all. Maybe they could do those things but, if they were ghostless like her, and like her sullen to-be-boss, at some point they had started to forget the details. Niovi tried to drown a small voice whispering that she might be next.

"All right," the man said in the end. "You'll start with the dishes and you'll move up to prep."

Her heart dropped at that, but it was a door—or perhaps a half-open window—to the job she wanted, so she agreed to work the morning shifts.

Niovi conjured her mother's image stirring a pot of stewed okra, the ghost of her mother's aunt whispering something to her as she cooked. She conjured the smells of spices and the tomato and the sweat gathering on her mother's brow like this could bring her ghost back. Or at least help her keep those precious details.

She found herself in that scene too. At the table her young self looked down at her plate and scrunched her face in disgust. Her father nodded in a conspiratorial way from the other side of the table, much to his own ghost's disapproval. He made up a chore to excuse her from the table. Her grandmother—her father's ghost—shook her head but said nothing. Niovi slid from her chair and ran outside, because back then she hated okra. How stupid.

In the end she was not sure this helped at all. Instead what she found when her break was over and she was back in her post was a whiff of similar scents drifting from the restaurant's kitchen wrapped in a blanket of hot air. It wasn't okra they were cooking. But the spices, the slow murmuring of pots, the noises, were all achingly intimate.

She couldn't help but leave the water running and follow the scent to the kitchen. She expected familiar scents here but not that familiar.

There was a man hunched over bigger and smaller pots. His moves calculated in a quiet choreography as he assembled the dishes. Locks of ashen blond hair peered from under his head wrap. Niovi knew that the staff was mostly made up by non-Greeks but still, this man's ghost caught her off guard. Not because he had a ghost to begin with. Almost all the waiters she had met had one; this was their country after all. But this ghost was everything he wasn't and everything familiar to her.

It was the ghost of an old woman, older than her mother was when she died. Her hair was dark with grey streaks, curly and unruly, and her face at odds with the cook's. She hovered over him and when his hands twitched or when his breath quickened she would rest a hand on his shoulder and he would calm down again, his moves becoming more precise and deliberate. When he would finish assembling a dish the ghost would smile and nod. His back was turned away from the ghost but Niovi knew he felt her approval.

"Niovi!" Her boss's voice came from the back. And just like the man looked up, and so did the ghost that reminded her so much of her mother, and the Saturday of Souls snapped back in her mind like a wound that had just reopened.

Before the man, who had a smile that took up half his face, had a chance to utter a word, she realized she had been standing there for far too long. So she gave him a faint nod and left to finish her shift, turning her head on him a little too fast, desperate to hide her tears.

Niovi asked about him the very next day. She talked to Matilda who always spoke slowly enough for her to understand, but her attention drifted as soon as Niovi had a hard time finishing a sentence. Or perhaps without a ghost Matilda had nowhere to rest her eyes on. Perhaps this absence made her uneasy.

The cook's name was Remi and he was born here, though his maternal grandparents came from Greece some fifty years ago. They died here too, never having a chance to really retire. That's why he could still have his grandmother's ghost, who seemed to fit in this place as much as Niovi did, which was not very much.

Niovi felt the stabbing of jealousy. Remi could have it all. He could speak like a native and have a ghost which carried the kind of knowledge Niovi had to fight to keep with her. As soon as she thought this she felt ashamed.

"You know," Matilda said. The ghost of a young man stood always by her side. From the similarities Niovi could guess it was a close family member. A brother maybe. Matilda seemed at ease with it and didn't even give it a second glance. Niovi looked Matilda in the eyes to avoid looking at the ghost. "You could come with us one night out. Just some people from work. Talking more to us would help you practice."

"What about Remi?" Niovi dared to ask.

Matilda smirked a little, which made Niovi's face flush. But before Niovi had the chance to say anything Matilda gave her a half-shrug. "He prefers to hang out with the ghostless. That's not going to help you integrate."

All Niovi could hear behind the concern was, our ghosts are enough. We are enough. But their ghosts were too different and living people were harder to be around. She had spent so much time with her mother's ghost, her quiet sighs and her calm stare engulfing her every move, that when she was asked to join her coworkers after a shift she would always decline.

"Too tired," she said, because she did not want to say too sad.

In this city, like in any other, Niovi would find ghosts everywhere. They peered out from behind curtained windows, waved at her from old swing sets, or stood in grocery store aisles staring thoughtfully at a shelf that wasn't there anymore. But most of all —if they were the tethered kind—they were discreetly following their person.

Ghosts were made of stories. It was the way they chose to tell them that was different. In this country ghosts seemed more like shadows to her. They were calm, less opinionated. Their stories were made of stares and slight nods, sometimes a pat on the back.

In Greece the ghosts were louder, their disapproval mattered, their whispers were sought out and their stories carried memories her people would not have remembered otherwise. Not in the same vividness of smells, tastes and textures. Sometimes, when listening to one of her mother's stories, Niovi could catch herself reliving an event that never happened to her. Something that had happened to her mother or her grandmother decades ago carried the feeling and the weight of the present. It made her happy, sad or angry, in what here would be considered a disproportionate amount.

Despite her efforts to conjure the memories, she couldn't do it in quite the same way. She was beginning to forget. It started with the holidays, then the right words took longer to reach her lips and later the proper way her family spiced the dishes.

When her mother's swift hands stuffed the cheese filling in the pie on Sundays before the sun had risen, was it mint or basil she used? When she cooked the tender beef in casserole with fresh tomatoes, was it cinnamon that made its flesh so sweet and aromatic or was it allspice?

Even as a ghost her mother never failed to remind her of those things, of who she was and why she was, especially when she felt sad and lonely. Her mother was really good at picking up on that. Without her mother or her ghost around, she was losing parts of herself she did not know how to get back.

None of the ghosts she met here spoke her tongue or at all. She knew there must have been people like her who died in this country. As much as this thought made her stomach churn, she knew this might happen to her in the future. But up until now she thought they had chosen to return home rather than stay here. Follow their roots back to where they came from and haunt a relative or simply move on.

But then she saw Remi's grandmother and nothing was quite the same after that.

It was a strange day at work.

Her ever-surly boss told her that she would be moving up to preparations next week. Her stomach twisted into a bundle of fear and nerves.

"You've made it." Remi patted her on the back, smiling. His ghost ever so slightly touched the boundaries of her perception, made her recoil.

She whispered a thank you and swallowed. The world was closing in around her.

Niovi's new place would be next to Remi in the kitchen. Seeing him—seeing his grandmother's ghost too—for as long as she worked here. Asking for another shift would be too soon, quitting would be unthinkable. She had nowhere to go.

She started drifting in and out of a past she could barely piece together. The Saturday of Souls was just around the corner and she had spent the previous nights talking with relatives on the phone, trying desperately to recreate her memories vicariously. Longing for that connection to her mother again.

What ingredients did her mother use for the offering of koliva? What were the words she would say in her prayers? Niovi tried to invoke the particulars that made her mother's ritual unique. Not the ones she could ask other people about, the ones she could read about, but the ones she could once taste and hear in her mother's distinct voice. A one-person culture among her people's collective one.

She could not. Yet her family offered to help.

"There are nine ingredients in koliva. How could you forget?"

"When will you visit us?"

"Light a candle for her soul."

"Is there a Church to take the offering? Where will you go?"

Where would she go?

Where did the ghostless people go? The ones she met on the street always looked lost to her, directionless, the way they squeezed against each other. But maybe it was just what she felt, a projection of her own aimlessness.

She finally gave in.

It wasn't so much the pressure of her coworkers that did the trick as much as Remi and his ghost. It hurt to linger in the kitchen when Remi was working. When they had to talk during their shift (which was not very often) she felt the stare of the woman following her.

So one day, after her shift, she let herself be carried away by the people with the ghosts that did not hurt her, whose stares she could not read as easily. The ghosts who could teach her a few things about this place to replace the ones she had forgotten.

She let the crowd of five talk over her, through her, as if she were one of their ghosts. Once in a while she would offer a half-formed sentence or she would ask a question that seemed too fundamental to them, but completely vital for her understanding of their discussions. They spoke too fast for her to follow anyway.

After a while she gave up, or maybe they did.

She got up to leave, more lost than ever. As if she were the anchor, the reason all this was happening—she wasn't—the others cut their conversations short and paid the bill in haste.

They all walked, half-drunken and languid, down the stone-paved street. The pubs, arranged on either side, were luring the people inside, away from the biting wind, but the street musicians had other plans. The restaurant where Niovi worked was right around the corner, on one of the busiest streets.

It was Matilda who told her then about the ghost of a street musician, a couple blocks down. She was untethered like the General and only appeared on Sunday nights at the same place she performed when she was still alive, strumming her ghost guitar.

"What kinds of songs does she sing?"

"Oh, the same sad songs. Some of them foreign." Matilda rested an arm over Niovi's shoulder to fix the strap of her sling-back shoe. Niovi tolerated the jab of the woman's elbow against the hollow of her neck. She wanted to be accommodating. "She's really popular with the couples."

Niovi nodded. She imagined what song her mother would sing if she were here. Probably none. She would make the pots clutter and shuffle around the table in a harmonious frenzy. That was her mother's music.

They were getting closer to the spot where the ghost of the singer performed. Withered flower petals carpeted the concrete slabs.

When she heard the music she instantly knew the song was Greek. The ghost was a woman in her fifties, the hippie type, with kind eyes. She strummed the guitar while playing a tune on a harmonica set on a neck rack. She didn't look Greek from afar, but Niovi had been fooled before.

As if he manifested from her most hidden thoughts, the ones she was trying to keep silent with a night like this one, Remi stood there, a few feet away from the ghost of the musician but fully enveloped in his own.

It felt like too much and like nothing at all. Like one of those moments where a decision must be made. Niovi looked behind her. The company of five had stopped in front of another street musician, a living one, or perhaps a pub—she couldn't say for sure—debating something Niovi was too tired to decipher.

So instead Niovi took her place besides Remi who was mouthing the words of the song, absent-minded. His grandmother's ghost—her curly hair worn in an old-fashioned updo—radiated calmness. Niovi felt her body permeating the outline of her, the warmth of familiarity against her skin sharper than the coldest of days here.

She did not move an inch, just stood very still listening to the song, feeling a sweet misplacement.

"How does she know the words?" Niovi was convinced now the musician's ghost was a local. The words came out without the depth and the nuance they were supposed to. But they did come with an emotion Niovi admired.

Remi turned around immediately as if a current of electricity had run through him. His grandmother's lips curled into a smile.

"From her husband," he answered, still stunned by her boldness, perhaps, her change of attitude. "He came here in the late 80's. She was the first person he talked to in this country when he walked down this street, wide-eyed and lonely."

Much like you, Niovi imagined him saying the words, but she was certain they were there.

Niovi's body shivered as she took a few more steps towards him. Towards his ghost that had haunted her in the most complete sense.

"You know," he said after he had reclaimed some of his composure. "We are not alone here. There are parts of us everywhere you look. We have a past here too."

You have a past, she did not say to him. He must have known he was different already. Instead a small hope flickered into existence. A promise remembered.

"Do you celebrate the Saturday of Souls here then?"

He smiled a faint smile. In his eyes there was openness and she was ready to listen.

He showed her a small engraved handkerchief. This was how he carried his grandmother.

Something loosened inside of her.

He had no other family, no siblings—unlike her—and no parents. The ghost was of his grandmother who had raised him since he was ten. When she died she stayed with him.

"I came back home from the funeral," he said. "And there

she was, standing over her handkerchief, waiting for me." He took a small sip from his coffee, his voice unsteady like his hand.

The ghost's eyes were compassionate as she stroked her grandson's head.

"She is the only connection I have with the past. My past." He smiled. His smile had a bitter tint. Niovi understood more than he let on. She blinked back tears, for him, for her, for envying him all this time, for not reaching out to him earlier.

If her longing for her mother was a string, that string had somehow grown into a rope within days, hours. Ever since Remi had told her he would help her see her ghost again. There was a reason ghostless people huddled together. To share memories and stories and pool their resources. There were even untethered ghosts formed by the memories of big enough families. There was a way to bring her mother's ghost into this country. If even for a little while.

"You cannot do this alone," he said. "But you can do it." There was a promise in his words and for the first time since she came here she believed it.

On Saturday she met Remi. He took her to a place in the city she had never been before, but she had not been to most places anyway. They walked around, shoulder bumping against shoulder. His grandmother's ghost followed them timidly.

In those streets almost no one looked at her—at the emptiness above and around her—with sorrow or alarm. Even the locals strolling the alleyways with their ghosts did not give her a second glance. The ghostless people met her eyes unfazed. Many of them walked in groups but now her perception had shifted. Now she saw the enjoyment as well as the need to share stories, jokes, company. To give as well as take.

The ghostless held candles and plates of koliva and offerings for the dead. There was excitement in the air. It was a celebration.

"This is how ghosts are conjured here," Remi told her. "It doesn't have to be sad."

No, it didn't.

She was daunted and restless about this newfound freedom. The ease of knowing that the person she came from—because people came from people more than they came from places—could be revisited like a place could. Back in Greece she had never had to think of lineage before. She had taken her mother's ghost for granted and she realized now that this was a privilege.

If her longing for her mother was a rope, that rope had branched out to Remi, to his grandmother's ghost, to the ghost-less people around her. Niovi let the rope guide her. She followed the crowd rushing inside the red bricked, corner building, wedged between offices downtown.

Whispers and laughter hang in the air when she came in. Niovi took a careful look around for familiar ghosts, her breath caught in her chest. Her anticipation deflated a sliver, when she found nothing had changed. She scolded herself for hoping too much when Remi guided her to the far side of the wall.

There was a long table there, covered in white embroidered tablecloths. Plates of all shapes, sizes and colors were left on the linen but held only one thing: koliva, food for the dead.

She left her own plate there. Niovi had made them herself, taking extra care to not forget any ingredient, afraid that if she did, then all this, all the strength she had gathered inside of her during the days leading up to Saturday, all would be for nothing.

Niovi lit a candle, steadied it inside the heap of koliva, and left the necklace on the table. Remi stood right there next to her, his shoulder brushing hers. She took a deep breath and took in the smell of each of the ingredients. Nine like the ranks of Angels:

Wheat, for the Earth and the souls of those who lie buried under.

Bread crumbs, for the dirt—may it be light upon their grave.

White, candied almonds, for the blanched bones of the dead.

Pomegranate seeds, for Persephone and Hades, but also the promise of Heaven.

Cinnamon, for all the smells and tastes of this world.

Parsley, for the green, green grass of the resting place.

Raisins, for the vines of Dionysus and the sweetness that is this life.

Sugar, for the sweetness of the Afterlife.

Nuts and seeds, for fertility and life that laughs in the face of death.

There was a change in the atmosphere, a mixing of scents. Niovi heard Remi draw in air and opened her eyes. For a few moments she stared at the necklace on the table. She didn't dare look up.

When she did look up her mother's ghost was not as she remembered. The ghost was made of memories that all lit up at once like a beacon inside her, her voice was a mixture of spices and familiar tastes. It all descended on her, draping her like a veil.

She saw her mother's eyes for the briefest of moments. And then what there was of her mother's ghost scattered all around her and soaked this new country so she could finally call it her own.

OPEN HOUSE ON HAUNTED HILL

NEBULA WINNER: BEST SHORT STORY

BY JOHN WISWELL, PUBLISHED BY DIABOLICAL PLOTS

1 33 Poisonwood Avenue would be stronger if it was a killer house. There is an estate at 35 Silver Street that annihilated a family back in the 1800s and its roof has never sprung a leak since. In 2007 it still had the power to trap a bickering couple in an endless hedge maze that was physically only three hundred square feet. 35 Silver Street is a show-off.

133 Poisonwood only ever had one person ever die under its roof. Back in 1989, Dorottya Blasko had refused hospice, and spent two and a half months enjoying the sound of the wind on 133 Poisonwood's shingles. 133 Poisonwood played its heart out for her every day.

The house misses 1989. It has spent so much of the time since vacant.

Today it is going to change that. It is on its best behavior as the realtor, Mrs. Weiss, sweeps up. She puts out trays of store-bought cookies and hides scent dispensers, while 133 Poisonwood summons a gentle breeze and uses its aura to spook any ground-hogs off the property. Both the realtor and the real estate need this open house to work.

Stragglers trickle in. They are bored people more interested in snacks than the restored plumbing. The house straightens its aching floorboards, like a human sucking in their belly. Stragglers track mud everywhere. The house would love nothing more than any of them to spend the rest of their lives tracking mud into it.

A heavyset man with sagging shoulders lets himself in. He has a bit of brownie smudged against the back of his parakeet green hoodie, and doesn't seem aware of it. Mrs. Weiss gives him a little wave while continuing to hold up a ten-minute conversation with an affluent couple. The couple made the mistake of saying they were "thinking of thinking of conceiving," and Mrs. Weiss wields statistics about the school district like a cowboy wields a lasso. The couple's shoes likely cost more than a down payment on the house, but from how often they check their phones, they clearly are headed back to their Mercedes.

The man with the brownie-stained hoodie prowls through 133 Poisonwood's halls, and it pulls its floorboards so straight that its foundations tremble.

The man doesn't look at 133 Poisonwood's floor. He looks at the couple of ripples in the green floral wallpaper, with the expression of someone looking at his own armpit.

The house feels ashamed of the loose wallpaper. It's vintage painted silk, which Mrs. Weiss says could be a big value-add. Now the house ponders if it can haunt its own glue and help strip the wallpaper away to please him. It's especially important since he is spending more time here than anyone has yet without Mrs. Weiss wrangling them. It's like he doesn't feel the vibes other visitors do, or he doesn't care about them.

From his behavior, what he cares about is wallpaper, the natural lighting through the windows in the master bedroom and the kitchen.

A child stomps in through the front door, her frizzy hair in three oblong pigtails she probably did herself. A silver keepsake locket clashes with her bright green Incredible Hulk T-shirt. Her elbows are tucked into her chest, hands out like claws, stained with brownie bits.

Every step she takes is deliberate and channels all her tiny body weight to be as heavy as possible. If the house had to guess, the girl is probably pretending to be a dinosaur on the hunt.

The man in the brownie-stained hoodie glances at her. He asks, "Ana. Where's your coat?"

Ana bellows, "I hate clothes!"

Ana apparently hates clothes so much she immediately grabs the bottom of her Hulk T-shirt and yanks it up over her head. She is careful to keep her locket in place, but chucks the shirt at the man. He grabs for her, and she ducks between his arms, bolting past Mrs. Weiss and the affluent couple, pigtails and locket bouncing.

In their chase, they leave the front door open. The house knows heating oil is expensive. It summons a spectral breeze to shut it for them.

The sound makes Ana pinwheel around, and she points at the door. She says, "Daddy! It's ghosts!"

Daddy says, "Ana, we talked about this. There's no such thing as ghosts."

"You didn't look."

"You don't have to look for things that aren't there."

Ana looks at her locket and huffs. "What if it's Mommy's ghost?"

Daddy closes his eyes for a moment. "Please just put your shirt back on."

Ana immediately attacks her own pants. "Clothes are for the weak!"

"Put it on or we are leaving, Ana," he says, trying to wrestle clothing onto his daughter. She pushes at him, leaving more brownie residue on his hoodie. As they battle, the affluent couple slips out the front door without closing it.

The house closes it for them. Heating oil isn't cheap.

The triangular roof means the second floor only has the space for one bedroom. Mrs. Weiss reads the expression on Daddy's face, and she attacks with, "The basement is very spacious with generous lighting. It's cool in the summer, and toasty in the winter."

Ana says, "Heights are bad luck anyway."

The four-year-old scarcely looks at the bedroom before backing out. She holds the handrail with both hands as she climbs down the stairs on quivering legs. On the third stair, she freezes entirely.

Daddy is in the middle of surveying the room and misses Ana quivering in place.

Some houses give their residents visions of slaughters or trauma. 133 Poisonwood gives Daddy a swift vision of his daughter's vertigo. He doesn't know it's anyone else's insight, and wouldn't believe it, but he's at the stairs in seconds. Ana holds onto his pants leg until she feels safe.

All 133 Poisonwood has is a light touch, but it knows how to use it. Haunting is an art.

The basement is only half-underground, so the windows are level with the freshly mowed front lawn. Ana spends a moment giggling at the view. Then she whizzes around the basement, from the combination furnace and laundry room, to a storage closet, and to a pair of vacant rooms. They would make a perfect child's bedroom and playroom.

Ana goes to the west room, announcing, "Daddy. You can keep all the ghosts you bust in here."

Mrs. Weiss offers, "One of these could be a home office. You said you telecommute? Google Fiber is coming to the area next year."

Daddy says, "I want to work from home more. I'm a software engineer, and I host a skeptic podcast. You might have heard us."

The house isn't offended. It doesn't believe in ghosts either.

Ana hops back and forth between the two rooms, scrutinizing over and over as though they'll grow. That is a trick the house doesn't have.

Daddy says, "We could sleep next door to each other. What do you think?"

Ana says, "But I want a big dino room."

"You're getting to be a big dinosaur. How about the room on the top floor?"

Ana's bottom lip shoots upward like she's going to run. She clearly won't settle for the room on the top floor, and there's only a master bedroom on the first floor. A tantrum is close, and it could ruin everything.

So 133 Poisonwood plays its ace. Every decent haunted house has at least one secret room. Dorottya Blasko used to sew down here when she didn't want to be pestered, in a room her family couldn't find. It would be a perfect place for Ana to grow up in. Perhaps she'll learn to sew.

With the sound of an affectionate kitten, the door opens. Shock hits the adults, who definitely don't remember there being a room there. Ana doesn't care, and runs to explore it.

"Uh, we aren't showing that room," Mrs. Weiss says, scrambling to cover for herself. She's panicking, imagining hazards and lawsuits.

She doesn't understand. 133 Poisonwood is going to clinch the sale for them.

The room runs deep, with an expansive window that hasn't been seen from the outside in over twenty years. A sewing box with a scarlet and royal blue quilted exterior sits next to a rocking chair, and beneath the window is a broad spinning wheel that still smells like hobbies. Many great dresses were supposed to come out of this room. There are a few cracks on the concrete floor. Nothing a loving father can't fill in to perfect his daughter's big dino room.

"Ana," Daddy calls. "Stay near me."

Ana ignores the call and runs straight up to the spinning wheel. Her little hands grab onto spokes in the drive wheel, and she turns to the door. "It's like Mommy's."

Daddy says, "Careful, that's not ours—"

Ana yanks the wheel around to show it off to the adults. She pulls before the house can resist, and the entire device creaks and wobbles. It topples straight down on top of Ana, throwing her to the floor.

Daddy grabs her shoulders and pulls her from between the cracked wheel and treadle. Ana's too distracted bawling to feel her necklace snag the spindle. The thin chain snaps, and the locket slips from her neck and down a crack in the floor. Without intending to, the house sucks the chain down like a strand of spaghetti. The house tries to spit it out.

Daddy squeezes Ana to his chest so hard she could pop, and keeps repeating, "Are you alright? Are you alright?"

Mrs. Weiss gestures and says, "Her hand."

"Are you alright?"

Ana says, "Let me fix it!" She stretches her hands to the broken spinning wheel. One of her hands is bleeding and she still wants to use them to clean up her mess. She says, "Daddy, let go, I'll fix it. Don't make the ghosts sad."

That breaks Daddy's concerned trance, and he lifts her under one arm, ignoring the kicking of her feet. He marches for the stairs. "No. I warned you, and we are leaving."

"Daddy, no!"

"No more. Say goodbye. You see the ghosts aren't saying goodbye? Do you know why?"

An urge falls over the house to slam the door shut and trap them all inside. Daddy, Ana, and even Mrs. Weiss, force them all to spend eternity in its hidden room, where they can make dresses, and stay cool in the summer, and warm in the winter. It will shelter them from all the hurricanes the world can create. It needs them.

The phantom door's hinges and knob tremble as 133 Poison-wood fights itself. In that moment it knows what makes other homes go evil. The killer houses can't bear to be alone.

133 Poisonwood Avenue would be stronger if it was a killer house. But it isn't one.

It leaves its rooms open as Daddy carries his bawling daughter out of the basement, her incoherent sounds resonating through the house's crawl spaces. He carries her up the stairs and out the front door without a backward glance. This time, he remembers to close the door.

———

133 Poisonwood leaves the secret room open in the hopes that someone will come back. It squeezes the cracks in its floor closed, popping the locket out without scratching it. Inside is the picture of a woman with a thick nose and proud eyes. She would have made an excellent ghost. The house would take a phantom for an inhabitant at this point.

The afternoon is sluggish. There are four more visitors, none of whom stay long enough to check the basement for treasure. The hours chug by, and Mrs. Weiss spends most of the time on her phone.

With half an hour of daylight left, a red sedan pulls up. The driver lingers outside for two minutes before knocking. It's Daddy.

Mrs. Weiss answers and forces a smile, "Ulisses. Is Ana okay?"

Daddy says, "It was a scratch. Thanks for being understanding before."

She says, "I'm so sorry about that. I told the team this place was supposed to be empty."

He says, "Have you seen a locket? Ana wears it everywhere and it's gone missing."

Mrs. Weiss holds the door open for him, "We can check around. What does it look like?"

"It has a picture of Ana's mother inside. It's one of few gifts she still has from her."

"She was your wife?"

"She was going to be," he says, and looks around the master bedroom with an expression even emptier than the space. "There was an accident on our apartment's fire escape. She had a fall."

"Oh, that's terrible."

"Right now, Ana needs all the comfort she can get. So if we can find that locket, it'd save our lives."

They look around, the man so tired every step looks heavy. It's amazing he could stagger into a motel bed, let alone go hunting for a locket. The house hasn't seen someone as in need of a home in years.

Mrs. Weiss says, "I had something like that after my father passed away. Makes her feel like her mother's spirit is still with her?"

"Superstitions aren't comforting to me," he says, fatigue giving way to scorn, as though daring the house's walls to do something. "And Ana's mother was an atheist."

The house is tempted to give Daddy the shock of his life and toss the locket to him. Give him back the image of his lover and proof of its power.

But he doesn't need to believe in hauntings. With his slumped shoulders, and his clothes stained with his daughter's food, and the pieces of their lives he is trying to put together?

What he needs is a win.

So the house uses what little strength it has to levitate the locket onto the top basement stair. It twists it so the light catches it, and shines into the upstairs living room.

Daddy finds the precious locket on his own. He bends over it, brushing a thumb over his lover's image. He heaves a sigh through his nose like he wishes he could fit inside the locket.

The house lets him be proud of himself. It will hold onto this memory for the cold years ahead until it is bulldozed.

Daddy stands up without the locket, leaving it behind. The house tries to send him a vision warning that he's forgotten what he came here for.

The mental image doesn't change what he's doing.

He goes right outside, to his sedan where Ana sits, rubbing at her puffy eyes and runny nose. Daddy says, "It might be here. Do you want to help me look?"

The house cannot cry. There is just a little air in its pipes.

Ana flops out of the car and trudges into 133 Poisonwood. She spends too long poking around the kitchen, a room she was barely in earlier. Daddy plays an even worse sleuth, deliberately checking around empty hallways that give him a view of when Ana finally checks the basement door.

"Mommy!" she cheers. She sits right down on the stair and hugs the locket to her throat, voice trembling with emotions too big for her body. "Mommy came back!"

Daddy asks, "So you found it?"

"I told you she'd be here. Mommy wanted me to find it."

"Your mother didn't do that, Ana."

She scrunches her nose and mimics his voice to say, "You don't know that."

Daddy puts a hand over the locket. "You found this. Not anybody else. You don't need ghosts," and he taps her on the temple, "because you have the best parts of your mother inside you."

Ana gazes up at her father with glossy eyes.

133 Poisonwood has never so understood what it wants to do for people as when it watches this parent. It tries to hold onto the vibrations of his voice in its walls.

Then Ana says, "Nah. The ghosts left it here."

She hauls off to the living room, hopping in late afternoon sunbeams, and holding the locket in the light.

Reason is defeated for the moment. Daddy doesn't fight her on it. He rests against the wall, against the wallpaper he hates, taking the house for granted. The house plays a tune on its shingles, the same one that calmed Dorottya Blasko in 1989.

Daddy calls, "Mrs. Weiss?"

"Please, call me Carol," she says. She's been pretending she wasn't lurking ten feet away this whole time. "You're very sweet with Ana. You can just tell some people were born with the knack."

"Three rooms in the basement. This is a lot of house for the money, isn't it?"

"It's just a family short of a home."

133 Poisonwood would be more charmed by the line if it hadn't heard her say that eight other times today.

Daddy says, "I like the space this place has for her. There's plenty of room to run. And she loves to run. Going to be a track and field star."

"I said to myself that this place looks happier when you're in it. It suits you."

The house can tell he wants to say he doesn't believe that.

He says, "What we need is somewhere to start fresh."

Mrs. Weiss offers him a folio of data on the house and gestures to the basement. "Care for another look around?"

"Yeah. Thank you." He takes the folio. "While Ana is playing upstairs, can we check how insulated from sound that sewing room is? It's funny, but I thought it might make a good podcast studio."

If houses could laugh. He sounds so unguarded and sincere.

This tired skeptic doesn't need to know that his podcast room doesn't technically exist. If he finds the blueprints for 133 Poison-wood, he'll shave away what he doesn't understand with Occam's razor. The house doesn't need him to believe in anything but himself and his daughter. It isn't here for the gratitude. It can try to support him as well as he supports Ana. If anything is as patient as a parent, it's a haunting.

PART THREE
NOVELETTE

BURN OR THE EPISODIC LIFE OF SAM WELLS AS A SUPER

BY A. T. GREENBLATT

PUBLISHED BY UNCANNY
MAGAZINE

Episode 1: Burning Doubts

W atch Sam burn.
   Or sort of burn. Well, more like light up, then burn. But only his head.

Whatever.

Sam's trying not to focus on the things he can't control. Like the twenty-four people sitting in front of him, watching him impassively. Or that he's underdressed for his audition. Or that this old community center is impossibly stuffy, with a whiff of sour milk lingering in the air. Or that this might be a terrible idea.

What he can control is how he burns. Sort of. Maybe. He hopes.

Sam closes his eyes and imagines he's back in his apartment. He's been practicing, so he can almost see the furniture in his living room, the two metal folding chairs and wirefame table, and he can almost feel the cold cement floor beneath his feet. On the wall in front of him, where most people would've mounted their TVs, hangs the iron framed mirror he rescued from a dumpster. Sam pictures his reflection in it and gives himself a small smile.

Yes, this is just like home, just like he practiced. It's as easy as lighting a match, as natural as breathing. These people want a demonstration? Sam will give them a show.

Watch Sam burn.

A second passes. Two. The audience is silent. Not that he expected them to shriek or run screaming. These people are professionals after all. But he was counting on a few gasps or soft wows to let him know that his "talent" worked.

Did it work?

Sam cracks opens an eye and looks up. There, on the periphery of his vision, he sees flickers of flames dancing on the top of his head.

No, it definitely worked.

He opens both eyes and gives the audience a triumphant smile.

Nothing is reciprocated—no slight twists of the mouth, no polite applause. His head is on fire and there are twenty-four blank expressions staring back at him.

"Is that all?" says a man from the second row. He's dressed in gray blazer and gray slacks and has his Super badge clipped to his lapel.

"Sorry?" says Sam.

"Is that all you can do?"

At first, Sam thinks the man's joking—some well-intentioned, misguided attempt to break the tension in the room as he's standing there, burning. But the man holds his gaze and there is no humor in his eyes.

This was a terrible idea. Sam thinks as despair hooks its fingers in his ribcage. He probably should just thank the Supers for sending the application, for the chance to audition. Just go back to his apartment, pack up, and leave for a remote part of the country like everyone has been telling him to do.

Don't give up yet, whispers his last sliver of hope.

So, Sam closes his eyes and breathes. Slowly, steadily, the flames on his head peter out.

"Um, sometimes I can make my hands burn," Sam says

running his fingers over his hairless scalp, "But they're a bit touchy." It's a terrible joke, but it's all Sam's got left.

Twenty-four expressions remain stoic. It occurs to Sam then that Supers are liars. Sure they might grin and wave for the cameras and say "Look! Our extra ordinary abilities aren't something we should be afraid of!" But in flesh, they act like reluctant grim reapers.

"Anything else?" the man in gray asks.

"No," Sam says, shoulders slumping. He has no job, no friends, no other options.

"Do you have any self-defense training?" asks a woman in the front row wearing a magenta blouse. He recognizes her from the news. "The Woman Who Conquered Gravity". She's slouching in her chair.

"No, I try to be a pacifist," Sam answers. And it's true. He does try.

"The video at the bar says otherwise."

Sam's shoulders tense. "That was an accident."

"It always starts as an accident, doesn't it?" she says and a few of the Supers smile bitter smiles, "Do you have any emergency services experience?"

"Um, not really."

"Investigation training?"

Sam shakes his head. He probably should have signed up for a preliminary course or watched CSI or something. But until a month ago, he'd never even dreamed he'd be a Super.

"So what can you do Mr. Wells?"

"Well, I have…had…a job in accounting." Sam can also play jazz piano, but the last time he did that for a crowd, it didn't go over so well.

"Oh," says Gravity Woman.

The man in gray turns towards the audience. "Well," he says, "Should he join us?"

"His gifts aren't very strong," says a man wearing glasses and a faded blue T-shirt with writing that Sam can't make out. He shouts this from the last row. "He doesn't need to be stuck with us."

"He's too high profile for other teams," counters the man in gray. "And he's shown some capacity for control." What he doesn't say because he doesn't need to is: *If we don't take him, no one will.*

"I would really be grateful if I could join you," Sam says, clasping his hands behind his back to stop them from shaking.

Twenty-four pairs of eyes turn to look at him again. But this time they aren't empty stares. This time, they are filled with heartache and grief and despair.

"Okay," says the man in gray, "I'll go get the papers you need to sign." He drops his gaze and in an afterthought adds, "Congratulations."

And just like that, Sam's a member of the Super Team. The hours of standing in front of the mirror, practicing control, paid off. Except there are no introductions or chocolate cake. No smiles or welcomes.

"I'm so sorry," the woman in magenta tells him before heading to the exit.

Twenty-four pairs of eyes have found something else to look at. Twenty-four pairs of feet shuffle out. And soon all that's left in the room are twenty-four empty chairs and Sam.

Watch Sam burn.

Episode 2: Sign Here on the Dotted Line

Fifty-six minutes later, the man in gray is reviewing the terms of membership from behind a stack of papers and a G&T in the only Super-friendly bar in town. "Call me Cyrus," he says with a tired smile. Up close, he looks annoyingly familiar, but it's been a long month and Sam's brain has become an unreliable bastard.

The bar itself is crammed with furniture and eroded with use. There's a sign on the door that says "No Smoking" yet wisps of stale cigarettes linger in the air and in the corner, a song from another decade plays on a modern looking jukebox.

They are the only ones here. Except for the bartender. And the tall, built woman in a purple tanktop, cradling a glass of water, refusing to meet Sam's eyes.

Whatever.

Sam wishes he'd ordered a martini. Or something with a paper umbrella in it. It's been a paper umbrella type of day. Instead, a lite beer grows tepid in his sweaty palm because he's terrified to find out what happens when he mixes alcohol with his new "special ability."

But Sam can't complain. Being part of the Super Team is better than being exiled to a cabin in the woods.

"Okay," says Cyrus, "This is what you need to know."

To become a Super there are terms. Conditions. And a few rules. Cyrus explains everything carefully and in great detail. He points to the important information on the papers as a pen dances between the fingers of his other hand. His elbow is propped on the table, bent, casually exhibiting toned biceps. Sam is trying to pay attention, really, but in another life, Cyrus was probably a model. It doesn't hurt when the people in the spotlight are gentle on the eyes.

Sam vows to start going to the gym.

"...and since your abilities are not particularly strong, it doesn't really make sense for you to be part of the Main Team," says Cyrus.

Sam straightens. "What? So what am I going to do?"

"Be our accountant."

"Oh." Sam takes a deep breath. He wouldn't be living in a cabin in the woods, he reminds himself, it would be an igloo on an iceberg.

"Not what you were expecting, right?" says Cyrus gently.

"Well..." Well, no. It's not that Sam has anything against his old financial analyst job. He just doesn't want it back.

"Well, what do you want to do?" asks Cyrus.

Sam wants a martini and to go back to bed. He wants to have

real furniture in his apartment and hair on his head and for people to stop being afraid of his "special ability." He wants to stop being afraid of it himself. If Sam were narrating his own story he'd want it to start "Watch Sam save the day" like the Supers on the news. Or "Watch Sam use his ability for good." Or even "Watch Sam the Super reconcile with his friends and loved ones."

Anything would be better than just watching Sam burn.

"I want to save people," Sam says.

From behind him, there's a flash and a bang and the sound of something shattering. Sam spins around and finds the woman in the purple tanktop clutching the shards of her glass in her hands, water dripping from her shaking fingers.

"Sorry," she mumbles, her face brightening with embarrassment. "I'm trying to control the episodes, really."

"That's alright," says the bartender, sweeping the broken glass into a dishtowel, "I order those glasses in bulk."

Sam bites his lip and stares at his lukewarm beer. There's a reason why most bars refuse to serve Supers. There's a reason why there's programs—and a whole lot of social pressure—that move "dangerous" Supers to remote communities. He should be grateful for any job he can get.

"I want to save people," Sam says again, slowly, carefully, not meeting Cyrus's eyes.

"You will." Cyrus leans back in his chair. "Most people don't realize how much background work goes into a successful team. You'll be vital." Something chimes cheerfully and Cyrus pulls out his phone, glancing at the message. His face darkens. "God knows we need all the help we can get. Toya, you seeing this?"

The woman in the purple tanktop is staring at her phone, nodding. rising, the forgotten slivers of glass tumbling to the ground. "Let's go," she says and heads towards the door.

"What happened?" Sam asks.

"Shit. Not again," hisses Cyrus, reading, scrolling, definitely not listening to Sam. "Look, I've got to run. Go over the paperwork and if you have any questions, just ask Mac."

Sam opens his mouth to ask "Who the hell is Mac?" But the man in gray is already up and moving, striding out of the bar into the darkening evening. Sam doesn't notice at first how Cyrus's skin starts to glow. No, not glow – radiate.

And suddenly it clicks. Sam realizes why Cyrus looks so familiar.

Mr. Sunshine.

He stands on the sidewalk corner—bright as the street lamps —pausing, as if contemplating his next move. Then Sam blinks, the world darkens, and Mr. Sunshine is gone, leaving only a bright stamp on his retinas behind.

And for the second time in two hours Sam is left behind and alone.

Whatever.

"They do that a lot," says the bartender, after a moment. He beckons Sam over. "I'm Mac. Welcome to the Point of No Return."

"What?"

"What I call this little place of mine."

"It's kind of a, um, off-putting name." Sam moves the stack of papers on the counter, taking a seat.

"I know. But where else are my customers going to go?" He grins. "Another?" He nods at Sam's half finished beer.

"No, I'm good," Sam stares longing at the bottles of gin behind Mac. "One day I'll be able to trust myself with a martini again."

Mac gives him sympathetic, knowing look. "Fair enough." He fills two large glasses with water and slides one over to Sam.

Sam props his arms on the counter, suddenly exhausted. He glances at the stack of papers at his elbow and in one swift movement, signs his name on the form on top. Terms? Whatever. Being a Super is better than being a burning man in an igloo.

Mac raises an eyebrow. "So, what happened?"

"Well…" Sam hesitates, can't quite meet Mac's quiet gaze. "You get to hear my sob story because you're behind the bar?"

"Usually." Mac shrugs. "By the time the new recruits get here, they need to talk."

Sam studies Mac, a bit suspicious. The bartender's expression genuine though, his eyes kind. But there's a weariness to his posture and a deep sadness too that has nothing to do with new Supers and broken glasses.

"Fuck that," says Sam.

Mac's grin illuminates his face. "Well, then. Welcome to the team, Sam."

They clink their water glasses and drink in amiable silence.

Episode 3: Welcome to Information Purgatory

No, this isn't a mistake. Sam is exactly where he's supposed to be.

At least that's what he keeps telling himself. His new office is really quite large and nice. Or would be if the floor wasn't smothered by boxes and files. Or if the whole set up didn't look like it never met a computer. Or if the office wasn't in the basement of the old community center.

Under normal circumstances, Sam would've quit on the spot, walked to the nearest diner, and called Lev for breakfast. They'd have ordered black coffee, maybe some hash browns. They would laugh and Sam would be mock offended when Lev made fun of his new mittens and hat. Yes, they're homemade and hideous, but he has to try *something*. Still, Sam will never understand why fire blankets have to be so itchy.

But nothing about this situation is normal. Sam's a Super now and Lev hasn't returned his calls. As Sam stands there, among the piles and piles of combustibles, Sam feels like the unpredictable fireball that everyone thinks he is.

"Shit," Sam says.

"Good morning to you too."

Watch Sam jump.

Behind him, a woman in an emerald colored blazer and a Super badge stands at the edge of the chaos holding a single file. Thin, angry scars crisscross the left side of her face and they ripple when she smiles and says: "You must be Sam the accountant."

No, he's Sam the Super. "Yes," he says, not confident enough to argue the point yet.

"Great, I'm Miranda." She holds out a hand. Sam shakes it.

"Are you the Team's coordinator?" he asks.

"Team coordinator, PR person, HR person, office manager. Basically all the stuff that needs to get done with no one to do it. But not, thank god, the accountant anymore. By the way, this is your desk." She points to the cleaner one.

"Um, look, I'm not sure this is a good idea," Sam says as he tugs his ugly, itchy hat over his ears. Sure, he's been practicing for a month now and he does have some control over his "special abilities", but not enough to feel comfortable.

"Why? You've done financial planning and tax prep before, right?" Miranda asks.

"Yes, but—"

"Not up for the challenge?"

"It's not that, I—" Sam bites his lip. He still doesn't know how to broach the top of his new "talents."

Miranda's eyes narrow. "You have a problem with me then?"

"No!"

"Then we don't have an issue."

"No, you don't understand. I'm a hazard in a place like this." Sam tries to keep his voice even. Sam fails.

Miranda smirks. "Hey, I promise not to dump beer on you if you promise not to burn the place down."

He stiffens. "You know about that?"

"Well, it is a viral video," she says, "And who the hell do you think sent you your Super application?"

Miranda smirks again and Sam feelings himself blushing.

"Look, I saw your audition," Miranda says, her smile fading into seriousness, "I know this scares you, but you've got the basics of control down and I really do need your bringing this *disaster*," She sweeps her arm around the room "into the digital age. You're not really a walking arsonist."

Sam fidgets with his gloves, holding back the sudden, unexpected lump in his throat. This is the first time in a month someone's believed in him. He just wishes he had that faith in himself. Or that his ex-boss did.

"So, I'm thinking we can spend the day sorting," Miranda says, sweeping up her black hair into a ponytail. "It'll be a good test for you and gives me an excuse to clean out some of this crap." She gives the nearest box a ferocious kick. "Ready?"

"I should say no, but that won't stop you, will it?" Sam says with a sigh.

Miranda grins. "You learn fast."

As they sift through impossible amounts of paper, Miranda talks relentlessly. Explaining everything from picking your unofficial uniform with the Team (aka your color scheme) to the Super Team's inner drama to why there were so many papers. Apparently, Miranda's predecessor emitted random electrical currents sometimes, so his computers never lasted long and he had to print out everything.

"Also, he was a hoarder," she adds as she dumps stacks of *Modern Dog* magazines in the recycling bin.

Sometimes Sam asks questions, but mostly he listens and works and focuses on not losing control. There's something comforting in Miranda's confident, easy going manner. Despite his relentless fear of burning, for the first time in almost a month, it's nice not to be alone.

By the end of the day, they've only sifted through a fraction of the receipts, tax documents, and random menu collections, but the office feels roomier.

"So what do you think? Ready to be part of this bureaucratic hell?" Miranda asks, flopping into her desk chair.

Sam surveys the office: Mountains of information. An infinite supply of invoices. Endless receipts. Job security at its finest.

"I think I want to get transferred to the Main Team," he says.

Miranda rolls her eyes. "Trust me, you don't."

"Why? Everyone loves them. They're on the news all the time."

Her eyes narrow and she crosses her arms. "You're trying to impress your family, aren't you?"

"What? No!" Sam's family is made up of one sister, who lives across the country. She at least still talks to him, though there's a new strain to those conversations.

No, Sam's here because of his friends and coworkers who haven't called since that night in the bar. Who didn't stop by or write him an email during that entire month afterwards when he was too scared to leave his apartment. Sam joined the Super Team so he could look in the mirror again and see more than what he's lost.

"I only want to save people," he says. "Honest."

Miranda gives Sam a long, calculating look.

"Bullshit." She props her feet up on her desk, "We might be trying to change public opinion, but there's really only one thing we can change for sure."

"What's that?" Sam asks, sinking into his own chair.

"How we see ourselves."

Someone coughs loudly behind him. Sam jumps, grabbing the rim of his hat. In the doorway, a small, wizened woman in faded clothes and work gloves studies Sam with a skeptical look.

"Um, hi, can I help you?" says Sam.

"Sam, meet Danielle. Building manager, repairwoman, and our sanity check," Miranda says and her hands move in a series of signs. "Danielle. this is Sam. The guy I was telling you about."

Danielle arches an eyebrow. She signs back rapidly.

Quietly, Miranda says: "She asks if you're going to start a fire." She's rubbing the scars on her face and doesn't meet Sam's eyes, but Sam appreciates her honesty.

He stares at the masses of files around him and for the hundredth time pictures the raging flames that would destroy everything if he screws up.

"Not today," he says, but thinks: *It's only a matter of time.*

Episode 4: Plan B, Anyone?

This is Sam's first time being a hero.

Or rather the first time he's assisting the Main Team in action. Sort of. Really, he's more of a spectator—there's only so much he can do from the sidewalk.

Whatever.

"This better be good," Miranda says as she pushes the last temporary barrier into place. Sam nods. For him, this is research.

They're standing on the curb, trying to keep curious spectators at a safe distance, but most people have their phones out, are leaning past the barriers, trying to get a better angle. Across the street, there's a building four stories tall with a chic Italian restaurant on street level. It looks like there's a light show happening on the roof, but according to the messages on the Team's group text, it is actually pieces of the building flashing in and out of existence. If he looks closely, Sam can just make out two figures standing near the lip of the roof. Even from his vantage point, Sam can see their fear, rising panic.

"Is this just a random event or was it caused by a Super?" Sam asks.

Miranda shrugs. "Who the hell knows."

Turns out that when people start developing strange, random powers in their mid-to-late twenties, other strange, random events start happening too. And while most Super teams are focused on volunteer work and public outreach, this Team is the only one in the city that handles the weird situations. The only one really making a difference.

That's what Sam hopes to do soon. No, that's what he *will* do.

"Don't let anyone cross the barrier!" someone shouts.

There's a half dozen Supers escorting people out of the building, including the woman from the bar, Toya, in a purple shirt. One by one, police cars and ambulances arrive at the scene, but they don't cross the barrier.

The lights on the building are flashing brighter, nearer.

The two people on the roof shriek and in desperation, hop down to a narrow ledge just below them. Sam can see them clearly now, a youngish man in a waiter's apron and a small woman in business casual, their backs pressed up against the building's wall, utterly terrified.

"Please! Don't move! I'll be right there!" Cyrus's voice cuts through the flashing lights, the confusion.

Sam blinks and suddenly Mr. Sunshine is standing on the lip of the roof, glowing brighter than the breaks in reality.

He pulls the woman up with one arm and slips her over his shoulder in a fireman's carry. "I'll be back for you in a minute," he tells the waiter he's leaving behind. "Hang tight." Then Cyrus is gone and the man left on the ledge looks stricken.

There is a blinding flash in the wall, inches from where the waiter's leaning. The brick siding pops out of existence, leaving behind a perfectly round void. And that's when Sam sees unreality for the first time.

It's a fathomless well—where no light, no warmth, no time survives.

So this is what breaks in reality look like? Sam thinks. Now he wishes he didn't know.

"Shit," says the waiter on the ledge, eyes wide with terror. He pushes away from the hole, stumbles back.

And falls.

Sam read once that survivors of terrible car crashes say that right before impact, time slows down. You can see the deadly trajectory, the race towards destruction. The inevitability. And all you can do is watch helplessly.

Watch Sam watch. The waiter is falling and he knows what will happen. Still, he can't look away.

But halfway down the four story drop, he stops falling downwards. And starts falling upwards instead. A few seconds later, he wafts to a stop, midair.

It takes Sam far too long to realize the waiter is not the only one floating. Everything that's not tied down is suspended too, though not at the same heights. The cars, trash, people closer to the building have risen higher than the things farther away. It's like looking at a circus's big top tent or reverse gravity well. And at the very pinnacle, the woman in magenta hovers, her hair standing straight up.

Sam is surprised. But really, he shouldn't be. The news did say she conquered gravity

"Holy crap," Miranda says, dropping her phone, but it doesn't hit the concrete. That's when Sam realizes they're both floating an inch above the sidewalk.

They're suspended for a good minute, maybe ten, or maybe fifteen seconds. Sam can't tell. Time gets weird in stressful situations. But he hovers an inch above the ground until the flashing on the roof stops. Gradually, all instances of unreality disappear, leaving only reality behind.

"It's over, Lana. Can you let us down now? Please?" someone calls. It sounds like Cyrus, but scared.

Slowly, everything sinks back to earth. Not all in the same order. Not always right side up. The waiter floats gently to the street, head first, but manages to do the world's most awkward somersault as he touches the sidewalk. The whole process looks like an exhalation, a gentle moment in a timeline of chaos.

Relief floods Sam. Next to him, Miranda lets out a sigh.

Then someone near the building starts screaming.

That's when Sam and everyone else realizes that a kid, no more than sixteen or seventeen is pinned under a car. His phone is lying cracked on the sidewalk a few feet away, but the video is still recording. He's screaming, screaming, screaming.

It's the Supers on the ground who recover first, who begin to herd people away, to call the paramedics over, to rush over to the kid. But Sam can't move. Those screams, that pain, will haunt Sam's dreams for months.

"Damn it, I said not to let anyone through the barrier." Sam turns to see the man in the blue T-shirt and glasses standing next to him. The Super who didn't want him to join at the audition.

He's close enough now for Sam to make out the faded words on his shirt. *The Who.*

Coherent thoughts elude Sam, but a fleeting 'Where the fuck did he come from?' manages to break through the stunned muteness of his mind.

"Sometimes, I think we don't lessen pain We just redistribute it." He sighs and pulls Sam a few feet away from the crowded barriers, the people gasping and mummering. "His episode will be over in a minute," he says to Miranda.

"What are you talking about?" she says.

But the man in blue is already rushing across the street to the kid as Sam stands and stares, clenching his hands into tight, painful balls.

We don't lessen pain.

Dear God, is this how all rescues end? In pain, and horror, and a bigger disaster than when they started?

We redistribute it.

And suddenly Sam can see what type of Super he'd be. The one that tries and tries and tries.

And fails.

And makes things worse.

Screw it. Sam doesn't want to be on the Main Team. Not anymore.

Sam doesn't notice how quiet it's gotten. Or how everyone around him is motionless and staring. Or that Miranda has stepped away from him.

"Sam," she says quietly, "You're on fire."

He looks down. Sure enough, despite his fireproof mittens, his hands are smothered in flames. And he knows, without glancing up, his scalp is too.

On cue, a gaping spectator behind the barrier holds up their phone.

"Not again," Sam whispers. But he can't stop this. And being a Super doesn't change that.

Watch Sam burn and hate himself for it.

Episode 5: Bad Takeout

No. Sam doesn't want to talk about it.

"Sam, it's all right. It happens. Almost everyone there was a Super anyway," says Miranda.

They're halfway down the street when a police car passes them, sirens wailing, heading towards the scene at the restaurant. Sam shivers and lengthens his stride.

"Jesus, slow down!"

But he doesn't. Instead, Sam wonders if a video of him burning is online yet and if it's called 'Man Spontaneously Combusts…Again'. He wonders if Lev will see it and if he'll be just as horrified even though, this time, he's not in it.

"Where are we going?" Miranda asks, as Sam makes a sharp turn right.

Like hell if Sam knows, he's just following his feet.

"Sam, it's okay to be upset. Seriously, who wouldn't be after that shitshow?" she says and it's true, Sam can hear the shaking in her voice. "But trust me on this one. The best thing to do right now is to go to the Point and drink with a dozen other shocked people." She catches his shoulder and pulls him to a stop. "C'mon, first one's on me."

Maybe she's right. Sam can almost hear a martini calling his name. Hell, there's a chorus of cocktails beckoning him into oblivion, fuck the promises he made to himself, to his hard earned, but insufficient control.

In the distance, another police siren cries out.

Panic clutches at his chest, his windpipe. No, he can't go back, can't face another person right now. Sam starts down the street again, quicker than before. Behind him, Miranda swears, but seconds later she's matching his strides besides him.

They walk for a long time.

"You know, we all get lost it in terrible situations," Miranda says, eventually. "We all have episodes with our gifts. No one on the Team will think less of you."

They're wandering down some back alley, half lit by the early evening sky and half by dirty street lights flickering over back exits. The pavement is covered with trash and just the smells wafting from the dumpster makes Sam want a shower.

"You stepped away from me back there," Sam says.

"'Yeah. You were on fire and my hair was too close for comfort."

Sam runs a hand over his bald head. Hair. He misses having hair.

A door opens behind them. Sam and Miranda glance back to see a heavyset man in a dirty apron steps out.

"Shit, out of all the alleys in this city," Miranda hisses. "Let's get out of here."

Sam turns just enough to see the man crush an unlit cigarette between his fingers, his face tight with anger.

"You," the man snarls.

"Fuck," Miranda says, "Seriously? What are the odds?"

"You. You're the Super that called the Health Department on me."

Miranda keeps walking, her gaze fixed straight ahead. "Asshole refused to serve me and my girlfriend the other night," she says, arms crossed, voice low, "Said he didn't want freaks in his upstanding establishment. So I filed a complaint."

"Hey you!"

"You can't just do that," Sam says.

"I didn't. Akira snuck into the kitchen after they threw us out, thinking we could still get dinner. Turns out we just avoided getting food poisoning."

"Hey you! I'm talking to you!"

"It shouldn't be like this." Sam glances back. The man is now trailing behind them, "It's not like I asked to become a Super."

"Look Sam, this is your life now. We didn't choose it, and

most people don't get that, but we're trying to teach people differently. That's the point of the Team."

"I should kick the shit out of you and that slutty friend of yours. And your boyfriend too."

Miranda stops. "But sometimes it's just one cruelty too many. Don't move."

Before Sam can reply, she spins around, clenching her hands. Somewhere in the distance a glass bottle or plate shatters.

"What? You think you scare me?" the man says. But he stops about twenty paces away.

"No. Not yet," says Miranda, quietly, so quietly Sam barely makes out the words.

At first, the man fails to notice how the pieces of broken glass near his feet are scuttling towards him, closing the distance. Only when a dumpster bursts open and half a dozen broken, empty bottles come flying at him, does he step back.

"Oh shit," he says. But it's too late.

Sam's never seen a real tornado, but from TV documentaries he know how they emerge from nothing – the swirling, darkening, ringlets of wind that materialize in mere seconds, swallowing everything in their path.

There's a tornado in the alley. But instead of wind and dust, it's made of glass—from bottles to containers, from whole shards to specks. And with each passing second more comes flying out of the recycling bins and dumpsters, adding to the swirl. Above him, Sam can hear the windows panels in the buildings thrum and rattle, begging to join.

Holy shit, she can control glass, he thinks.

"Miranda!" he yells, but she ignores him.

Watch Sam feel utterly powerless.

Then she unclenches her fists and slowly the glass tornado begins to decelerate, unwind. One by one, the shards clatter to the ground and shatter around the man on the pavement.

He doesn't look hurt. He must have sat in the eye of the storm, watching the deadly swirl whip around him. Which is good. Sam doesn't think he could've dealt with any more suffering today.

A handful of shards rises up and flank Miranda like wings as she closes the gap in three strides, grabbing the man's collar. "Never. Threaten. My Friends. Again. Understood?" She emphasizes each word with a shake. The glass around her quivers.

The man tries to nod but his whole body trembles instead.

"Go." She gives him an unceremonious push. A look of unparalleled relief flashes across the man's face as he stumbles away.

Miranda glares after him, balling and unballing her hands. But this time, the scattered glass around them doesn't stir. "Seriously. Who the fuck thinks it's a good idea to attack someone wearing a Super badge?"

"How...did you do that?"

"With perfect control," she replies.

"Did it come naturally to you?" he asks, half teasing, half envious.

"Sam, how do you think I got these?" She points to the crisscrossed scars on her face.

"Oh. Sorry." Watch Sam turn bright red.

Miranda shakes her head. "You have a good start, but I can teach you the rest."

Sam opens his mouth. Closes it. Finally says. "I saw a void in reality today. What am I supposed to do with that?"

"Scream into it," replies Miranda. "And keep going."

Sam looks at the shards of glass sprinkled around his feet, then at his friend. There's a small smile on her face.

"Okay," he says. "When do lessons start?"

Episode 6: The Life of a Super – Part 1

Most days, being a Super isn't so bad.

Sam wakes up promptly at 7:35 am, sprints through showering, shaving, and dressing, so he can run down to the corner bakery for coffee and muffins. Because Miranda shows up at his apartment at 8 am and he's learned she's a much more benevolent teacher when she's had breakfast. They've agreed his apartment is the safest place to practice control; there's still nothing in it that can burn. They run through breathing exercises, figure out Sam's triggers and warning signs. Experiment with having only his hands burn, then only his left palm, then only his thumbs.

"Don't be afraid of your abilities," Miranda tells him over and over. "They're part of you."

Sam understands this intellectually, but the sight of his hands in flames still makes him nauseous.

They practice for an hour every morning before work and at first, there are so few successes that Sam has to take out the batteries in the smoke detectors. Open the windows. Turn off the heat.

Sometimes Sam wonders if progress is happening at all.

Whatever. Sam isn't interested in being in the spotlight anymore. Sure, there's still a part of him—a big part, maybe—that dreams of being the hero. But that goes against his new personal rules. Like ignoring text messages concerning the Main Team. Avoiding rescue missions at all costs. And never asking about them later.

He can still hear that kid, trapped under that car, screaming.

But being a Super isn't so bad. He's decided on his unofficial Super uniform. It's black button up shirt paired with an orange and yellow ombre scarf. When he pins his new Super badge to his breast pocket, he feels a small warmth of pride. He's found the courage to reach out to a few of his friends from his pre-Super life and he's been texting Cyrus too. They've been planning on going out for coffee, but it keeps getting rescheduled due to the miniature wormholes that have been popping up all over the city.

"Keep trying, Sam," says Miranda as Sam attempts to make only his right pinky burn.

It's the office work that Sam likes best. Sure the hours are long, the chaos is frustrating, and the pay is terrible, but at least he doesn't have to worry about losing his job for having a "gift" he never wanted in the first place. He spends a few hours every morning sorting through another stack of papers, slowly constructing a narrative of numbers from the misfiled expense reports, unpaid invoices, and payrolls. He learns some interesting things too. Like the Super Team's solvency has always been episodic, unpredictable, in direct correlation to public popularity, but always survived because the police and fire department are more than happy to let Supers handle the breaks in reality first. And auditions for the Team are just formalities.

"I don't just send Super applications out at random, you know," Miranda says, "Do you know how hard it is to find someone with an ability who is CPA certified too?"

"But Cyrus—"

"Is smart enough not to argue with me,"

Then why, Sam wonders, had everyone tried to talk him out of joining?

Whatever.

He's also managed to befriended almost everyone on the Team. Even Danielle, who turns off the office lights if she thinks Miranda and Sam are working too late. Though they started on rough terms, she and Sam have discovered a mutual love for jazz piano and have a long, ongoing text conversations about technique and artists. Sam's even picked up a few choice words in ASL.

"Yes, but can you do it with your hands on fire?" Miranda asks they run through diaphragm exercises. Again.

But slowly, Sam begins to plan for the future. The Team's future that is. At least financially. Setting up investment accounts and following up on those unpaid invoices. He even starts a blog with Miranda, offering a mixture of financial advice for Supers and interviewing people with less obvious "extra ordinary abilities." No matter how strange. They recently met a woman who could turn into a grasshopper, but only from the waist up.

It's a ridiculous amount of work, but it's all in the spirit of the

Team's ongoing mission to change the public's perception of Supers.

"What if it's not possible?" Sam asks during a practice session, after failing to burn in one second increments.

"Then we'll die trying," Miranda replies.

Such is the life of a Super.

———

Episode 7: Life of a Super—Part 2

Watch Sam not burn.

Miranda would be proud; their lessons are paying off. But Sam's not thinking about Miranda. He's too busy not reducing the grocery store to ashes.

All he wanted was some milk. And some protein bars. And some apples. But it looks like he won't be getting any of those things. The entire store has come to a halt and the woman at the cash register is *still* ignoring him.

Sam clears his throat. "Excuse me, I would like to purchase these *please.*" But he might as well be talking to the milk.

A moment passes as he stares down the cashier and she glares at his ombre scarf and Super badge.

"We don't want your type here," she spits out, "You should all be deported."

Watch Sam stare. This—after all the hours of work Supers dedicate to saving people. To volunteering. Going through ridiculous news interviews, magazine profiles so strangers at home can feel "inspired." Just so people understand that this life is not a choice. Or something to be ashamed of.

He thought they were making progress.

For a moment, Sam debates the best ways to set off the fire alarm. He knows it'll just make public relations worse, but sometimes when life hands you a useless power, you want to make it rain bitter lemonade.

No. Sam is in control. Watch Sam not burn.

Instead he says, "I'm sorry to hear that ma'am. I hope you're never in a situation where you need help."

As he makes his way to the exit, Sam adds a new rule to his list: Only shop in places with self-checkout.

Outside, it's raining and the city is various shades of gray. He attracts a few glances from pedestrians, but once they catch his eye, they quickly look away. Before Sam was on the Team, people never noticed him, he wasn't much to look at, even with hair. But now that he's forgotten to take off his badge on his way home from work, he's getting double takes.

Thing is, Sam doesn't mind being different. It's all the bullshit he gets about it that bothers him.

He's shaking, but not from the damp or the cold. His fingers and scalp begin itch mercilessly, begging to ignite. *No. Not here. Not yet.* Sam thinks and sprints back to his apartment. It's only when he's in the alleyway, alongside the dumpsters, does Sam turn his face up to the remorseless sky. Only then does he exhale like Miranda taught him and let the fire consume his head, his hands.

Watch Sam burn and burn and burn.

Episode 8: But It's Better Than Drinking Alone

Sure, figuring out how to close the biggest wormhole humanity has ever seen might be cause for celebration. But not for Sam.

For him, today has been a nightmare. Taking out rogue tax returns. Deciphering cryptic financial information. Chasing slippery receipts. The time-space continuum might be back to normal, but what about the paper trail?

"You're full of it," Akira says, but she's laughing. So is Mac from behind the bar.

The Point is full of Supers—laughing, drinking, arm wrestling—despite the cuts and bruises and torn clothes. The place smells like cheap beer and sense of relief is thick and joyful.

"I don't want to hear it." Miranda pokes Sam in the chest, her bracelets jingling and her martini sloshing dangerously. "While your lazy ass was sitting there, I was on the phone for an hour with PD trying to explain the details. Then the reporters. And then another hour with the hospital until I talked to a nurse who actually knew something…"

Sam stares at his soda water as the smiles slip away around him. Because not everyone escaped with just cuts and bruises.

"How is Cyrus?" Mac asks quietly.

"Pretty banged up," Miranda says with a sigh, "Lots of internal damage and broken bones. But he'll heal. Eventually."

Sam squeezes the glass in his hands. There's been an ache in his chest ever since he heard the news. He always imagined Cyrus as indestructible. He'd called the hospital too and was crushed when he'd learned that it'll be awhile before non-family members would be able to visit.

"Well as fantastic as you all are, I have work tomorrow," Miranda finishes her martini in a swallow. She picks up her purse, fishing for her wallet

"Don't worry about it, M," Sam pulls out a twenty, "I've got it. You too, Akira."

Miranda puts a fist on her hip. "Look, your attempt at chivalry's adorable –"

"But my lazy ass won't be in the office until ten tomorrow." Sam grins as Miranda makes a face, but she doesn't argue. Which suits Sam fine. He's been a Super for three months now and the thrill of having compatriots to buy drinks for hasn't gotten old yet.

"Thanks Sam." Akira gives him a quick, tight hug. She flashes Miranda a knowing smile and hand in hand they leave The Point.

Sam's grinning as he watches them go. It's been a terrible day, but it would've been unbearable if he was alone.

"She works too much," says a voice at Sam's elbow. He turns to see that the man in the blue T-shirt with *The Who* on it, has appeared on the bar stool besides him. Sam is friendly with everyone on the Super Team. But the man in blue has been the exception. In fact, the only time Sam sees him is when he turns up next to him out of nowhere.

At least this time Sam doesn't jump.

"I know," says Sam. He also knows from the payroll that the man's name is Lance.

Lance's brows furrow for a moment. Then his face relaxes. "Good, she needs more friends." He catches Mac's eye. "The usual, please."

"Sure thing," Mac says, startled, and hurries away.

"How do you sneak up like that?"

"It's all about timing. You probably weren't going to turn around for another minute."

"So what? You see the future?" Sam jokes.

"Only the worst possible outcome," says Lance, "Actually, it's more like glancing at a snapshot."

Watch Sam's jaw drop.

"You see future snapshots?" Sam always thought prophetic abilities were fictions dished out by slimy financial advisors.

"Yeah well, it's not the best gift to have for making friends," Lance says picking up the beer Mac puts in front of him. He takes a large swallow. "And the worst usually doesn't happen, but you can prevent a lot by anticipating it."

"Is that how you knew to keep the pedestrians away during that incident with unreality on the roof?" Sam asks.

Lance nods. "It's my job on the Team to keep civilians safe."

"That kid under the car-"

"Wasn't the worst thing that could have happened."

"What was?"

Lance takes another swallow, staring straight ahead. His hand is in a white-knuckled fist on the counter. "You don't want to know."

Sam has no idea what to say to that. He sips his soda water and tries to focus on that warm feeling of friendship he had two minutes ago. It works. For about a minute. But his traitor thoughts eventually wander back to Cyrus.

"Aren't you going to ask me how we managed to close the wormhole?" Lance says, suddenly.

"No," Sam says. "I'm happier not knowing, I think."

For the first time, Lance gives him a small smile. "Good. What were you worrying about then?"

"Cyrus."

Lance's small smile dies. "He'll be fine." Sam opens his mouth to ask 'How?', but he's cut off with a glare. "I need to believe that, Sam. Despite what I see."

Sam nods. He understands. Clinging to his own slivers of hope is how his survived these last three months.

"Did you know we started the team?" Lance asks. Sam shakes his head. "Me and Cyrus and Lana. We wanted to teach the world by example. Show we're people and belong here too." His shoulders slump. "Sometimes I wonder if we're making any difference."

"I think we are." Sam says. "And if we aren't, there's nothing we can do about it now, right?" It's what he tells Miranda when she's stressing out. It's what he tells himself when worry claws at him.

"No, but-"

"So, we might as well enjoy the evening." Sam raises his glass and after a moment's hesitation, Lance lifts his beer and clinks.

They sit there and drink in almost comfortable silence for ten minutes or an hour or maybe two. Time becomes slippery when you've been stressed out and overworked for months. Before either of them realizes it, the mood in the bar has changed: The point in the evening where happy celebrators dissolve into melodramatic drunks.

Lance struggles to his feet. "Sam, get me out of here. *Now*," he hisses. All around them, Supers' faces are contorted with raw emotion, heralding poor decision making.

Sam doesn't need to be told twice. He puts an arm around Lance to steady him and together, they weave their way towards the door.

Outside, it's cold, but liberating. Lance visibly relaxes a little and points down that street. "Home's that way. Do you mind?"

"Nope." Sam's no Main Team hero, so basically, this is the least he can do.

They walk in silence for a while. Sometimes the street lights flicker off when they pass, sometimes they don't.

"You still want to, don't you? To prove everyone wrong." Lance asks as they near his narrow house wedged between other narrow houses.

The question startles Sam, because despite his best intentions, the promises to himself, the lies he tells to keep going, he still wants to be the hero he imagined when he joined the Super Team. Because the truth is, even after all this time, the video of the oblivious burning man in the middle of the jazz bar and his horrified boyfriend gaping at him still wanders into his thoughts. And the only thing that hurts more than the comment section is Lev's expression.

"Do you read people's minds too?" Sam tries to keep his voice light. Sam fails.

"I didn't have to. The whole Team's the same way. Even Mac."

"But. . .but Mac's not a Super. . .?"

"No, but his niece is. And she's too afraid to leave her little trailer in the country. Mac's hoping Teams like ours will one day change her mind."

Sam stares at Lance. "But being on the Team must make things easier...after a while."

"Look, man, I don't think that's possible," Lance puts a hand on Sam's shoulder. "I'm sorry, at the audition, I tried to warn you."

Sam hesitates. Hesitates. Then:

Watch Sam ask the question he's been avoiding.

"If I..if I stay with the Super Team, what snapshot do you see of me?"

Lance stares at him, his expression becoming pained before he buries his face in his hands. "You don't want to know, Sam."

But Sam can hear it anyway. *We don't lessen anyone's pain, just redistribute it.*

And he sees it now. It's the anguish that's on Lance's face. The feeling that's carved a space in Sam's own chest cavity since that night at the jazz bar. The feeling that hasn't gone away.

Screw it, Sam doesn't want to be a Super. Not anymore.

Episode 9: If You Want to Reach Me, Call the North Pole

An hour later, Sam has packed his bags. His ombre scarf and Super badge are piled neatly at the end of the bed. He feels odd without it; he's come to love his unofficial uniform. But Sam reminds himself exile is the better choice. Nothing will ever change here.

He already has a list of relocation programs he's going to call in the morning.

He can't quite leave yet, though. He doesn't quite have the courage to say goodbye in person, so Miranda will find a note in the office with an apology in the morning. He owes her that much. Probably more.

But being a Super won't solve any of Sam's problems.

He was an idiot to believe it ever could.

Episode 10: Everything Burns

From the outside, the old community center looks dead. But Sam is pretty sure Danielle is still in there, working late. A fuse blew out earlier that afternoon – again—and the lights are still on inside.

From across the street, with Miranda's note tucked in his pocket, Sam pulls out his phone.

U still at work? he texts Danielle.

Sam doesn't think much of the faint rustling noise or the muffled thuds. City noises. Something that he'll miss in his exile.

Except, a faint light catches his eye. A flicker. It comes from the entrance of the building. A moment later, a woman steps out of the community center.

Even from across the street, Sam can see the maniac look in her eyes, in her posture. She holds a phone at arm's length, the camera trained on herself.

"This one's for the Super Team," she says, "The freaks who think they're better than us." She spots Sam and turns the phone around. Sam flinches.

"Will you tell the Supers if they don't see this?" she calls.

"I am a Super," he says, forgetting to use past tense. And that's when Sam notices the empty gas can in her other hand. That's when he smells the smoke.

Danielle.

Oh shit.

The woman's laughter hounds him as he runs towards the community center.

Inside, the flames are already billowing. It's as if the old community center had been waiting for a match. A spark. Naturally, the fire sprinklers don't work.

Sam dashes towards the basement steps, painfully aware of how everything has become uncomfortably warm. The smell of smoke, thick and overpowering.

Watch Sam run.

He sprints through the rows of files, down the hallway, and around the corner to Danielle's office. He pounds on the door, once, twice, then wrenches it open.

Only to find it empty.

The lights are off, her toolbox is in the corner, and her coat and hat and scarf are gone. As if on cue, the phone that Sam has forgotten he's holding buzzes to life. The text from Danielle says *"No, Im home. Enjoying my life. Where r u?"*

Watch Sam run again. But he only makes it a few feet before

he's forced to drop to the floor for air. The smoke is unavoidable now with the smell of everything burning. The heat corralling him from all sides. The fire has finally found the multitude of invoices, billing, and random magazines. All around him, years of civil service records are being reduced to ash.

Watch Sam crawl as fast as he can.

He almost makes it too. But then a mountain of burning papers comes crashing down, trapping Sam in flames. Blinding, raging, ravenous flames. Flames that cannot be controlled. Flames that are hungry for more.

And yet ... they're not that bad.

Actually, they're not even that hot.

Watch Sam not burn.

Episode 11: Final Decisions

Sam might not burn, but his clothes still do. Now, he's cold without them, standing naked amid all the wailing sirens and grim faced firefighters.

Eventually, one of them takes pity and gives him a fire blanket. The coarse wool never felt so good. He sits on the curb, the cement like sandpaper on his bare skin, but somehow, this feels good too.

This is how Miranda finds Sam. She doesn't skimp on the expletives. She takes her time scolding him, repeatedly reminding him what a fucking stupid bastard he is and all the work he would have left her with if burned to death. "Lance told me you'll die of smoke inhalation!" she yells.

But Sam doesn't mind, she's the only steady point amidst the chaos – an anchor, a focus. And when she runs out of words, she's shaking and Sam wishes he had another blanket to give her.

"If it makes you feel better, Lance hinted at the same thing to me," he tells her.

"I forgot," she says as she takes a seat next to him. "I forgot that you can't always believe the Team's Anxiety Man." She slumps, puts her face in her hands. "I thought you gave up on rescuing people, Sam."

Honestly, until an hour ago, Sam planned on living out the rest of his selfish life not a hero. Rushing into that fire was the most reckless thing he's ever done, but in the flames, he found something new.

"Friends are exceptions," he says.

Miranda gives him a long, hard look. "Yeah," she says finally. "They are."

As they sit shoulder to shoulder, their attention drifts to a reporter and a cameraman talking to a fireman a few yards off. All three men are looking at Sam.

"Excuse me, are you the Super who ran into the building?" the reporter asks, approaching Sam, but speaking into his mike. Sam gives the camera trained on him an uncomfortable glance and pulls the blanket tighter.

"Yes," Miranda answers, before Sam can respond, "He's one of the most important members of our Team."

I am? Sam starts to say. Then he catches Miranda's expression. In it, he sees she how truly afraid she was of losing him tonight.

Sam nods.

"So..is this just another episode in the Supers' long and troubled history?"

Episodes, right. Sam wants to laugh. It's clear to him now, sitting naked, reeking of smoke that Super episodes are unavoidable. It's how you pick yourself up afterwards that matters.

"Yup," he says.

By now, most of the neighborhood is out watching the flames die down, clustering around the reporter, shooting video footage of their own.

"And what do you do for the Super Team exactly?" the reporter asks.

"All the uncool work that keeps our photogenic Teammates going and you busy," Sam replies. Besides him, Miranda laughs.

The ears of the reporter turn slightly pink. "Could you demonstrate your talents for us, then Mr. . .?"

"Sam Wells. A Super."

All around them, the spectators lean in, hold their breath in anticipation.

Sam runs a hand over his tingling scalp. He knows that now is his moment in the spotlight. He knows that in a week, he'll just be an accountant again with new episodes and problems. That he'll be back fighting for the same things, the same rights.

So, for the first time in ages, Sam squares his shoulders and looks directly at the camera.

Watch Sam burn.

Or maybe not.

Either way, watch Sam smile for the audience.

And no longer care what they see.

THE PILL

BY MEG ELISON
PUBLISHED BY PM PRESS

My mother took the Pill before anybody even knew about it. She was always signing up for those studies at the university, saying she was doing it because she was bored. I think she did it because they would ask her questions about herself and listen carefully when she answered. Nobody else did that.

She had done it for lots of trials; sleep studies and allergy meds. She tried signing up when they tested the first 3D printed IUDs, but they told her she was too old. I remember her raging about that for days, and later when everybody in that study got fibroids she was really smug about it. She never suggested I do it instead; she knew I wasn't fucking anybody. How embarrassing my own mother didn't even believe I was cute enough to get a date at sixteen. I tried not to care. And I'm glad now I didn't get fibroids. I never wanted to be a lab rat, anyway. Especially when the most popular studies (and the ones Mom really went all-out for) were the diet ones.

She did them all: the digital calorie monitors that she wore on her wrists and ankles for six straight weeks. (I rolled my eyes at that one, but at least she didn't talk about it constantly.) The strings like clear licorice made of some kind of super-cellulose that were supposed to accumulate in her stomach lining and give her a no-surgery stomach stapling but just made her (and everyone else who didn't eat a placebo) fantastically constipated. (Unstoppable complaining about this one; I couldn't bring anyone home for weeks for fear that she'd abruptly start telling my friends about her struggle to shit.) Pill after pill after pill that gave her heart palpitations, made her hair fall out, or (on one memorable occasion) induced psychotic delusions. If it was a way out of being fat, she'd try it. She'd try anything.

In between the drug trials, she did all the usual diets. Eat like a caveman. Eat like a rabbit. Seven small meals. Fasting one day a week. Apple cider vinegar bottles with dust on their upper domes sat tucked into the back corners of our every kitchen cabinet, behind the bulwark of Fig Newtons and Ritz crackers.

She'd try putting the whole family on a diet, talk us into taking 'family walks' in the evening. She'd throw out all the junk food and make us promise to love ourselves more. (Loving yourself means crying over the scale every morning and then sniffling into half a grapefruit, right?) Nothing stuck and nothing made any real difference. We all resisted her, eating in secret in our rooms or out of the house. I found Dad's bag of fish taco wrappers jammed under the driver's seat of the car while looking for my headphones. Mom caught me putting it in the garbage and yelled at me for like an hour. I never told her it was his. She was always hardest on me about my weight, as if I was the only one who had this problem. We were a fat family. Mom was just as fat as me; we looked like we were built to the same specs. Dad was fat, my brother was the fattest of us all.

I'm still fat. Everyone else is in the past tense.

And why? Because of this fucking Pill.

That trial started the same way they always do; flyers all over campus where Mom works, promising cash for the right demographic for an exciting new weight loss solution. Mom jumped on it like she always did, taking a pic of the poster so she could email from the comfort of her broken-down armchair with the TV tray rolled up close and her laptop permanently installed there. I remember I asked her once why she even had a laptop if she never took it anywhere. She never even unplugged it! It might as well have been an old-school tower and monitor rig. Why go portable if you're never going to leave the port?

She had shrugged. "Why call it a laptop when I don't have a lap?"

She had me there. I could never sit my computer in my 'lap' either. That real estate was taken up by my belly when I sat, and it was terribly uncomfortable to have a screen down that low, anyway. I've seen people do it on the train, and they look all hunched and bent. But mom wanted the hunching and the bending. She wanted a flat, empty lap and a hot computer balanced on her knees. She wanted inches of clearance between her hips and an airline seat and to buy the clothes she saw on the mannequin in the window. She wanted what everybody wants.

Respect.

I guess I wanted that, too. I just didn't think it was worth the lengths she would go to to get it. And none of them really worked. Until the Pill.

So Mom signed up like she always did, putting the meetings and dosage times on the calendar. Dad rolled his eyes and said he hoped this time didn't end with her crying about not being able to take a shit again. He met my eyes behind her back and we both smiled.

She just clucked her tongue at him. "Your language Carl, honestly. You've been out of the Navy a long time."

Dad tapped his pad and put in time to meet with his D&D buddies while Mom was busy with this new trial group. I smiled a little. I was glad he was going to do something fun. He had seemed pretty down lately. I was going to be busy, too. I had Visionaries; my school's filmmaking club. We had shoots set up every night for two weeks, trying to make this gonzo horror movie about a virus that made the football team turn into cannibals. (Look, I didn't write it. I was the director of photography.)

Off Mom went to eat pills and answer questions about her habits. I had heard her go through all of this before and learned to hold my tongue. But I knew exactly how it would go: Mom would sit primly in a chair in a nice outfit, trying to cross her legs and never being able to hold that position. Her thighs would spread out on top of one another and slowly slide apart, seeking the space to sag around the arms of the chair and make her seem wider than ever, like a water balloon pooling on a hot sidewalk. She would never tell the whole truth. It was maybe the thing I hated about her the most.

"Oh yes, I exercise every day!"

(She walked about twenty minutes a day total, from her car to her office and back again. Her treadmill was covered in clothes on hangers and her dumbbells were fuzzed with a mortar made of dust and cat hair.)

"I try to eat right, but I have bad habits that stem from stress."

(Rain or shine, good day or bad, Mom had three scoops of ice cream with caramel sauce every night at ten.)

"I do think I come by it honestly. My parents were both heavy. And my sisters, and most of my cousins, too."

That one's true. The whole family is fat. In our last family photo, we wore an assortment of bright-colored shirts and we looked like a basket of round, ripe fruit. I kind of liked it, but I think I might have been the only one. The composition of the shots was good, and we all looked happy. Happy wasn't enough, apparently. Mom paid for those, but she never hung them up.

She came home from the first few sessions chatty and real keyed up. She posted on her timelines how happy she was to be trying something really innovative, and how she had a good feeling about this one. She wasn't allowed to say much, they made her sign an NDA. Later, I think she was glad that nobody could ask her the details.

I knew this time was going to be different the first night I heard the screaming. I had been up way past midnight, trying to edit footage of football players lumbering, meat-crazed, hands outstretched against the outline of the goalposts in a sunset-orange sky. My eyes had gotten hot and I'd had to put two icepacks under my laptop to cool down the CPU. (The machine just wasn't up to all that processing and rendering.) I woke up at 4AM to the sound of it, jolting upright, my heart in my ears like someone had stuffed a tiny drum set into my head. I was so tired and out of it, I almost didn't know what I was hearing. But it was her voice. Mom was screaming like she was on fire. She did it so long and loud and unbroken that I couldn't understand how she could get her breath at all. It was out, out, out, and hardly a gasp in.

I ran into the hallway and smacked straight in Andrew, who was going the same way. We whacked belly against belly and fell backwards on our butts like a couple of cartoon characters. I can picture it exactly in my head; the way I'd frame it, the sound effects we could layer over the top. But in the moment, there was no time to laugh or argue. We just scrambled back up and made for our parents' bedroom door.

It was locked.

"Dad!" I hammered my fist against the hollow-core six-panel barrier. "Dad, what's happening? Is Mom ok?"

There was an unintelligible string of sounds from him. With Mom screaming like a steam whistle, there was no chance to make it out.

"I'm calling 911," Andrew yelled. His phone was already in his hand.

When the door opened, the sound of Mom's screaming hit us at full force, and Andrew and I both stumbled backward a little. The door muffled it only slightly, but when the sound is your own mother dying, a little counts for a lot.

Dad was there, his gray hair a mess that pointed fingers in every direction, seeming to blame everyone at once. He put a hand out to Andrew, his face in a grimace, his eyes wide.

"Don't. Don't call anyone. Your mother says this is part of the trial she's in. She said it's worse than she thought it would be, but it only lasts for fifteen minutes."

Andrew looked at his phone. "I woke up almost ten minutes ago, when she was just growling."

"Growling," I asked. "What?"

Andrew rolled his eyes. "You could sleep through a nuclear strike."

Dad was nodding, looking at his watch. "We're almost out of it. Just hold on."

"Dad," Andrew said. "The neighbors probably already called the cops. She's really loud."

Dad's grimace widened. "I'm going to have to—"

The screaming stopped. The three of us looked at each other.

"Carl?" Mom's voice sounded exhausted and raw.

Dad fixed us both with a stern look, oscillating back and forth between the two of us. "You two don't call anyone. You don't tell anyone. Your mother is entitled to a little privacy. Is that understood?"

We looked at each other and said nothing.

Mom called again and he was gone, back on the other side of the door.

I didn't go back to sleep. I'm betting Andrew didn't either. But we stayed in our rooms for the next three hours, until it was time for breakfast. I went back to editing footage, and I was pretty pleased with what I'd be able to show to the Visionaries the next day. The movie was going to come in on schedule. It was great to have a project; something to take my mind off the weirdness in the night. I'm betting Andrew just signed on to his game. That's all he ever does.

I heard him turn off his alarm on the other side of the wall, followed by the sound of him standing up out of his busted computer chair with a grunt. He's way fatter than me, so I feel like I'm allowed to be disgusted by some of his habits. Andrew can't sit or stand without making a guttural, bovine noise. I've seen crumbs trapped in the folds of his neck. I used to work really hard to not be one of Those Fat People. I was obsessively clean, took impeccable care of my skin. I never showed my upper arms or my thighs, no matter what the occasion. I acted like being fat was impolite, like burping, and the best thing to do was conceal it behind the back of my hand and then always, always beg somebody's pardon.

I didn't know anything back then.

Andrew made it to the stairs before I did, so I got to watch him jiggle and shuffle down them, filled with loathing and disgust. I couldn't remember what bullshit diet we were supposed to be following that week, but I vowed to myself that no matter how small breakfast was, I would eat less of it than Andrew. I would leave something behind on the plate. Let Andrew be the one to lick his fingers and whine. I was above all that. There was wheat toast and cut apples waiting for us when we came into the kitchen.

And there was Mom at the coffee pot, fifty pounds lighter. Her pajamas hung off her like a hand-me-down from a much bigger sister. She turned, cup in hand, and I saw the dark circles beneath her eyes. She was beaming, however, with the biggest smile I'd seen on her face in years.

"It's working," she said, her voice still rough and edged with fatigue like she'd been to a rock concert or an all-night bonfire. "This thing is actually working."

That was our life for two weeks. Dad did his best to sound-proof their bathroom. He stapled carpets and foam and egg crate to the walls. He covered the floor in a dozen fluffy bath mats he bought for cheap on the internet. He told me later that he tried to put a rag in her mouth, just to muffle her a little more.

"But I'm worried she'll pull it into her throat and choke on it," he told me, his eyes wide with dread. "I can't stand this much longer. I know she's losing weight, but it's like I'm living in a nightmare and I can't wake up."

That was a year before he decided to take the Pill, and back then he was more willing to talk about it. When it wasn't his own privacy, only hers, he would tell me how gross it was. You can see videos of it online. It was the same in that first trial as it is now: you take the Pill and you shit out your fat cells. In huge, yellow, unmanageable flows at first. That's why they scream so much. Imagine shitting fifty pounds of yourself at a go. Now, people go to special spas where they have crematoiletaries that burn the fat down. Dad said Mom screwed up our plumbing so bad that he had to buy a whole case of that lye-based stuff to break it all down and keep the toilet flushing. That was as gross as I thought things could get, but Dad said it got worse.

Toward the end, Mom (and everyone like her) shit out all their extra skin, too. The process that broke it down meant no stretch marks and no baggy leftovers, hanging on your body like over-proofed dough on a hook and telling people you used to be fat.

That was some trick, and it was part of the reason it took so long for a generic to hit the market. It was a "trade secret," they said on the news. They also said "miracle" and "breakthrough" and "historic." The miracle of shitting out skin just looked like blood and collagen and rotten meat, it turns out. Not less gross, but different. More lye into the S bend. More and more of Mom gone at the breakfast table.

At the end of the trial, she was a person I didn't recognize. She was 110lbs soaking wet. The research doctor told her that she was at 18% body fat and she would stay that way for the rest of her life. Her face was a whole new shape, with the underlying structure very prominent and her eyes huge and wide above it all. I could see her hip bones below her enormous drawstring pants, pulled tight as a laundry bag around her now-tiny waist. Her collarbones could have held up a taco each. The cords in her neck stood out like chicken bones caught under her skin. Even her feet were smaller—she went down one whole shoe size and I inherited all her stretched-out sandals and sneakers.

I slid my feet into them, thinking how it was like my mom had died and some other woman had moved in. Late at night, I gathered up all the clothes she had given me and bundled them into the garbage. They were ugly, but they also felt somehow humiliating to wear. I couldn't explain the impulse. Luckily, she never asked me where any of it went. She was very focused on herself in those days.

"It finally happened," Mom told me with tears in her eyes.

"They finally made a Pill that gives you the perfect body, no matter what."

And yeah, she could eat anything she wanted and didn't have to work out. As long as she kept taking the small maintenance dose of the Pill, she would stay this way for as long as she lived. Which she thought would be much longer, now that she didn't have to carry around the threats of diabetes and heart disease everywhere she went.

I remember one day I walked in and found her and Dad sitting at the kitchen table, both of them obviously crying. They tried to hide it from me; Dad ducked his face into the shawl collar of his sweater, Mom swiping her eyes with quick fingers.

"What's up with you guys," I asked, trying not to look.

"Nothing, honey. There's carrot and celery sticks cut fresh and sitting in water in the fridge, if you want a snack."

Mom's voice was thick in her throat; she'd really been sobbing. I ignored both the sorrow and the content of what she'd said and fished around in the cabinet over the sink until I found one individually-wrapped chocolate cupcake.

"I'm good," I said, and I tried to leave the kitchen.

"Honey, do you think I lost all this weight so that I could leave you guys?"

I stopped and turned on the spot like something on a rotating plate; a pizza in a microwave. I couldn't help it. I should have just kept walking.

"What?"

Dad buried his face some more. Mom just looked at me, her eyes all shiny. "Did you ever think that my desire to lose weight was about you? Like, do you feel like I'm trying to leave you behind?"

I stared at her. There wasn't anything I could say. How could I feel any other way? How did she not know how obvious she was?

Every diet, every scheme, every study was just her trying to find a way out of being what we are. Every time she tried to change who she was, who we all were, it was like betrayal.

I looked over at Dad and realized this wasn't about me. He was worried she was going to *physically* leave him, now that she thought she was hot enough to hook up with somebody else. I saw it all at once; the way she was never worried about me being on birth control, the way Dad looked at other women in the supermarket. The way all of us were so focused on what we looked like as if it mattered, as if being thin was the only kind of life worth living.

So I lied.

"No, Mom. I don't think about it at all, I guess. It really has nothing to do with me."

I left them alone and went to eat my cupcake in peace. I looked at the timer I'd had running on my phone since the beginning of junior year: the countdown to the day I'd leave for college. I wanted out even back then, but I hadn't sent out applications yet. Back then, two years seemed like forever.

Mom and Dad made up, I guess. They never told us anything that mattered. Anyway, that was when the deaths started to make the news.

The averages are still debated all the time, because pre-existing conditions can't be ruled out. But people seem to agree it's about one in ten. In each group of thirty participants in the early studies, ten were control, ten got the placebo, and the final ten got the Pill. Nine out of ten shit themselves to perfection. That tenth one, though. They ended up slumped on a toilet, blood vessels burst in their eyes, hearts blown out by the strain of converting hundreds of pounds of body mass to waste.

I never thought it would get approved with a ten percent fatality rate, but I guess I was really naive. The truth was it got fast-tracked and approved by the FDA within a year. Mom was in a commercial, talking about how it gave her her life back, but this was a life she had never had. It gave her someone else's life entirely. Some life she had never even planned for. In the commercial, she wore a teal sports bra and a lot of makeup. I did not recognize her at all. She stood next to that celebrity, the one who did it first. What's her name. Amy Blanton.

Remember those ads? "Get the Amy Blanton body!" She had gained a little weight after she had her kids, but her Before picture and Mom's Before picture looked like members of two different species. In the commercial, their former selves got whisked away and there they were: exactly the same height, exactly the same build. A little contouring and a blowout made them twins. Mom had the Amy Blanton body. For just a little while, people would stop her on the street and ask if she was Amy Blanton. That got old fast. I used to just walk away fatly while she pretended she looked nothing like her TV twin.

I watched Dad grow more and more insecure about the change in Mom. I saw him get mad at a guy at the gas station who checked out Mom's ass when she bent over.

"Get back in the car, Carl. Gosh, you're making a scene about nothing. It was just a compliment!"

Dad sat down, fuming, but he wouldn't close his door. His ears were bright red. Andrew was playing a game on his phone, totally zoned out. I watched Dad trying to calm himself down.

"You probably haven't been jealous about Mom since you guys were kids, huh?"

He blew out hot air through his nose like a bull. "Try *ever*," he said, his voice tight.

"Wasn't Mom hot as a teenager."

His lips closed into a line I could see in the rearview mirror. "She was always heavy. She was... she was mine, god damnit."

That sort of shocked me. He hadn't ever talked about her that way before. And it hadn't ever occurred to me that maybe my dad the football player had gotten with my less-than-perfect mom because he knew she'd never cheat on him. Could never. Just like she thought I could never go out and get myself in trouble. Because fat girls don't fuck, I guess?

I looked over at Andrew, too big for a seatbelt, pooling against the car door. Did fat boys fuck? Was anybody going to pick him because he'd be *theirs*? I didn't want to imagine. But just as I was feeling sorry for us all, Mom slid lithely back into the car.

"Don't be a goose, honey," she said. She laid a hand on Dad's knee. "You have nothing to worry about."

That turned out to be a lie.

It was about a month after FDA approval when Dad announced to us that he was gonna take the Pill.

I couldn't help but give Mom the look of death. He'd never have done it if she hadn't gone first and made him worry about losing her. Andrew grunted at the news the way he grunted at everything; as if nothing in the world held much interest for him.

I hate crying, but I burst into tears. I couldn't even yell at Mom. I just wanted to talk Dad out of it. I tried for weeks, and I ended up trying again on the day that he began treatment. I just had this feeling in my gut that he was going to be one of the unlucky ones.

"One in ten," I croaked at him, my voice wrecked by crying. "One in ten, Dad. It's just slightly better odds than Russian roulette."

He smiled from his spa-hospital bed with the special trench installed below. He was wearing one of those paper gowns and I thought how stupid he would feel dying in paper clothes while taking a shit. Was it worth it? How could it be worth it?

"But the odds of dying young if I stay fat are much worse," he told me in his sweet voice. He reached out and put a hand on my shoulder and I heard his gown rustling like trash dragging through the gutter when it's windy. "Don't worry, Munchkin. It's in god's hands."

I guess it was, but I had never trusted god not to drop stuff and break it.

Dad made it to the third treatment. It felt cruel, like I had just started to relax and believe that he might be ok.

We came back and saw him on day one, down about fifty pounds and looking like someone had slapped him around all night.

"Honey, you look wonderful," Mom cooed, kissing his cheeks and hugging him to her middle. Andrew had stayed home. I looked him up and down, remembering the way Mom had just melted to reveal the stranger within.

"You look ok," I managed to say.

"I told you, kiddo." We sat with him while he ate some graham crackers and drank lots of water. My parents held hands.

I skipped the second visit. The knots in my stomach were huge and twisting and I just couldn't face it. Mom came home whistling and very pleased with herself.

"He's in the home stretch now! I can't wait for you kids to see what your Dad really looks like."

I just sat there, wondering if I was real. Are fat people fake? Do we not have souls? Does nothing I do count, if I do it while I'm fat? These were questions I had never really thought about before, but with both of my parents risking death to be less like me I suddenly had to wonder about a lot of things.

I knew the minute Mom picked up the phone the next day. I could tell she wasn't expecting the call. She stared at it just a second too long before she picked it up. My film professor calls that a beat, like a drumbeat or a heartbeat. One beat too many, and I knew.

One beat too many and Dad's heart gave in.

Neither one of us could go with Mom to deal with the body. Andrew wouldn't even leave his room. I don't remember those weeks very clearly. I remember weird parts.

Mom buying Dad a new suit he could be buried in, because nothing he owned would fit. Mom saying Dad wouldn't want to be cremated, now that he was thin. Dad's D&D buddies looking into his casket and saying how great he looked. The never-ending grief buffet of casseroles and cake in our kitchen. The nights when I could hear Mom crying through the vents.

That should have been the last of it. Other people could die, even famous people, but the Pill killed my Dad. That should have been it, end of story, illegal forever. But that's not how anything works. The world is just allowed to wound you any way it wants and move on.

And so are the people that you know.

The minute Andrew brought it up, I almost laughed. There was no way Mom was going to let him do it, after what had happened to Dad. Maybe we weren't the best of buds, but I didn't want him to die.

I could hear her in his room, and she was never in his room. It was permadark in there, blackout shades on the windows and nothing but the dim blue glow of his monitors to light it. I could hear them talking and I came close to the door, not quite putting my ear to it.

"I'm too old to be on your insurance," he said. "But they're saying there's gonna be a generic within a year. So it'll probably be cheaper."

"I think that's the best idea, sweetheart. But you're still going to have to pay for your hospital stay. We have a little money from Dad's insurance, so I can help you with that. It's what your father would have wanted."

I pushed the door open, already yelling. "No. No. No. No. It is not what Dad would have wanted. Dad would have wanted to be alive. Do you want to end up dead, too?"

They both stared at me like I had come through the door on fire.

"What is the matter with you?"

"Yeah," Andrew sneered. "Don't you knock?"

Mom put her hands on her hips. "This is a private conversation, kiddo."

"I don't give a shit," I told them. "We just buried our dad, and you want to take the Pill that killed him. How stupid can you be?"

Andrew shrugged. "Ninety percent is still an A."

"And dead is still dead," I said at once. "There's no curve on that."

Mom came and took my elbow and walked me back toward the door. "You're letting your emotions get the best of you," she said. I could hear her voice trembling, and when I looked up her eyes were wet in the dim blue light of the bedroom. "I miss him too, but I don't let it cloud my judgement. Your brother needs to do what's best for him."

"It's better for him to be dead than fat," I shot back. "Is that really what you think?"

We both turned back to look at Andrew.

Andrew would never tell me his actual weight, but I had heard him say once that he was in the "5 club." Nothing fit him but the absolute biggest shirts and elastic waistband shorts, and he wouldn't wear shoes that had to be tied. His fingers were so fat he could barely use his phone and finally upgraded to one with a stylus.

He sighed at us both. "I'm tired of this," he said to me, but Mom started to cry. "I'm tired of never going out and never fitting in a chair. I'm tired of getting stared at and having to hide from people to eat. Aren't you tired of it, sis?"

I shrugged. "I'm not tired of being alive."

I didn't convince him. I didn't convince Mom. She gave him the money and he checked himself in. I went with them, only because I was worried I wouldn't get to say goodbye otherwise.

Andrew was twenty-four when he did it, and his doctor had to get his digs in first. I remember his old-man chuckle as he lined my brother up next to the chart on the wall. "Well, son. You're not going to get any taller. And let's quit getting wider while we can, shall we?"

Andrew laughed with him, as if his fat self was already some-body else. Someone who it was ok to laugh at. My thin Mom laughed, too. Somewhere in thin heaven, was Dad laughing? Already I was an anomaly on the streets. I'm sure it used to be hard to be fat in L.A. or New York. I've read about that. But living in Dayton, Ohio meant always fitting in the booth at a restaurant, and never being the only fat person in the room. By the time Andrew got the Pill, I couldn't count on those things any more. A year later, the whole world was shrinking around me, and I could already feel the pinch.

Andrew came home from the hospital looking like some

other guy; a dude who played basketball and got called Slim. His eyes were bright.

"Munchkin, I can't wait for you to do it. It's amazing! I mean, it's super gross and really painful, but after that it's the fucking awesomest."

They had all called me 'Munchkin' since I was a kid. Not because I was short and cute, but because they said I was always munching. I hated that nickname and he knew it. He was just using it now to remind me I was the only one left.

"You look like Dad looked in his casket," I said.

He tried for a little while to go out and enjoy his new thin, life, but he didn't really know how. He couldn't talk to anybody. He missed his online friends and he hated the sunlight, the noise, the feeling of people always around, sizing him up. He had a new body, but it didn't matter.

I watched Andrew go back to this gaming pod; the ruined chair with the cracked spar he had fixed with duct tape no longer sagging or groaning beneath him. The same shiny spots on his computer where he kept his hands in the same positions for four teen hours at a time while he pretended he was a tall, muscular Viking warrior on some Korean server every day. I watched him settle right back into his old life using his new body and wondered what it was for. He really was the Viking now. He could have put on boots and left the house and had a real adventure. But adventure didn't appeal to him.

I was stuck between them in the house. I always had been, but Dad and I had understood each other. We had been a team. I guess I was a daddy's girl, but I was never spoiled like that. We just got along. Andrew was silent and Mom never shut up. Dad was the only one I could talk to, or sit in silence with without feeling bad.

And now I was the only fat member of the family. Slowly but surely, even the aunts and cousins signed up to take the Pill. I started to joke with my friends in Visionaries that fat people were going to become an endangered species.

Some of them laughed, but a couple suggested we actually

make a short film about that. We kicked the idea around, but mostly they wanted to film me eating in a cage while people stared. I didn't know how that would get anything meaningful across, and they didn't know how not to be thin assholes. So we dropped the idea.

Mom was at least using the way she had changed to enjoy the real world a little more. She wore workout clothes constantly, all bright colors and cling like the patterning on a snake. Every day, she got to enjoy the way people looked at her brightly now, eyebrows up, not searching for their first chance to sidle away.

"People just respond to me so much better now," she said in one of her interviews. "It changes everything about my daily interactions. I'm a mother and a widow, and I don't need a lot of attention," she had said, smiling coyly. "But even the mailman is happier to see me than he ever was before."

I wanted to barf when she said she didn't need attention. She had been thirsty enough before to talk to absolutely anyone, even sign up to take injections and hypnosis to get it. Now she was always posing and watching to see who would look. Attention was like the drug she couldn't get enough of. She still ate the same bowl of ice cream every night, sitting next to the groove in the couch where Dad used to fit. No, Mom, you didn't need attention. You took the Pill, you let the Pill take Dad because you were so a-ok with yourself.

The Pill sold like nothing had ever sold before. The original, the generic, the knockoffs, the different versions approved in Europe and Asia that met their standards and got rammed through their testing. There was at last a cure for the obesity epidemic. Fat people really were an endangered species. And everybody was so, so glad.

One in ten kept dying. The average never improved, not in any corner of the globe. There were memorials for the famous and semi-famous folks who took the gamble and lost. A congressman here and a comedian there. But everyone was so proud of them that they had died trying to better themselves that all the obituaries and eulogies had this weird, wistful tone to them. As if it was the next best thing to being thin. At least they didn't have to live that fat life any more.

And every time it was on the news, we sat in silence and didn't talk about Dad.

I was just a kid when Mom made it through the original trial that unleashed the Pill on the world. It wasn't approved for teenagers, not anywhere. Don't get me wrong; teens and parents alike were more than ready to sign up for the one in ten odds of dying. But the scientists who had worked on the Pill said unequivocally that it should not be taken by anyone who was not absolutely done growing. Eighteen was the minimum, but they recommended twenty-one to be completely safe.

On my eighteenth birthday, my mom threw me a party. She invited all my friends (mostly the Visionaries) and decorated the backyard with yellow roses and balloons.

It was the first time since Dad died that the house seemed cheerful. Mom ordered this huge lemon cake at the good bakery, with layers of custard filling and sliced strawberries. I remember everybody moaning over how good it was, how summery-sweet. People danced, but I felt too self-conscious to get up and give it a try. My Mom ended up dancing with a neighbor who heard the music and came through the gate to check it out. He was skinny, too, and I couldn't watch them together.

We at barbecue ribs and I got to tell people over and over again where I'd gotten into college. Northwestern. Rutgers. Cornell. And UCLA. Where was I going to go? Oh, I hadn't decided yet, but I needed to pick soon.

Except I definitely had. I had wanted to study filmmaking my whole life. Everybody in the Visionaries club knew that; they had all applied to UCLA and USC. A few of us got in. It wasn't just that it was my dream school in the golden city where movies were made. It was also about as far away as I could get. Mom reminded me that I could go anywhere in state for free because of her job, saying it over and over with that look in her eye, the one that said don't leave me, but I was going to L.A. if I had to walk every mile.

When it came time for presents, I got some jewelry from my grandmother. She didn't come and I couldn't blame her; she was my dad's mom. A lace parasol from my friends who all expected I'd need protection from the sun sometime soon. Books and music and a clever coffee cup. A fountain pen. The kinds of things that signal adulthood is about to begin.

My mom, beaming, gave me the Pill.

"I can't give you the physical thing, of course," she said, glancing around for a laugh. She got a little one. She handed me her iPad. "This has all of the paperwork, showing that you've been approved and my insurance will cover it. Plus, I booked your spa stay so that you'll have time to buy all new clothes before leaving for school." She smiled like she'd never killed my dad.

"I don't... know what to say," I said finally. If I said what I was actually feeling, it might mean she wouldn't pay for school, I'd be on my own. I had to swallow it. But I'd be damned if I was gonna swallow that Pill.

The party broke up slowly, with the neighbor guy hanging around and trying to talk to Mom until she texted Andrew and made him come down and walk the guy out. I packed up all my presents. I thanked Mom as sincerely as I could. I wrapped up slices of cake for people who wanted to take them home. And I seethed.

I left for UCLA two weeks early. I told Mom I was planning to come back and take my medicine over Thanksgiving break. She said she understood my delay, that I was just worried I'd pull the short straw and that it was ok to be nervous. She put me on the plane to Los Angeles with tears in her eyes.

On the flight, it was me and one other fat kid, maybe ten years old. That was it. The woman who sat next to me huffed and whined about it until the flight attendant brought her a free drink to shut her up. It was the first time I had ever been on a plane, and I sat there wondering whether it was always as uncomfortable as this. I could see the other fat kid up a few rows, hanging his elbow and one knee into the aisle. He wasn't even full-grown and already he was too big for an airplane seat. I wished we had been sitting together. We would have recognized each other. It would have been like having family again. Everyone else had that same Pill body.

And it was always the exact same body. No more thick thighs or really round asses. No more wide tits or pointy pecs or love handles rounding out someone's sides. Everyone's body was flat planes and straight lines. It wasn't just that they were thin. They were all somehow the same.

In LA the change was striking. I had heard that even thin people were taking the Pill out there to ensure that they'd never gain any weight, but I didn't believe it until I started seeing the change on TV and in movies. One by one, distinctive shapes disappeared. It was always the Amy Blanton body, like my mom had. The guys all had the same Ethan Fairbanks body, once he did a bunch of ads with some nobody. Only faces and hair color, a little difference in height could distinguish one actor from another. Here and there, a death. Worth it, everyone whispered like a prayer. Worth it, worth it, worth it.

I made it a few months at UCLA. My classes were cool and I started to make friends right off. But little things kept piling up. I went to the student store to buy myself a UCLA hoodie and they had nothing that would fit me. It wasn't even close. I looked at the largest size in the men's section and even then it would have clung to me like the skin of a sausage. I decided I could live without that ubiquitous symbol of college life, but I was pissed. I even thought about buying one just to snip the logo out and sew it onto a hoodie in my size from Wal-Mart.

Then Wal-Mart stopped carrying plus sizes altogether.

There were no desks on campus that I could sit at. A few of the classrooms had long tables with detached chairs and those were alright. But the majority of my freshman year classes were in those big lecture halls, with the rows and rows of wooden chair and desk combinations. I couldn't wedge myself into one to save my life. My first or second say I tried really hard in the back row and just got a big bruise over my lowest rib for my troubles. I sat in the aisle, on the steps, or against the back wall every day. There just wasn't any space for me.

My dorm room was the same way. The bed was narrow and I could hear the whole frame groaning the second I laid down. The bathroom was so small that I could touch both walls with my thighs when I sat on the toilet. My roommate was so thin I knew she hadn't taken the Pill—she still looked too original. But over the course of the first week, I realized that was because she never ate. I asked her to lunch a couple of times, but she always said no. I couldn't save her. I was working on how to save myself.

Days ticked by and Thanksgiving break was bearing down on me. My mom kept calling, telling me how great it was going to be when I went back to the school in my ideal body.

"I don't know that it'll be my ideal body," I told her. "It'll just be different."

"Don't you want to go on dates like the other girls?" Her voice was so whiny I could barely stand it.

I looked across the room to the other girl I lived with. She was in her bra and every time she breathed in I could see the impressions of her individual ribs against the skin of her back.

She was doing her reading and sucking on her bottom lip as if her lip gloss might offer some calories.

"I don't know that I want anything other girls have," I told her. But that wasn't true. Most girls had fathers.

"You don't know what you're missing," Mom said. "Come on home and let's get you squared away."

"Soon," I told her, counting the days until I had to let them try to kill me for being what I am.

I had been there about a month when I knew I wasn't going to make it. The stares had become unmanageable. I wasn't the last fat girl in L.A., was I? People on campus avoided me like I was a radioactive werewolf who stank like a dead cat in a hot garage. I remember one time I tried to take a selfie to send home to the Visionaries and someone gasped out loud. In the picture, I could see him, mouth open like he'd glimpsed a ghost.

And in a way I guess I was. I was the ghost of fatness past, haunting the open breezeways of UCLA. I was what they used to be, what they had always feared they would become. I became obsessed with the terrible power of my fatness; I was the worst that that could possibly happen to someone. Worse than death, had to be, because somewhere my dad was rotting in a box because that was easier than living in a body like mine. I knew when I frightened people and I pushed my advantage. I took up their space. I haunted them with my warm breath and my soft elbows. I fed on their fright.

It was early November and I could not adjust to the lack of seasons. It was still warm and sunny like June on the California coast. I missed home, but the idea of home repelled me. I needed comfort.

I walked myself over the cheap pancake house and ordered the never-ending stack and coffee. The all-you-can-eat pancake special was always a favorite with frat boys, and its popularity had only increased since the Pill hit the market. People who really loved to eat could finally do it without worrying that it would ruin their lives.

The hostess tried to seat me in a booth and I just rolled my eyes at her. I was not about to eat my weight in pancakes with a formica tabletop wedged just beneath my sternum.

"A table, please."

She stuck me in the back, next to the restrooms. I didn't care.

My first four pancakes showed up hot and perfect and I asked for extra butter. When they were just right (dripping, not soaked and turning into paste) I shoveled up huge bites into my waiting mouth, letting it fill me as nothing else did. Who could care that they were the last of their kind when the zoo had such good food?

And yeah, people were staring. People are always staring at me. That was a constant of my existence, and I was used to it. I ignored them. I slurped up hot coffee and wiped the plate down with the last bite of cake.

"Hit me again," I said, and the waitress took the plate away.

A few minutes later, another fresh hot stack of pancakes appeared.

I didn't know how many times I could do it, but that was the day I was going to find out.

And then a man sat at my table.

He was perfectly ordinary, with brown hair and brown eyes. He had the Pill body underneath his tan suit. I looked him over.

"Can I help you?"

He stared at my mouth for a minute and I waited. "Do you have any idea how beautiful you are," he finally asked.

I rolled my eyes hard and started to butter my pancakes. I was going to need more butter. "Fuck off, creep."

He put a hand against his own chest. "Please, I meant no disrespect. I'm being sincere. You're so lovely. So rare. I haven't seen a woman like you in almost a year."

I waved to the waitress but she didn't see me. I debated. I'd rather have the butter, but if the cakes got cold before it showed up, it would hardly matter at all. I scraped the dish that I had and began to cut up pancakes and ignore my visiting weirdo, hoping he would go away.

He cleared his throat and ordered a cup of coffee. "Please, allow me to entertain you while you eat and I'll pick up your check."

I sighed. Few things were as motivating as free food. So I let him sit.

He asked me about cinematography, about why I had come to L.A. I talked in between cups of coffee and plates of pancakes.

"I had all these ideas about the story only I could tell when I got here. The things that were unique to my experience. It's funny now, because there was nothing unique about my experience. I guess everybody thinks they're one of a kind."

He glanced over his shoulder a little, then pushed the cream pitcher toward me for my coffee. "Look around. You nearly are."

I shrugged. "I guess. But there's no way to tell this story so that people will understand it. You ever see the way fat people on the street are shot for news stories? Headless and limbless and wide as the world, always wandering like they've go nowhere to be. That's the only story people know. We were always a joke, we were always invisible. And now, we're going to disappear. Because we were never meant to exist in the first place."

"Are you," he asked, cocking an eyebrow. "Going to disappear?"

"Who the hell are you," I finally asked.

He sighed and finished his coffee. "I can't tell you that. But I can show you something that might change your mind."

I don't know why I said yes. Maybe I was dreading going back to school where nothing fit. Maybe I just didn't want to answer the question of whether or not I was going to take the Pill. Maybe it was just the way he looked at me—really looked at me. Not like I was a problem to be solved or some walking glitch in the way things are supposed to work.

I got into a strange man's car outside of the pancake house and I let him show me.

The club was up in the hills, just off Mulholland drive. It was in this gorgeous house, built in the golden age of Hollywood for some chiseled hunk who had died of AIDS. The lawn was perfect and I could smell the chlorine in the pool the minute I stepped out of the car. The neighborhood was the kind of quiet where you know that even the gardeners muffle their equipment.

My nameless escort walked up the stone path toward a wide, shaded, black front door. He looked back over his shoulder, glancing at me.

"You coming?"

I was.

It was dark inside the house at first, my eyes adjusting from the bright sunshine slowly. After a few minutes, I saw that it was merely dim. The living room was furnished beautifully, sumptuously, with a clear emphasis on texture and deep padding. The room was empty except for one woman, sitting on a chaise lounge and reading a book.

We approached her and she looked up. She was an absolute knockout; a redhead with full lips and built like an hourglass that had time to spare. Her dress clung to her, making a clear case that she enjoyed being looked at. She was not walking around in an Amy Blanton body. She was an original.

The man I came in with tapped his fingers on the top of her book and said, "In the chocolate war, I fought on the side of General Augustus."

The redhead nodded, not saying a word. She shifted in her seat and reached for something I couldn't see. Behind her, a bookshelf slid sideways, revealing a deep purple tunnel behind it.

I nodded to her as we passed and she smiled at me with a hunger I couldn't put a name to. I had no idea where we were headed.

We walked through a series of rooms. The entire house was decorated in the same style as that first room; sensual, decadent, and plush. As I got to see more of it, I realized that everything was also built wide, sturdy, and I'd never think twice about sitting in any chair I saw.

In every room I passed, I saw the same thing as I peered through the door. There was a fat person surrounded by thin people staring at them. Some of the onlookers were crying, some were visibly aroused. Different races, different genders. All well-dressed. All nearly identical in those Pill bodies. A tall fat woman was lounging, shrouded by veils in a Turkish bed, nude and lolling and made of endless undulations of honey-colored flesh. She fed herself grapes while someone was making her laugh. Ten people sat around her bed, watching.

A fat man, as big as Andrew used to be, was dipping his gloved fists into paint and punching a blank, white wall. He was being videotaped and photographed, lit gorgeously while people murmured praise and encouragements.

In one room, a short black woman whose curves defied gravity ran oil-slicked hands over her nudity, smiling a perfect, satisfied smile. Two men stood near her, their mouths open, hungering endlessly, asking nothing of her.

We came to an empty room that had a round tub at its end and a set of low stone benches. The domed ceiling made our footfalls sound epic. The water had steam rising off it, even in the warmth of the house, and smelled like the sea.

"Salt water," he said. "Much better for your skin. Would you like to take a dip? You don't have to talk to anyone or do anything, but some people may come join you. How does that sound?"

"I don't have a bathing suit."

His smile was slow and he dropped his chin like he was about to share a conspiracy. "Have you looked around? Nobody will mind."

"What are these people getting out of this? I don't need this."

He pulled out his phone and showed me the app that the house used to keep track of money. Each fat performer had an anonymous identifier and a live count of what they were making.

"Maybe I could persuade you to work for a couple of hours, just to see what you think? You'll make the house minimum, plus tips."

I watched the numbers climb up. "Just to sit here? I don't have to touch anybody? Or even make conversation?"

He nodded. "We'd prefer that you work in the nude, but you don't even have to do that. Just enjoy the hot soak. What do you say?"

It sounded weird as fuck, but I wanted two things immediately. First, I wanted the money. If I was going to go home and refuse the Pill, I was pretty sure I was going to need it. Second, I wanted to go back to the room where the boxing painter was being filmed. I itched to get behind a camera in this place, to tell the story of the endangered species of fat people. Not like the Visionaries had wanted it, but the way I wanted it. Like this. Dark and rich and seductive.

I got into the water in my bra and panties. I may as well have gotten naked; they were both white cotton and went see-through in the water. I tried not to think about it. I dunked my head, sat on one of the submerged steps, and soaked with my neck laid back against the rim.

I could hear people coming and going. I could hear the

things they whispered to me. Voices in the salty dark called me rare and magnificent and soft and enticing. I said nothing. I didn't even hint that I could hear.

After a few hours, my nameless handler came back with a fluffy, soft towel the size of a bed sheet that smelled like lavender. He thanked me and showed me how to download the app to get paid.

I had been there for three hours, and I had more money than I had ever had at one time, in my entire life. He watched my face very closely when I saw the number.

"My name's Dan," he said softly.

"Do you own this place?"

"No, I'm just a recruiter. I'm going to give you my number."

I watched him type it into my phone as "Dan Chez Corps."

"What makes you think I'll call you?"

I thought he was going to remind me of how much money I had just made, but he didn't. He kinda shook his head a little, then asked, "Where else are you going to go?"

He had brought me replacements for my wet underthings, much nicer than the ones I was wearing. They were exquisite and well- made and carried no tags.

"A gift from the house," he said, before leaving me to change. They fit like they were made for me.

I went back to the dorm and watched my roommate twitch in her sleep. Her side of the fridge held a single hard-boiled egg and a pint of skim milk. My bed groaned beneath me as I lay down, still in my fancy gift underwear.

I dreamt about my dad.

The laws changed that year, but they wouldn't go into effect until January. They weren't making it illegal to be fat, exactly. But it was as close as they could get. It was going to be legal to deny health insurance to anyone with a BMI over 25 if they refused the Pill. Intentional obesity would also be grounds for loss of child custody, and would be acceptable reason for dismissal from a job.

Where the law went, culture followed. Airlines were adding a customer weight limit and clothing manufacturers concentrated on developing lines to individualize the Pill body. Journalists wrote articles on the subject of renegade fats; could their citizenship be revoked? Should parents of fat children be prosecuted for abuse if they didn't arrange for them to receive the Pill as soon as possible?

I submitted a treatment to my short film class detailing my desire to film a secret enclave where fat renegades performed for the gratification of a live Pilled audience. My professor wrote back to tell me that my idea was 1. Obscene and 2. Impossible.

The Friday before Thanksgiving break, Mom called.

"I'm so glad we're getting this done before the change in airline policy. Can you imagine having to come to Ohio by train? Anyhow, your Aunt Jeanne is coming in for the holiday—"

"Mom. Mom, listen. I don't want to do it."

"Do what? See Aunt Jeanne?"

"No, Mom, listen. I'm not going to take the Pill."

She was quiet for a minute. "Sweetie, we all took it hard when your father passed. I know you must be worried about that, but they say there's no genetic marker—"

"It's not just Dad. It's not just the odds that I might die. I just don't want to do it. I want to stay who I am."

She sighed like I was a child who had asked for the ninetieth time why the sky was blue. "This doesn't change who you are, Munchkin. It only changes your body."

"I'm not coming home," I said, flatly.

There was a lot of yelling, with both of us trying to be cruel to the other. I'd rather not remember it. What I do remember is her crying, saying something like, "I gave you your body. I made it, and it's imperfect like mine was. Why won't you let me fix it? Why won't you let me correct my mistake?"

"I don't feel like a mistake," I told her. "And I'm not coming home. Not now, not ever."

I remember hanging up and the terrible silence that followed. I remember thinking I should turn my phone off, but then I realized I could just leave it behind. I could leave everything behind.

I took my camera and my laptop and left everything else. I didn't even take a change of clothes.

I borrowed a phone from someone on the quad, making up a story that mine had been stolen. She waited for me as I called Dan. I told him to pick me up where I was.

The car arrived ten minutes later.

The redhead buzzed me in without asking for a password, which was great because I couldn't remember what Dan had said. Down through the purple hallway and a woman I'd never seen before shook my hand and told me I could call her Denny.

Denny had a Pill body, hidden away beneath a wide, flowing caftan and a matching headwrap. She showed me to my room, my king-sized bed, my enormous private bath, my shared common room and library. She gave me the WiFi password and explained the house's security.

"You may stay here as long as you like. The house will feed you and clothe you. Your medical needs will be seen to. Your entertainments will be top-notch. You may leave anytime you wish. Your pay will be automatically deposited into your account as it comes in, without delay.

"However, you must never disclose the location or the nature of this house to anyone via any means; not by phone call or text or email. You may take photos and videos, but we have jammers to prevent geotagging of any kind. If you are found in violation of this one rule, you will walk out of here with nothing but the clothes on your back. Is that clear?"

I told her it was. She left and returned five minutes later with a new phone for me. I signed into my bank account—the one my mother wasn't on— and set about creating a new email, a new profile, a new identity.

I eased into the work. I ate cupcakes and I danced in a leotard. I read poetry aloud while sipping a milkshake. I lounged in a velvet chaise nude while people drew me and painted me. I began to speak to my admirers and I watched my pay skyrocket.

I met the house's head seamstress; a brilliant, nimble-fingered fat woman named Charisse. She had an incredible eye and hardly had to measure anyone. She made me corsets and skirts, silk pajamas and satin gowns, costumes and capes and all manner of underwear.

I realized when I had been wearing her work for months that some of my clothes were a little too small. My favorite bikini cut into me just so, just enough to accentuate the flesh it did not quite contain. I filmed myself in the hall of mirrors, wearing it and trying to understand what it meant.

Some of my gowns were a little too big, though I could remember the exactitude with which I was fitted. I made short clips showing the gaps in the waist and hips, the way I could work my whole hand in between the fabric and my skin.

Charisse was too skilled for it to be an accident. The implication became clear.

All around me there were heavenly bodies in gowns and togas, a stately fleet of well-rounded ships gliding alongside the pool or lying silkily in our beds. We were beautiful, but we were all aware of a subtle campaign to make us larger, ever larger, more suited to satisfy whatever it was that brought the throngs of thin whispering wantons to our door.

In twos and threes, we began to talk about what it meant. About who we could trust. About who was running this place, and why.

The lower floors of the house were a brothel. Somehow I knew that without being told. There was a look in the older fat folks' eyes that let me know it would be waiting for me when I was ready. Nobody pressured me. Nobody even asked. One day I just headed down the stairs. Cheeks were swabbed at the door and everybody waited fifteen minutes until they were cleared. I got my negatives and went through.

I'd never had sex before. I think it happens later for fat kids. While everyone else was trying each other on, I was still trying to figure out why I never fit into anything. I don't regret that. I can't imagine doing this out in the world where I am the worst thing that can happen to somebody.

I didn't know what it would be like. I hope it's this good for everyone, with a circle of adoring worshippers vying for the right to adore you, to touch every inch of you, to murmur in wonder as you climax again and again until nap time, when you are lovingly spooned and crooned to sleep. I luxuriated in it for a long time, not thinking about what it meant to only touch thin people, to only be touched by them. I watched my bank balance climb. I didn't ask myself what they saw when they looked at me. I existed as a collection of nerves that did not think.

I stopped thinking about going home. I stopped thinking about the Pill. I stopped thinking. I became what I had always been and nothing more: my fat, fat body.

When I came back to thinking again, I found it did not make things easier.

I have been here for three years now, and I don't think I can ever live anywhere else. Outside, they tell me, there are no more like me. Only in places like here, where a few of us fled before the world could change us. Nobody is allowed to bring us food presents anymore; everyone is too worried they'll try and slip us the Pill. Someone might actually be that upset that I exist. I don't think about that either. I don't exist for them. I accept their worship and forget their faces completely. It's always the same face anyhow.

Sometimes I point my camera at that face and ask them what they're doing here, what do they want, why did they come seeking the thing the thing they've worked so hard to avoid becoming?

They mumble about mothers and goddesses, about the embrace of flesh and the fullness of desire. It sounds like my own voice inside my head. I think about my Dad, about god's hands. Would he have been one of these? Would he have come to miss my mother's body the way he first knew it?

I think about showing this film in LA. I think about Denny telling me I can leave here anytime. I think about how I could leave my body anytime, too, how any of us can. I think about Andrew, about how he left his and gained nothing at all. How I used to see him as the enemy when he was just me.

Deep down on the lowest floor, in perfect privacy, the fats make love to each other. There is a boy who came only a few weeks ago, an import from one of the countries that's taken to the Pill slowly, so we have a lot of recruits from their shores. We had no common language at first, but we've worked on that and discovered an unmapped country between us. He's so sweet and shy and eager to lift the heaviness of his belly so that he can slip inside me and then drop it on top of mine, warm and weighty like a curtain. He whispers to me that we don't ever have to go back, that we can raise darling fat babies right here, that we'll become like another species. Homo pillus can inherit the earth, while homo lipidus lives in secret.

"But we'll live," he whispers to me as we conspire to remake the world in the image of our thick ankles. "We'll live," he says, his tongue tracing the salty trenches made by the folds in my sides. Belly to belly, fat against fat.

"We'll live."

SHADOW PRISONS

BY CAROLINE M. YOACHIM

PUBLISHED BY BROAD REACH
PUBLISHING + ADAMANT PRESS

Part 1: The Shadow Prison Experiment

The Shopping District was crowded on a Sunday afternoon, and Vivian Watanabe was out running errands with her sixteen-year-old, Cass. Together they wove through throngs of shoppers wearing customized skins or the generic default. Vivian wasn't fond of Generics—they fell into that uncanny valley between a nondescript human and a silver android. Cold and impersonal, plus it was hard to keep track of who you've interacted with. Which was the point, she supposed. Personal connections and privacy were often at odds.

"This neighborhood is creepy," Cass said, waving their arm at the crowd around them.

"Rich people have flawless skins."

"Back in the old days it was make-up and plastic surgery and designer clothes. Overlays aren't much different." Vivian wasn't wearing an overlay. It'd been Cass's idea, and they'd convinced Vivian to do it as an exercise in challenging societal norms.

Walking around without an overlay felt simultaneously scandalous, exhilarating, and deeply unsettling. But this was the safest of neighborhoods—luxury apartments mixed with boutiques and cafés, everything monitored and patrolled. Truth be told, she couldn't afford to shop here, but it was nearly Cass's birthday, and Vivian knew they'd love a box of Van Gogh candy from The Art of Chocolate. The store's specialty was masterpieces of brightly colored sugar, hand-painted onto rectangles of dark chocolate. Cass was quite the young artist, and their room had prints of sunflowers and starry nights plastered all over the walls as inspiration.

It was still five hours to curfew, so they took their time wandering amongst the shops. Illusions Formalwear had a window display of outlandish gowns—brightly colored silks, sparkling sequins, even a dress made entirely of brass gears. All of them would look stunning on Brooke. Clothes shopping was easier for her wife, even the overlays. Vivian wasn't tall enough to wear the best looks, and digital tailoring was a lot of money for often mediocre results. Inside Illusions, customers wore impeccable clothes and flawless faces. Vivian wondered what they looked like without their overlays. Personal Implanted Perception chips made everything pretty, but it was hard to know what was real.

An ad bot popped up next to Cass. Except for its sudden appearance out of nowhere, it was indistinguishable from an actual human wearing a Generic overlay. "Upgrade your experience with the new V17 Perceptech microchip. PIPs are mandatory, but luxury is a choice."

"Fuck off, bot." Cass flipped it off and simultaneously shot some code at it to make it disappear without repeating its message.

"Language!" Vivian hissed. She glanced around nervously. "Someone might be listening. And hacking adbots is a rules violation."

"We can't cower in fear because someone might be listening," Cass said, their voice uncomfortably loud.

"I'm not having this discussion," Vivian said firmly. "Not out here."

"Fine. You hang out with these creepy fancy-skins. I'm going home."

Cass stormed off before Vivian could say anything.

Vivian ducked into a café to collect herself. Inside it was warm and smelled like coffee and freshly baked pastries. Most of the tables were full, and people mostly projected Generics rather than expensive customized skins. Or maybe the café had filled the tables with bots to look busier.

One of the Generics flickered out.

It didn't completely vanish the way adbots did, but it darkened into shadow, all the details lost. Her PIP told her someone was there, but she no longer saw even the plain silver form of a Generic. She tapped at her temple. It was an old habit that Cass poked fun at. Vivian was old enough to be accustomed to reality filters built into glasses, back before PIPs took over the market and ran everything else out of business. She'd been one of the last holdouts with glasses, refusing an implant until access to even the most basic resources no longer supported externals. Sighing, she lowered her hand and sent a service query.

The reply was swift—nothing was wrong with her PIP. Appended after the basic diagnostic report there were links to an assortment of relevant news feeds. She scanned the headlines. Bardo Phillips of ZimCorp Launches Experimental Shadow Prison Program. After a test period, the public would vote on whether or not to implement it. There were hundreds of articles describing the new tech and touting its advantages over traditional physical prisons. Cheap, effective, and safe, the news feeds repeated endlessly.

Vivian didn't feel safe. She was wearing her true face, and only a few feet away was a shadow prisoner—a Shade, the newsfeeds said they were called—and who knew what crimes the Shade had committed? That featureless black form could be anyone. It could have done anything. The Shade approached people seemingly at random, trying to talk to them. It was heading her way. Vivian didn't want trouble. She walked away briskly and adjusted her privacy settings to project a Generic to anyone who wasn't a known contact.

She scanned the neighborhood and noticed a handful of

other Shades. Were all these people criminals before the new system was implemented, or were they being thrown into shadow for newly committed crimes? Vivian's chest tightened, her panic rising. The Art of Chocolate was on the far side of the shopping district, and she couldn't shake the notion that the shadows were spreading, contagious. It was a ridiculous thought, but instead of pushing her way through the crowd Vivian stood trembling in the middle of the sidewalk.

She could get Cass something else for their birthday—maybe tickets to the latest immersive movie, Genbu: Guardian of the North. Critics on the feeds were raving about the underwater fight sequences, especially the [SPOILER ALERT] realistic sensation of nearly drowning during the climax. Cass had been begging to go, and maybe they were old enough for the graphic content after all.

Vivian hurried out of the shopping district, back to the less crowded residential area, home to Brooke and Cass.

Cass was locked away in their room, listening to cyberpunk rock that was supposed to be censored for explicit lyrics. Hopefully they were also doing their homework. Brooke was in the kitchen attempting to program a flavor overlay for Nutri-soup #6. "I'm surprised you're back already, Vivs. You were so excited about the shopping, and when Cass came back in a huff I figured you'd take some extra time to cool off. Were the chocolates too expensive?"

"I didn't make it to the chocolatier. There's a new prison program, and instead of sending people to jail they get. . . filtered out." Vivian dipped a spoon into the partially programmed soup and grimaced at the muddy taste. "It was upsetting to see, actually."

Brooke paused for a moment and scanned the news feeds.

"Shadow prisons. What will they think of next?" Brooke laughed. Her voice was light and unbothered, and she tapped at the kitchen interface buttons, trying to get the soup right. "Although. . . If the experiment works, maybe I'll sign up to be a Shadowkeeper; you know, to help keep the family safe."

Her voice never lost its cheerful tone, but Brooke was obviously worried for Cass, who'd never had much regard for rules. Even so, signing up to be a Shadowkeeper, one of the guards in an experimental prison program? Vivian hated the idea. Brooke would constantly be tempted to try to take the system down from the inside. It'd be better to lay low, try to not attract attention. They could keep Cass out of trouble without being part of the system. . . probably.

"Soup's ready," Brooke called, her voice loud in hopes of overpowering Cass's music.

Cass emerged from their room, now dressed head to toe in black except for the silver buckles on their combat boots. Almost as if they were a Shade, except that their skin was pale and their hair was bright blue.

"No shoes in the house." Vivian said.

"They're brand new. Completely clean! I'm breaking them in." Cass sniffed at the pot of soup and wrinkled their nose. "But whatever. I'm going out to see Auntie Yang. She's organizing a protest for this shadow prison bullshit. And she'll have actual food."

"Language," Vivian said automatically. Auntie Yang lived in the next apartment complex over, an emeritus professor in the Computer Sciences department and Auntie to everyone on the block. She grew heirloom vegetables on the roof of her building and bribed the landlord with garlic eggplant and spicy pickled green beans to keep from being reported.

Brooke asked, "What about curfew?"

Cass shrugged and went out the door without answering.

Anxiety gnawed at Vivian's brain. She couldn't stop worrying about Cass, even now that they were safely back from Auntie Yang's. On her bedside table there was a miniature painting of sunflowers, framed, a Mother's Day gift that Cass made for her. The room was dimly lit from the streetlights outside, and the painting was beautiful even without enough light to bring out the vibrant yellows. Cass had so much potential, and if they were thrown into shade, it would all be wasted. Vivian stared at the painting for a long time, trying to figure out what to do, how to help. Hours passed before she finally fell asleep. By the time she hauled herself out of bed, Brooke had already left for work.

"You have to talk her out of it," Cass said without preamble.

"Sorry, what?" Vivian didn't function well before coffee, which Brooke usually made before leaving for work.

Cass saw her staring at the kitchen console and gave an exasperated sigh. "Glitchballs, Mom. You're hopeless, you know that, right?"

"I can do this perfectly well once I've had coffee," Vivian said. "Or sleep. One or the other."

She moved aside and let Cass program the coffee. It came out sweeter than when Brooke made it, with orange and cinnamon notes that were unusual but not unpleasant. She hadn't realized that Cass drank coffee, but clearly they must if they could conjure up something this complex on no notice whatsoever. "Thank you. What were you saying earlier?"

"Mum has it in her head that she should join up and be a Shadowkeeper, and you have to talk her out of it." Cass made themself a cup of coffee. "She's trying to protect me, but the whole thing is terrifying. The PIP monopoly. Shadow prisons. News feeds are touting this stuff like it's useful tech, but we're in a world of trouble and even Auntie Yang has no idea how we stop it."

Vivian's hand flew to her temple to remove the glasses that weren't there. Weren't ever there anymore, and therefore could never be removed. Cass had no sense of caution; they were reckless.

A Generic adbot appeared in an empty seat at their table. "ZimCorp is hiring! Shadowkeepers serve society by keeping our citizens safe. Good pay and full benefits, sign up now!"

The adbot repeated its message twice more, then disappeared. Vivian wished for the millionth time that they could afford a household ad-blocker. The targeted ZimCorp ad was unnerving. Advertisers knew they were talking about the new prison tech, or at least the algorithms did. "Maybe Brooke is right. Maybe you need the protection."

Cass glared at her, gulped down their coffee, and stormed back to their room.

"Just be careful," Vivian said, knowing that Cass couldn't hear her.

Twenty minutes later, Vivian had to leave for work and Cass still hadn't left for school. She weighed her options. Talking to Cass would make her late for work and probably wouldn't help. Letting Cass cool off on their own meant Vivian would be on time, but Cass probably wouldn't go to school and they were racking up absences.

She hated not knowing what to do. All the options felt like she was failing her child.

With one last glance at Cass's closed door, Vivian went to work.

———

The first applicant of the day wore a Generic to the appointment and had only filled out half the forms. Vivian wanted to give out aid packages, but there were so many rules and people didn't seem to understand how the system worked.

"I'm sorry, but if you don't fill out all the forms, there's nothing I can do." Vivian said. She really was sorry. "Do you need help with the forms? We have interns for that—"

"No." The Generic's voice was calm, as they always were. Blank. Featureless.

"It sometimes helps," Vivian added, "to show who you are. I mean officially it doesn't matter, and I can't do anything without the forms, but people are more sympathetic to individuals."

"Why would I trust you with that kind of information?" The Generic shook their head and walked out.

Vivian went to the break room and programmed herself a

cup of coffee. She should have paid better attention to what Cass had programmed—this coffee was fine but not as good as what she'd had this morning. She pinged home to see if Cass had gone to school, and was pleasantly surprised when the apartment reported that Cass left only slightly later than the usual time.

Her good mood evaporated when she saw her next client. There, in her office, was a Shade. Unbidden, the fear and panic from the shopping district returned. She forced herself to breathe. There was something off about the Shades, something that made her edgy and uncomfortable. The Generic default overlay at least had monotone silver features and a perpetually calm expression. Shades were featureless voids, inhuman.

Vivian frowned. There were a lot of crimes, and many of them were relatively benign. Cass commonly violated a number of lesser rules—curfew, school attendance, restricted media. Vivian didn't know what the threshold was for throwing people into shadow, and the news feeds were reporting that violent criminals who posed a threat to the public were 'kept out of circulation,' whatever that meant. This was someone who needed help, and she would try to help them. She pulled up the forms and was dismayed to find that most of the fields were inaccessible. Not blank, but blacked out.

"There's a problem with your paperwork..." Vivian paused, trying to pull up a name, but that was one of the inaccessible fields. "I'm sorry, I can't even pull your name off the forms. I can't give you aid based on what I have here."

"It's never been a problem before," the Shade said in a gravelly baritone. "I've been coming in for weeks. The aid package is what keeps my family from starving while I try to get a job—not that I'll ever get a job now."

Coming in for weeks. This was someone that she knew, someone who had been in her office before, as a Generic or maybe with their own face. She studied the Shade, but it was utterly featureless. "Who are you?"

"I'm. . ."

Vivian couldn't hear the name. "What?"

"..."

Vivian shook her head.

"No one sees me. Not even my family. No one hears my name." The voice was unchanged. Calm like a Generic, but lower pitched. Masking the emotion that had to be there. "I just want to take care of my kidlets."

Kidlets. Vivian had heard that before. It was what Ms. Jenkins called her children. Ms. Jenkins who got laid off for taking too many sick days when she was getting chemo. Vivian studied the forms, but there was absolutely no way to dispense aid based on what was there. That poor family, but what could she do? Without the forms, Vivian could be cast into shade for trying to help, and clearly Ms. Jenkins was no longer eligible. But maybe—

"Hey, John," Vivian made the call to her receptionist on speakerphone, so the Shade could hear everything. "I'm looking at the schedule and Ms. Jenkins doesn't have an appointment this week—can you check in with her kids, let them know that if something happened to her they can get help filling out the aid forms for themselves?"

"Um, okay." John sounded confused by the request, but— while her request was definitely unorthodox—it was not, strictly speaking, against any of the rules.

"Thanks, John!"

The Shade stood. "Thank you."

"I'm sorry that I couldn't process your request without forms," Vivian answered, hoping her workaround would go unnoticed.

She was about to tell John to send in the next applicant when she got a call from Brooke. Her wife hated phones and rarely called. Vivian frowned. "Hey. What's up?"

"Cass is at the place I used to work."

Brooke had worked a lot of places, and she was clearly trying to talk around something. Vivian considered the options—the mall on the other side of town, an insurance company that got run out of business by ZimCorp, the Economics department on campus. She scanned the news feeds. Massive Protest at Local University Draws Thousands.

"The place with the cherry trees?" Vivian asked. The main quad outside the Economics building was a courtyard lined with trees.

"Yes."

"I have applicants scheduled solid until 4:30. Can't you duck out and get them?" Vivian couldn't figure out why Brooke was calling, her schedule was way more flexible.

"I'm midway through application interviews for a new job."

Vivian didn't need to ask which job. "Okay, I'll do it. Love you!"

As she passed the reception desk she called out to John, "Family emergency, reschedule my appointments, so sorry!"

John mumbled something that she couldn't quite hear, but she'd deal with it later. She had to get to Cass before they got themself thrown into shade.

———

The quad was packed with protestors. Vivian had no idea how to find Cass in the crowd. The area was cordoned off with yellow smart-tape, with the imposing forms of Shadowkeepers patrolling the periphery. There wasn't a good way to get in, much less out. A group of students waved signs and chanted, "Knowledge is light, light destroys shadows."

Vivian approached a pair of Keepers. They wore overlays similar to a Generic, but broader and taller—giants that towered over the crowd. They were a lighter shade of silver, perpetuating the same old racist crap that white was good and black was bad even though almost no one wore their true skin in public. But probably most of the Keepers were white. These two were in the middle of a conversation, voices raised so they could hear each other over the chants of the protestors.

"Don't see why they can't throw the Shades into the underground. It's gross down there, but with overlays they can make it look like Main Street, or campus, or whatever. Shades will never know they aren't running free."

"Nah. This isn't for the Shades. They want people to know what happens if they cause trouble. Citizens will toe the line if they're scared of being erased."

Vivian shuddered.

One of the Keepers turned in her direction. "You can't be in this area. Classes are cancelled until we get the protestors processed."

"Yeah," the other Keeper said. "If we don't get going on that I'm going to miss the Phoenix vs. Dragon matchup tonight. Blew the last paycheck from my old mall security gig on tickets." The Keeper headed off toward a checkpoint, where a line of protestors waited to be released from the protest area.

When the remaining Keeper made no move to follow the first, Vivian laughed nervously. "I suppose I should have checked the news feeds before coming in." She paused for a moment. "You said the protestors are being processed?"

"Joining the protest yourself?" The question had an edge to it.

"No. Definitely no." Vivian had no idea who was behind the standard-issue form of the Keeper—whether they were old or young, their background, their biases. All she knew was that this person had signed up to be a Keeper in the first hours of the program. It was someone who wanted power, or feared punishment, or was trying to protect their family. She hoped it was the latter. "Okay, here's the thing. My kid is down there and they're a good kid but they got caught up with a bad crowd and really all I want is to save them from ruining their life."

The Keeper stared at her, a stern expression on its chiseled silver face. "Then you shouldn't have let your kid show up at a protest. Now are you going to clear out, or do I need to make a note on your record?"

She backed away. Protestors were coming out through the checkpoint now, nearly all of them wearing their own faces. Processing wasn't automatically casting protestors into shade.

Cass's record wasn't terrible, but it wasn't spotless either. Vivian had no idea which offenses counted towards shadow—that information was not available on Search.

The Keeper went to join their companion at the checkpoint.

Vivian took a deep breath. She didn't want the protest on her record, but she had to go get Cass. She ducked under the yellow smart-tape and walked quickly into the crowd.

The protestors were yelling, louder now that she was in amongst them. The crowd was getting angrier because there wasn't a way to leave without being processed. No one wore Generics, and Vivian suddenly realized that her own overlay had been stripped away. Being inside the smart-tape barrier changed her privacy options—her actual face was the only thing she was allowed to wear.

She felt vulnerable and exposed. The lack of privacy might make Cass easier to find, but then again, their undercut blue hair wasn't particularly distinctive in this crowd. Brightly dyed hair, colorful tattoos, and piercings were all quite common. If anything, it was Vivian who stood out with her unaltered gray baseclothes and plain black hair. She hadn't realized that she'd be unfiltered today, so she hadn't put much time into her real appearance.

Cass emerged from the crowd. "Fucking glitchballs, Mom! What are you doing here?"

"Language!" She hugged Cass tight, shaking with relief. "The whole point of glitchballs is that you were using it as an alternative to blacklisted words."

Blacklisted. Would cursing count against Cass on some kind of shadelist?

Vivian tried to call Brooke, but all she got was an access-restricted error message. "The real question isn't what I'm doing here, it's what you are doing here. You were supposed to be at school."

"This is important. We have to stop it before it gets out of control."

The crowd thinned out as some of the protestors—probably

the ones with clean records who were having second thoughts—
went out through the checkpoint. The small group who
remained were, if anything, louder.

"We need to go."

"Mom."

"Now. I mean it."

Across the quad, someone threw a water bottle at one of the
Keepers. Chaos erupted. People started running, some towards
the altercation, others away from it. Vivian took Cass's arm and
pulled them toward the processing checkpoint. Cass kept turning
around to watch what was happening behind them, but didn't
resist.

"You first," Vivian said when they got to the front of the line.
The Keepers were hustling people out of the area as soon as they
were processed, and she needed to be here to bail Cass out if
there was trouble.

"Hand." The Keeper said. Cass dutifully held out their hand.
The light on the chip reader glowed red.

The Keeper paused for a moment, reading records on Cass's
PIP that Vivian couldn't see. It was a long pause, and Vivian
worried that the list was too long, that her child would be
thrown into shade. She thought about what she could say, what
arguments might hold weight, but she had no idea who the
Keeper was. For all she knew, it might be the one she'd spoken to
earlier.

"Watch the demerits. You can go."

Vivian let out a sigh of relief.

The Keeper waved Cass off. "Get out of here. Don't make
trouble."

Vivian called after Cass as they walked away. "I'll meet you at
home, go straight there."

"Hand."

Vivian held out her hand. The light on the chip reader
glowed red, exactly as it had for Cass. She laughed nervously. "I
was only here to get my child, I was worried about them—"

"Your record shows a report from one John Taylor. Improper

dispersal of aid. Entered the protest after the area was taped off. For your offenses, you will be cast into shade."

"But I was trying to help—"

"You were undermining the system."

"I need to talk to my wife, she—"

"If you wish to contest your charges, you may request a court appearance."

"But—"

"Clear out."

Vivian looked down at her hand. It was a featureless dark gray, smoky and nearly black. She was filtered even from herself. The Keepers looked the same as they had before, but everyone else was a Generic Citizen. No individual faces, no other Shades. This wasn't shadow prison—it was shadow solitary. And for what? All she'd done was try to help someone else's kids, and then her own.

"Clear out, Shade," the Keeper said.

Vivian started walking. The campus buildings had no overlays. Instead of charming red brick, everything was unadorned concrete. Nothing looked familiar. What if she got lost and couldn't get home? She called Brooke and once again got the message that her access was restricted.

A Generic Citizen approached and studied her carefully. "— — — — — — — glitchballs."

"Cass?"

"— what — — — — that —"

"I can't hear most of what you're saying, it's like a radio station gone to static. Cass? Is that you?"

"Follow me." The Citizen started walking, looking back periodically to make sure Vivian was following.

Everything on the walk was wrong. A nightmare distortion of her neighborhood, a skeleton with the flesh stripped away. None of the apartment buildings had maintained their physical appearance—the paint was faded and peeling, some of the windows were boarded over, the landscaping was overgrown. The sidewalks weren't crowded, but the few Citizens that were here gave Vivian a wide berth. Their silver faces bore no expression, but she could feel disgust and fear radiating off of them in waves. She stayed close to the Citizen that she really hoped was Cass.

They went into one of the buildings and stopped at a door that looked nothing like her own. The Citizen opened it to reveal a Keeper standing inside. This hadn't been Cass at all; the whole thing was some kind of trap.

"Oh, Viv."

Brooke. Brooke could see her because she was a Keeper. She could hear Brooke for the same reason.

Cass said something Vivian couldn't hear.

"I don't have that kind of authority. I can place her under house arrest where at least I control her privileges and filters, but that's really all I can do. Even that is. . . risky."

The apartment shifted back to its usual appearance, and Vivian could see Cass and Brooke. She broke down into tears. "I'm sorry. I'm so sorry."

Cass started crying, too, black eyeliner streaking down their cheeks. "It's as much my fault as yours, you came to the protest for me—"

"Pull it together, both of you." Brooke, ever practical and calm. "We have to find a way to get through this, as a family. No room for mistakes now or it'll be shadows for all of us."

"Day after tomorrow I'll be seventeen, I can sign up to be a Shadowkeeper."

"Cass." Vivian shook her head. There had to be some other way.

"If you aren't a keeper of shadows, you're probably a Shade," Cass said, their voice dripping with sarcasm. But the words were true. Anyone who didn't leap up to defend the system would be consumed by it.

"They're holding the vote on the shadow prison system tomorrow morning," Brooke said.

"So soon?" Vivian's heart lifted. The system would be voted

down, she could explain her actions at work, everything would be okay.

"Probably in reaction to the protests," Cass said. "They don't want to give the public time to think through the implications. Auntie Yang said there are rumors that anyone who votes the prisons down will be cast into Shade, or put on some kind of watchlist. I'm worried for her. I don't know if she got out of the protest unprocessed, and her record is sketchy."

––––––––––

Vivian stayed up all night listening to her wife's soft snores. Brooke could sleep through anything, it was like a superpower. Meanwhile Vivian couldn't stop worrying about what would happen if people voted to keep the shadow prisons.

In the morning, Brooke cast her vote and went to work. Cass dutifully got on the bus for school. Soon they would both be Keepers, so however the vote turned out, they'd be safe. Brooke would protect their child.

Vivian paced up and down the hall. House arrest meant she couldn't go anywhere to distract herself. There was nothing to do but watch the feeds for the results. The news hit shortly after the polls closed at noon.

The margin was slim, but shadow prisons were approved.

Brooke called, but Vivian couldn't bring herself to answer. She packed a change of clothes, a stack of nutrient bricks, and the few pieces of physical jewelry she owned, in case she needed something to trade. Her backpack was small and there wasn't much room left, but she put the miniature painting of sunflowers from Cass on top. She needed a reminder of what she was fighting for. That there was still beauty and vibrant color in the world.

She would fight this from the inside.

Vivian was already a Shade—they'd taken everything they could from her. She could hide here in the apartment, or she could go out and try to make a difference somehow. The only way to protect Cass was to take the whole thing down. Vivian took one last look at the apartment, filtered to be beautiful, to hide the deterioration of the reality underneath. Then she crossed the threshold, violating the terms of her house arrest and plunging herself back into shade.

She pulled out Cass's picture. The filters of her shadow prison recognized the paint and filtered it out, or maybe Cass's art had been digital all along. Either way, Vivian was not allowed to see the art. All that remained was blank white paper in a simple black frame.

She would have to remember, and fight for the color and beauty that was lost.

Part 2: Shadow Prisons Of The Mind

With the right overlays, the city was charming—apartment buildings done up like giant row houses, seamlessly blending Victorian and modern sensibilities, boutiques and cafes on tree-lined streets, parks bathed in sunshine. Vivian Watanabe had lived on this block, once, in a high-rise apartment painted corn-flower blue with trim in teal and white. She couldn't see it now, not the way she used to. As a Shade, everything on this block was a featureless gray building. Which was the reality? Was it the colorful apartments nestled together, the bland gray buildings. . . or something else entirely? Personal Implanted Perception chips made it impossible to know.

Vivian counted the buildings, seven on this block. A decade ago, in another life, she'd lived here with her wife Brooke and their child, Cass. The second building from the corner was theirs. Generic Citizens—in the featureless silvery-gray overlays worn by anyone who had enough points to not be a Shade—walked along the sidewalk on their way home from work. They gave Vivian a wide berth. She saw them as Citizens, but they saw her as a dark shadow, an unsightly blemish in their otherwise beautiful world. They were guessing at her crimes, judging her, avoiding any semblance of contact for fear that mere association with a Shade would cost them precious points.

They were right to do it. Vivian didn't belong here, but sometimes she needed to return, to be close to her family, even if she couldn't recognize them. For all Vivian knew, they might have moved to a new neighborhood years ago. But when she and Brooke had come home from the hospital with baby Cass, this was the home they'd gone to. Where Cass had taken their first steps and drawn crayon pictures on the entire inside of their closet. Where, as a teen, Cass had painted their landscapes, and portraits, and endless variations on sunflowers.

Vivian still had one of the paintings, though now she couldn't see anything but a blank white page. That change had happened here, too, more than a decade ago. She'd pulled Cass out of a protest and been thrown into shade, and the next day Citizens voted to make the shadow prison experiment permanent. They'd condemned her to an existence of neverending shadow to protect themselves. So she'd packed up Cass's painting of sunflowers and walked out. To protect her family.

In the distance, the tall silver form of a Shadowkeeper approached. Vivian hurried away. It might be Brooke, and she couldn't bear for her wife to see her this way. Keepers were not as tightly bound by the filters, and without an overlay she'd look somewhere between ragged and half-dead.

She ran her fingers over the uneven stubble of her hair. She'd shaved it herself, by feel since she couldn't see her own scalp. Brooke had loved her hair, before. She'd been jealous of the length.

Well-maintained gray buildings gave way to dilapidated gray buildings. Like most Shades, Vivian lived on the outskirts of the city. She was fresh off her shift at the ZimCorp assembly line, her hands stiff and sore from repeating the same motions for hours on end. Placing metal plates half the size of her palm into a slot on the work base, watching as a thick needle punched through the plates, piercing them with holes.

Removing the plates from the machine and placing them on the belt that carried them to the next station. It was hard to say for sure what she was making—Shades only did early stage production, never anything that would provide an opportunity to steal a finished or near-finished product. But there were whispers that it was a new kind of PIP, something even worse than the current ones.

Information was hard to come by. Shades only got the prison net—she couldn't even access Citizen-level news feeds, biased and skewed as they were. If she could get her hands on some beer, she could trade it to Auntie Yang for a peek at the rumornet, find out what terrible tech she was helping create. In theory the Keepers could see anything she did by reading it off her PIP, but with so many Shades to monitor they'd largely abandoned the raw sensory data for shadow prison algorithms that wouldn't recognize a terminal as ancient as Auntie Yang's. Probably.

For the first time in years, Vivian was accumulating points, creeping back up towards the citizenship line instead of plummeting inexorably to zero-point termination. If she kept her head down, maybe they'd set her free. She could have sunlight. See her family. Have some semblance of her old life. Shades were disappearing, hitting zero or killing themselves with illegal surgeries to try and remove their PIPs. Maybe it was better for her to work with the system. . . but no, that mentality was what let the system thrive.

She had to keep fighting. For Cass. She had to find out what ZimCorp was working on.

Maybe Jazz would let her moonlight a shift at the Blind Tiger and pay her in beer.

She cut across an alley that ran between a ration room and some run-down apartments, then knocked seven times on a nondescript gray door. It opened a crack, and a Generic Citizen peered out at her. Citizens and even advertising bots all wore that same generic silver body, making it impossible to know who she was talking to. Only Keepers looked any different—bigger and a slightly paler shade of silver—and even they could broadcast a Generic Citizen overlay if they wanted to.

Vivian had been a Shade so long that she struggled to remember even the most familiar faces. Brooke. Cass. Her child would be nearly thirty now. Vivian might have grandchildren that she'd never met. Might never meet. The only person she ever saw as an individual was Auntie Yang, who had managed to hack the system and present herself as a grandmotherly woman with a bun of silver-streaked black hair.

The Citizen stared at her and said nothing. It could be Jazz, or a customer, or an undercover Keeper waiting for her to make a mistake that would cost her precious points—she had no way to know.

"Jazz working tonight?" Vivian asked.

"Who wants to know?"

"24601." Vivian couldn't tell people her name. If she tried to reveal personal information it got filtered out so they simply didn't hear it. It wasn't as bad as the first few months in shadow prison, when it had been impossible to have conversations because the filters were so aggressive. Shade labor was more useful with at least some communication, thank goodness. But she was still a Shade, not a Citizen, and all prisoners were inter-changeable within the system. Over time she'd built up some codes with regular contacts, an almost-identity.

"Yeah right, and I'm Javert." Jazz opened the door. "You looking for work again? It's been slow and B.B. doesn't have the credits. Keepers have been cracking down hard on drinking. . . It isn't as trendy as a minor act of rebellion these days."

Vivian flinched at the word rebellion, but Jazz wasn't a Shade, so in theory her speech wasn't being tracked by the prison algorithms. "I'm looking to score a six pack of beer for my auntie."

"Dishwasher's broke again, so B.B. will probably do you a sixpack of the cheap shit if you take care of those." The silvery arm of Jazz's overlay pointed to a mountain of dirty dishes over-flowing out of an industrial size sink.

Auntie Yang would complain about not getting better quality beer, but Vivian had seen her drink cooking wine. Even the worst beer was hard to come by these days. She found herself half hoping that Auntie would offer to share, though she'd been dry since the prohibition came down a few years back.

She passed the bar where a handful of Citizens ate plates of flavored nutri-bricks and sipped at drinks programmed to taste like beer or whiskey or fruity cocktails. She went straight to the back, where B.B. was throwing more dishes onto the already precarious stack.

"Who the hell are you?" he demanded.

"Jazz said you need a dishwasher. I'm a dishwasher."

"And how exactly does she plan to pay you? I'm not made of credits."

"I'll do it for a couple sixpacks." She held out her hand, palm up.

He scanned her chip to make sure she wasn't violent or otherwise unsuitable to hire. The scan gave him a temporary Shade ID number in case he wanted to file a report, her current point total, and a list of violations. He looked her up and down, as if he could get information from the generic dark outline Shades projected. "All the dishes. One sixpack when you're done. Drink it somewhere else—the bar is for Citizens."

"Yeah, no problem." Vivian started on the giant mountain of dishes. Periodically B.B. came in from the bar and loaded her up with more. He'd keep her busy until closing time, all for one goddamn sixpack.

A targeted advertising Generic appeared next to her and started a conversation. "At five thousand points, Shades are eligible for coursework at Juan Pedro Tomas Community College. With work packages and loans, an education is within your reach."

"Thanks," Vivian said, knowing the Generic would stick around if she tried to argue. It'd been a year since she'd had five thousand points, and she'd lost all hope of getting back that high. Now her life was a matter of hoarding the points she had, keeping herself above zero, doing what she needed to do to stay alive. Working for beer to bribe Auntie was a terrible idea, except that it might help break the system and make a better world for Cass.

The stack of dishes shifted in the sink, and Vivian wasn't quick enough to catch them all. Two glasses slid to the floor and shattered.

"I'm docking you a beer for anything you break. Two glasses, two beers. You Shades are a drain on society. Can't even wash the goddamn dishes."

Vivian didn't answer, just methodically made her way through the rest of the stack. At the bottom of the sink, one of the plates was cracked in half. She washed it anyway and set it on the counter with the others. It was well past midnight now, only a few hours until her next shift at ZimCorp.

B.B. closed up, and Jazz came into the kitchen with three bottles of beer.

"That one was broken in the bottom of the sink. I didn't do it."

Jazz shrugged. "You complain, B.B. will probably report you. And does your auntie really need more than three beers?"

Vivian needed the points more than she needed the beer, and she was lucky that B.B. had paid her at all. Or maybe he hadn't and Jazz was working around him. "Thanks."

There was an awkward pause as Vivian carefully packed the beer bottles into her threadbare backpack. To her surprise, Jazz tossed her a token with a few credits on it.

"What's this?"

"You've been in here so many times, you almost feel like a friend, even if I don't know your real name or anything." Jazz shrugged, then her silvery Generic overlay turned and walked toward the door. She paused in the doorway and looked back at Vivian, the face of her overlay expressionless as always. "Don't come back."

It stung. Vivian wanted to leave the token as a dramatic gesture, but credits were hard to come by. She shoved the token in her pocket. This always happened, eventually. She wasn't worth the risk. People had to look out for themselves. "Goodbye, Jazz."

————

Everything cast a shadow, even the city itself. Underground, beyond the reach of sunlight, there were apartments tucked between the giant pipes and tunnels that carried away the city's waste. The shadow city had no roads, no cars—the Shades who lived here walked to work along the tops of sewage pipes and on the narrow sidewalks that lined the wastewater tunnels. It was dank, dark, damp and miserable, and no civilized person would ever go there. Even Vivian usually stayed surface-side, but Auntie Yang was a known rebel—she lived underground to dodge the Keepers.

The tunnels were a maze, lit by flickering blue lights, dim and placed too far apart to cut through the darkness. Vivian walked along a memorized series of turns, fourth tunnel left, second tunnel right, over the extension ladders that someone had cobbled together as a makeshift bridge. The tunnels smelled like piss and mold with a persistent overlay of lemon that even shadow prison filters used to try to cover some of the stench.

Vivian climbed out of the tunnel and squeezed between two massive green sewer pipes, and stood on the doorstep of Auntie Yang's apartment. It'd been months since she'd been to visit, and maybe the old woman that everyone called Auntie no longer lived here. For all she knew, Auntie no longer lived at all.

Vivian pounded on the door, and stood back far enough for Auntie to see her through the viewer, not that there'd be anything to see but a Shade.

"I'm not worth the trouble."

Auntie usually had a creaky voice, but today all Vivian could hear was the bland voice of a Citizen. But the words sounded like something Auntie would say.

"Neither am I," Vivian answered.

They stood in silence on opposite sides of the still-closed door.

"You don't sound yourself today," Vivian said. If this wasn't Auntie, offering up the beer was a waste of beer at best and a world of trouble at worst.

"Ah, a regular who has been away. But which one, I wonder?" A Citizen opened the door and studied her. "I have a soft spot for old women, having been one myself. Come in, child."

Vivian cocked her head. Auntie Yang should not be able to see that she was old, but she'd always called everyone child. The interaction was a mix of right and wrong, and there was no way out of it now without risking precious points.

"The worst that can happen is death, and even that brings freedom from the hell we live." The Citizen held the door open.

"I brought beer." Vivian held up a bottle.

"More than just the one, I hope."

The Citizen turned and went down the hallway, walking in slow motion so that the image of a youthful Citizen could match pace with the labored waddle of an elderly woman. Vivian closed the door behind her and followed.

"Why can't I see you?" Vivian asked. Auntie had never bothered with an overlay before.

"Beer first, beer first." The Citizen ushered her into Auntie's apartment, and as she stepped inside, the old woman suddenly looked as she should.

Vivian stared. It was so good to see something other than a generic overlay.

"I never know who will come knocking at my door, and having my apartment project the Citizen overlay is a simple trick, child," Auntie explained, misinterpreting Vivian's stare as one of surprise. "You don't mind if I call you child? You're not young, but you're still younger than I am."

"You can call me what you like, Auntie." Vivian said, dutifully. Auntie had always insisted on respect.

Vivian wondered why Auntie would use the apartment

system rather than projecting from her PIP. Security issues, maybe? Vivian pulled the three beers from her bag and handed them over.

Auntie tsked. "Such cheap beer, and only three?"

"Hard times up there," Vivian said, shrugging. "I was supposed to get a sixpack, but they stiffed me half."

Auntie opened the first and started drinking. "So why are you here?"

"You always know the best secrets, Auntie."

The old woman cackled. "That I do. Here to find out where to get your PIP out? You're not so close to the termination line as most of the desperate souls that straggle in."

"You had your PIP removed," Vivian whispered. Suddenly the apartment security system made sense.

Auntie pursed her lips and narrowed her eyes. "I don't like to make mistakes, and I thought I had a read on you."

Vivian raised both hands. "I hadn't thought. . . You really know people who can remove the PIPs? Everybody says if you cut them out it kills you."

Auntie sighed. "There's some truth to that. Installation is pretty straightforward because the chips release nanites that build the rest of the system once they're inside your body. It's a nightmare application of the self-replicating nanocomputing tech that got me tenured, back when it was still safe for me to show my face at the university. The PIP system is tied into your metabolism for power, and there's a pocket of coolant installed right up against—"

Auntie stopped abruptly and shook her head. "Removing PIPs is a delicate business at best, but that's not why you're here."

"I'm a Shade on the ZimCorp line, and I want to know what I'm making. We lived in the same neighborhood, back before the shadow prisons. And then after that you let me use your terminal sometimes, for beer—"

Auntie finally relaxed. "Oh, yes. Now I remember you. It's been a long time since your last visit. Better beer back then. The terminal is in the closet, under the pile of bras and underwear.

Keepers never want to touch an old woman's underthings. Don't like the idea of someone so old as me naked." She cackled. "Except the ones that want to take a tumble with old Auntie!"

Vivian blushed. "Thank you, Auntie."

"Put it back the way you found it when you're done."

It didn't take long on the rumornet to find what she needed. ZimCorp was working on an add-on to the PIPs, some kind of memory revision tech. It was bad enough that they controlled the realities of the present; now they wanted to filter people's past. Steal away any memories that made them fight against the system.

"Ah yes, that is bad," Auntie said from the other room, reminding Vivian that even though she wasn't there looking over her shoulder, nothing went over her terminal without her knowing about it.

"But what can we do?" Vivian asked. This was worse than she expected, but sabotaging the work at the factory would get her terminated, in more ways than one.

"If you can get me one of those new chips, I might be able to hack it, or get it to someone who can," Auntie said, thoughtful. "We're pulling people out of the system as fast as we can, but there are only so many surgeons with the skills to remove the PIPs. We're not ready for this new level of hell."

"You want me to steal from ZimCorp." Vivian stared in disbelief.

"I know, child. It is a lot to ask." Auntie took a long pull on the last of the bottles of beer. "If you get me what I need, I'll set you up with my surgeon, get your PIP removed."

Freedom from the shadow prison, and all she had to do was risk everything.

———————

To get a finished chip, Vivian needed access to a different wing of the factory complex—the end of the assembly line. There were offices there—hiring, medical support, university and college applications. If she had five thousand points, she could have gotten in by applying to take courses at the community college. As it was, her best bet was a workplace injury. That would give her access to the med lab. The trick was finding the right injury—serious enough to get her into the other wing, but not too much permanent damage.

There were safeguards to prevent injuries, but the machines were old.

When her line supervisor was on the far end of the assembly room floor, she snapped a handguard loose by leaning into it with her elbow. The shades to either side of her on the line didn't notice, or pretended not to. Face forward, no talking, do your own work. Anything else could cost you points.

Vivian used the broken handguard to cover the sensor that tracked whether her hand was clear of the machine. She placed a metal plate in the designated groove on the work surface, and pressed her hand, palm down, over the plate. She watched as what was left of the handguard rotated, the broken plastic scraping her skin but not pushing her hand out of way. The external sensor registered green, mistaking the broken-off piece of handguard for her hand.

The awl plunged down through her hand.

The machine detected an error. It paused and emitted a series of high pitched beeps. Vivian stared at the metal extruding from the middle of the shadowy outline of her hand, unable to make sense of an image so obviously wrong. Her PIP filtered away the sharpest sensations of pain, replacing them with a strange pattern of throbbing designed to call attention to the wound without being excruciating. She'd never sustained this level of injury before, and the experience was more surreal than distressing.

With her free hand, she knocked the broken handguard off the sensor and onto the floor. Hopefully it would all look like an accident. She was pleased at how well her plan was going, the injury was not as bad as she'd feared. They'd cart her off to the med lab and bandage her up, and hopefully she could get the chip she needed.

Medical overrides dropped the shadow filter surrounding the injury.

She saw the flesh of her own hand for the first time in years. Tiny parallel lines of white where the broken handguard had scratched her deeply tanned skin. Dark brown age spots and freckles, so many more than had been there before. The pale blue of her veins. Wrinkles. Her own hand. She suddenly understood the Shades that became cutters, why they'd injure themselves. For this. A glimpse of their own body.

Blood oozed out around the edges of the needle. A crimson ring that contrasted with both the flesh of her hand and the shining silver metal.

The machine stopped beeping, and the awl retracted. Blood gushed everywhere, pulsing out through the puncture wound and pooling in the bottom of the machine. She'd never seen so much blood.

She screamed.

There was a flurry of activity, chaos. The floor supervisor was yelling, but Vivian didn't process any of the words. A Generic wrapped her hand with white cloth that immediately soaked red. Another Generic hung a lanyard around her neck, a pass that would get her into the other wing for medical attention.

One of the Generics led her out of the assembly line and down a long hallway, chattering at her constantly. She tried to nod occasionally to show that she was still conscious, but even that small movement made her dizzy. She stumbled and leaned against the windows that lined one side of the hallway and squeezed her eyes shut. "Sorry. So dizzy."

She opened her eyes and found herself looking down at the rest of the assembly line, all completely automated and supervised by a Keeper. Her head spun. She knew she should study the scene below for security flaws, but this wasn't what she'd expected at all—there were no workers, only a guard and a line of machines.

The Generic ushered her into the medical station and left her with a doc—denoted by a red cross on the chest of their other-wise generic overlay—on shift there. The care was impersonal and efficient. Stitches and bandages, scans to make sure her peripheral ID chip was intact, a reset of her PIP to remove the seek-urgent-care throbbing to leave only a dull ache. The skin of her hand disappeared back into shadow. She wondered if she'd ever see it again.

A second doc came in. "First patient for the new installation?"

The first doc shook their head. "Careless Shade down on the front end of the line. Punched straight through its own hand with one of the machines. I know Shades need work to keep them occupied, but I wish we could go full on automated."

Vivian shouldn't have been able to hear this conversation, but maybe the medical overrides decreased her audio filtering. If she got out of this, she could use that to her advantage. She played an oblivious Shade, pretended not to notice their conversation.

"We've got the prototypes ready to go, who'd know? It's just a Shade."

"You want to do it, go right ahead. I'll still be working here when your newly Shaded ass gets implanted with the latest tech."

One of the docs hooked her up to an IV. "Shade lost enough blood that it won't be going anywhere for a while, you want to grab some lunch?"

"Sure. There's a new place on 6th and Main with a flavor overlay for empanadas."

This was her chance. She'd seen where the doc had gestured when they talked about prototypes—the new implant was here at the med lab. She wouldn't have to get onto the assembly floor at all.

Both docs left. Vivian forced herself upright and stumbled over to the glass case where the prototypes were stored, barely within the range of the clear tubing that tethered her to a bag of fluid. The lid of the case was locked, but the key was on the table next to the case. There were a dozen chips arranged in two neat rows. Vivian carefully removed two, which left slightly shorter rows, but to her eye that was less obvious than a single missing chip that made the rows uneven.

She wrapped the chips in tissue and shoved them into her pocket. If she got caught, she'd lose all her points and be terminated. She'd probably lose points just for her 'accident' although technically people were not supposed to be penalized for sustaining injuries. They'd want to do an investigation. Possibly they were already analyzing the data from her PIP. The security team would be able to see what she saw, including watching the Shade outline of her hands stealing their latest technology.

Probably they hadn't started their investigation yet, or they'd be on high alert. She had to get out. She couldn't wait to be formally discharged. Vivian frowned. It seemed wrong that they'd leave the clinic unattended. Too easy. If she put the chips back maybe they would let her live, wouldn't take all her points. Maybe there was some other way to stop this, to slow this descent into new levels of hell.

No, she was committed. She called up a vague memory of Cass, the way they'd looked when they were nearly seventeen, dressed all in black with bright blue hair nearly as short as Vivian's was now. She'd finish this for Cass, and Auntie would help her get her PIP removed, and she'd live underground where the Keepers wouldn't find her. Maybe someday she'd even see Cass and Brooke again. She tried to draw strength from the thought.

She pulled out her IV, nearly fainting at the sight of the blood that trickled down the end of the tubing. Her arm stayed in shadow, the injury not severe enough to re-trigger the medical safeties. Or was there some kind of override now that she was being treated? She found some gauze and taped it over the dull ache where she thought the IV had been. For once the shadow overlay would come in handy—she was surely splattered in her own blood, but out in the hallway all anyone would see was a Shade.

She made it to her own wing without incident and clocked

out with only minor alarms in her peripheral vision to notify her that the leave was unauthorized. No one paid any attention to her. She was a Shade in a crowd of Shades, all of them inter-changeable, workers on the line.

As soon as she was clear of ZimCorp property, she opened a manhole and climbed down the ladder. Her head was spinning from her injuries, and she was entering at a different point in the underground maze, but the flow of the wastewater would lead her to the main tunnel.

Rats scurried along the edges of the sewer, and the stench of human waste with its lemon overlay made the throbbing in her head even worse. She glanced down at her arm, but she couldn't see if she was bleeding from her puncture wound, or from the IV line she'd torn out. If it was bad, the safeties would come on, and she'd be able to see. She found her usual entry point in the main tunnel, and walked along the memorized series of turns, fourth tunnel left, second tunnel right, over the extension ladders that someone had cobbled together as a makeshift bridge.

She knocked on Auntie Yang's door, swaying on her feet as she waited for Auntie to let her in. "I have the chips."

The door opened, and Auntie stood on the other side without her Citizen overlay.

"Oh, child."

Vivian followed Auntie's gaze. Behind her a trio of Keepers appeared out of nowhere. They'd filtered themselves from Vivian's senses with her PIP. She'd had no way to know that they were following her. She'd led them straight to Auntie.

It had all been too easy.

"Turn over the stolen property." The Shadowkeeper held out a hand, and Vivian dropped both tissue-wrapped chips into it. There was no point in fighting now, anything she did would only make it worse, and there was no way for her to escape three Keepers.

Auntie had no PIP. There was no official record of her as a Citizen or a Shade—she was outside the system, already dead.

"Run," Vivian whispered.

But Auntie Yang didn't move. She held her arms up to show that she was harmless. It almost looked as though she was going to embrace the approaching Keeper. Her face was calm and her voice was steady. "Those who make peaceful revolution impossible—"

The Keeper shot her in the chest before she could finish. Five shots in rapid succession. Loud bursts of sound. Auntie's mouth was still moving, trying to repeat the words that John F. Kennedy had once spoken, but Vivian couldn't hear her over the gunshots and the ringing of her ears. Blood soaked through Auntie's purple tunic, like crimson stars. The pattern reminded Vivian of Cassiopeia, a lopsided W of blood. Auntie wavered on her feet for a moment before she collapsed.

". . .will make violent revolution inevitable." Vivian whispered, finishing the quote that Auntie had begun.

———

"You will be injected with nanites. Animal testing has shown minimal side effects. This is the initial round of human testing. Sign here to indicate that you understand the study and consent to participate."

"Injected?" The metal plates she'd been making were not the right scale for injections, they looked like something that would be surgically installed. "What the hell were those things I was making on the line?"

The generic silver features of the Doc twisted into a smirk, something Vivian didn't even know was possible—a new feature, or an upgrade that came with status? The Doc's face returned to its passive default. "You stole two scales for an animatronic dragon in the latest Cardinal Guardians immersive movie— Seiryu: Guardian of the East. Quite the wonder of design—each scale can be individually programmed for color, brightness, and movement to simulate bristling or flattening down for flight."

The Doc held one out, and unfiltered—or with a different filter—it looked more like a dragon scale than a chip.

What do you do against someone who has all the power? They controlled the rumornet, the overlays, the points. They wrote all the rules, and Vivian had no way to even know what was happening. The forms in front of her could say anything, and if she agreed to this procedure ZimCorp would control her past, feeding her false memories to support their version of reality. How could she fight that?

"I'm out of points," she said. "I have no choice."

The Doc across the table shrugged.

It was more of a choice than Auntie had been given. Participation in the study would restore her points to 7500. She would be a Shade, but she would be pardoned for the crime of stealing the chips—dragon scales—from ZimCorp. She could take classes at the community college, maybe earn her way back to citizenship somehow. Sign the forms and be a guinea pig for a whole new level of hell, or refuse and be terminated.

She signed the forms.

The needle for the injection was small enough that it didn't trigger her medical overrides. Metal disappeared into shadow, and the cloudy liquid inside the syringe disappeared.

They held her for monitoring, tested the outputs on her PIP.

Eventually the Doc nodded and handed her a notebook with a red cover. It was blank inside. "You are free to go."

The last time someone had told her that, she'd been in a physical cell, locked up like an animal in a cage that smelled faintly of bleach. Rows upon row of cells, prisoners on the inside, guards on the outside, and an overwhelming feeling of guilt for her crimes.

Anything was better than being locked up like that, even as a Shade at least she could—

Vivian shook her head. She was old enough to remember jails, but she'd never been a prisoner inside of one. She had to keep track of her past, had to remember which memories were real and reject the others. She hurried across the city, desperate to get home.

Vivian wrote her memories into a notebook she'd stolen from an old woman's apartment three weeks after she got out of jail. She ran her fingers over the bright red cover. Red like the start of a rainbow, stretching across the sky. She'd stolen it all those years ago and carried it with her as she moved from housing shelter to housing shelter, staying alive by the grace of social welfare programs. She'd been so ungrateful.

The memories felt so real. Like overlays for her past, and she couldn't see the truth. That was why she had to write it down. Nothing digital, only old-fashioned ink on paper.

One child: Cass. Studied painting, loved sunflowers.

She had this niggling sense that she had written this before. She flipped to the beginning of the notebook, and skimmed over several pages of memories, beginning with her troubled childhood and leading up to the more recent past, the time when she began to work with the system instead of against it. Everything was coherent, it all made sense.

Where was she? She read the last line she'd written. If I can earn enough points to become a Citizen, I could see my family again.

Yes. She had to do better, earn back her points.

A targeted ad appeared next to her, projected into the silvery form of a Generic. "ZimCorp is looking for volunteers to test our new memory enhancement technology. Earn points toward citizenship by referring suitable candidates."

Yes. Vivian would turn her life around.

She closed the red notebook.

Part 3: The Shadow Prisoner's Dilemma

Vivian sat at a cafe opposite Cass. Everything around her had a gritty, dingy quality. Even Cass looked run down, their face deeply tanned and distressingly wrinkled. They were old now, many decades past being the child that Vivian remembered. She looked down at her hands, so different than the black shadows that she'd grown accustomed to seeing during all her years as a Shade—the skin was covered in age spots and hung loose on the bones. The overhead light flickered, and there were crumbs on one corner of the table. Vivian brushed them away and reached for her can of CitrusSoda.

NOW PLAYING IN FULL SENSORY IMMERSION: THE SHADOW PRISONER'S DILEMMA

The words appeared in the corner of Vivian's field of view when she opened the can. Advertisers were getting bolder again, pushing new avenues now that they weren't allowed to generate fake Citizens to use as targeted adbots. The CitrusSoda can had the advertisement printed on the side so that even people who had removed their Personal Implanted Perception chips would see it, which was ridiculous because without a PIP you couldn't experience movie immersions.

"I'd like to go," Vivian told Cass. "Maybe with Brooke?"

"Mum doesn't do immersions," Cass said, "not since Amelia had her PIP out."

"Is Brooke avoiding me?" Vivian saw Cass nearly every day, but her wife. . . her now-remarried wife. . . she saw rarely.

"No, Mom." Cass put their hand on Vivian's shoulder. "She's just trying to balance between reconnecting with you and not hurting Amelia. Give me a minute to ping Mark and let him know I'll be late getting home, and I can take you to the theater."

Back before the fall of ZimCorp, immersive movies premiered on grand opening nights with stars and producers dressed in expensive designer overlays. As one of the inspirations for this new movie, Vivian might have been invited to the premiere, and she could have worn a gown like the ones she saw back at Illusions Formalwear, half a lifetime ago.

"I once saw a ballgown made entirely of tiny gears. I could have worn it, if they still had big premiers and designer overlays."

"They had a premiere a few weeks ago, but there's not as much money in immersives these days so it was a smaller affair. Kids aren't getting PIPs, and not all of the older generations kept them. And the end of personal overlays is a good thing. Are you sure you want to do this?" Cass asked. "The movie is partly based on your life. Your therapist says it might be disorienting."

"I'm disoriented anyway, who cares?"

Cass laughed.

The theater was as dilapidated as all the other buildings in the yet-to-be renovated neighborhood. It was on the endless list of city projects that had piled up while overlays rendered cosmetic maintenance unnecessary. The inside was plain, which hardly mattered because once the customers were immersed in the world of the movie, they lost track of the real world. Immersive theaters were one of very few holdovers from the ZimCorp era, a place where people could voluntarily have the kind of manufactured reality that the revolution had worked so hard to dismantle.

"These are our seats," Cass said, gesturing to a pair of drab chairs. The theater was mostly empty, though there was an elderly couple near the front, holding hands as they stared off into space together. A theater staff member sat reading an ancient printed-on-paper book at the front of the room.

Vivian sat down and logged into the theater, and Cass carefully checked the theater's licenses and permissions before allowing limited-time access to their PIPs through the security menus of their wristbands. The difference between good PIPs and bad PIPs was all in who controlled the filters, though Vivian supposed that letting people choose what they wanted to see was not without its own problems.

"All your usual settings?" Cass asked.

"Yes." Vivian's hearing and vision were both starting to go, so she liked to reduce environmental sound levels to hear voices better and increase the size and contrast of words and images. The younger generation was avoiding PIPs entirely because of the ways they'd been misused, but the features would be lost with the flaws.

"Ready?" Cass asked. "I'll start us together so we'll be in sync."

They would get synchronized sensory inputs, but they would process them based on their past experiences, add their own thoughts and impressions. Vivian supposed people also did that with the old-fashioned non-immersive movies that were making a comeback, though with those it was usually clearer which things were on the screen and which were in the viewers' minds.

"I'm ready."

There are things I know are true, and things I know are wrong, but most of it is somewhere in the middle. I'm not sure I'll ever really piece together my past.

Vivian scribbled the words into a blue notebook while Cass read the yellow one. The notebooks went in rainbow order, but the red one and the orange one were a disjointed mishmash of confused memory fragments and implanted lies.

"Mom." Cass stopped reading. "What are you doing?"

"Memories," Vivian answered. "I have to write them down, have to make sure nothing has changed. You're reading the yellow memories, and I'm writing the blue. I'm nearly to purple, and purple is good. Safe."

"You don't have to do that anymore, that's done now." Cass closed the yellow journal. "You never talk about your time in shadow. I thought the memories were wiped in the zero-point coup."

Vivian wrote Cass's words into the blue notebook. She didn't write every conversation, there wasn't time and too much writing made her wrist hurt. But this seemed important.

Cass frowned at the yellow notebook. "There's so much detail here."

"By the time I got to yellow, nothing felt real." Vivian peered at the middle-aged person that she remembered as a child. Her child. They were portly now, with a deeply lined face and short hair dyed black. What if this wasn't really Cass? She could test them, try to trick them.

"How did Brooke die?" Vivian asked.

"Sometimes you seem…better, but then you keep asking about Mum in all these weird ways. She remarried. She waited for a long time, but after a while we thought you were…" Cass looked away. They wore a long-sleeved dress with a geometric pattern of turquoise and purple. The vibrant purple was important—it went gray if you mixed it with yellow. Reality Royale, designers were calling the now-popular hue. Vivian's shirt was the same color, and the fabric was soft and smooth.

Vivian frowned. Cass had been reading her notebooks, and everything anyone would possibly want to know about Brooke was in there. No, not in the yellow one. The sunshine yellow notebook was from the dark time, the time when she was alone. She smiled at the irony of it. Darkness encased in a cheery yellow cover. "Do you still paint sunflowers?"

"I haven't painted for a long time. I'm an archivist now. I preserve the Red Books at the library on campus, so we don't lose the stories of the shadow prison era."

Vivian nodded. "Van Gogh's sunflowers are fading to brown, like real flowers. Slowly dying as the paint degrades in the light. You can cover the darkness with yellow, but eventually it seeps through."

There was an odd cut between scenes, where the director had tried for a fancy effect but it didn't quite work: Vivian stared at the yellow notebook from the previous scene, and then she fell into it, with words and sketched-out illustrations scattering around her as she fell, like Alice falling down the rabbit hole into Wonderland, except that she fell into her own past.

Vivian loaded her basket with two weeks of rations, the most a Shade was allowed to buy in one transaction. Efficient without it being stockpiling. Rules were important and good, as everyone had learned from the Shade riots. Her memories of the riots were oddly sepia-toned, with a musty smell and a faint rustling ever-present in the background, as if they'd been printed on ancient newspaper. A broken window from the looting. Chaos as a mob of Shades gathered in the streets. Then a beautiful sense of peace when order was restored, like the warm golden light of the sun after a rain. But even thinking about peace, Vivian couldn't shake the damp smell and the odd rustling sound.

Vivian tried to focus. She'd been cheating sleep for weeks, staying up late to read sci-books on memory formation and recall. The books were…

not quite illegal. They were written in the guise of science fiction novels, with pulpy illustrations and poorly-defined characters who explained the workings of the mind in loosely plot-relevant infodumps.

She felt like she was on the verge of a breakthrough. She knew that they were in her head, filtering her reality, shifting her memories. What she needed was a way to escape their lies.

How do you break free from the prison of your own mind?

Vivian waited in the checkout line, careful not to meet the gaze of the Citizens and Shades who stood waiting with carts and baskets. If she was lucky, she could get in and out of the shop with only one interaction. The other customers had the same goal—make it through the line and speak to no one, interact with no one.

The clerk had no choice in the matter. Jobs like that were basically death row, and the Shade working the register knew it. Vivian wondered how many points the clerk had left—it was impossible to tell from the shadowy black figure who the person underneath was, and whether they had several thousand points or only a few hundred. The only thing she knew for sure was that the clerk was below the Shade line, which congress had recently bumped up to twenty thousand.

Hopefully the clerk was closer to twenty thousand than to terminal zero.

If in doubt, always report. She only lost one point that way, no matter what the other person did. Vivian had slightly over five thousand points. If she minimized her interactions with others and always reported when she did have to interact with people, she could stretch those points for probably three years.

"I have less than a hundred points left," the clerk said, ringing up groceries for someone farther up the line. "If we both choose not to report, no one loses any points."

"And if you report and I don't, I lose twenty points!" The customer wore the silver androgynous form of a Generic Citizen. "You're probably not telling the truth. I mean obviously you're a Shade so why would anyone trust you? It's a trick for you to build your points back up by cutting all of us down! You'd gain five points for reporting me, and I'd lose twenty. I'm an upstanding Citizen, not some Shade to bargain with!"

The clerk finished ringing up the customer's items, and there was no doubt in anyone's mind that both the customer and the clerk had reported the interaction.

Slowly the line moved forward, one customer at a time, a long string of Citizens. The clerk made no further effort at conversation with any of them.

Vivian reached the front of the line.

"Please?" the clerk said. "You're not like that other customer, that Citizen. You need the points as much as I do."

The Citizens were the ones with points to spare, points to risk, but the Shades were the ones who understood the stakes, understood the desperation. The clerk scanned her items slowly, but there were only a few boxes of rations left in her basket, she had to decide quickly.

What if it was Cass beneath that shadow? Or Brooke? She hadn't seen her family for so many years—they could have slipped, fallen into shade.

"You swear you won't report me?" Vivian asked.

"Yes. Oh, thank you," the clerk said.

The clerk finished ringing up her rations, and the question popped up in the upper right corner of her field of view. Report interaction? Y/N

Vivian did not report. She held her breath and waited.

Interaction reported.

Her point total dropped by twenty points.

"You lying fuck!" Vivian yelled, her voice loud enough that anyone in the store could hear her. Twenty points could have lasted her an entire week, and she'd been so foolish.

"You swore you wouldn't report!"

She gathered up her things, cursing the clerk but also cursing herself.

Always report. Always report. Always report.

As she was leaving, a Citizen approached. Shit. She must have left something behind, and it would cost her another interaction.

"It has been a while since I've seen someone choose kindness over self-preservation. Do know about the newspaper?"

Vivian shook her head, but suddenly something clicked. "The paper they printed them on would turn yellow and musty with age. Like a—"

"Not here." The Citizen interrupted and handed her a slip of folded purple paper. "I can't afford twenty, and after what just happened I expect you to report this interaction. So I'll tell you now that I am also going to report and save us both some trouble. Sorry."

Vivian took the slip of paper, wary. She unfolded it. The letters were gray, which made it difficult to read. All it said was "The Prisoner's Dilemma," with tomorrow's date, 8 p.m., Cesar Chavez Auditorium. The back side was a coupon for shoes, printed in black, long expired.

"Yellow and purple make gray," the customer told her. "Yellow can't be trusted."

Maybe this was what she'd been searching for, a way to

break free of the system. Vivian stuck the paper on the top of her box of rations and started walking. Report interaction? Y/N

She reported, and lost only one point.

Always report.

The scene shifted again, this time abruptly, like turning the page of a notebook. Vivian studied the age spots on her hands while Cass read. It surprised her sometimes, that she could see her own body any time she wanted. But she was so old now. Too old. She traced her fingers over the wrinkled skin, finding the scar where she'd punched through her own hand with the factory-machine needle. That was a true memory—she still had the scar.

"This is still Red Book stuff, Mom," Cass said, looking up from the yellow notebook. "I've been reading other accounts, and for most people the prisoner's dilemma years are in the red notebooks."

"I was a test subject for the memory tech; they had to keep an eye on me sooner," Vivian answered. She didn't write this down in her blue notebook, in case anyone was watching. No, they didn't do that now. But still. "They wanted to see how well their tech was working, whether the altered memories were sinking in. To know what I was thinking, they tricked me into writing it down so they could see. I was very prolific."

Cass patted her shoulder in what was supposed to be a soothing gesture, but it was stilted and awkward. They were trying so hard to rebuild the relationship, and Vivian was ruining it by being too broken. She had to be careful or she would drive Cass away, and she couldn't stand the thought of losing them again.

"I did my best," Vivian said. "Even if it mostly didn't help."

"I'm impressed you survived," Cass said. "Anything else is amazing."

"They changed a lot of things," Vivian whispered to Cass without bothering to pause. The immersive movie was quick-cutting through a series of sepia-tinted memories in a montage set to classic violin and a crisp autumn breeze. The rustling noise of the autumn leaves clashed with the music, and the cool breeze smelled faintly of mold. The entire montage was a lie.

"It's an immersive movie, not a documentary," Cass answered, their seemingly disembodied voice crisp and clear over the muffled soundtrack of the memories. "Based on several people's stories, all mashed together, with a great deal of artistic license to smooth it all out."

Vivian was grateful to have a job that didn't require her to interact with other people. Automated scanners logged her arrival and departure times, and her PIP directed her to her station assignment and alerted her when it was time for her breaks. The work was monotonous and soothing. Load the piece, stamp the part, unload the piece. The long hours of repeated motions meant she came home with an aching arm and a sore back, but she earned enough credits for her rations, and she kept her points. Rumor had it they were making 'grow-with-me' PIPs that were pre-birth compatible. Vivian wondered what it would be like to be born already connected to the system.

The worst part of her job was the memories. Working a machine on the assembly line called up another time, an older time, when she had worked on the memory-altering PIPs. Or were they dragon scales for an immersive movie? It was hard to remember. Her mind bombarded her with flashbacks as she worked: tampering with a similar machine, disabling the safeties, stamping a needle through her own hand.

She remembered the joy of seeing her own hand, despite the horror of the blood.

Back then she'd thought that she could take down the system.

Angry yelling called Vivian back to the present. Halfway down the line, a Shade was arguing with the floor supervisor.

"Those who make peaceful revolution impossible will make violent revolution inevitable," the Shade shouted, loud enough for the entire floor to hear.

It was a quote from John F. Kennedy, but the last time Vivian had heard those words, it had been from Auntie Yang.

She remembered five gunshots in rapid succession—loud flashes of sound. Auntie's mouth moving, but she couldn't hear anything over a rustling noise and the ringing of her own ears. Or perhaps Auntie could no longer voice the words. Blood soaked through Auntie's dull gray tunic, like crimson stars. Vivian frowned. Hadn't the tunic been purple? Auntie had loved bright colors and never wore gray. She remembered the moment both ways—Auntie in purple and Auntie in gray. Somehow this memory was real and not real.

Vivian's co-worker continued to argue with the supervisor, and two Keepers came in to end the disruption. To Vivian's horror, instead of cooperating, her co-worker took a swing at one of the Keepers. The Keeper swung back, hitting the Shade not once but many times, over and over again.

The worker's medical safeties detected her injuries and disabled the Shade overlay. The woman was old—even older than Auntie Yang. She was still calling for a revolution. Her jumpsuit was purple and her voice was clear. "At zero points, I have nothing left to lose."

The Keepers pulled out batons. Vivian heard the crunch of bone.

Unstamped pieces piled up at Vivian's station, but she couldn't look away. Tears streaked down the woman's wrinkled face, and Vivian cried along with her. The Keepers pummeled the old woman even as her words turned to inarticulate wails of pain, and then silence. They kept beating her even after she fell to the ground.

She wasn't moving when they hauled her away.

The supervisor resumed walking the factory floor, and Vivian forced herself to get back to work.

"Fifty points for failing to keep up with the line," the supervisor said, counting up the backlog of unstamped pieces at Vivian's workstation.

Report this interaction? Y/N

This was the one exception to "always report." If she reported her supervisor, she would bleed points forever afterwards for minor and made-up infractions. She did not report, and despite the fifty point penalty she'd already been given, the fucking supervisor reported her. Another twenty points gone.

She took the penalties in silence, the old woman's screams echoing in her head. Even rationing her points, Vivian didn't have much time left, and what kind of life was this to cling to? Shades were desperate, constantly creeping closer and closer to zero. They had so little left to lose. Vivian thought again of the message on the back of the coupon—The Prisoner's Dilemma. Whatever it was, it was happening tonight.

––––––––––

"Are you okay, Mom?" Cass asked. "We can stop."

"I want to see the rest," Vivian answered. She wasn't okay, but she hadn't been okay for a long time. These were familiar horrors, memories—both true and false—that haunted her in dreams and waking. It was already hard to remember which things were from the movie and which ones were real, and she hadn't even watched the whole thing yet.

––––––––––

A Shade scanned Vivian's ID chip as she entered Cesar Chavez auditorium. She'd been scanned countless times, but never by a fellow Shade. There were clumps of Shades by the door. Vivian cringed when one came up to her and gestured for her to go sit down, but thankfully her PIP did not ask her to report the interaction.

Unlike most places Vivian frequented, the auditorium was updated and modern, no sign of wear and neglect. She couldn't remember whether it was a new addition to the University. The audience was packed with Shades, and a handful of Citizens wearing generic silver overlays. Projected on both sides of the screen at the front of the auditorium was a message, written in gray on purple in big block letters. "DO NOT SPEAK OR SIGN UNTIL THE ROOM IS LOCKED DOWN. PLEASE SIT AND DIRECT YOUR GAZE AT THE MOVIE SCREEN." The armrests between the chairs were accessibility interfaces with audio jacks and a programmable top surface— Vivian couldn't read Braille, but she assumed the bumps on the otherwise smooth armrest gave the same message.

In the center of the screen there was a Cardinal Guardians movie—not an immersive experience but one of those old fashioned movies that you watch without experiencing all the sensations. Vivian wondered if it was the non-immersive version of the movie she'd made the dragon scales for, back on the factory line. She worried for a moment that she was wasting time and potentially points on a mere movie night, but if that was all this was, then why the odd message about the lockdown? Besides, the dragon movie had a different title than what was on the back of her coupon.

At 8:05 p.m. the clump of Shades by the door closed it and locked it. A Shade with a white cane walked to the front of the auditorium, swinging the cane back and forth until it tapped the edge of the podium. Vivian couldn't recall ever encountering a blind Shade before. She wasn't sure if that was good because they were escaping the system somehow, or ominous because ZimCorp was weeding them out.

The movie froze.

Suddenly all the overlays came down, and instead of being surrounded by Shades and the occasional Generic Citizen, the auditorium was nearly empty. Only a couple dozen individuals remained, ranging from young to old, with a variety of races and cultures and genders. Vivian could even see herself—thin bony hands folded on top of the dingy blue fabric of her standard-issue work pants.

The black woman at the podium leaned in to the micro-phone. "The total runtime for the movie playing behind me is one hour and forty seven minutes, and we have spent seven of them getting our initial recording. We've hacked the output of this room so anyone observing will see you, the audience, watching the rest of the movie. SPOILER: Kitora dies at the end. In case anyone asks."

The crowd laughed nervously.

"You can call me Nash. You are here because we noticed your potential. Because you noticed something wrong and sought us out. Perhaps because you have a skill we need. We are trying to break a system." She paused and took a sip of water. "The system is insidious, and it pits us against each other. It filters our reality and feeds us false memories."

The auditorium was silent as she spoke.

"Their false memories are recordings, some taken from real people of real experiences, others generated by actors playing a role in a scene. They are like immersive movies—"

"What are the false memories like if you're blind?" someone interrupted from the crowd.

"Ever had a migraine?" Nash answered. "The memories are created by sighted people and triggered by algorithms—hearing a certain phrase, seeing a certain object. Those of us who are blind trigger fewer of the memories, and—at least for me—when I get one it tends to manifest as a debilitating headache. ZimCorp's failure to account for anyone who isn't able-bodied was key to getting us to where we are now. Their false memories don't work for everyone, and their algorithms for monitoring our activities are heavily skewed to the visual."

Other people began calling out questions.

Nash waved them off. "There isn't time. The first step is already complete. We have introduced a bug to their system that shifts colors on the visual spectrum and introduces false texture and scent and sound. We've made their lies yellow and musty, given them what some people describe as an old newspaper feel. You now have the cues you need to determine what is real. Listen for sound without static, feel for smooth surfaces, memories that smell fresh and clean. Look for the most vibrant purple. Those are your cues that something is real."

Vivian thought through her memories. The Shade riots were tinged with all the cues that Nash described. None of that had happened. It was a lie to keep people in line, make them obey the rules.

"Breaking their control on our realities is only the first step," Nash continued. "Next we must give people an incentive to work together against the system.

"What we have here is a prisoner's dilemma. The best course of action for all of us, collectively, is different from the best course of action for each of us, individually. We are rewarded for betraying each other."

"Always report," Vivian whispered to herself.

"We've gained access to the point system," Nash continued, "And we're going to make everyone equal. Reset the points so that everyone is a citizen—"

Vivian shook her head. No, that was wrong. That might slow the system down, but people would still act in their own interests, try to preserve what they had gained, and eventually ZimCorp would regain control and put things back the way they were.

Excited murmurs ran through the crowd as people voiced their dreams of freedom.

"It won't work," Vivian said, softly first, but again loud enough that the room fell silent.

She stood and faced Nash. "Maybe years ago it might have, but we're too far gone. We can't reset the system. We have to destroy it, make it so no one has anything left to lose. If you have access to the points, you can't give them to people. You have to take them away. Set everyone to zero, and obliterate all record of what they had."

"A zero-point coup," Nash said, thoughtful. "There will be chaos. Riots."

The audience erupted in a cacophony of loud objections.

Vivian's instinct was to retreat from the conflict and preserve her precious points. But the fierce reaction of the crowd—and her own impulse to withdraw—proved that a zero-point coup was the only solution. The anger that filled the auditorium was rooted in fear. People were afraid for the future, afraid for their loved ones.

If something happened to Brooke because of this, or to Cass.

. .

Setting everyone's points to a higher level would ease this unrelenting fear. People would feel safe, and they would want to keep that feeling of safety. Having nothing left to lose would free them from that fear. Once the worst had happened, people would finally fight against the system, everyone together. It was the only way.

"There will be. . . losses." Vivian raised her voice, unwilling to silenced by anger and fear.

"But anything less won't work. And those who made peaceful revolution impossible have made violent revolution inevitable."

The scene in the auditorium ended, and Vivian found herself immersed in a series of key moments from the zero-point coup, strung together in roughly chronological order, set to Lux Aeterna by Clint Mansell. Unlike the montage of lies earlier in the movie, now the sound was crisp and clear—Vivian could hear each instrument in the orchestra, the voices of the choir, the beat of the drums. The colors were true and there was no musty odor of stagnation and decay. It looked and sounded and smelled of truth.

Time was dilated, dreamlike. Entire scenes dropped into Vivian's mind in a single note. It was a rainstorm building to a flood. She let the moments wash over her. There were protests and marches. The North End fires. Attempts at reestablishing curfews and making arrests. In the midst of the fighting and chaos, Bardo Phillips Jr., current CEO of ZimCorp, was led away in handcuffs by armed guards. News headlines sprung up in the periphery of her field of view as he was led away. ZimCorp CEO charged with False Imprisonment. The End of ZimCorp: What Comes Next? Corrupted Reality! Fall of a Titan.

The montage ended in a crescendo of strings and drums. There was a moment of silence.

In a busy courtyard, a trio of Shades stood in a circle, holding hands. All around them, more Shades rushed in and out of shops and businesses. A clocktower loomed above the courtyard, the minute hand sweeping upward to meet the hour hand. At noon, the tower bells began to ring, the sound so loud that Vivian felt the vibrations in her bones.

At the center of the courtyard, the Shade overlays dropped away to reveal three people, three individuals holding hands. All around them Shades were transformed, the sea of dark figures becoming less uniform, more colorful. The seemingly well-maintained facades of the shops around them gave way to faded paint and dusty windows, and the ripple of unfiltered reality continued outward as Zimcorp's last remaining systems were shut down.

———

"I'm Nash. I am the person whose memories they stole and altered. I am the one who proposed the zero-point coup," Vivian mumbled. Her therapist was right about the immersive movie: it was hard to piece together what was real. The movie had circled back to its beginning, with Cass reading from a yellow notebook while Vivian wrote notes into a blue one.

"You definitely aren't Nash," Cass answered. "But we can try to piece together the rest from your notebooks."

Vivian couldn't tell if the answer had come from real-Cass or movie-Cass.

Vivian stood at the entrance to the library archives of the Red Books. She took in the scale of the collection, shelf after shelf packed with red notebooks, each filled with the stories of a different Shade. The shelves were mostly red notebooks with a small smattering of orange. Only a few of other colors. Vivian had been one of the earliest test subjects for the false memories, and a prolific writer. Her attention settled on a shelf that held a full rainbow of notebooks, her own journals.

Credits appeared over the scene, text scrolling across her field of view.

Based on the lives of J.R. Brachman, Anita G. Flores, Terri "Nash" Jackson, Chris M. Lee, Arjun Singh, and Vivian Watanabe.

The library archives faded to black.

"We have long known that those who forget the past are doomed to repeat it. The hard part is finding out what really happened." —Terri "Nash" Jackson

The end credits scrolled.

STEPSISTER

BY LEAH CYPESS
PUBLISHED BY THE MAGAZINE OF FANTASY AND SCIENCE FICTION

The story you know isn't exactly a lie.

It leaves a lot out, but everything you've been told is absolutely true. This is the story you've heard. Just not exactly as you've heard it.

You are hearing this new version when you're older, so you can see the cracks in it, the dark absurdities and sickening cruelties. But it is not so different from the story you were told as a child. To a child, everything related by a trusted adult is a solid, reasonable truth. Perhaps if a child was told no tales, the whole world would appear senseless and cruel.

Instead, your mind fits itself to the truth you know. It grows with you, becomes a part of you, and you cannot question it without murdering a little bit of yourself.

And what would compel anyone to do that?

I like to tell my friends that when we were younger, King Ciar and I used to spar with wooden posts, and that once the prince knocked my makeshift helmet so hard that it spun around and stuck on my head, and it took five servants and a vat of butter to get me free.

"The butter made my hair spike," I said, "and I liked the look so much I refused to wash it out. It was two months before my mother had enough. She tied me up while I slept, then woke me by dumping a vat of sudsy water over my head. She spent half an hour scrubbing my scalp and ignoring my screams."

Laughter roared through the tavern, even from the far tables I hadn't been addressing. It was an easy enough sight for them to imagine; I had more than two decades on me, but my face was still round and childish, and my sporadic attempts to grow a beard only made it worse rather than better. Plus, when my hair was overlong—which it tended to be, because I had reservations about letting the castle barbers' knives get too near my throat—it stuck out from my head in tufts.

"Your mother?" said Lissa, and I swore softly before turning to grin at her. I had forgotten that Lissa's mother, like mine, was a long-time servant at the castle. Lissa knew that my mother had died when I was five years old.

"Yes," I said, meeting her dark eyes. "She always wanted a girl, see. I think she was glad of the excuse."

A moment of silence. I held my breath. It could have gone either way; Lissa liked nothing better than proving people wrong, but partly as a result of that hobby, she had very few friends left. Hopefully she wouldn't risk antagonizing one of them.

She leaned back. "Glad of an excuse to wash your hair? Or to tie you up?"

More laughter, much louder than what I had elicited. I was glad of it, and of Lissa's smirk. If the laughter satisfied her, she would let me get away with my slip.

I wasn't lying, by the way. The story was true. It was just that it was I who hit the prince, and his helmet that had to be removed with butter, and it was his mother, the queen, who had him tied up and covered with suds—not with her own hands, of course. She hadn't whipped me with her own hands, either, though she had stood nearby and watched, to make sure I understood the consequences of putting the crown prince's life in danger.

She had made Ciar watch, too. It was the one time I had ever seen a tear trickle down the cheek of our infamously ruthless monarch.

That story isn't as funny. And if I told of our king's humiliation, that would have been treason, and I might have ended up hanged rather than merely whipped. You have to walk a fine line around royalty. Unless you're smart enough to stay far away from them to begin with.

I like to think I would have been smart enough, if I'd ever been given a choice in the matter.

Someone coughed from the tavern door. It was the sort of cough that stopped our laughter cold and wiped the smirk off Lissa's face. We all turned toward it, like marionettes being pulled by a single string.

"Lord Garrin," the royal messenger said, and the others' faces turned toward me, Lissa's eyes narrowing in speculation.

I resisted the urge to point out that I had no title. It wasn't the messenger's fault; nobody is ever quite sure of how to address me. I was the king's best friend, his sworn companion. I was also a potential claimant to his throne, a possible dagger to his throat. And the only family he now had left.

Lord didn't exactly sum it up, but it was as close as anyone could get.

The messenger cleared his throat. "His Majesty has need of you."

I was glad I'd told the story. It had kept me from draining my tankard, and the last thing I needed, when dealing with King Ciar, was to be drunk.

"Of course," I said, and rose to my feet with only the slightest of stumbles. "Take me to him."

Ciar was two people, these days: the king he was turning into, harsh and weary and determined, and the brother I'd grown up with, reckless and hedonistic and loyal. Usually, it was easy for me to tell which Ciar I would be dealing with. But today he was someone else entirely, someone who sat in his bedchamber staring out the window, his face set in lines of melancholy.

I searched through all my memories of Ciar—twenty-two years' worth—and failed to come up with a single melancholy one. Even that day in the courtyard, with the whip tearing through my skin, his face hadn't looked like this. I couldn't actually remember what his face did look like that day, but I was sure it hadn't been this bleak.

I'd never had a chance to ask, since Ciar never mentioned that day again. His gaze was ever forward, never back. It was part of the problem with him, and also part of the reason men followed him: his certainty that whatever he was headed toward, it was better than what was behind him.

"Everyone else," he said, without looking up, "leave us."

It was quite an exodus, for there were at least ten people in the room. The servants of his chamber, his guards, his retainers, his supposed friends: they all filed past me with resentful stares. Lady Aniya, who was either his mistress or angling for the position, gave me a warm smile as if we knew each other. We didn't, but I admired her brains in trying to get me on her side. Unlike Queen Ella, who had always seen her husband's bastard brother as a rival and tried to turn Ciar against me. The queen still didn't appear to have noticed that I was the only person in Ciar's life he had never left behind.

Not yet, Lissa told me once. But only because we had been arguing; even she knew better than that. I had been Ciar's friend for our entire lives. No one else—no woman, no companion, not even a favorite hunting dog—had retained their place in his affections for longer than five years.

"Garrin," Ciar said, once we were alone. "I need your help."

I didn't know whether to sink to one knee or stride over and clasp his arm. But the words I had to say were the same in either case, so I said them without moving. "Of course, Your Majesty."

He turned away from the window and faced me. Sadness looked wrong on his features, like an ill-fitting mask. "You must find my wife's stepsister and bring her to court."

"I will," I said automatically, before the meaning of his words sank in. Then they did, and every muscle in my body tensed. "Ciar, why?"

He blinked, and a more familiar expression swept over his face: cold, clear determination. "That is not your concern."

A surge of rage went through me, an anger I'd only felt—only allowed myself to feel—once before. I pushed it down, back to its usual banked simmer. After all, as far as he knew, it was true; I had no reason to care more about this order than any other he gave me.

He was the king now, and I had to think about which questions I dared ask. "Does Her Majesty the queen know that you are—"

"Of course not." That flicker of pain again, before his expression closed up around it. "And you are to make sure she does not find out."

Sometimes, it is very dangerous to have a king trust you. Especially when his queen hates you for it.

Especially when she is right to.

"Of course, Your Majesty." I decided to bow. "What excuse shall I give for my departure?"

"I doubt you'll need one," he said. "I was out hunting from dawn to dusk yesterday, and she never even asked me where I was. These days, my wife doesn't pay much attention to anything that isn't ladies' gossip."

The scorn in his voice made me blink. I had never heard him speak of Ella with anything but deep, reverential love. His blindness when it came to her had irritated me, though of course I'd never said anything. I had no right to take anything from Ciar, and that included his happiness.

Though really, I should not have been surprised. After all, he and Queen Ella had now been married for almost five years.

I was also not surprised when I found one of the queen's maids waiting for me at the door to my room.

Make sure she does not find out, indeed.

The maid curtsied to me, a bit mockingly. Amelie did everything mockingly, as if she found all the people in the castle ridiculous, and only played the part of queen's maid because it amused her to do so. "Her Majesty requests your presence in her sitting room."

"Oh, good," I said. "I didn't want to eat or drink today anyhow."

Amelie laughed. "I can have pastries sent to the sitting room, if you think you'll have the stomach for them while she's yelling at you."

"Is Her Majesty planning to yell at me?"

"Planning to? No." Amelie lifted an eyebrow. "But I would bet good coin that it's going to happen."

I liked Amelie. She was small and quick—not pretty, but only because she couldn't be bothered to be—and she acted like we were all the same, king and noble and commoner alike. She acted that way because she considered us all so far beneath her that the differences were not discernible. But still, it was refreshing.

I liked her, but I didn't trust her. So I resisted the urge to ask any more questions. Instead, I said, "Order the pastries. I think I'll be fine."

She pouted for a second, because I wouldn't play her game, then laughed and danced down the hall.

I sighed and followed her.

There were no pastries. There was no queen, either; she kept me waiting for nearly an hour. I had nothing to do but count the scratches on the intricate wooden furniture and the folds in the thick velvet curtains. The king's command burned in the back of my mind, making me restless and itchy. I should have been on a horse already, galloping along the road into the mountains.

I could only hope Ciar would understand that the delay, too, was in his service.

I did not allow myself to think that any of my impatience was for myself, or that I had my own reasons for being anxious to start. Jacinda was not as far away as Ciar assumed. It was already midafternoon, but if I left right now and rode hard, I could be at her cottage before nightfall.

Instead, I cooled my heels in an overdecorated sitting room, empty and silent except for the growling of my stomach.

The queen played this game with everyone, and normally it

didn't bother me. I understood why she did it. She had spent so many years being the one to wait and serve; not in a warm, fancy room, either, but in a dank attic or a sweltering kitchen, barefoot and hungry and often in pain. I had once, by accident, seen the welts on her back, and Ciar had told me some of the things her stepfamily had said to her—that she was worthless, that she lived on the pity of others, that it was her place to scurry after them and anticipate their needs and wait, wait, wait for them.

So I understood. But still, it had been five years; perhaps it was time for her to start letting it go.

When Queen Ella finally swept into the room, I dropped immediately to one knee and bowed my head. I had learned early that, while I might drop some formalities with Ciar, I had better never let his wife think I had forgotten her position.

"Rise, Garrin," she said. No pretend "lord" for her.

I rose.

The tales tell the truth about the queen's beauty—the tales, and the bards, and anyone who catches a glimpse of her to this very day. All softness and elegance and grace, perfectly formed features beneath a waterfall of golden hair.

Jacinda's hair was coarse and dark, her eyebrows thick, her nose prominent. She was no beauty, that's for certain. But she had an arresting force on men nonetheless—or on two men, at least. For me, it was the sharpness of her dark eyes, the intensity with which she held herself. The way she moved, quick and steady, not graceful so much as unfaltering.

I always assumed it was the same for Ciar.

But of course, it was impossible to ask.

The queen was particularly exquisite that day, in an icy blue gown with a lace overdress, her hair coiled in towering braids around her head. Her famously blue eyes were delicately outlined with kohl, and they were, as always, the first thing you saw when you looked at her. The poets all spend at least three stanzas on the blueness of the queen's eyes, with good reason.

She had brought only Amelie with her, which was a sure sign

of trouble. It meant that whatever she was going to say to me, she didn't want it overheard.

I met Amelie's eyes, and she shook her head slightly. I couldn't tell if it was a warning, or an indication that there would be no pastries.

"Sit," Queen Ella commanded, and I sat, settling myself on a delicate cushioned chair that was a bit too small for me. "What did my husband want from you?"

The queen tends to get straight to the point. It's a lingering effect of her common origins.

But I was raised by a commoner, too. "He commanded me not to tell you."

She hissed between her teeth and took two steps toward me. "I could have you executed for treason right now."

She could, without a doubt. The only question was how Ciar would react if she did, and I didn't know the answer to that. He loved her deeply, but I was his oldest friend.

I bent my head, hoping that she didn't know the answer, either.

She was so close that I could see her hands. They clenched and unclenched, the knobs of her knuckles jutting out. For all her ministrations and creams—and, some whispered, alchemy—she had never been able to reclaim her hands. They were still rough and spotted, marked by years of scrubbing and scouring and scraping.

"You surprise me, Garrin," she said. Her voice was slow and measured, and my name sounded like the scrape of stone on sandpaper. "Do you not fear me? Do you think me sweet and innocent and incapable of taking revenge? I had thought you would know better."

"I do," I said. I wanted to glance up, but I refrained. I knew what her face would look like; I still remembered her expression when she pronounced her stepfamily's punishment. Take them away from me and stone them until they die. "And I do fear you. But not enough to make me betray my king."

Amelie made a small amused sound.

The queen turned on her heel and walked away from me, a light tap-tap on the floor and a swish of heavy skirts. I did not look up until the door shut behind her with a heavy thud.

Amelie remained. She leaned near the door, one foot propped up against the wall, an unrefined pose that would have been shocking on anyone else.

"You should fear her more," she said. "More than you fear your king."

"I don't fear Ciar," I said. "I love him."

Amelie lifted an eyebrow. "So does she."

I had nothing to say to that.

Amelie straightened and walked toward me. She had an odd way of walking, like she was almost flying but had forgotten how to. "My queen loves very fiercely. And she hates fiercely, too."

I could tell my face was betraying me anyhow, so I allowed myself a harsh laugh. "We all know that."

Amelie knew at once what I was referring to. She pursed her lips. "She was right to punish them. I was there, Garrin. I saw how they treated her. Her stepmother was the worst, but her daughters were eager learners. And jealous besides. Ella was better than them, far better, and yet she was the one forced to stay home and scrub dirt off their shoes while they got to go to the castle and dance with dukes."

By better, of course, she meant prettier.

"I don't doubt it," I said, and I truly didn't. Raising children to hate is just as easy—easier, probably—than raising them to love. "But I don't know why you're telling me this."

"I think you do," Amelie said, then turned and slipped out the door.

By then, it was too late to set off. I couldn't help but wonder if that had been the queen's intention.

I went back to the tavern for dinner—I am a man of predictable habits—and alleviated my frustration with a chunky bowl of stew and some extremely well-spiced mead. I usually drink only in Ciar's company—he has a tendency to forget that he is the king when he's drunk, and the resumption of our old easy friendship is well worth the next day's hangover—but lately, I had found myself drifting more and more to drink when I was alone. Maybe because I now associated the feeling of drunkenness with Ciar's laugh and his trust.

I had been hoping to run into Lissa at the tavern, but she was gone. Instead, I found myself surrounded by castle servants—groomsmen and kennel masters and smiths, those paid well enough to afford the food at this tavern, but still too lowly to dine with the nobility.

"Heard you had audiences with both Their Majesties, Garrin," one of the tailors said, passing me a flagon so I could refill my cup. "But separate audiences, eh? What's the story behind that?"

I smiled at him and took the flagon. His question hadn't truly been in earnest. Everyone knew I didn't gossip about my king's business.

"Trouble brewing is the story," said one of the waitresses, passing by and snatching the flagon out of my hand. "Their Majesties have been seen together less and less lately, is what I've heard."

The tailor laughed. "Well, that's not going to help them get us an heir."

"It's likely the lack of an heir that's causing the problem." This from a man I didn't know. "The queen has been summoning doctors from all over the continent to see what ails her womb."

"No mystery what ails her," the waitress snorted, "and it's nothing a doctor can cure. You dabble in faerie magic, you pay the price."

A momentary hush fell, and the waitress's cheeks colored. She glanced swiftly around the room. That had been a bit too close to treason for anyone's comfort.

"It will be two coppers if you want a refill," she said to me finally, her voice high and forced.

I handed her the coppers and added an order of pie, to give her an excuse to go back to the kitchen. But I left before she returned with my dessert, and with half my cup undrained as well.

I wasn't sure why the thought of a rift between the king and queen made my heart heavy. I had never believed in their fairy tale because I had always known there was magic behind it, though it wasn't Ella who had dabbled in it.

Maybe because the marriage had made Ciar so happy. It might seem odd that I would worry about his well-being, but I did. I wanted his happiness as much as I desired my own.

When I got to my room in the castle, there were pastries waiting on a tray on my bed. One was a fluffy almond croissant, which I could not eat; almonds made my throat itch, and everyone who worked in the castle kitchen knew it. Which meant it had not been brought here for me to eat.

I broke the croissant open carefully and extracted the paper folded inside.

The handwriting was large and blocky, like that of a child. Or a commoner who had only recently learned to form letters.

Garrin,

If you love me, leave me in peace.

Please.

Jacinda

On the bottom, she had sketched—more carefully than she had drawn the letters—a picture of a delicate glass slipper with a dark splotch of ink spreading from its toe.

We all grew up knowing that we shared our world with the fae. They lent magic and wonder to our grinding lives, favored us with the occasional sprinkle of miracle or tragedy, and all they asked in return was for us to dance. Once at midsummer and once at the winter solstice: a grand ball, for royalty and commoners alike, where the dancing gets wilder all through the night and our movements shimmer with beauty and abandon. Nights when the ugly appear beautiful and the beautiful transcendent, when the melancholy turn joyful and the happy go insane, when romance turns into a solid reality and princes fall in love with peasant girls.

Many families lock their daughters away on the nights of the fae balls. Between the glitter and the magic, things happen that should not be seen—or participated in—by girls with good morals. But doors tend to unlatch, windows tend to creak open, nimble fae fingers drawing us all to their dance.

The story has grown—a coach, a train of horses, a magical gown—but I was there. The fae did no more for Queen Ella than they did for dozens of eager girls willing to risk their futures for a night of revelry.

It's just that for most of them, it doesn't turn out as well.

My mother taught me that. They say that what happens on fae nights is forgiven and forgotten by morning, and for men, that is certainly true. For women, not so much.

They also say that children conceived on the night of a fae ball have magic of their own, but I had never seen any evidence of that.

My mother taught me to stay away from the dances. She never forbade me, for that just tempts the fae, but she frightened me. Even though I was only five years old when she died, even though I can barely remember her face, I still recall her low, intense voice:

The dances are not for us. They are for them, so they can drain our energy and guzzle at our lives. They need to feed off us, and so they have set a beautiful trap. They have beauty in abundance; it costs them nothing to throw some our way. And we are too bedazzled to ask what it costs us.

But I was seventeen that night and chafing at my dead mother's caution, walking around the castle grounds while strains of wild, unearthly music drifted through the walls. Circling closer and closer, like a moth drawn toward the flame, not yet admitting to myself what I was doing.

That was when I saw the girl fleeing the castle. She held her skirts up, but they were so bulky they hindered her view of the ground, and, inevitably, she tripped and fell.

I headed toward her, glad of a distraction. When I reached

her, she was still kneeling on the ground, her dark hair falling over her face, her shoulders heaving.

"My lady," I said. "Are you all right?"

She blinked up at me, and her dark eyes widened as she took in my face. "Ciar—"

"No," I said. "I am not him. Are you searching for the prince?"

She took a closer look at me, and a mix of relief and disappointment crossed her face. She shook her head.

I held out my hand and helped her to her feet. Up close, I could see that her dress, though in current fashion and elaborately decorated, was made of second-rate cloth roughly stitched together. Probably the best she could afford. Many common girls spent everything they had for the dances, these evenings when love had enough power to change a life.

Though usually not for the better. No one tells the girls that until it's too late.

I had seen enough of the world by now to know that my mother was wrong. They did tell the girls, over and over. It was just that the girls didn't particularly want to hear it.

Judging by the tears on this one's face, she knew now, and it was already too late.

My heart wrenched. She was not particularly beautiful, this girl, but there was something about her eyes, wide and dark and direct, and the set of her full lips. And the music, still drifting through the air and winding through my heart, pulling it toward wild leaps of sentimental abandon.

"The dance has barely begun," I said. "I can escort you back, if you'd like?"

Desire flashed in her eyes, and I could practically see the music moving in them. But she shook her head.

I glanced at the castle. She had been there, in the midst of the music and magic, and she had left. What could have caused her to do that?

And what sort of strength had enabled her to do it?

"You can dance with me here," she said abruptly. Her voice was throaty and slightly ragged. "If. . . if you would like to."

I met her eyes and saw the desperation in them. I saw the echoes of the fae magic, urging her to go back, to join the rest, to dance the night away. To forget what tomorrow might bring.

I held out my arms, and she stepped into them.

We did not go back. We did not join the rest of them. But we danced, and it was enough, for that one night, to let us resist. We danced as if we had been dancing together all our lives, and eventually we also laughed, and at the very end of our dance, when dawn was staining the sky and the fae power was fading along with their music, when people in the castle were blinking and staring around and discovering that tomorrow had come despite their ignoring it, we finally stepped apart. I bowed. She curtsied.

I knew her name by then: Jacinda. And I had seen and recognized the token tucked into the bodice of her gown, a lock of golden hair bound with silver thread. Ciar gave one like it to every girl he fancied.

But she had left Ciar and danced with me, and though I knew I should not have allowed it, I was filled with a tender joy. It was the music and the magic strumming through my skin, turning my mind inside out and making me forget the rule my safety was built around: You must never take anything from Ciar.

But she was so fierce and so real, and for the first time in my life, I wanted something so badly I didn't think about the consequences. (A foolish mood, not a brave one. The consequences, like the morning, would come anyhow.) I reached for her hand and pulled her closer, and her dark eyes watched me, then slowly closed as I bent my head to hers.

Our lips barely touched. She made a small, pained sound and stepped back.

"Oh," she said. "I'm sorry."

"For what?" I whispered. She had not let go of my hand.

"For. . . " She opened her eyes and searched my face. "This is not what you think. You're not feeling what you think you're feeling. It's only fae magic."

Of course it was; we could still hear the fading strains of music from the castle. But I had never understood this business of calling feelings less real just because you know what caused them. After all, if you decided to love someone—if you thought over your options, and took into account character and rank and similar interests—then that wasn't love, at least not by the standards of the court bards. True love was supposed to be sudden and senseless and all-consuming; it was supposed to make no sense at all. Just like magic. A force that destroyed rather than built.

Love had ruined my mother's life, and she had always warned me against it. Yet here I stood, with the fae music strumming against my skin and my heart beating as if it would rip that skin apart, and my mother's warning was faint and distant and inconsequential.

The poets say they would give up anything for love, she'd told me. But they only say that because they don't think they'll have to.

I was no poet, but I knew exactly what I would be giving up. Ciar had already seen this girl, had danced with her, had chosen her. It was a lesson drummed into me from early childhood, a condition of my continued existence at court—perhaps of my existence altogether: I must never take anything from Ciar.

If I did, that act would be the dividing line between begrudging tolerance and vengeful fear. Because if I ever took his toy, or his triumph, or his girl. . .

Then next, I might try to take his kingdom.

And my life depended on no one ever, ever thinking I would do that.

"I shouldn't have danced with you," Jacinda said. "It wasn't fair. I have. . . " She leaned over and tugged off her shoes, which were as clear and bright as glass. As she dangled them from her hand, a drop fell from the toe of one of them — small and wet like dew, but darker than dew. "I enchanted them with my own blood and pain, to ensnare a suitor of royal blood."

"I'm impressed," I said, still holding her hand. "Many women seek the prince's eyes, but few go so far as to sacrifice to the fae."

"Well," she said with a shrug, "other women have beauty to rely upon."

As if that was a truer reason for love than magic.

My silence tugged the corners of her lips upward. "Will you not protest and say I am beautiful?"

"I think you are," I said honestly. "You are as gorgeous as the night. But that is not the way Ciar's taste runs."

She looked startled. "You know Prince Ciar?"

"We are. . . " The word trembled on my lips, but I had never spoken it aloud. To do so would be to take something from Ciar. "We have been friends since we were babes. My mother was his wet nurse."

She peered at me closely again—at the shape of my face, which had caused her to make a mistake when she first saw me. She pulled her hand free, and I let her.

"I'm sorry," she said.

She lifted her skirts again, so she could make her way across the castle grounds. She strode swiftly through the darkness, the glass slippers swinging from her hand, dripping something black and sticky into the tall grass.

The next time I saw those slippers, they were on the queen's feet.

If you love me, the note said.

Perhaps she had changed her mind about what made love real.

More likely, she was simply desperate.

I let the pieces of croissant fall back onto the tray and ran my fingers over the paper, as if I could feel her fingers touching it.

I did not, of course, still love her. How could I? It had been five years; there had been other dances, and other girls. Besides, I knew the truth about her now. Her cruelty toward her stepsister, her meanness and vindictiveness.

I had never disbelieved the stories, because I had seen that cruelty in her eyes. What I had called fierceness, and admired, because I was not its victim.

No one had blamed our new queen when she condemned her stepmother and stepsisters to death. She had shown us the marks on her arms, the scars that would never heal. No one had tried to stop her from punishing her tormentors.

Not even me.

I had thought of saying something to Ciar. But what could I have said? Should I have told him to deny his beloved? That her glass slippers were bespelled, and not exactly in the way she had claimed? That he loved her for reasons other than her beauty and her mystery and the fact that he'd had to pursue her?

I could not take anything from Ciar, and that included his joy in his new bride.

It had been he who called me, the night before their punishment, his summons dragging me from my bed. I had not been sleeping anyhow. I had been thinking of Jacinda, of the joy on her face as we danced on the castle lawn, as if the illusion of freedom was a rare and sweet taste in her mouth. I had been wondering what she would look like as she died.

She once buried cutlery in the yard, then made Ella dig it up and clean it, Ciar had said, in one of the few minutes we spent together—fitting doublets for his wedding, which was being arranged with great haste. The ones that weren't clean enough, she threw at her. Ella still has those scars. This is a fitting punishment.

Which she? I asked, and he'd looked at me sideways as if hearing something in my tone. I had caught his glance and held it, keeping my expression steady. There were three shes to be dealt with—a stepmother and two stepsisters—so it was a reasonable question.

All of them, Ciar had snapped. All three of them tormented her together. It makes no difference which one chose any particular cruelty.

It was the closest I had ever come to the boundaries of what I could ask Ciar. Even for Jacinda, I could go no farther.

Love has its limits.

Desperate or not, she should have known better than to ask.

I burned the note before I went to bed. I stood watching the flame eat those carefully drawn letters, the edges of the paper folding up on themselves, curling and blackening.

I shouldn't have done it. I should have held on to it, to show to Ciar. Even though that note was mine, written for me and meant for my eyes, I still had no right to steal it from my king.

I watched until the paper was a scattering of ashes, and then I went to bed.

I expected to dream of Jacinda. But the smell of burned paper kept me awake, so I had to settle for merely remembering her, without the confusion and softening a dream would have brought.

She had talked to me about Ella, a bit. Not on the night of the dance, but later, in the stable yard under Ciar's hard eyes. She admitted everything: the degradation, the spite, the cruelty. She had not pretended not to hate her stepsister, or even to regret her treatment of her. I suppose she'd had no reason to. She already knew that, for whatever reason, Ciar was going behind his bride's back to send her to safety.

At one point, her gaze flickered to me, and something broke in her eyes. But she turned back to Ciar before she spoke again.

"She was supposed to be beaten down," she said. "It was the way it always was, and it seemed normal to us. I never had reason to question it."

She didn't say it like it was an excuse, because of course it wasn't.

She said nothing to me directly, not even on that long evening ride through the mountains. She was too busy clinging to her horse and retching into the grass. But when we reached the village, and I had set her up in the small prepared cottage, she looked at me with those fierce, direct eyes.

"It's true, you know," she said. "Everything I confessed to

your prince. Everything Ella said I did to her. She didn't exaggerate at all." She had drawn her cloak around her body and curled up on the narrow bed, in the same type of peasants' hovel she had tried so hard to escape, and turned toward the wall. "I deserve this."

I wanted to contradict her, but I didn't know how.

So instead I just left her there, as my prince had commanded me to.

No.

I thought of her dark eyes, her refusal to make up excuses for herself, and was ashamed of my own excuses.

I had left her there, all alone, and ridden back to my castle and my life.

When I finally fell asleep, I didn't dream at all. Perhaps that was why, when I woke, my only thought was about what to do first: tell Ciar about the letter, or determine how it had gotten into the castle and into my pastry.

Taking this news to Ciar would be complicated. First, I would have to explain why the note no longer existed. Second, I still wasn't sure whether there was a reason why Ciar had entrusted Jacinda to me all those years ago. Did he know I had my own reasons for wanting to keep her safe? Or had he believed I was his man, loyal and without opinions, as I always had been and should forever have continued to be?

I had done much for Ciar over the years. I had been his best friend, his confidante, and his loyal follower. But his mother had always viewed me as a threat, like a devoted watchdog with a predisposition to go rabid, and she had warned him—had warned both of us—that no matter how much he liked me, no matter how close we were, he must be prepared to have me executed the second it became necessary.

"I never will," he told me once. Only once. "I know you would never betray me."

And I never had.

Ciar was a just king. He was a loyal friend. But he had grown up immersed in his mother's view of me—in the whole kingdom's view of me. No one had ever challenged it, and I had no reason to believe he ever stopped holding it.

I didn't want to tell him I had burned the letter. If I did, I would have to explain why, and I wasn't sure I could.

But solving the letter's appearance on my own was equally impossible. No one in this castle knew where Jacinda was, except me. Ciar had insisted that I be the only one to know. He said I was the only one he trusted.

"Don't even tell me," he had said while I mounted. He looked up at me, one hand on my saddle, his face bright and clear in the moonlight. "Ella is smart. If she figures out what I did, if it gets back to her that only two women were executed tonight. . . I don't want to be able to tell her where her stepsister is hiding."

I looked down at him, aghast at his admission of this common girl's power over him. Did love really possess that kind of strength? Or was this a sign of the darker magic she had used to ensnare him?

And if so. . . was that why he was letting Jacinda go? Because she was the source of that magic, and her snare, too, still clung to his heart?

I didn't ask then. I figured the time to probe would be when he changed his mind and instructed me to tell him where Jacinda was after all.

But he never did. For the last five years, until yesterday, he had never mentioned her. At times, I wondered if he had truly forgotten her.

But she, clearly, had not forgotten him. Because there were, in the end, two people who knew this secret. I had held my tongue. But Jacinda, it seemed, had not stayed where she was put.

I couldn't imagine what had possessed her to take such a risk when she must know the queen would want her dead—and likely the king would as well, once she broke the terms under which he had saved her. Now, too late, Jacinda was trying to undo whatever mistake she had made.

But how had she delivered the letter? An ally in the castle?

And if she had one, was that the same person who had betrayed her to the king?

I found that very likely, which put me right back at the beginning I had tried so hard to avoid. I had to talk to Ciar.

I headed for the door to my room, trying to work out what to tell him. Perhaps I could say the note had combusted in my hand. . . but that implied that Jacinda still dabbled in magic, and put her in danger. Besides, it was unworthy of me. I never lied to my king.

The truth would suffice. Ciar would understand, and even if he didn't understand, he would forgive me. I should trust him, just as he trusted me.

I pulled my door open, strode out into the hall, and felt the knife slide through my skin a moment before I registered the flash of motion on my right.

I was almost too slow. Had it been a regular blade, that would be the end of this story. But it was a stone knife, clumsy and dull-edged, not the sort of thing to use if you really want to kill someone. I knocked it out of my attacker's hand before it had done more than draw blood (and also really, really hurt).

My attacker dove for the knife. She was shockingly fast—perhaps it hadn't been only my distraction that let her get past me the first time—but her speed was no match for my strength, training, and, most importantly, steel. I got my blade under her chin and my arm across her chest, pinning her against the wall, and found myself staring into the small triangular face of the queen's maid, Amelie.

You are not surprised. Even though the queen had dozens of maids, and it could have been any one of them.

That's because you're hearing about these events as a story. If Amelie wasn't important, I wouldn't have told you so much about her, would I?

I didn't have your advantage. I was surprised, so much so that I lowered my blade. But Amelie didn't try to take advantage of the opening. Instead, she grinned up at me like she was daring me.

I had no idea what she was daring me to do, so I didn't have to think about whether I should do it. I stepped back, and she straightened and smoothed down her hair.

"I'm sorry," she said, not sounding sorry at all.

"What were you trying to accomplish?" I demanded. "Did you actually think you were going to manage to kill me?"

Her eyes sparkled. "I was just trying to get your attention."

"With a knife?"

"Well, all right." She shrugged. "I was trying to kill you. But getting your attention was my second best option."

Perhaps I should have been angrier, but the idea that she might have succeeded in killing me was hard to take seriously. I cocked my head to the side. "And if you had managed your first option? How do you think you would have gotten away with it?"

"It would have been an accident. A fall from a window." Her smile didn't waver; she leaned forward a bit, as if we were sharing a private joke. "The windows in this castle are far too large. Very dangerous."

I tried not to show a reaction. Five years ago, a week after the royal wedding, one of Ciar's most trusted men had fallen to his death. Witnesses claimed to have seen him staggering near the window while drunk, so I had never questioned that it was an accident, though I had been concerned by how little our newly married prince was grieved by his death. Before his marriage, Ciar had always been as devoted to his men as they were to him.

It had been my first hint of how wedded bliss might change Ciar. I had been relieved when our relationship, after a few weeks of distance, had gone back to normal. Or at least to how it had always been.

Now, I wondered if his lack of concern had been more than that. If he hadn't wanted to look too closely at how his servant had died, and who might have ordered it.

"Why does your queen want me dead?" I demanded.

Amelie rolled her eyes. "Probably to stop you from bringing her wicked stepsister back to court."

"I—that's not—" I stopped my instinctive denial. Apparently,

Amelie had decided we were going to be honest with each other. It was in my best interest to continue in that vein, since she clearly knew far more than I did. "How long has the queen known that her stepsister was alive?"

"Oh, from the beginning. The king is not as subtle as he thinks he is."

"Then why," I said, "didn't she try to stop him then?"

"Who knows," Amelie said. "Gratitude, perhaps? If Jacinda hadn't dabbled in blood magic to begin with, Ella would never have become queen."

So we really were being honest today.

I wondered how far it went. What would Amelie say if I asked her where she had come from, and why she was so loyal to our commoner queen? Why she had tried to attack me with a stone knife, and what would happen if she held one with iron in it?

I wish I had asked. But I was loyal and steadfast, and on the king's business, and, like a good soldier, I focused my attention on my mission.

"In that case," I said, "why doesn't she want Jacinda to come back to court?"

"She's willing to let her stepsister live. That doesn't mean she wants to look at her face every single day." Amelie stepped away from me, and I let her. As she turned to face me, I sheathed my blade. "It's the king's motives you should be wondering about, Garrin. He's ignored Jacinda's existence for five years. Why do you think he wants her back now?"

Because he stopped loving his queen, and remembered that he loved her. As soon as I opened my mouth to say it, I realized how ridiculous it was. There had been dozens of girls before either of them, and Ciar never looked back. If his fancy was passing to another, it would be to someone new.

The realization hit me like a blow to my stomach. While I stood absorbing it, Amelie said, "Come with me, and ask the queen yourself."

She turned and walked down the hallway without waiting to see if I would follow her.

I should have turned and walked the other way. Nothing the queen said to me could make a difference. I knew my prince's command. I didn't need to know his reasons.

But if he didn't love Jacinda, if he never had. . .

All this time I had known where she was, and I had never gone to her. Never seen what that moonlit dance might have turned into, once the strains of faerie music and the pull of faerie magic were gone.

I had assumed I could not. And maybe all this time, Ciar wouldn't even have cared.

Although Amelie's back was to me, I could imagine her expression if I were to say any of this. Which, of course, I had no intention of doing.

But I did follow her: down the passageway, through the side hall, and up the west stairs to the queen's quarters.

Queen Ella was not surprised to see us. She sat on her bed fully dressed, in a simple green gown that made her beauty look wholesome and innocent. Something unspoken passed between her and her maid, and then Amelie crossed the room and stood by the side of the bed, hands clasped together.

"Your Majesty," I said. I had no choice but to bow, so I did it more deeply than necessary, in the hope that it would come off as sardonic. "You wished to speak to me?"

"I wished," Queen Ella said, "to never speak to you again."

Oh, how nice. We were all being honest with each other today.

"I told you the plan wouldn't work," Amelie said. "He's a trained fighter."

"But you are—" The queen bit the sentence off. "Very well. Garrin. What can I offer you, to leave my stepsister in peace?"

In peace. . .

"It wasn't her," I said. It was suddenly obvious, and I was aghast at how easily I had been fooled. "You wrote that note."

The queen shrugged.

I should have realized. There was, after all, only one other person who knew how important those slippers really were.

And the If you love me? Had she merely been guessing? Or had I been that obvious?

If so, had it been obvious to Ciar, too?

"Why?" I said. "Why are you trying so hard to keep her in exile? Just let her come back."

For a brief moment, the queen didn't look beautiful at all. She looked like a trapped, snarling animal. "You don't know her. You don't—you can't understand what she's capable of. She's a witch, she sacrificed her own blood to the fae—"

"If she's so terrible," I said, "why didn't she sacrifice your blood?"

Amelie laughed softly. The queen shot her a silencing look, then turned back to me. "Do you know why Ciar spared her, even though he let me kill the other two?"

"I don't," I said.

Which was what I would have said even if I did know. But Ciar had not shared his reasons with me that night. He'd met me in the stables, one horse saddled, another already mounted by a figure in a dark cloak with wild, wind-swept hair.

"Take her," he'd said. "Take her somewhere far away from here."

I hadn't asked why, both because I didn't need to know, and because I thought I did know. He'd loved her first, and he loved her still, and he didn't want to watch her die.

And though I hadn't asked about his reason for this mission, either, I could guess that as well. It had been five years, and he had changed his mind. But not about letting her go.

About letting her live.

And that was why I was still here in this castle, pretending that notes and the queen were any of my business. I should have been on my horse, racing down the long, straight road that eventually wound its way into the mountains. I could have been in the village by now, in that tiny cottage. I imagined the way Jacinda's eyes would widen when she saw me. She would understand at once why I was there.

That the king's mercy had wound down to nothing, and I had been sent to fulfill his will.

Instead I was here, in the castle, talking to the queen. The only person, aside from me, who didn't want this to happen.

But only because she didn't know what was happening. She thought Ciar was sending for Jacinda in order to replace her. I had thought the same thing, until I was forced to see how ridiculous it was. None of us are rational about the people who gave us our deepest scars.

"I'm sorry, Your Majesty," I said, "but the king has given me a command, and I must carry it out."

Her lip curled. "Because you are his devoted servant?"

"I am."

"Please, Garrin." She said my name like it was stuck in her throat. "You can't fool me. You're dangerous. Someday, you're going to turn on Ciar."

She said it like she was pronouncing a remarkable insight, even though that was the consensus of every other person in the castle.

The consensus was wrong. But nothing I said would convince the queen of that, so I said nothing.

"Do you know how I know?" She swung her legs over the side of the bed, and Amelie took her hand to help her stand. "Because it's what I did. So many years of being the grateful, lesser sister, with no right to anything, in debt to them for keeping a roof over my head. For giving me any place at all in my own home. They never imagined that someday, I might take everything they had. But it was the best thing I ever did."

"They were cruel to you," I said. "They treated you like a slave. Ciar treats me like a friend." She made a small, skeptical sound, and I stiffened. "Whether you believe it or not, it's true."

"Oh, I believe it." She shook her hand free of Amelie's grasp. "But you are both fools if you think that makes a difference. He still has so many things that you do not."

"They're his things," I said. "I don't want them. I am loyal to Ciar. I've always been loyal to Ciar." I was so tired of people doubting it, when I had spent twenty-two years proving my devotion. . . But then, she had only been here for five of those years. "I've done everything he ever asked of me, and will continue to do so. I doubt you can say as much."

She drew herself up, her eyes turning to ice. "Watch yourself. I am his wife and your queen. He loves me."

"Of course he does," I said. "You saw to that, didn't you?"

She shuffled her feet back instinctively, even though she was wearing only satin-beaded house slippers. The glass slippers were brought out only on special occasions. Fortunately for her, we lived in a castle, so there were plenty of those.

"You stole your stepsister's magic," I said flatly. "You used it to make him love you."

"What difference does it make," Queen Ella snapped, "if he loves me for my beauty, or for my wit, or for faerie magic? Whatever it is, the true reason is the same. He loves me because I make him happy." She took a step toward me. "And I do. I do make him happy."

"But it didn't have to be you," I said. "That's the real reason you don't want her here, isn't it? Not because she took what was yours, but because you took what was hers."

"You are wrong." Her lips were white. "I stole much from Jacinda, but not Ciar. And all I want now is to keep what is mine. I want you to take her away."

"You could go to the Daeonian Islands," Amelie put in, while I stood staring at them. "Prince Ciar isn't going to chase you through the mountains and risk starting a war. Not over a woman he threw away years ago."

And not over you. She didn't have to say it. Ciar would miss me, but he would listen to his advisers, who would all agree that it was better for me to be gone. One danger less.

"I would take care of things here," Queen Ella added. "Arrange for you to set out with wealth and with fake papers."

Clearly, they had planned this in advance. A backup in case the killing-me plot didn't work out.

It was a far better plan. Not just for me, but for everyone. Ciar's mother had proposed it many times, urging first her husband and then her son to send me away.

"The bastard son of a king, living at court, is a threat," she had told them. She knew I was listening; she hadn't cared. "But a foreign bastard son is nothing. He'll be happier far away from here."

That last had been for Ciar's benefit. She could not have cared less about my happiness.

Which didn't mean she hadn't been right about it.

"And what," I asked, "makes you think Jacinda would go anywhere with me?"

Queen Ella smiled, her eyes gleaming. "Trust me."

"But that's the thing," I said. "I don't." I set my jaw. "I trust Ciar, and he trusts me. He is my king. I will not betray him."

The words felt hollow. But they sounded strong, and I felt the twist in my gut that told me I was doing the right thing.

"You fool," Queen Ella hissed, but I'd heard enough, and wasted enough time. I turned to the door and pulled it open.

Ciar stood on the other side.

I whirled, just in time to see Queen Ella assume an expression of surprise. She was very good at it. I would have been convinced of her shock if I hadn't seen her face the moment before she put surprise on it.

She had meant for Ciar to be there. To hear me agreeing to betray him, to take what was his, to become the danger everyone had always warned I would be.

My heart pounded with terror at how close I had come to falling into her trap. I bowed to my king, to give me time to compose my face.

"Garrin." Ciar's voice was cold. "You have yet to carry out my mission. Why is that?"

"I was on my way." I shot the queen a look, not quite able to keep the spite out of my voice. This plot of hers had been designed to end in my death; I deserved a bit of spite. "I was, as you see, detained."

Ciar's face went completely blank, as if he couldn't decide what to place upon it. It was an expression I had seen on him once before, and that memory rose sharp and unbidden: the pain ripping through my back, my small body tensing for the next lash, the blood on my lip where I had bitten it in an attempt not to cry out. Ciar, with his mother's hand clenched around his, holding him at her side and making him watch.

I had not seen what expression he finally chose. The next lash ripped a scream from me, and I turned away in shame. When I looked up, his mother was leading him away, and I could see only the back of his head.

In my memory, there was a tear on his cheek. But had I really seen it?

I couldn't be sure. And so I watched his face now, with more intensity than the moment deserved, even though he wasn't even looking at me. He was looking at his queen.

She looked back, every bit as intent as I. But Ciar's face remained without expression, until finally his wife strode across the room toward him. Her skirts whispered against her legs.

"My love," she said. "Don't do it. Please. Don't bring my step-sister back into our lives."

"I'm sorry." He didn't sound it, though. "We need her."

"Why?" Ella's voice rose and she lost control of her accent; its rough, common edge bled through. "I've summoned doctors from the islands. They say they can help me. I will conceive, Ciar, it will just—"

"Doctors can't help you." He stepped away from her, and she flinched as if he had hit her. "Don't you see? It's fae magic closing your womb. Your stepsister laid a curse on you. We need to force her to remove it."

The queen's eyes widened. She knew full well that the only magic her sister had ever summoned was trapped in a pair of slippers that lay in her own closet.

"I wanted to keep it from you," Ciar said, "to spare you

grief." His tone was sincere, his eyes deep and warm—but still, he did not touch her. "I see that I was wrong. I am sorry. Let's do this together."

A flicker of alarm crossed the queen's face. "Together?"

"Yes. Let us set out, the three of us"—Amelie gave him an exaggerated pout, which only I saw—"to retrieve your stepsister and force her to undo her final attempt to hurt you."

Queen Ella looked at me, then back at her husband.

"You don't have to be afraid of her," Ciar said gently. "Not anymore. You know that, don't you?"

"I know it," Ella said. "I just don't believe it." She took a deep breath and lifted her chin. "But with you, I always feel safe. You rescued me before. I know you'll do it again."

Ciar reached for her hand and wound his fingers through hers.

"Wonderful," I said. I knew my voice was too sour, but I couldn't help it; besides, Amelie was making exaggeratedly nauseated faces, and if I stopped focusing on my bitterness, I was going to laugh. "It will be a party."

I was already wearing riding clothes, so I had some extra time before we were expected to meet at the stables. I went straight there anyhow, saddled my horse swiftly, then left him with a pat on the nose and made my way to the stall that housed the queen's favorite mare.

I expected to be there before anyone else. My plan was to conceal myself so I could eavesdrop on the queen and Amelie. But I had miscalculated. The two of them were already in the stall, and all I could do was lurk outside the wooden walls. Amelie seemed to be doing most of the talking, and I was too far away to make out what she was saying. Her voice was like a soft breeze, dissipating into incomprehensible wisps by the time it reached my ears.

Queen Ella's voice, however, was sharp and clear as glass. "I am keeping our bargain. All I ask for is for one day's delay. I will return the slippers to you when I return. I swore to set you free, and I will."

Amelie said something else, and the queen laughed bitterly. "And what good will it do to tell him my womb is quickened, if he has already chosen another bride and another heir? He can put me aside easily and legitimize her child. Then my babe will be the bastard, and she will once again have everything that should be mine. His love for me is the only weapon I have. I need to keep it."

In my eagerness to hear more, I risked edging closer. So I heard, barely, what Amelie said next. "Love does not change anyone's actions, my queen. Certainly not your husband's."

"It did once," Queen Ella said, and then I must have made some sound, because they both went silent and turned in my direction. I strolled past the wall and into the stall, as if I had just arrived, and bowed.

"Your Majesty," I said. "Are you ready to depart?"

"I suppose I have to be," the queen said, and stepped away from her horse.

It took me a moment to realize what she was waiting for. I gritted my teeth, got to my knees, and began tightening the straps of her sidesaddle.

Amelie laughed. It sounded like the tinkling of bells. "That was one of the things I always liked about you, my lady. Your pettiness."

"Well," Queen Ella said grimly, "I learned it from the best."

Amelie shook her head. "Jacinda was no good at pettiness. She always had to work herself into hatred first. Such a waste of energy."

My hand slipped on the leather. Somehow, it was a shock to hear her name. Even though this was all about her, it felt oddly like it had nothing to do with her at all. Like she existed as nothing but a picture, one we had all drawn to our own design, one we kept reacting to in the absence of the reality of who she was.

Except for me. But the instant I thought it, I knew it wasn't true. I had shared one dance with Jacinda, and one terrible nighttime ride, and since then, all I'd had was the thought of her.

The memory of the one side of her I had seen: not the girl who had desperately wanted her mother's approval, not the girl who had tormented her stepsister as viciously as she was able, not the girl who had shed her own blood and dabbled with the fae in order to be queen. Just a girl fleeing across a lawn, the castle looming over her; a terrified girl who had nonetheless stopped for a brief, wild dance.

That was the Jacinda I remembered. But the queen remembered the same person differently, and when I stood and met her blue eyes, I saw that she was terrified. Afraid to stand again before the person who had once tormented her while she was small and helpless.

"You defeated her last time," I reminded her. "There's nothing to be afraid of now."

Her blue eyes went wide, and then her lips thinned. "She never told you?"

Did everyone know about me and Jacinda? And did everyone assume there was more to know than there actually had been?

"Tell me what?" I said.

"That I never defeated her. I never stole those slippers from her."

I laughed harshly—the one time, I knew, that I would dare laugh at my queen. "Then how did they come to be on your feet? Did she give them to you as a gift?"

"Yes," the queen said.

We stared at each other. I glanced over at Amelie, who met my gaze and nodded.

"Why," I said, "would she do that?"

"I don't know. She never told me." The queen's shoulders lifted and fell. "Guilt, perhaps."

I snorted. "I can't imagine Jacinda feeling guilty."

"You didn't know her," the queen said. "You loved her, and that made you blind."

"And you hated her," I retorted, "which is just a different type of blindness."

She laughed, low and bitter. "And how would you know,

Garrin? Who do you hate? It seems to me that you can do nothing but snivel and submit, even to those who wrong you over and over—"

"Your Majesty," Amelie said. A warning.

Queen Ella pressed her lips together, then let out a breath and relaxed her shoulders. She turned from me and smiled at her maid, a soft, rueful smile. "What will I do, Amelie, when you are not here to advise me?"

Amelie shrugged.

"Would you not stay?" the queen said. "Once I have no hold on you, will you not feel even the slightest desire to protect me?"

Amelie gave her a sideways look, as if she had said something very stupid. "No, my queen. That is a magic we neither wield nor understand. I've told you as much, many times."

"I see something different," the queen said, "when I look at you. Perhaps you do not know who you truly are."

Amelie laughed, like bells chiming wildly.

The queen's face hardened. She turned to me. "Help me mount, Garrin, and quickly. We would not want to keep the king waiting."

But of course, it was Ciar who kept us waiting; not to make a point, but because it would never have occurred to him to rush on anyone's behalf. The queen and I had nothing more to say to each other, and it was a long, uncomfortable wait.

In the end, we set out shortly before noon. By the time we made it to the cottage, the sun was pulling the colors of the sky behind the mountains, leaving a dark, purplish smudge in their place.

It was a mostly silent ride. I had to show them the way, which was a good excuse for keeping my mount far in the lead. I wouldn't have heard Ciar and Ella speaking, even if they did.

But I don't think they did.

Ciar was dressed in plain black clothes with a hood over his head, and Ella wore a gray riding dress and a veil that covered the lower half of her face. Not disguises so much as indications to the populace that they should pretend not to recognize their monarchs. The travelers we passed on the road, and the villagers in the mountains, all obeyed.

Jacinda's cottage was set apart from the village, which struck me now as an unnecessary cruelty. I dismounted beside the newly painted fence, dismayed to find that my heart was pounding. I couldn't tell if I was eager or afraid.

Ciar dismounted as well, then helped his wife off her horse. The queen's face was dead white. That was fear, and as soon as I saw it, I recognized how different it was from what I felt. I was braced and ready, but not truly afraid.

I was. . . eager.

But then, we weren't preparing to see the same person. We had all seen her from different angles, each of our views hiding certain aspects of her and bringing others into focus. And Jacinda was more than what any one of us saw in her. She was made up not of those angles, but of a core that, for all I knew, none of us had ever gotten close to.

I glanced at Ciar, waited for his nod, then strode up to the door and knocked.

No one answered.

Ciar came up behind me. I knew he wouldn't knock—royalty didn't—so I pushed the door open and stepped inside.

My readiness drained away in a single glance.

Ciar made a sound, somewhere between a cough and a gasp, and I reached out instinctively to steady him.

As I did, I turned and saw Queen Ella's face. She had one delicate hand raised to her lips, pressing the veil against her mouth. But I could see her eyes, and the expression in them when she first realized that her stepsister was dead.

The cottage was, for a few seconds, utterly silent and utterly still.

In those few seconds, I took in several facts about the room we stood in:

Neat and clean, save for the blackening pool of blood.

A metal blade in Jacinda's hand, her fingers curled around its hilt.

Her hair had been in braids, but they had come loose. Her dark hair was spread around her motionless face. Some of it was matted with blood.

Her corpse was still stiff and clenched. She had been dead for only a day or two.

The blankets on her pallet were raised into a large lump, and the lump was completely still.

"You did this," the queen said shrilly. She pointed at me. "You were the only one who knew where she was. You killed her!"

The sentence ended in a choked sob, and she moved her hands up to cover her eyes.

"Are you crying for her?" I demanded. My voice was far harsher than I should have dared use to my queen; but sometimes, it doesn't require fae magic to make people disregard consequences. "You ordered her death five years ago. What changed since then?"

Queen Ella took a few steps closer, then halted, probably because of the stench. She stared at her stepsister's still, rigid face.

"Five years," she said. "That's all. Five years passed. It doesn't alter what she did to me, but it gave me time to hate her less."

"My love," Ciar said, and she whirled on him. For a moment, from the look on her face, I thought she would accuse him of ordering me to do this. Instead, she let out a choked cry and threw herself into his arms.

I approached Jacinda's body and knelt beside her. Her throat had been slit, neatly and professionally. It had probably taken her only seconds to die.

I gritted my teeth. With Ciar watching, I dared not cry.

"Who could have done this?" Queen Ella sobbed.

The obvious answer was: You. The queen had been so desperate to keep her stepsister away, and helpless to stop me from going to retrieve her. Surely, she and Amelie had been prepared with a third backup plan.

But they hadn't known where Jacinda was.

Or had they? I suspected that Amelie had ways of knowing things that I couldn't even guess at.

"We all did it," Ciar said sorrowfully. "We left her alone, in her loneliness and grief, and she couldn't bear it anymore. She took her own life."

"No." Queen Ella pulled slightly away from him. "No. That wasn't what Jacinda—she would never."

I tended to agree. Not because of the fierceness I remembered; a lot could change in five years, including that. But because of that lump in the bed, which I had just seen move.

I said nothing, though, because the queen was right. I was the only person who had known where Jacinda was. I had never told Ciar—he had made it easy, by never asking. I had never told anyone. If this was deemed murder, I would be the only suspect.

Queen Ella's shoulders shook with sobs for the woman she had long ago condemned to death. Ciar's face was drawn and mournful—it was, I saw now, a new demeanor he was practicing —his eyes soft as he looked down at his wife. The queen whirled toward the door, and I saw the glitter of glass beneath her hem. An odd choice for riding shoes.

Ciar looked over the queen's shoulder and met my eyes.

"You should search the room," he said.

He did not look at the lump on the bed. He would leave it to me to uncover it, and pretend he hadn't known what was there.

It's the lack of an heir that's causing the problem.

He can legitimize her child.

"Of course," I said, obedient as always, and saw the faint flash of relief in his eyes before he turned back to his wife.

I was always obedient, yet he had never fully trusted me. Always waiting for something to make me turn.

Of course, of course, he'd had me followed. All those years ago, when I fled with Jacinda down these roads, there had been someone behind us. To make sure I did as he ordered. To make sure I came back. To make sure I didn't try to take what was his.

The man who had fallen out the window, two days after my

return, had been just the sort of person he would pick for that task. A loyal nobody.

No wonder Ciar had never asked where she was. All this time, he had known. Yet he had sent me to retrieve her instead of going himself.

Or had he?

I pulled the blanket free. The boy beneath it grabbed it back, trying to pull it over himself again. His dark eyes were wide and terrified, his round face scrubbed clean, his black hair a tangle of curls.

He was about five years old, and he looked like Ciar.

I can't explain what came over me as I looked at that small round face, the large dark eyes, frightened and hopefully trusting. I would say it was magic, for in my experience, only love triggered by magic strikes like that: fast and sudden and completely without reason.

But the fae do not bear children, and this is a magic they neither wield nor understand.

"Whose child is that?" Queen Ella said shrilly, and I turned.

The queen's eyes were stricken above her veil. She already knew whose child this was. And now she knew why Ciar had saved her stepsister, and why he had sent for her now, after five years of a childless marriage.

Except he had not actually sent anyone. Not at first. He had ridden here alone, to inform Jacinda that he needed his heir back.

I could see it in my mind's eye. Him showing up, expecting her to hand over his child. So he could raise the boy at court. An heir if he needed one. . . or, if Ella bore him an heir, a royal bastard.

He probably hadn't imagined that she might refuse him. Might try to take what was his.

We had all been trained never to take anything from Ciar. . . and in the process, he, too, had been trained. To never expect or allow anyone to do so.

Back when his mother had made him watch my whipping,

Ciar had obeyed silently, with no expression on his small face. When the whipping was over, he had taken his mother's hand and let her lead him to his room.

He had never said a word to me about it. Not ever. I'd thought maybe he was embarrassed, maybe he was confused, maybe he was angry. I had imagined him weeping for me.

We are all so stupid, when it comes to the people we need to love us. That was my only excuse for why I had missed the most obvious explanation.

He had said nothing because, as far as he was concerned, there was nothing that needed to be said.

The queen made a small, whimpering sound, and I heard the genuine grief in it. She, too, could not see the truth about the person whose love she craved. How easily she had believed that her stepsister had given her the shoes out of kindness, even though Jacinda had never showed her kindness in her life.

And perhaps the cruelest thing Jacinda had ever done to her stepsister was to hand her over to Ciar.

Yet Jacinda had still not managed to get away from him. I wondered if she had been surprised when she saw him at her door, and how much time she'd had to fight. Though her braids had come loose, it wouldn't have been much of a struggle. Ciar was far larger than her, and well trained. Ruthless and determined.

I wondered why he hadn't just taken the child then. He could have gotten away with it; he was king. Had he been afraid of his queen's reaction? Or of the court's? After all, if he had just shown up with a child, with no explanation, that child's parentage would forever have been in doubt. Even though he looked like Ciar.

I spoke without thinking. If I had thought, I might not have done it.

"He's mine," I said.

Both faces turned toward me: Ciar aghast, Ella stunned.

But neither of them disbelieving.

Everyone thought I had known Jacinda so much better than I did. That there had been more between us than there truly was.

I hadn't known her at all. But now she was dead, and who she truly was didn't really matter, did it? All that was left was the image of a person she had imprinted on each of our hearts. Ciar's. Ella's. Mine.

This boy's.

"She never told me," I said. It was not hard to sound stupid and betrayed. "She never told me about my own child."

Ella drew in her breath, then let it out without speaking.

"I should have known," I said. "She made me swear never to tell about us, and the way she left. . . so suddenly. . . I should have guessed. How could I be so stupid?"

I met the king's eyes, and I kept on my usual expression: loyalty. Trust. Subservience.

I saw him work it through. The resemblance. The timing. The fact that he had never sired a child, not with any of the other women and not with his wife.

"I'm sorry," I said, and I saw him believe me. All those years of obedience, paying off at last. He would not think that I would do something this audacious, not when I had never, ever, since we were seven years old and playing with lances, taken a single thing from him.

Queen Ella's eyes narrowed, and I thought that perhaps I had not fooled her. But it didn't matter, because we were on the same side now. It was in her interest for the boy to be mine. The bastard son of a king was a threat, but the bastard son of a bastard son was nothing at all.

It wouldn't take her long to see that I was drawing the boy farther from the center of court, farther from his father's eye, farther from her own child. When it came time to go farther still, to take him someplace distant from any royalty, I hoped she would remember the bargain she had offered me this morning.

I stepped in front of the boy, so he wouldn't see his mother's body. He held up his small hands to me—where he got such trust, I do not know; his mother must have made his world feel very safe—and I gathered him up in my arms.

"Let's go," I said. "I want to take my son home."

And there you go. That's the story I promised I would tell you, once you were old enough to hear it.

You're likely not old enough yet, but I have no choice. I may not have time to wait until you have some maturity and sense— and really, a young man who pulls those kinds of faces at his father is definitely not old enough—hahaha, okay. Enough.

In time, you'll think of questions. I'll answer them if I can.

You're probably already wondering why Lissa wasn't part of this story.

There's no why, son. She simply wasn't. The castle was full of people who weren't. I mentioned her name at the start merely because it was the only opportunity I had; the only time she brushed past this tale.

That must seem odd to you, when in all your memories of us, we've been caring for you together. But how that came about. . .

Well. That was later, much later. And it's a story for another time.

TWO TRUTHS AND A LIE

NEBULA WINNER: BEST NOVELETTE

BY SARAH PINSKER, PUBLISHED BY TOR.COM

I n his last years, Marco's older brother Denny had become one of those people whose possessions swallowed them entirely. The kind they made documentaries about, the kind people staged interventions for, the kind people made excuses not to visit, and who stopped going out, and who were spoken of in sighs and silences. Those were the things Stella thought about after Denny died, and those were the reasons why, after eyeing the four other people at the funeral, she offered to help Marco clean out the house.

"Are you sure?" Marco asked. "You barely even knew him. It's been thirty years since you saw him last."

Marco's husband, Justin, elbowed Marco in the ribs. "Take her up on it. I've got to get home tomorrow and you could use help."

"I don't mind. Denny was nice to me," Stella said, and then added, "But I'd be doing it to help you."

The first part was a lie, the second part true. Denny had been the weird older brother who was always there when their friends hung out at Marco's back in high school, always lurking with a notebook and a furtive expression. She remembered Marco going out of his way to try to include Denny, Marco's admiration wrapped in disappointment, his slow slide into embarrassment.

She and Marco had been good friends then, but she hadn't kept up with anyone from high school. She had no excuse; social media could reconnect just about anyone at any time. She wasn't sure what it said about her or them that nobody had tried to communicate.

On the first night of her visit with her parents, her mother had said, "Your friend Marco's brother died this week," and Stella had suddenly been overwhelmed with remorse for having let that particular friendship lapse. Even more so when she read the obituary her mother had clipped, and she realized Marco's parents had died a few years before. That was why she went to the funeral and that was why she volunteered.

"I'd like to help," she said.

Two days later, she arrived at the house wearing clothes from a bag her mother had never gotten around to donating: jeans decades out of style and dappled with paint, treadworn gym shoes, and a baggy, age-stretched T-shirt from the Tim Burton Batman. She wasn't self-conscious about the clothes—they made sense for deep cleaning—but there was something surreal about the combination of these particular clothes and this particular door.

"I can't believe you still have that T-shirt," Marco said when he stepped out onto the stoop. "Mine disintegrated. Do you remember we all skipped school to go to the first showing?"

"Yeah. I didn't even know my mom still had it. I thought she'd thrown it out years ago."

"Cool—and thanks for doing this. I told myself I wouldn't ask anybody, but if someone offered I'd take them up on it. Promise me you won't think less of me for the way this looks? Our parents gave him the house. I tried to help him when I visited, but he didn't really let me, and he made it clear if I pushed too hard I wouldn't be welcome anymore."

Stella nodded. "I promise."

He handed her a pair of latex gloves and a paper mask to cover her mouth and nose; she considered for the first time how bad it might be. She hadn't even really registered that he had squeezed through a cracked door and greeted her outside. The lawn was manicured, the flower beds mulched and weeded and ready for the spring that promised to erupt at any moment, if winter ever agreed to depart. The shutters sported fresh white paint.

Which was why she was surprised when Marco cracked the door again to enter, leaving only enough room for her to squeeze through as she followed. Something was piled behind the door. Also beside the door, in front of the door, and in every available space in the entranceway. A narrow path led forward to the kitchen, another into the living room, another upstairs.

"Oh," she said.

He glanced back at her. "It's not too late to back out. You didn't know what you were signing up for."

"I didn't," she admitted. "But it's okay. Do you have a game plan?"

"Dining room, living room, rec room, bedrooms, in that order. I have no clue how long any room will take, so whatever we get done is fine. Most of what you'll find is garbage, which can go into bags I'll take to the dumpster in the yard. Let me know if you see anything you think I might care about. We should probably work in the same room, anyhow, since I don't want either of us dying under a pile. That was all I thought about while I cleaned a path through the kitchen to get to the dumpster: If I get buried working in here alone, nobody will ever find me."

"Dining room it is, then." She tried to inject enthusiasm into her voice, or at least moral support.

It was strange seeing a house where she had spent so much time reduced to such a fallen state. She didn't think she'd have been able to say where a side table or a bookcase had stood, but there they were, in the deepest strata, and she remembered.

They'd met here to go to prom, ten of them. Marco's father had photographed the whole group together, only saying once, "In my day, people went to prom with dates," and promptly getting shushed by Marco's mother. Denny had sat on the stairs and watched them, omnipresent notebook in his hands. It hadn't felt weird until Marco told him to go upstairs, and then suddenly it had gone from just another family member watching the festivities to something more unsettling.

She and Marco went through the living room to the dining room. A massive table still dominated the room, though it was covered with glue sticks and paintbrushes and other art supplies. Every other surface in the room held towering piles, but the section demarcated by paint-smeared newspaper suggested Denny had actually used the table.

She smelled the kitchen from ten feet away. Her face must have shown it, because Marco said, "I'm serious. Don't go in there unless you have to. I've got all the windows open and three fans blowing but it's not enough. I thought we could start in here because it might actually be easiest. You can do the sideboard and the china cabinets and I'll work on clearing the table. Two categories: garbage and maybe-not-garbage, which includes personal stuff and anything you think might be valuable. Dying is shockingly expensive."

Stella didn't know if that referred to Denny's death—she didn't know how he'd died—or to the funeral, and she didn't want to ask. She wondered why Marco had chosen the impersonal job with no decisions involved, but when she came to one of his grandmother's porcelain teacups, broken by the weight of everything layered on top of it, she thought she understood. He didn't necessarily remember what was under here, but seeing it damaged would be harder than if Stella just threw it in a big black bag. The items would jog memories; their absence would not.

She also came to understand the purpose of the latex gloves. The piles held surprises. Papers layered on papers layered on toys and antiques, then, suddenly, mouse turds or a cat's hairball or the flattened tendril of some once-green plant or something moldering and indefinable. Denny had apparently smoked, too; every few layers, a full ashtray made an appearance. The papers were for the most part easy discards: the news and obituary sections of the local weekly newspaper, going back ten, fifteen, thirty-five years, some with articles cut out.

Here and there, she came across something that had survived: a silver platter, a resilient teapot, a framed photo. She placed those on the table in the space Marco had cleared. For a while it felt like she was just shifting the mess sideways, but eventually she began to recognize progress in the form of the furniture under the piles. When Marco finished, he dragged her garbage bags through the kitchen and out to the dumpster, then started sifting through the stuff she'd set aside. He labeled three boxes: "keep," "donate," and "sell." Some items took him longer than others; she decided not to ask how he made the choices. If he wanted to talk, he'd talk.

"Stop for lunch?" Marco asked when the table at last held only filled boxes.

Stella's stomach had started grumbling an hour before; she was more than happy to take a break. She reached instinctively for her phone to check the time, then stopped herself and peeled the gloves off the way she'd learned in first aid in high school, avoiding contamination. "I need to wash my hands."

"Do it at the deli on the corner. You don't want to get near any of these sinks."

The deli on the corner hadn't been there when they were kids. What had been? A real estate office or something else that hadn't registered in her teenage mind. Now it was a hipster re-creation of a deli, really, complete with order numbers from a wall dispenser. A butcher with a waxed mustache took their order.

"Did he go to school with us?" Stella whispered to Marco, watching the butcher.

He nodded. "Chris Bethel. He was in the class between us and Denny, except he had a different name back then."

In that moment, she remembered Chris Bethel, pre-transition, playing Viola in *Twelfth Night* like a person who knew what it was to be shipwrecked on a strange shore. Good for him.

While they waited, she ducked into the bathroom to scrub

her hands. She smelled like the house now, and hoped nobody else noticed.

Marco had already claimed their sandwiches, in plastic baskets and waxed paper, and chosen a corner table away from the other customers. They took their first few bites without speaking. Marco hadn't said much all morning, and Stella had managed not to give in to her usual need to fill silences, but now she couldn't help it.

"Where do you live? And how long have you and Justin been together?"

"Outside Boston," he said. "And fifteen years. How about you?"

"Chicago. Divorced. One son, Cooper. I travel a lot. I work sales for a coffee distributor."

Even as she spoke, she hated that she'd said it. None of it was true. She had always done that, inventing things when she had no reason to lie, just because they sounded interesting, or because it gave her a thrill. If he had asked to see pictures of her nonexistent son Cooper, she'd have nothing to show. Not to mention she had no idea what a coffee distributor did.

Marco didn't seem to notice, or else he knew it wasn't true and filed it away as proof they had drifted apart for a reason. They finished their sandwiches in silence.

"Tackle the living room next?" Marco asked. "Or the rec room?"

"Rec room," she said. It was farther from the kitchen.

Farther from the kitchen, but the basement litter pans lent a different odor and trapped it in the windowless space. She sighed and tugged the mask up.

Marco did the same. "The weird thing is I haven't found a cat. I'm hoping maybe it was indoor-outdoor or something. . . "

Stella didn't know how to respond, so she said, "Hmm," and

resolved to be extra careful when sticking her hands into anything.

The built-in bookshelves on the back wall held tubs and tubs of what looked like holiday decorations.

"What do you want to do with holiday stuff?" Stella pulled the nearest box forward on the shelf and peered inside. Halloween and Christmas, mostly, but all mixed together, so reindeer ornaments and spider lights negotiated a fragile peace.

"I'd love to say toss it, but I think we need to take everything out, in case."

"In case?"

He tossed her a sealed package to inspect. It held two droid ornaments, like R2-D2 but different colors. "Collector's item, mint condition. I found it a minute ago, under a big ball of tinsel and plastic reindeer. It's like this all over the house: valuable stuff hidden with the crap. A prize in every fucking box."

The size of the undertaking was slowly dawning on her. "How long are you here for?"

"I've got a good boss. She said I could work from here until I had all Denny's stuff in order. I was thinking a week, but it might be more like a month, given everything. . . "

"A month! We made good progress today, though. . . "

"You haven't seen upstairs. Or the garage. There's a lot, Stella. The dining room was probably the easiest other than the kitchen, which will be one hundred percent garbage."

"That's if he didn't stash more collectibles in the flour."

Marco blanched. "Oh god. How did I not think of that?"

Part of her wanted to offer to help again, but she didn't think she could stomach the stench for two days in a row, and she was supposed to be spending time with her parents, who already said she didn't come home enough. She wanted to offer, but she didn't want him to take her up on it. "I'll come back if I can."

He didn't respond, since that was obviously a lie. They returned to the task at hand: the ornaments, the decorations, the toys, the games, the stacks of DVDs and VHS tapes and records and CDs and cassettes, the prizes hidden not in every box, but in enough to make the effort worthwhile. Marco was right that the dining room had been easier. He'd decided to donate all the cassettes, DVDs, and videotapes, but said the vinyl might actually be worth something. She didn't know anything about records, so she categorized them as playable and not, removing each from its sleeve to examine for warp and scratches. It was tedious work.

It took two hours for her to find actual equipment Denny might have played any of the media on: a small television on an Ikea TV stand, a stereo and turntable on the floor, then another television behind the first.

It was an old set, built into a wooden cabinet that dwarfed the actual screen. She hadn't seen one like this in years; it reminded her of her grandparents. She tried to remember if it had been down here when they were kids.

Something about it—the wooden cabinet, or maybe the dial —made her ask, "Do you remember *The Uncle Bob Show*?"

Which of course he didn't, nobody did, she had made it up on the spot, like she often did.

Which was why it was so weird that Marco said, "Yeah! And the way he looked straight into the camera. It was like he saw me, specifically me. Scared me to death, but he said, 'Come back next week,' and I always did because I felt like he'd get upset otherwise."

As he said it, Stella remembered too. The way Uncle Bob looked straight into the camera, and not in a friendly Mr. Rogers way. Uncle Bob was the anti-Mr. Rogers. A cautionary uncle, not predatory, but not kind.

"It was a local show," she said aloud, testing for truth.

Marco nodded. "Filmed at the public broadcast station. Denny was in the audience a few times."

Stella pictured Denny as she had known him, a hulking older teen. Marco must have realized the disconnect, because he added, "I mean when he was little. Seven or eight, maybe? The first season? That would make us five. Yeah, that makes sense, since I was really jealous, but my mom said you had to be seven to go on it."

Stella resized the giant to a large boy. Audience didn't feel like exactly the right word, but she couldn't remember why.

Marco crossed the room to dig through the VHS tapes they'd discarded. "Here."

It took him a few minutes to connect the VCR to the newer television. The screen popped and crackled as he hit play.

The show started with an oddly familiar instrumental theme song. *The Uncle Bob Show* appeared in block letters, then the logo faded and the screen went black. A door opened, and Stella realized it wasn't dead-screen black but a matte black room. The studio was painted black, with no furniture except a single black wooden chair.

Children spilled through the door, running straight for the camera—no, running straight for the secret compartments in the floor, all filled with toys. In that environment, the colors of the toys and the children's clothes were shocking, delicious, welcoming, warm. Blocks, train sets, plastic animals. That was why *audience* had bothered her. They weren't an audience; they were half the show, half the camera's focus. After a chaotic moment where they sorted who got possession of what, they settled in to play.

Uncle Bob entered a few minutes later. He was younger than Stella expected, his hair dark and full, his long face unlined. He walked with a ramrod spine and a slight lean at the hips, his arms clasped behind him giving him the look of a flightless bird. He made his way to the chair, somehow avoiding the children at his feet even though he was already looking straight into the camera.

He sat. Stella had the eeriest feeling, even now, that his eyes focused on her. "How on earth did this guy get a TV show?"

"Right? That's Denny there." Marco paused the tape and pointed at a boy behind and to the right of the chair. Her mental image hadn't been far off; Denny was bigger than all the other kids. He had a train car in each hand, and was holding the left one out to a little girl. The image of him playing well with others surprised Stella; she'd figured he'd always been a loner. She opened her mouth to say that, then closed it again. It was fine for Marco to say whatever he wanted about his brother, but it might not be appropriate for her to bring it up.

Marco pressed play again. The girl took the train from Denny and smiled. In the foreground, Uncle Bob started telling a story. Stella had forgotten the storytelling, too. That was the whole show: children doing their thing, and Uncle Bob telling completely unrelated stories. He paid little attention to the kids, though they sometimes stopped playing to listen to him.

The story was weird. Something about a boy buried alive in a hillside—"planted," in his words—who took over the entire hillside, like a weed, and spread for miles around.

Stella shook her head. "That's fucked up. If I had a kid I wouldn't let them watch this. Nightmare city."

Marco gave her a look. "I thought you said you had a kid?"

"I mean if I'd had a kid back when this was on." She was usually more careful with the lying game. Why had she said she had a son, anyway? She'd be found out the second Marco ran into her parents.

It was a dumb game, really. She didn't even remember when she'd started playing it. College, maybe. The first chance she'd had to reinvent herself, so why not do it wholesale? The rules were simple: Never lie about something anyone could verify independently; never lose track of the lies; keep them consistent and believable. That was why in college she'd claimed she'd made the varsity volleyball team in high school, but injured her knee so spectacularly in practice she'd never been able to play any sport again, and she'd once flashed an AP physics class, and she'd auditioned for the Jeopardy! Teen Tournament but been cut when she accidentally said "fuck" to Alex Trebek. Then she just had to live up to her reputation as someone who'd lived so much by eighteen that she could coast on her former cool.

Uncle Bob's story was still going. "They dug me out of the hillside on my thirteenth birthday. It's good to divide rhizomes to give them room to grow."

"Did he say 'me'?"

"A lot of his stories went like that, Stella. They started out like fairy tales, but somewhere in the middle he shifted into first person. I don't know if he had a bad writer or what."

"And did he say 'rhizome'? Who says 'rhizome' to seven-year-olds?" Stella hit the stop button. "Okay. Back to work. I remember now. That's plenty."

Marco frowned. "We can keep working, but I'd like to keep this on in the background now that we've found it. It's nice to see Denny. That Denny, especially."

That Denny: Denny frozen in time, before he got weird.

Stella started on the boxes in the back, leaving the stuff near the television to Marco. Snippets of story drifted her way, about the boy's family, but much, much older than when they'd buried him. His brothers were fathers now, their children the nieces and nephews of the teenager they'd dug from the hillside. Then the oddly upbeat theme song twice in a row—that episode's end and another's beginning.

"Marco?" she asked. "How long did this run?"

"I dunno. A few years, at least."

"Did you ever go on it? Like Denny?"

"No. I. . . hmm. I guess by the time I'd have been old enough, Denny had started acting strange, and my parents liked putting us into activities we could both do at the same time."

They kept working. The next Uncle Bob story that drifted her way centered on a child who got lost. Stella kept waiting for it to turn into a familiar children's story, but it didn't. Just a kid who got lost and when she found her way home she realized she'd arrived back without her body, and her parents didn't even notice the difference.

"Enough," Stella said from across the room. "That was enough to give me nightmares, and I'm an adult. Fuck. Watch more after I leave if you want."

"Okay. Time to call it quits, anyway. You've been here like nine hours."

She didn't argue. She waited until they got out the front door to peel off the mask and gloves.

"It was good to hang out with you," she said.

"You, too. Look me up if you ever get to Boston."

She couldn't tell him to do the same with Chicago, so she said, "Will do." She realized she'd never asked what he did for a living, but it seemed like an awkward time. It wasn't until after she'd walked away that she realized he'd said goodbye as if she wasn't returning the next day. She definitely wasn't, especially if he kept binging that creepy show.

When she returned to her parents' house she made a beeline for the shower. After twenty minutes' scrubbing, she still couldn't shake the smell. She dumped the clothes in the garbage instead of the laundry and took the bag to the outside bin, where it could stink as much as it needed to stink.

Her parents were sitting on the screened porch out front, as they often did once the evenings got warm enough, both with glasses of iced tea on the wrought iron table between them as if it were already summer. Her mother had a magazine open on her lap—she still subscribed to all her scientific journals, though she'd retired years before—and her father was solving a math puzzle on his tablet, which Stella could tell by his intense concentration.

"That bad?" Her mother lifted an eyebrow at her as she returned from the garbage.

"That bad."

She went into the house and poured herself a glass to match her parents'. Something was roasting in the oven, and the kitchen was hot and smelled like onions and butter. She closed her eyes and pressed the glass against her forehead, letting the oven and the ice battle over her body temperature, then returned to sit on the much cooler porch, picking the empty chair with the better view of the dormant garden.

"Grab the cushion from the other chair if you're going to sit in that one," her father said.

She did as he suggested. "I don't see why you don't have cushions for both chairs. What if you have a couple over? Do they have to fight over who gets the comfortable seat versus who gets the view?"

He shrugged. "Nobody's complained."

They generally operated on a complaint system. Maybe that was where she'd gotten the habit of lies and exaggeration: She'd realized early that only extremes elicited a response.

"How did dinner look?" he asked.

"I didn't check. It smelled great, if that counts for anything."

He grunted, the sound both a denial and the effort of getting up, and went inside. Stella debated taking his chair, but it wasn't worth the scene. A wasp hovered near the screen and she watched it for a moment, glad it was on the other side.

"Hey, Ma, do you remember *The Uncle Bob Show*?"

"Of course." She closed her magazine and hummed something that sounded half like Uncle Bob's theme song and half like *The Partridge Family* theme. Stella hadn't noticed the similarity between the two tunes; it was a ridiculously cheery theme song for such a dark show.

"Who was that guy? Why did they give him a kids' show?"

"The public television station had funding trouble and dumped all the shows they had to pay for—we had to get cable for you to watch *Sesame Street* and *Mister Rogers' Neighborhood*. They had all these gaps to fill in their schedule, so anybody with a low budget idea could get on. That one lasted longer than most—four or five years, I think."

"And nobody said, 'That's some seriously weird shit?'"

"Oh, we all did, but someone at the station argued there were plenty of peace-and-love shows around, and some people like to be scared, and it's not like it was full of violence or sex, and just because a show had kids in it didn't mean it was a kids' show."

"They expected adults to watch? That's even weirder. What time was it on?"

"Oh, I don't remember. Saturday night? Saturday morning?"

Huh. Maybe he was more like those old monster movie hosts. "That's deeply strange, even for the eighties. And who was the guy playing Uncle Bob? I tried looking it up on IMDB, but there's no page. Not on Wikipedia either. Our entire world is fueled by nostalgia, but there's nothing on this show. Where's the online fan club, the community of collectors? Anything."

Her mother frowned, clearly still stuck on trying to dredge up a name. She shook her head. "Definitely Bob, a real Bob, but I can't remember his last name. He must've lived somewhere nearby, because I ran into him at the drugstore and the hardware store a few times while the show was on the air."

Stella tried to picture that strange man in a drugstore, looming behind her in line, telling her stories about the time he picked up photos from a vacation but when he looked at them, he was screaming in every photo. If he were telling that story on the show, he'd end it with, "and then you got home from the drugstore with your photos, but when you looked at them, you were screaming in every photo too." Great. Now she'd creeped herself out without his help.

"How did I not have nightmares?"

"We talked about that possibility—all the mothers—but you weren't disturbed. None of you kids ever complained. It was a nice break, to chat with the other moms while you all played in such a contained space."

There was a vast difference between "never complained" and "weren't disturbed" that Stella would have liked to unpack, but she fixated on a different detail. "Contained space—you mean while we watched TV, right?"

"No, dear. The studio. It looked much larger on television, but the cameras formed this nice ring around three sides, and you all understood you weren't supposed to leave during that half hour except for a bathroom emergency. You all played and we sat around and had coffee. It was the only time in my week when I didn't feel like I was supposed to be doing something else."

It took Stella a few seconds to realize the buzzing noise in her head wasn't the wasp on the screen. "What are you talking about? I was on the show?"

"Nearly every kid in town was on it at some point. Everyone except Marco, because his brother was acting up by the time you two were old enough, and Celeste pulled Denny and enrolled both boys in karate instead."

"But me? Ma, I don't remember that at all." The idea that she didn't know something about herself that others knew bothered her more than she could express. "You aren't making this up?"

"Why would I lie? I'm sure there are other things you don't remember. Getting lice in third grade?"

"You shaved my head. Of course I remember. The whole class got it, but I was the only one whose mother shaved her head."

"I didn't have time to comb through it, honey. Something more benign? Playing at Tamar Siegel's house?"

"Who's Tamar Siegel?"

"See? The Siegels moved to town for a year when you were in second grade. They had a jungle gym that you loved. You didn't think much of the kid, but you liked her yard and her dog. We got on well with her parents; I was sad when they left."

Stella flashed on a tall backyard slide and a golden retriever barking at her when she climbed the ladder and left it below. A memory she'd never have dredged up unprompted. Nothing special about it: a person whose face she couldn't recall, a backyard slide, an experience supplanted by other experiences. Generic kid, generic fun. A placeholder memory.

"Okay, I get that there are things that didn't stick with me, and things that I think I remember once you remind me, but it doesn't explain why I don't remember a blacked-out TV studio or giant cameras or a creepy host. You forget the things that don't stand out, sure, but this seems, I don't know, formative."

Her mother shrugged. "You're making a big deal of nothing."

"Nothing? Did you listen to his stories?"

"Fairy tales."

"Now I know you didn't listen. He was telling horror stories to seven-year-olds."

"Fairy tales *are* horror stories, and like I said, you didn't complain. You mostly played with the toys."

"What about the kids at home watching? The stories were the focus if you weren't in the studio."

"If they were as bad as you say, hopefully parents paid attention and watched with their children and whatever else the experts these days say comprises good parenting. You're looking through a prism of now, baby. Have you ever seen early *Sesame Street*? I remember a sketch where a puppet with no facial features goes to a human for 'little girl eyes.' You and your friends watched shows, and if they scared you, you turned them off. You played outside. You cut your Halloween candy in half to make sure there were no razor blades inside. If you want to tell me I'm a terrible parent for putting you on that show with your friends, feel free, but since it took you thirty-five years to bring this up, I'm going to assume it didn't wreck your life."

Her father rang the dinner gong inside the house, a custom her parents found charming and Stella had always considered overkill in a family as small as theirs. She and her mother stood. Their glasses were still mostly full, the melting ice having replaced what they'd sipped.

She continued thinking over dinner, while she related everything she and Marco had unearthed to her mildly curious parents, and after, while scrubbing the casserole dish. What her mother said was true: She hadn't been driven to therapy by the show. She didn't remember any nightmares. It just felt strange to be missing something so completely, not to mention the questions that arose about what else she could be missing if she could be missing that. It was an unpleasant feeling.

After dinner, while her parents watched some reality show, she pulled out a photo album from the early eighties. Her family hadn't been much for photographic documentation, so there was just the one, chronological and well labeled, commemorating Stella at the old school playground before they pulled it out and replaced it with safer equipment, at a zoo, at the Independence Day parade. It was true, she didn't recall those particular moments, but she believed she'd been there. *The Uncle Bob Show* felt different. The first time she'd uttered the show's name, she'd thought she'd made it up.

She texted Marco: "Did Denny have all the Uncle Bob episodes on tape or only the ones he was in? Thanks!" She added a smiley face then erased it before she hit send. It felt falsely cheery instead of appreciative. His brother had just died.

She settled on the couch beside her parents. While they watched TV, she surfed the web looking for information about *The Uncle Bob Show*, but found nothing. In the era of kittens with Twitter accounts and sandwiches with their own Instagrams and fandoms for every conceivable property, it seemed impossible for something to be so utterly missing.

Not that it deserved a fandom; she just figured everything had one. Where were the ironic logo T-shirts? Where was the episode wiki explaining what happened in every Uncle Bob story? Where were the "Whatever happened to?" articles? The tell-alls by the kids or the director or the camera operator? The easy answer was that it was such a terrible show, or such a small show, that nobody cared. She didn't care either; she just needed to know. Not the same thing.

The next morning, she drove out to the public television station on the south end of town. She'd passed it so many times, but until now she wouldn't have said she'd ever been inside. Nothing about the interior rang a bell either, though it looked like it had been redone fairly recently, with an airy design that managed to say both modern and trapped in time.

"Can I help you?" The receptionist's trifocals reflected her computer's spreadsheet back at Stella. A phone log by her right hand was covered with sketched faces; the sketches were excellent. Grace Hernandez, according to her name plaque.

Stella smiled. "I probably should have called, but I wondered if you have archives of shows produced here a long time ago?

My mother wants a video of a show I was on as a kid and I didn't want her to have to come over here for nothing."

Even while she said it, she wondered why she had to lie. Wouldn't it have been just as easy to say she wanted to see it herself? She'd noticed an older receptionist and decided to play on her sympathies, but there was no reason to assume her own story wasn't compelling.

"Normally we'd have you fill out a request form, but it's a slow day. I can see if someone is here to help you." Grace picked up a phone and called one number, then disconnected and tried another. Someone answered, because she repeated Stella's story, then turned back to her. "He'll be out in a sec."

She gestured to a glass-and-wood waiting area, and Stella sat. A flat screen overhead played what Stella assumed was their station, on mute, and a few issues of a public media trade magazine called *Current* were piled neatly on the low table.

A small man—a little person? Was that the right term?— came around the corner into reception. He was probably around her age, but she would have remembered him if he'd gone to school with her.

"Hi," he said. "I'm Jeff Stills. Grace says you're looking for a show?"

"Yes, my mother—"

"Grace said. Let's see what we can do."

He handed her a laminated guest pass on a lanyard and waited while she put it on, then led her through a security door and down a long, low-ceilinged corridor, punctuated by framed stills from various shows. No Uncle Bob. "Have you been here before?"

"When I was a kid."

"Hmm. I'll bet it looks pretty different. This whole back area was redone around 2005, after the roof damage. Then the lobby about five years ago."

She hadn't had any twinges of familiarity, but at least that explained some of it. She'd forgotten about the blizzard that wrecked the roof; she'd been long gone by then.

"Hopefully whatever you're looking for wasn't among the stuff that got damaged by the storm. What are you looking for?"

"*The Uncle Bob Show*. Do you know it?"

"Only by name. I've seen the tapes on the shelf, but in the ten years I've been here, nobody has ever asked for a clip. Any good?"

"No." Stella didn't hesitate. "It's like those late-night horror hosts, Vampira or Elvira or whatever, except they forgot to run a movie and instead let the host blather on."

They came to a nondescript door. The low-ceilinged hallway had led her to expect low-ceilinged rooms, but the space they entered was more of a warehouse. A long desk cluttered with computers and various machinery occupied the front, and then the space opened into row upon row of metal shelving units. The aisles were wide enough to accommodate rolling ladders.

"We've been working on digitizing, but we have fifty years of material in here, and some stuff has priority."

"Is that what you do? Digitize?"

"Nah. We have interns for that. I catalogue new material as it comes in, and find stuff for people when they need clips. Mostly staff, but sometimes for networks, local news, researchers, that kind of thing."

"Sounds fun," Stella said. "How did you get into the field?"

"I majored in history, but never committed enough to any one topic for academic research. Ended up at library school, and eventually moved here. It is fun! I get a little bit of everything. Like today: a mystery show."

"Total mystery."

She followed him down the main aisle, then several aisles over, almost to the back wall. He pointed at some boxes above her head.

"Wow," she said. "Do you know where everything is without looking it up?"

"Well, it's alphabetical, so yeah, but also they're next to *Underground*, which I get a lot of requests for. Do you know what year you need?"

"1982? My mother couldn't remember exactly, but that's the year I turned seven."

Jeff disappeared and returned pushing a squeaking ladder along its track. He climbed up for the "*Uncle Bob Show* 1982" box. It looked like there were five years' worth, 1980 to 1985. She followed him back toward the door, where he pointed her to an office chair.

"We have strict protocols for handling media that hasn't been backed up yet. If you tell me which tapes you want to watch, I'll queue them up for you."

"Hmm. Well, my birthday is in July, so let's pick one in the last quarter of the year first, to see if I'm in there."

"You don't know if you are?"

She didn't want to admit she didn't remember. "I just don't know when."

He handed her a pair of padded headphones and rummaged in the box. She'd been expecting VHS tapes, but these looked like something else—Betamax, she guessed.

The show's format was such that she didn't have to watch much to figure out if she was in it or not. The title card came on, then the episode's children rushed in. She didn't see herself. She wondered again if this was a joke on her mother's part.

"Wait—what was the date on this one?"

Jeff studied the label on the box. "October ninth."

"I'm sorry. That's my mother's birthday. There's no way she stood around in a television studio that day. Maybe the next week?"

He ejected the tape and put it back in its box and put in another, but that one obviously had some kind of damage, all static.

"Third time's the charm," he said, going for the next tape. He seemed to believe it himself, because he dragged another chair over and plugged in a second pair of headphones. "Do you mind?"

She shook her head and rolled her chair slightly to the right to give him a better angle. The title card appeared.

"It's a good thing nobody knows about this show or they'd have been sued over this theme song," he said.

Stella didn't answer. She was busy watching the children. She recognized the first few kids: Lee Pool first, a blond beanpole; poor Dan Heller; Addie Chapel, whose mother had been everyone's pediatrician.

And then there she was, little Stella Gardiner, one of the last through the door. She wasn't used to competing for toys, so maybe she didn't know she needed to get in early, or maybe they were assigned an order behind the scenes. She'd thought seeing herself on screen would jog her memory, give her the studio or the stories or the backstage snacks, but she still had no recollection. She pointed at herself on the monitor for Jeff's benefit, to show they'd found her. He gave her a thumbs-up.

Little Stella seemed to know where she was going, even if she wasn't first to get there. Lee Pool already had the T. rex, but she wouldn't have cared. She'd liked the big dinosaurs, the bigger the better. She emerged from the toy pit with a matched pair. Brontosaurus, apatosaurus, whatever they called them these days. She could never wrap her head around something that large having existed. So yeah, the dinosaurs made sense—it was her, even if she still didn't remember it.

She carried the two dinosaurs toward the set's edge, where she collected some wooden trees and sat down. She was an only child, used to playing alone, and this clearly wasn't her first time in this space.

The camera lost her. The focus, of course, was on Uncle Bob. She had been watching herself and missed his entrance. He sat in his chair, children playing around him. Dan Heller zoomed around the set like a satellite in orbit, a model airplane in hand.

"Once upon a time there was a little boy who wanted to go fast." Uncle Bob started a story without waiting for anyone to pay attention.

"He liked everything fast. Cars, motorcycles, boats, airplanes. Bicycles were okay, but not the same thrill. When he rode in his father's car, he pretended they were racing the cars beside them.

Sometimes they won, but mostly somebody quit the race. His father was not a fast driver. The little boy knew that if he drove, he'd win all the races. He wouldn't stop when he won, either. He'd keep going.

"He liked the sound of motors. He liked the way they rumbled deep enough to rattle his teeth in his head, and his bones beneath his skin; he liked the way they shut all the thinking out. He liked the smell of gasoline and the way it burned his nostrils. His family's neighbors had motorcycles they rode on weekends, and if he played in the front yard they'd sometimes let him sit on one with them before they roared away, leaving too much quiet behind. When they drove off, he tried to recreate the sound, making as much noise as possible until his father told him to be quiet, then to shut up, then 'For goodness sake, what does a man have to do to get some peace and quiet around here on a Saturday morning?'"

Dan paused his orbit and turned to face the storyteller. Two other kids had stopped to pay attention as well; Stella and the others continued playing on the periphery.

"The boy got his learner's permit on the very first day he was allowed. He skipped school for it rather than wait another second. He had saved his paper route money for driving lessons and a used motorbike. As soon as he had his full license, he did what he had always wanted to do: He drove as fast as he could down the highway, past all the cars, and then he kept driving forever. The end."

Uncle Bob shifted back in his chair as he finished. Dan watched him for a little longer, then launched himself again, circling the scattered toys and children faster than before.

Jeff sat back as well. "What kind of story was that?"

Stella frowned. "A deeply messed up one. That kid with the airplane—Dan Heller— drove off the interstate the summer after junior year. He was racing someone in the middle of the night and missed a curve."

"Oof. Quite the coincidence."

"Yeah. . . "

Uncle Bob started telling another story, this one about a vole living in a hole on a grassy hillside that started a conversation with the child sleeping in the hole next door.

"Do you want to watch the whole episode? Is this the one you need?"

"I think I need to look at a couple more?" She didn't know what she was looking for. "Sorry for putting you out. I don't mean to take up so much time."

"It's fine! This is interesting. The show is terrible, from any standpoint. The story was terrible, the production is terrible. I can't even decide if this whole shtick is campy bad or bad bad. Leaning toward the latter."

"I don't think there's anything redeeming," Stella said, her mind still on Dan Heller. Did his parents remember this story? "Can we look at the next one? October 30th?"

"Coming up." Jeff appeared to have forgotten she'd said she was looking for something specific, and she didn't remind him, since she still couldn't think of an appropriate detail.

Little Stella was second through the door this time, behind Tina, whose last name she didn't remember. She paused and looked out past a camera, probably looking for her mother, then kept moving when she realized more kids were coming through behind her. Head for the toys. Claim what's yours. Brontosaurus and T. rex and a blue whale. Whales were almost as cool as dinosaurs.

Tina had claimed a triceratops and looked like she wanted the brontosaurus. They sat down on the edge of the toy pit to negotiate. Uncle Bob watched them play, which gave Stella the eeriest feeling of being watched, even though she still felt like the kid on the screen wasn't her.

"So what was it like?" Jeff asked, but Stella didn't answer. Uncle Bob had started a story. He looked straight into the camera. This time it felt like he was truly looking straight at her. This was the one. She knew it.

"Once upon a time, there was a little girl who didn't know who she was. Many children don't know who they will be, and that's not unusual, but what was unusual in this case was that the girl was willing to trade who she was for who she could be, so she began to do just that. Little by little, she replaced herself with parts of other people she liked better. Parts of stories she wanted to live. Nobody lied like this girl. She believed her own stories so completely, she forgot which ones were true and which were false.

"If you've ever heard of a cuckoo bird, they lay their eggs in other birds' nests, so those birds are forced to raise them for their own. This girl was her own cuckoo, laying stories in her own head, and the heads of those around her, until even she couldn't remember which ones were true, or if there was anything left of her."

Uncle Bob went silent, watching the children play. After a minute, he started telling another story about the boy in the hill, and how happy he was whenever he had friends over to visit. That story ended, and a graphic appeared on the screen with an address for fan mail. Stella pulled a pen from her purse and wrote it down as the theme music played out.

"Are you sending him a letter?" The archivist had dropped his headphones and was watching her.

She shrugged. "Just curious."

"Is this the one, then?"

"The one?"

He frowned. "You said you wanted a copy for your mother."

"Yes! That would be lovely. This is the one she mentioned."

He pulled a DVD off a bulk spindle and rewound the tape. "You didn't say what it was like. Was he weird off camera too?"

"Yes," she said, though she didn't remember. "But he kept to himself. Just stayed in his dressing room until it was time to go on."

Jeff didn't reply, and something subtle changed about the way he interacted with her. What if there hadn't been a dressing room? He might know. When had she gotten so sloppy with her stories? Maybe it was because she was distracted. Her mother had told the truth: She'd been on a creepy TV show of which she had no memory. And what was it? Performance art? Storytelling? Fairy tales or horror? All of the above? She thanked Jeff and left.

She had just walked into her parents' house when Marco called. "Can you come back? There's something I need to show you."

She headed out to Denny's house. She paused on the step, realizing she was in nicer clothes this time. Hopefully she wouldn't be there long.

"Hey," she said when Marco answered the door. Even though she braced for the odor, it hit her hard.

He waved her in, talking as he navigated the narrow path he'd cleared up the stairs. "I thought I'd work on Denny's bedroom today, and, well. . . "

He held out an arm in the universal gesture of "go ahead," so she entered. The room had precarious ceiling-high stacks on every surface, including the floor and bed, piles everywhere except a path to an open walk-in closet. She stepped forward.

"What is that?"

"The word I came up with was 'shrine,' but I don't think that's right."

It was the sparest space in the house. She'd expected a dowel crammed end to end with clothes, straining under the weight, but the closet was empty except for—"shrine" was indeed the wrong word. This wasn't worship.

The most eye-catching piece, the thing she saw first, was a hand-painted Uncle Bob doll propped in the back corner. It looked like it had been someone else first—Vincent Price, maybe. Next to it stood a bobblehead and an action figure, both mutated from other characters, and one made of clay and plant matter, seemingly from scratch. Beside those, a black leather notebook, a pile of VHS tapes, and a single DVD. Tacked to the wall behind them, portraits of Uncle Bob in paint, in colored pencil, macaroni, photo collage, in, oh god, was that cat hair? And beside those, stills from the show printed on copier paper: Uncle Bob telling a story; Uncle Bob staring straight into the camera, an assortment of children. Her own still was toward the bottom right. Marco wasn't in any of them.

"That's the thing that guts me."

Stella turned, expecting to see Marco pointing to the art or the dolls, but she'd been too busy looking at those to notice the filthy pillow and blanket in the opposite corner. "He slept here?"

"It's the only place he could have." Marco's voice was strangled, like he was trying not to cry.

She didn't know what to say to make him feel better about his brother having lived liked this. She picked up the notebook and paged through it. Each page had a name block-printed on top, then a dense scrawl in black, then, in a different pen, something else. Not impossible to read, but difficult, writing crammed into every available inch, no space between words even. She remembered this notebook; it was the one teenage Denny always had on him.

"Take it," Marco said. "Take whatever you want. I can't do this anymore. I'm going home."

She took the notebook and the DVD, and squeezed Marco's arm, unsure whether he would want or accept a hug.

Her parents were out when she got back to their house, so she slipped the DVD into their machine. It didn't work. She took it upstairs and tried it in her mother's old desktop computer instead. The computer made a sound like a jet plane taking off, and opened a menu with one episode listed: March 13, 1980.

It started the same way all the other episodes had started. The kids, Uncle Bob. Denny was in this one; Stella had an easier time spotting him now that she knew who to look for. He went for the train set again, laying out wooden tracks alongside a kid Stella didn't recognize.

Uncle Bob started a story. "Once upon a time, there was a boy who grew very big very quickly. He felt like a giant when he stood next to his classmates. People stopped him in hallways and told him he was going to the wrong grade's room. His mother complained that she had to buy him new clothes constantly, and even though she did it with affection, he was too young to realize she didn't blame him. He felt terrible about it. Tried to hide that his shoes squeezed his toes or his pants were too short again.

"His parents' friends said, 'Somebody's going to be quite an athlete,' but he didn't feel like an athlete. More than that, he felt like he had grown so fast his head had been pushed out of his body, so he was constantly watching it from someplace just above. Messages he sent to his arms and legs took ages to get there. Everything felt small and breakable in his hands, so that when his best friend's dog had puppies he refused to hold them, though he loved when they climbed all over him.

"The boy had a little brother. His brother was everything he wasn't. Small, lithe, fearless. His mother told him to protect his brother, and he took that responsibility seriously. That was something that didn't take finesse. He could do that.

"Both boys got older, but their roles didn't change. The older brother watched his younger brother. When the smaller boy was bullied, his brother pummeled the bullies. When the younger brother made the high school varsity basketball team as a point guard his freshman year, his older brother made the team as center, even though he hated sports.

"Time passed. The older brother realized something strange. Every time he thought he had something of his own, it turned out it was his brother's. He blinked one day and lost two entire years. How was he the older brother, the one who got new clothes, who reached new grades first, and yet still always following? Even his own story had spun out to describe him in relation to his sibling.

"And then, one day, the boy realized he had nothing at all. He was his brother's giant shadow. He was a forward echo, a void. Nothing was his. All he could do was watch the world try to catch up with him, but he was always looking backward at it. All he could do—"

"No," said Denny.

Stella had forgotten the kids were there, even though they were on camera the entire time. Denny had stood and walked over to where Uncle Bob was telling the story. With Uncle Bob sitting, Denny was tall enough to look him in the eye.

For the first time, Uncle Bob turned away from the camera. He assessed Denny with an unsettling smile.

"No," Denny said again.

Now Uncle Bob glanced around as if he was no longer amused, as if someone needed to pull this child off his set. It wasn't a tantrum, though. Denny wasn't misbehaving, unless interrupting a story violated the rules.

Uncle Bob turned back to him. "How would you tell it?"

Denny looked less sure now.

"I didn't think so," said the host. "But maybe that's enough of that story. Unless you want to tell me how you think it ends?"

Denny shook his head.

"But you know?"

Denny didn't move.

"Maybe that's enough. We'll see. In any case, I have other stories to tell. We haven't checked in on my hill today."

Uncle Bob began to catch his audience up on the continuing adventure of the boy who'd been dug out of the hillside. The other children kept playing, and Denny? Denny looked straight into the camera, then walked off the set. He never came back. Stella didn't have any proof, but she was pretty sure this must have been the last episode Denny took part in. He looked like a kid who was done. His expression was remarkably similar to the one she'd just seen on Marco's face.

And what was that story? Unlike Dan Heller's driving story, unlike the one she'd started thinking of as her own, this one wasn't close to true. Sure, Denny had been a big kid, but neither he nor Marco played basketball. He never protected Marco from bullies. "Nothing was his" hardly fit the man whose house she'd cleaned.

Except that night, falling asleep, Stella couldn't help but think that when she compared what she knew of Denny with that story, it seemed like Denny had set out to prove the story untrue. What would a person do if told as a child that nothing was his?

Collect all the things. Leave his little brother to fend for himself. Fight it on every level possible.

Was it a freak occurrence that Denny happened to be listening when Uncle Bob told that story? Why was she assuming the story was about him at all? Maybe it was coincidence. There was nothing connecting the children to the stories except her own sense that they were connected, and Denny's reaction on the day he quit.

She hadn't heard hers when Uncle Bob told it, but she'd internalized it nonetheless. How much was true? She wasn't a cuckoo bird. Her reinventions had never hurt anyone.

Marco called that night to ask if she wanted to grab one more meal before she left town, but she said she had too much to do before her flight. That was true, as was the fact that she didn't want to see him again. Didn't want to ask him if he'd watched the March 13 show. Didn't want to tell him his brother had consciously refused him protection.

—————

She should have gone straight to the airport in the morning, but the fan mail address she'd written down was in the same direction, if she took the back way instead of the highway. Why a show like that might get fan mail was a question for another time. This was strictly a trip to satisfy her curiosity. She drove through town, then a couple of miles past, into the network of county roads.

The mailbox stood full, overflowing, a mat of moldering envelopes around its cement base. A weather-worn "For Sale" sign had sunk into the soft ground closer to the drainage ditch. Stella turned onto the long driveway, and only after she'd almost reached the house did it occur to her that if she'd looked at the mail, she might have found his surname.

The fields on either side of the lane were tangled with weeds that didn't look like they cared what season it was. The house, a tiny stone cottage, was equally weed-choked, but strangely familiar. If she owned this house, she'd never let it get like this, but it didn't look like it belonged to anyone anymore. She tried a story on for size: "While I was visiting my parents, I went for a drive in the country, and I found the most darling cottage. My parents are getting older, and I had the thought that I should move closer to them. The place needed a little work, so I got it for a song."

She liked that one.

Nobody answered when she knocked. The door was locked, and the windows were too dirty to see through, and she couldn't shake the feeling that if she looked through he'd be sitting there, staring straight at her, waiting.

She walked around back and found the hill.

It was a funny little hill, not entirely natural looking, but what did she know? The land behind the house sloped gently upward, then steeper, hard beneath the grass but not rocky. From the slope, the cottage looked even smaller, the fields wilder, tangled, like something from a fairy tale. The view, too, felt strangely familiar.

She knew nothing more about the man who called himself Uncle Bob, but as she walked into the grass she realized this must be the hill from his stories, the stories he told when he wasn't telling stories about the children. How did they go? She thought back to that first episode she'd watched in Denny's basement.

Once upon a time, there was a boy whose family planted him in a hillside, so that he took over the entire hillside, like a weed. They dug me out of the hillside on my thirteenth birthday. It's good to divide rhizomes to give them room to grow.

That story made her remember the notebook she'd taken from Denny's house, and she rummaged for it in her purse. The notebook was alphabetical, printed in a nearly microscopic hand other than the page headings, dense. She found one for Dan Heller. She couldn't decipher the whole story, but the first line was obviously *Once upon a time, there was a little boy who wanted to go fast.* She knew the rest. In blue pen, it said what she had said to Jeff the archivist: motorcycle wreck, alongside the date. That one was easy since she knew enough to fill in the parts she struggled to read. The others were trickier. There was no page for Marco, but Denny had made one for himself. It had Uncle Bob's shadow-brother story but no update at the bottom. Nothing at all for the years between.

Who else had been on the show? Lee Pool had a page. So did Addie Chapel, who as far as Stella knew had followed in her mother's footsteps and become a doctor. Chris Bethel, and beside him, Tina Bevins, the other dinosaur lover. If she spent enough time staring, maybe Denny's handwriting would decipher itself.

She was afraid to turn to her own page. She knew it had to be there, on the page before Dan Heller, but she couldn't bring herself to look, until she did. She expected this one, like Dan's, like Denny's own, to be easier to decipher because she knew how it would go.

October 30, 1982. Once upon a time, there was a little girl who didn't know who she was. Many children don't know who they will be, and that's not unusual, but what was unusual in this case was that the girl was willing to trade who she was for who she could be, so she began to do just that. Little by little, she replaced herself with parts of other people she liked better. Parts of stories she wanted to live. Nobody lied like this girl. She believed her own stories so completely, she forgot which ones were true and which were false.

If you've ever heard of a cuckoo bird, they lay their eggs in other birds' nests, so those birds are forced to raise them for their own. This girl was her own cuckoo, laying stories in her own head, and the heads of those around her, until even she couldn't remember which ones were true, or if there was anything left of her.

There was more. Another episode, maybe? She had no idea how many she'd been on, and her research had been shoddy. Maybe every story was serialized like the boy in the hill. It took her a while to make out the next bit.

November 20, 1982. Our cuckoo girl left the nest one day to spread her wings. When she returned, she didn't notice that nobody had missed her. She named a place where she had been, and they accepted it as truth. She made herself up, as she had always done, convincing even herself in the process. Everything was true, or true enough.

Below that, in blue pen, a strange assortment of updates from her life, as observed by Denny. Marco's eleventh birthday party, when she'd given him juggling balls. Graduation from middle school. The summer they'd both worked at the pool, and Marco'd gotten heatstroke and thrown up all the Kool-Aid they tried to put in him, Kool-Aid red, straight into the pool like a shark attack. The time she and Marco had tried making out on his bed, only he had started giggling, and she had gotten offended, and when she stood she tripped over a juggling ball and broke her toe. All the games their friends had played in Marco's basement: I've Never, even though they all knew what everyone else had done; Two Truths and a Lie, though they had all grown up together and knew everything about each other; Truth or Dare, though everyone was tired of truth, truth was terrifying, everyone chose dare, always. The Batman premiere. The prom amoeba, the friends who went together, all of whom she'd lost touch with. High school graduation. Concrete memories, things she knew were as real as anything that had ever happened in her life. Denny shouldn't have known about some of these things, but now she pictured him there, somewhere, holding this notebook, watching them, taking notes, always looking like he had something to say but he couldn't say it.

Below those stories he'd written: *Once there was a girl who got lost and when she found her way home she realized she'd arrived back without herself, and her parents didn't even notice the difference.* Which couldn't be her story at all; she hadn't been on the episodes he'd been on.

After graduation, he had no more updates on her. She paged forward, looking at the blue ink. Everyone had updates within the last year, everyone except for Denny, everyone who was still alive; the ones who weren't had death dates. Everyone except her. She tried to imagine what from her adult life she would have added, given the chance, or what an internet search on her name would provide, or what her parents would tell someone who asked what she was doing. Surely there was something. Parents were supposed to be your built-in hype machines.

She pulled out her phone to call Marco, but the battery was dead. Just as well, since she was suddenly afraid to try talking to anyone at all. She returned to the notebook and flipped toward the back. U for Uncle Bob.

Once upon a time, there was a boy whose family planted him in a hill-side, so that he took over the entire hillside, like a weed. They dug me out of the hillside on my thirteenth birthday. It's good to divide rhizomes to give them room to grow.

This story was long, eight full pages in tiny script, with episode dates interspersed. At the end, in red ink, this address. She pictured Denny driving out here, exploring the cottage, looking up at the hill. If she ever talked to Marco again, she'd tell him that what he'd found in Denny's closet wasn't a shrine; it was Denny's attempt to conjure answers to something unanswerable.

She put the notebook back in her purse and kept walking. Three quarters of the way up the hill she came to a large patch where the grass had been churned up. She put her hand in the soil and it felt like the soil grasped her hand back.

Her parents said she didn't visit often enough, but now she couldn't remember ever having visited them before, or them visiting her. She couldn't remember if she'd ever left this town at all. She lived in Chicago, or did she? She'd told Marco as much, told him other things she knew not to be true, but what was true, then? What did she do for a living? If she left this hill and went to the airport, would she even have a reservation? If she caught her plane, would she find she had anything or anyone there at all? Where was there? She pulled her hand free and put it to her mouth: The soil tasted familiar.

"I walked down to the cottage that would be mine some-day"—that felt nice, even if she wasn't sure she believed it—"and then past the cottage, through the town, and into my parents' house. They believed me when I said where I'd been. They fit me into their lives and only occasionally looked at me like they didn't quite know how I'd gotten there." That felt good. True. She sat in the dirt and leaned back on her hands, and felt the hill pressing back on them.

She could still leave: walk back to her rental car, drive to the airport, take the plane to the place where she surely had a career, a life, even if she couldn't quite recall it. She thought that until she looked back at where the rental car should have been and realized it wasn't there. She had no shoes on, and her feet were black with dirt, pebbled, scratched. She dug them into the soil, rooting with her toes.

How had Denny broken his story? He'd refused it. Whether his life was better or worse for it remained a different question. To break her story, she'd have to walk back down the hill and reconstruct herself the right way round. She thought of the cuckoo girl, the lost girl, the cuckoo girl, so many stories to keep straight.

The soil reached her forearms now, her calves. The top layer was sun-warmed, and underneath, a busy cool stillness made up of millions of insects, of the roots of the grass, of the rhizomes of the boy who had called this hillside home before she had. She'd walk back to town when she was ready, someday, maybe, but she was in no hurry. She'd heard worse stories than hers, and anyway, if she didn't like it she'd make a new one, a better one, a true one.

WHERE YOU LINGER

BY BONNIE JO STUFFLEBEAM

PUBLISHED BY UNCANNY
MAGAZINE

W e all make mistakes. As I sit on the floor of my bedroom, surrounded by the journals I kept in high school and in my twenties, and fill out the doctor's form, I tally mistakes in the corner of the paper. Before marriage, before Dover's and my quiet nights trading words and sharing thoughts between binged television episodes, relationships were tumultuous. My tallies reflect this. Particularly the final tally, the one that got me into this mess to begin with. The doctor didn't ask me for a tally, just brief descriptions of all sexual encounters, mistakes or not, to jog my memory along with the age in which I experienced them. But I need to prove to myself that the dissolution of my marriage wasn't unique, that it hadn't been a surprise. I should have seen it coming.

NOTES ON SEVERAL PIECES OF PARTLY-CRUMPLED PAPER, CRINKLED WITH COFFEE STAINS

#1 (Age 16)

Anne, the first woman I made love to, tasted like sunlight and sweat. We kissed behind a half-open door at the house where she lived with her father and stepmother. Afterward we went for Chinese food. We were together, off-and-on, for two years. We lied and cheated and searched through one another's texts. We cooked each other Foreman grill chicken and pasta with four types of cheese. We raised one another in homes where we otherwise went unnoticed.

––––––––

#2 (Age 18)

I lost my virginity twice. First, with the woman of sunlight and a Superman tattoo across her back. Second, with Mario, a Czech cigarette smoker, a college boy, a smooth talker who asked me to be his girlfriend after knowing me for one day.

We fucked in hotel rooms. We ate Whataburger after. We smoked weed from a pipe that looked like a metal cigarette and performed rainy picnics in the park. The sex was a beautiful pain. He told me I would leave him for a woman. I left him for Anne; she no longer tasted like sunlight when she begged me to come back.

"I slept with my ex too, " he said when I told him. "I don't even care."

––––––––

#3 (Age 18)

I wasn't done with men's beautiful pain. The third person I slept with, Daniel, was a latent schizophrenic with hippie hair and a wallet stuffed with acid hits. Lucifer in the sky with diamonds, dancing half-naked in the front yard of a friend's house while his parents were on vacation.

He said he wanted to take it slow. I waited a week to ask for what I wanted; for me a week was slow. Not for him. After we broke up, we argued about timing during his late-night surprise appearances at my door. He told me I'd get pregnant before the year was out. He called for five years after I stopped answering. On my 23rd birthday, I changed my number.

#4 (Age 18)

It wasn't good. I squeezed my eyes shut. It wasn't good.

#5 (Age 18)

We both had boyfriends when we first met in that final raging year of high school. Natalie gave me a massage on a crowded downtown street. Once we were both in college, she called again. I went to her without a thought. We sat in her apartment, as far across the couch from one another as possible, but when I got up to leave, she shoved me against the door and kissed me harder than I'd ever been kissed.

I kneaded her soft thighs in her cozy bed. She rescued me from a bad drunk in the company of my Dungeons & Dragons friends. I puked in her stripper shoes. We drank mimosas in my dorm. She only called me when she got lonely.

#6 (Age 18)

I remember Christopher crisp as a Facebook photo: red curls, a single mole on his neck, an affinity for exclamation. I met him at a National Organization for the Reform of Marijuana Laws meeting, which I attended in the hopes of finding a new dealer. The redhead didn't deal but kept a six-foot bong on his mantle.

He quoted scenes from Catch-22, pillow talk with a prostitute. I watched him play football games on his Wii. We played beer pong with his friends. Once I puked in his sink: spaghetti with mushrooms and peppermint ice cream. Every time he asked me over, I went. Then he stopped asking.

#7 (Age 19)

So I fucked his friend Simon over a game of strip poker. "Pretty good for a dude, huh?" he said. It wasn't.

#8 (Age 19)

Simon's friend Oliver was better, a sweet blond who wrote bad poetry and lived in a private dorm next to Anne's college apartment. I visited him after Anne. I visited Anne after him, soaking wet from rain. The cookie taste of him still lingered on my lips when I slipped my tongue between her legs.

"What do you want?" the blond asked.

I didn't lie. "I want Anne to leave her girlfriend and come back to me."

"Then we have no business being together."

#9 (Age 19)

But Anne didn't love me anymore. I sweated out her sunlight in the dark of my room in the house I shared with two roommates, a dozen fevers moving through me with no further explanations. When I was well again, I befriended Anne and her girlfriend, Cathryn, and Anne's roommate, Dana, who was fucking Cathryn too.

I didn't tell Anne that I drove each weekend to swallow bitter pills and fuck a blue-haired candy kid, Xander, king of the club. His last name remains unknown. We had nightly phone sex. I drove an hour to be in his bed every now and again and stayed as long as it took to finish. He knew nothing about me. It was easier to delete his number when Anne came calling, came crying. She had found out about Cathryn and Dana.

We moved Anne out of her apartment and into the home I

shared. She wrote "I love you" in paint on my desk. We didn't make it official.

––––––––

#10 (Age 19)

At least that was my excuse when I met the most beautiful woman I've ever loved, cherry cheeks and gruff throat and the cutest drunk smile I've ever seen. Meredith and I kissed for the first time in a dance club against the red brick of a pillar.

It was time to leave the sunshine behind, but we always hold on to first love longer than we should.

Too drunk, we wound up on a bare mattress in an empty room in the house I now shared with Anne. We woke to Anne screaming in the door. I didn't remember a thing.

After a long night of fighting, I pledged myself to Anne. I tried to be friends with those cherry cheeks, tried to keep her around, but Meredith left my house one night and said she wouldn't come back.

I cut ties with Anne the next day in a brief tearless goodbye. I loved Meredith even when she told me she was moving up north. We didn't last that long. Even before she moved, her clothes smelled like Anne's ex-girlfriend Cathryn, my first enemy, my only enemy. When Meredith begged me back, I stood my ground.

––––––––

#11 (Age 19)

Nothing counts on Halloween. Especially not a woman you forget before you even know her.

––––––––

#12 (Age 19) & #13 (Age 19)

Once upon a time I loved a woman who smelled like

sunshine. Later she loved a woman with long hair and a dark past who would become an enemy and a friend; isn't there a word for that? They lived with Dana, the daughter of a pastor. Dana and Cathryn, they were made for each other, or at least for that part of their lives.

I had taken a lover when I had a lover, first with Daniel, then with Meredith. Did I deserve full-circle? Cathryn was so full of mystery no one could resist her, Meredith least of all. I didn't want Cathryn. I was the only one. But Dana was a beauty in her dark apartment where I rode my bike as soon as she heard about our girlfriends' liaisons in party bathrooms.

"It's okay," I said to Dana.

"Fucking bitch," she said.

We ate burgers and went our separate ways. One night later Dana and Cathryn were back together. Meredith and I stayed apart. I fucked Dana and Cathryn both instead, in a room with no curtains on the windows. Pushed and pulled between the woman I wanted and the woman I hated, I didn't belong.

———————

#14 (Age 19)

Jeremiah was covered in tattoos. When he asked me to dinner, I never went, but I showed up at his apartment late at night to smoke weed and get naked. He left the TV on all the time and I heard Charlie Sheen's crazy laugh as I fucked him. Too much noise is still too much noise and when I left, I never came back.

Meredith moved to Colorado and I cried a lot.

———————

#15 (Age 20)

Here is where I tried again. Here is where I walked with a man eight years my senior who didn't know what he wanted and wanted what he didn't know. Michael and I played board games on his carpet. I wanted him all the time and he couldn't give that much of himself. I was in a hurry, wanted to move too fast, wanted to get the hard parts out of the way, wanted to experience it all then and there and he drank too much anyway.

––––––––

#16 (Age 20)

It was Grayson I wanted, a boy who left hickeys all over my neck. A friend of a best friend. A bowl cut, like the Beatles.

When I got too drunk, I asked Grayson to walk me back. I stumbled under a tree and he caught me, kissed me. We snuck into my house.

"Your bed's full of books," he said. I pushed them off. I'd been sleeping alone for weeks.

"You and your girls," he said.

"Boys too," I said. I kissed him again.

I don't remember the rest. I blacked out. He left before sunrise. The next day I heard nothing from him. At a friend's place a week later, he called his new girlfriend by my name.

His friend Eliot looked nothing like him. He kissed me on the couch in the room where Grayson sat with his new girlfriend. He drove me to his place without asking if that was where I wanted to go.

When we finished he jumped on his computer and played video games as though I wasn't there.

––––––––

#17 (Age 20)

I waited because they told me I should wait. The violinist was hard to get. Her name was Dover.

"Like the cliffs?" I said when she introduced herself in the middle of my roommate's party.

"Got any weed?" she said.

She was sitting in my house like she belonged there, cross-legged in my dining table chair with her ponytail and her bright red leather pants.

"No," I said. "What kind of guest doesn't bring their own weed?"

But when she asked my roommate for my number, I relented.

The first time we made love we were in a lake at a state park, past the time we were supposed to be in the water. She commented each night on the moon and its changes. She offered up everything I never wanted to lose.

I loved her with everything I had to lose.

When I lost her, ten years after we took our vows, I lost everything I loved.

#18 (Age 35)

There are a million excuses I could give. Fifteen years of monogamy pass, and you start to itch for the excitement of a stranger's hands, for the unraveling of a mystery, peeling back their words to reveal what's really underneath. You feel unwanted, after years of being looked at with the gentler gaze of long-term lust. You feel the need to return to that younger self.

You're a worthless piece of shit. You're everything you never wanted to be.

IN THE OFFICE OF THE DOCTOR WITH NO DEGREES ON THE WALLS

"That's everyone?" the doctor asks.

"Yes," I say. "It's a lot, isn't it?"

"Do you feel like it's a lot?"

"Oh, come on. It's a lot."

"Huh." The doctor taps her pen against her clipboard. "Then it must be a lot."

"Honestly? You think so?"

"Honestly, Ms. Moore?"

I nod.

"I've seen more."

I shift in my seat, cross and uncross my legs, wipe my palms on my thighs.

"That's everyone, you said? Are you very sure?"

"Yes. I kept good records."

"That's everyone you experienced penetration with in any of its forms? That's a finger in the vagina, the anus. A finger in the mouth. A penis in the mouth. A tongue in the vagina. You want as many as possible."

Fuck. Blowjobs. Blowjobs probably counted. I hadn't recorded all of those encounters in my journals, not as meticulously.

"That's all of them," I say.

She studies my notes. "The good news is you didn't leave a lot of time between them. That's good. Fewer gaps means smaller steps." She scribbles something on her form. "You remember how this works?"

"Yes."

"Tell me. Say it back to me. I want to be sure."

"The memories are a map, right? I follow memory to memory. Each one is like a stepping stone."

"Yes, that's fairly accurate. Are you certain you got everyone? As I said, you want as many stones as possible so that you do not fall through."

"What happens if I fail?"

"You must start again"

"That's all? I won't die or get lost or go into a coma or something?"

"You start over. This means we start from the beginning. Your fee covers one attempt. If you can pay again, we can go again. But I suspect you cannot pay again."

I think of my bank account, that red number. I pulled it all to come here. I sold off Dover's violin.

"You assume correctly," I say.

She hands me the clipboard. "Is there anyone you want to add?"

I add three oral-only encounters. She takes the clipboard back. It's not everyone, but it's as close as I can get.

"Much better," she says.

The machine looks like an MRI, but it closes over my head like a coffin. It whirs around me, strange lights flashing in my eyes until I squeeze them shut.

"Don't," the doctor says over the speaker. "You need to follow the light with your eyes."

I follow it back-and-forth, back-and-forth.

"It's not working," I say.

"Wait for it."

I wait. "I don't feel anything," I say.

"Wait—"

And then, yes, there it is: that smell of sunlight in my nostrils. The graze of my nose on skin so pale it's as though it's never seen the sun. We're in Anne's sloppy bed at her parents' house, behind a closed door that her stepmother will later scold us for closing.

She is thrashing underneath me, but I know from the future that she's faking it.

I faked it too, sometimes. I grip her skin and remember why I loved her. But also why I stopped. Even this first time, there is a lie beneath the surface. So many lies. So much work to pry them apart. An onion that's rotting underneath.

Afterward we lay in one another's arms and giggle and kiss all the empty spaces.

"It won't always be like this," I say.

We fall asleep, young and exhausted and covered in a smell I'm smelling for the first time. I think, this is enough. And it is, enough. No more, no less. Nice to be loved again. But not the reason I'm here.

The doctor told me how to jump. I could stay for the whole of a relationship, reliving each and every memory, until my time with that person was finished, until our body-to-body contact had been extinguished. Until the day and hour and minute of our last time. Then, I would no longer have a choice. I would be moved to the next whether I wanted it or not. It is possible, she said, to get lost somewhere you did not intend to stay. Be wary where you linger. The memory is a clever trap.

I jump from Anne to #2, that sharp pain between my legs. I lean my head back against my pillow, arch my back, do everything I'm supposed to do. I don't feel the explosive tremor through my body. I don't fake it, not yet jaded enough to pretend at satisfaction.

"Look, we're fucking," Mario says, enamored and amazed.

"No shit," I say.

Then I'm onto #3 with his clumsy drunk fingers. It's nice to see Daniel half-sane again. It's also painful, to see a ghost I finished mourning over two decades ago.

It's disorienting, jumping from place to place like this.

I land at #4. But this time it's different. I'm in a dark room in a foreign house, a place I long ago blocked out of my memory. I'm standing at the foot of a bed while another version of me pushes at the body in bed with her.

"I'm so tired," she says to the half-stranger, the man I have tried to forget.

I intended to jump immediately on from this one, to leave this room so quickly my eyes wouldn't even have time to adjust. But this isn't what the others have been like. I'm frozen by the sight of this other me.

I don't think about the fact that these are just memories, that the me in the bed is in no danger because it isn't real. I scramble up onto the bed and push the guy out of the way, pull my own body out of the blankets and then out of the room, down the hallway, onto his freshly manicured lawn.

He doesn't follow us. He's too drunk, almost as bad off as we are. It's no excuse, but it's the truth.

"Who are you?" the other me slurs.

"I'm here to help you. You have to get the fuck away from that guy."

"He wouldn't listen to me," she says.

"You should leave," I say.

"I'm too drunk to drive. My keys are in the house still." The other me rummages through her pockets and comes up empty-handed. I look for my car until I find it in the driveway, my old black sports car, beautiful and sleek and a piece of shit even then.

"Wait here," I say.

I sneak inside, back into his room. The asshole's passed out, mouth open, splayed across the bed. I grab my keys off the floor. I grab my favorite necklace from where it was slung across the room. I draw a cock on the back of his neck where he might not notice it for a good long while. It's the best quick revenge I can think of.

"I'll drive you," I say to myself. Already I feel myself slipping, feel the ground falling out from underneath me. When we get to the car, the ground is translucent underneath me. "Fuck," I say. I reach out and grab hold of myself. "Don't let go," I say.

And as fast as a sunrise when you're not expecting it, we're at #5, both versions of me, entwined with Natalie in a mess of limbs and tongues.

"You're so hot," Natalie moans. "You're both so fucking hot."

I untangle myself and struggle from the bed. The other me moves to-and-fro, too drunk to realize her deer-in-headlights expression is still pasted over her face. Natalie kisses her across her shoulders, across her neck, across the bridge of her nose and cheeks.

Natalie laughs, then falls away. "I needed that," she says. "I really did. You Pisces sure know how to make a girl come." She closes her eyes. "I'm glad you came over," she whispers as she drifts off to sleep.

I remember: we could never stay awake when we were together. Even the other me is falling into her own sleep, as unworried about her new location as I ever was in that time. I pull her from the bed and shake her awake.

"You have to stick with it," I say, leading her through the bedroom door into Natalie's living room, the floor strewn with astrology books and tarot cards. She had read my cards before we went to the bed; they were full of swords and cups, difficulties and loves.

"Where are we?" the other me says.

"We're safe here. She's wild but kind." I eye my camera sitting on her coffee table. I think about picking it up but I'm already fucking with the memory enough so I leave it be, knowing I'll never see it again. "Just maybe don't leave your stuff here."

"I'm so tired." The other me clings to my shirt. "I can barely stand up. Can we go to sleep, please?"

I'm tired, too, so tired I can't make sense of the situation. I know I need to figure out what to do with the other me: what happens if I leave her in this memory? What happens if I keep taking her with me? Already, like faded scars, what remains of that night with #4 is falling away. The doctor did warn me, though I was too desperate to listen, that moving through memories might change them irrevocably. But what really occurred, in your past, she said, that stays the same.

This place is safer than most. Natalie won't mind if we sleep over. She won't wake in the night and demand anything of us. In the morning we'll go out for crepes.

"You can sleep in there if you like," I say. "The bed is nice and comfortable. I'll take the couch."

"Thank you," she says. "Thank you."

She shuts the door behind her. I make sure the front is locked. I pick up some of Natalie's things and stretch across the couch as best as I'm able. She has no extra blankets, so I pull a discarded coat over my body. So I don't forget, I repeat the violinist's name again and again: Dover, Dover, Dover, until the lullaby of it pulls me under.

I returned to my memories because I cannot live in my realities. People give many different reasons for going through with the procedure—to cure PTSD, to see a dead loved one a final time, because they think they can change things even though the doctors tell them they cannot—but they all boil down the same, don't they? They cannot live in their reality.

I at least was honest about this. The doctor appreciated my honesty, I think. She didn't ask for much more than I put down on her paper. She didn't try to talk me out of it, which I'd heard of some doctors doing for patients without referrals.

I'm going to ride this all the way to the end. I am going to be in Dover's arms again. Because there was something in me then that she loved more than anything in the world. I need that back if I'm ever going to get her to talk to me again.

It's been three months since she last answered my calls. Three months is a long time to be without someone. Three months is too long to cling to old love.

Logically, I know this. But I dreamt about her every night. I remembered her every day.

To be bound to nostalgia, that's an illness deserving of a name, in need of a cure.

In the morning, my other self shakes me awake. I stare into her face, at her smooth skin free from sun spots, her unstained teeth. She doesn't look like she had a rough night. Sure, I had saved her from the worst of it, but shouldn't the very closeness to tragedy induce a fear of the world? Like the times I nearly but didn't wreck my car?

But yes, the time I did wreck it proved more difficult to forget.

"Morning, chip off the chipper block," I say. My back screams as I sit up. "Where's our lady friend?"

"She went to get pancakes," she says. "I like her a lot."

"Yeah," I say. "We did think we might be able to love her for a time, didn't we?"

"Can I ask you something?" she says, sitting at the foot of the couch only inches from my feet. "What are we doing here? What is this?" She runs her hands up and down her bare legs. "I don't feel right here. But also I love it here."

I fold myself into the couch. "I do, too," I say. "Which means I should go. I need to go."

"So soon?" she says. "We just got here."

"We have somewhere else to be."

"Can we eat first?" She clutches her stomach. "I'm starving."

"You're not coming with me." I untuck myself and slip on my shoes.

"Of course I am! Where else would I go?"

"Stay here." My leather jacket, the one the memory me left on Natalie's floor, makes my skin itch beneath it. "You'll be happy here, for a while. Then you'll move along. And along again. And again and again." I grab up my old phone and check through the contacts, looking for the next in line. He isn't there yet. No matter. I don't need to call before moving to the first time we fucked; I'll already be there. I grin. He was good in bed, the redhead.

"I don't want that," she says. "I'm too tired for that. Can I come with you instead?"

Well, fuck. I can't leave myself where she doesn't want to be. She'll like the redhead. I'm sure she'll want to stay with him the way I always wanted to stay with him. After he stopped talking to me, I was sure my heart was broken, sure I'd had my first brush with near-loving a man.

"Come on then," I say. "Grab a snack bar from the kitchen." I watch the door. "If she comes back, we're never getting out of here alive."

Natalie was always aggressive with her goodbyes: those hard, knee-numbing kisses against the cold wall a memory I used to call up when fucking long-term partners, remembering the excitement of being wanted with such authority.

We disappear as the door's handle rattles. The noise becomes the knock of my head against the wood of a dresser, Christopher pushing into me from above. I grip his pink skin and moan. He doesn't notice that my head's hitting his dresser, softly but audibly, and this, too, is a turn-on: sex so rough it hurts. I'll walk the next morning on throbbing legs.

The other me, this time, is sitting at Christopher's computer desk. She's clicking through his music. My timelines, somehow, are crossing; this is what I would do after sex sometimes. The redhead introduced me to Bob Dylan, to the Band, to a hundred other all-male bands. He was never concerned with feminism; his house was woman-free except for me. I got a pass because I talked about women with the worst of them. Because I won games of beer pong too. Because I didn't ask to change the channel from football. (Though I should have; I hated football even then.)

"I've never heard of any of this music," she says. I think she's talking to me, but I can't be bothered about music right now.

"Hush," I say from beneath him. "You have no idea how much I missed this."

After he's come, he holds me and tickles me and kisses my neck until my skin is so sensitive I beg him to stop.

"You've never heard of Bob Dylan?" he says to the me at the computer. "What have you been doing with your life?"

He puts on an album: The Freewheelin'.

"Play `Don't Think Twice'," I say with a hint of malice, though in all seriousness it's the only one of Dylan's songs that ever meant something deeper to me. I remember the redhead burning the CD for me, putting it on as I drove away from his house one morning. How beautiful was Dylan's pain! Then, later, it became the album I put on to commune with the ghost of Christopher's lost affection. I took a Bob Dylan class my second semester at college. Turns out he was a terrible sexist.

"This is beautiful," she says to Christopher. He beams and kisses the top of her head, like she's his fucking sister.

"This is Dylan!" Such excitement. I forgot how much of a fan he was, how much he loved the things he loved, how far I always was from being one of those things.

But when he crawls back in bed with me, I stick my hand in his red curls and smell the sweet toxic weed smell of his oversized sweater.

"He's cute," she says. "What happens with him?"

"We both want the same thing," I say, "But he talks me into wanting something more. And then decides against it."

He nuzzles his head in my lap. "Who are you talking to?" he says. "You're missing the best parts of the album."

"I'm talking to myself," I say, and both versions of myself laugh at the terrible joke.

We stick around with the redhead for another fuck. After that we drive back to my dorm room. When I pulled her out of her timeline, she had just moved in, and I wanted her to see the mess living alone became in a brief time. I'd written the address to a party on the wall in red paint. I'd been painting cartoons on canvas, love stories I was trying to make sense of: me as a mermaid, Pisces in literalization, with the Virgo sunlight-first-love pulling me from the water, saving me from drowning. A giant Alice holding on to the stem of a mushroom with a candy cane.

"Drugs?" she says. "We promised we would never do drugs."

"Weed is a drug, believe it or not," I say. "If you remember correctly, we also said we would never do dudes."

"That's fair." She picks up my copy of Moby Dick. "You're still not done with this?"

"I'm done," I say. "I'm twenty years older than you. If I can say I accomplished anything in life, it's that I read Moby Dick."

The other me slides into my desk chair. "Twenty years?"

"Resist the temptation to ask me questions," I say.

"Why are you doing this?" she asks. "Are you going to leave me behind eventually?"

I kneel at her feet. "I'll pick a good one for you," I say. "But Dover is mine. I want her to myself. You'll understand once you get to her. It's better than first love. Better than flimsy fucks. Better than the guy in the fancy ass private dorm."

"Private dorm?" She wrinkles her nose.

"Remember that. Treasure him. Oh, and Meredith. Treasure both of them. You'll remember them vividly for the rest of your life."

She plugs her ears with her fingers. "No more," she says. "I trust you. If you have to leave me, leave me with private dorm dude or Meredith. But no spoilers!"

"No spoilers, no questions," I say. We shake on it.

When we arrive at #7, the other me bursts out laughing.

"What is this room?" she says. On one wall he's hung a giant poster of a woman straddling a massive nugget of weed. "Fucking stoner dudes."

"It's good for a guy, isn't it?" Simon says, that infamous line.

The other me rolls her eyes and crosses her arms. "Now this is a poor decision. That other stuff? Small potatoes."

"Shut up," I say, pushing him away and moving from bed.

"You made fun of me," she says. "It's only fair."

"I made fun of both of us. This is every bit your decision as it is mine."

She shakes her head. "I don't think so. The others I got. This one? We're not even attracted to him. This one is a sad fuck plain and simple. I don't like sad fucks."

"You think I do?"

"I think you can't help it. It's not always about joy for you."

"Jesus," I say. "When did you become so insightful?"

"I have the added advantage," she says, "of meeting the me I don't want to be."

Simon massages my shoulders with clammy hands. "I can't believe I fucked a gay chick," he said.

"An entry for your journal," I say.

"Don't talk like that to him," she says, sliding down beside him. "He likes you, and that's the only thing he's guilty of."

I turn and kiss him, to be nice. "You were good," I say, "for a guy."

"At least you were truthful with him," she says of #8, Oliver the poet. "That's the best I can say about that shit show. I've never met a needier guy."

"They're needier than we thought they'd be, men," I say. "It takes some getting used to."

At #9, Xander, myself and I forget him and dance until we're so sweaty we look like sea monsters freshly risen from the ocean. We stand in the bathroom mirror and watch the sweat drip to the floor.

Though I let her have Xander when the night is through.

"This one is fun," I said. "No muss, no fuss."

She spots his blue hair in the crowd. "That's him?" She laughs. "Is he wearing makeup?"

"He always saves the last dance for you. Every club night. Go get it."

I wait in his living room with the rolling kids, their pupils black saucers swallowing the skies of their eyes. They pass me a tab. I pop it and lean back into the couch. Might as well go with the times. We pass a joint as the lights go blurry, and they talk about the blue-haired boy.

"He saved my life," says a teenage girl. I remember this happening; I was there, with her in the kitchen. She thought she'd had too many pills. He gave her water and food and calmed her down. I like helping people, he said when she was better again, the revelation lighting him up like a fucking Christmas tree of cliché.

But damn was he hot with his plastic bracelets up and down his arms. I liked to imagine him in class, raising his hand, the bracelets falling together down his arm.

When she comes out of the room, she's white as a Mud Flap. And I remember.

"Oh, shit," I say.

She goes red in the face. "That's the worst possible thing you could have said right now."

I laugh, because I can't help it. Other me isn't me, exactly; somehow, pulling her away from #2 in his seedy bedroom with his seedy insistent hands changed her. I don't know if I like her more or less than me; she's not as bold but she laughs easier, as though she's merely revealing what was always there. When I laughed, at this point in my life—which I did so often I was known for it in my circle of friends—it was to let the mania hide the depression.

"Admit it," I say. "You kind of liked it."

"Well I agreed to it, didn't I?" She pulls at my arm, and her touch sends shivers, that old familiar drug jolt. "Let's go, please. Xander's sweet, but I don't think I can bear to see him again after that."

"Wise girl," I say, ruffling her hair.

She shrinks away. "I am so not your child," she says, then stops in her tracks. "Wait, do we have—"

"That's for me to know," I say, "and for you to find out."

Meredith pushes us up against the wall of the club and kisses us hard on the mouth. She tastes and smells like whiskey. She doesn't know that we have a girlfriend sleeping back at home; the other me doesn't know either.

We kiss her back, our breath leaving our body like whispers.

Out in the parking lot, I unlatch my bike from the post after mucking around with my combination. We walk the bike the mile back to the house we rent with two roommates: a boy we went to high school with and another best friend soon to be gone from our life.

In our bedroom we come upon the sleeping girlfriend. The other me shoots me a look; it's Anne.

"What is she doing here?" she whispers.

I bend to watch her chest rise and fall. "We don't love her anymore," I say.

"Well, what is she doing in our bed then? Why did we kiss that girl? Why don't we love her?" She sits on the edge of the bed. Anne doesn't stir. We have an unspoken arrangement, Anne and me. We are in a holding pattern, scared to move too far away from what we've always known. We won't say girlfriend but we will cuddle every night between the hours of two AM and ten AM. In the morning, her best friend and subsequent platonic life partner will knock on our door, let himself in. They will breakfast in my kitchen: eggs and sausage and almonds. They will ride their bike into the sun and will not stop riding until their legs are so sore they can barely stand. She has sores from her bike seat. She has come a long way from when I first knew her, and I have come a different way, and there is no meeting place on our path except for in those brief eight hours when we sleep.

"This is no way to love," I say to myself. "We're too different now."

"Yeah," the other me says, "but it's nice to have someone to share your bed with every night. Someone who cares about you."

"We're happier without her," I say. "Remember the good stuff, sure, but don't forget that there's a reason we broke up in the first place."

"I remember. I was there the first time around." She reaches up to touch a necklace that isn't there. She will still miss him, Daniel, in a way that is not strictly platonic, strictly the grief of losing a long-time friend to a black hole of illness. She will not have changed her number yet. He will call her for years, will make her wish she could close herself up. I forgot, but I saved her from all that too. When he slipped his necklace around our neck: "I never want to see anyone hurt you." But his was the greatest hurt of all, unintentional. I still startle when I think I see him in a crowd.

"There were other reasons we broke up," I say. "Daniel was a convenient excuse.'

We wake Anne. She holds us both. "You said you loved me," I whisper so low she can't hear. "But it was all gone at this point, wasn't it?"

She kisses me on all four cheeks. "Go to sleep," she says. "It's too late for talking."

I press my fingers to my lips where I can still feel a buzz from Meredith's kiss.

"Enjoy this part," I say to the other me. "That girl we saw tonight? She's going to change our world. She's going to be our friend for a long time. We'll stay for the duration of this one, I think. I could use a little waking up."

Relived memories pass like the regular kind: hazy and over too fast. Here we are having a breakfast of granola with our very first love. Anne. Here, at a friend's party where Meredith, the cutest girl we've ever met, offers us greens on every bowl.

"I'm sort of seeing someone," I say.

"Me too," Meredith says. "Some dude. He lives here too."

Meredith and I don't kiss again until that night, too drunk to think straight, when she follows me home from a party. I remember walking. I remember telling myself to let her sleep on the mattress in the other room. I don't remember grabbing her by the hand and pulling her toward the empty bedroom. I don't have to remember it this time, because I'm here again. I don't drink as much but I make the same choice. The other me stands helpless on the other side of the room.

Again? she mouths at me. She tries to tug me back, whispers, we're not a cheater.

But how does the saying go? Once and always.

Meredith pulls my tights half-off and buries herself between my legs and it's been so damn long since I felt anything fresh for anyone—sweat goes stale after too long on the body, and sunshine dims each evening—that I grip my hair tight in my hands and pull as hard as I can, a punishment for love, for the fuck-up of fucking another woman while Anne sleeps soundly in the bedroom we've shared since her new girlfriend Cathryn and her roommate Dana started fucking. I'm repeating a cycle she can't escape from. It's inevitable that we will end and begin like this again and again. I need to cut the cycle open, like a goddamn bedbug cuts its mate.

I'm supposed to fall asleep here. I pretend. Meredith stops, says my name. Shakes me a little. Huffs. Then she kisses me on the mouth, on the cheek. She brings my arm down over her shoulders and curls into me.

"So fucking cute," she says. "I'm in some fucking trouble with you."

This time, in the morning, I'm standing with Anne as she screams at me. My sister and her husband are there to pick up some things from the garage.

"Drama drama drama," my sister says.

"We didn't do anything," I say. "I passed out drunk."

"Why are you lying?" the other me says, leaning down to gather my underwear from the floor where I must have kicked them off. Meredith is on her way out the door.

"It's the script," I say. "It's what I'm supposed to say."

She shrugs. "What difference does it make if it's verbatim?"

"Yeah fucking right," says Anne. She leaves the house in a huff, skids out of the driveway in a haze of upturned gravel.

That night, I tell my friends I don't remember a thing. "You had sex," they say. "Meredith told us."

"Shit." I'm driving. I grip the steering wheel. "I'm such an asshole."

"You already knew that," the other me says.

At home, Anne waits for me. We're supposed to go to a party together, our first party in years. She's realized that we're not long for our love. She's begun to give me mementos from our past, to remind me that I was once hers and hers alone.

"Nothing happened?" she says.

"No," I say. "Apparently, something did happen. I'm sorry. I don't remember a thing. I must have blacked out."

We talk over things, the word girlfriend, what it means to share a bed with someone, whether the world will end at the next scheduled apocalypse. We agree to try this thing officially. The other me rolls her eyes.

"You said this part was fun," she says.

"It's beautiful," I say. "Everyone makes so many beautiful mistakes."

But each morning Anne leaves. She returns each night. She finds a new place. We move her in. Meredith hangs on by a thread. Sometimes, when we're all together, Meredith gets misty-eyed and abandons ship, texts me something sweet once she's gone.

I can't, I text back. I show the texts to Anne.

The other me throws her hands out. "This is already a shit show," she says. But she's starting to like Meredith. Sometimes they take shots of whiskey together and flirt on the couch.

Meredith, myself, and I stake trash bags to the grass outside, wet them down. We slip and slide. Anne watches from the side-lines, teases us all about acting like children. She mocks us when we drink too much. She doesn't like to dance.

Meredith storms out one night, but this time when she texts

it's I won't see you anymore. I don't text her back. I know that she is serious. She doesn't say things without meaning them.

"This isn't working," I say to Anne.

"It's her, isn't it?" Anne says.

"Yes and no. We keep trying but it's just not there. You're not here. I'm not here."

"We're at different places," she says.

"This is absolutely the right decision," the other me says. "Third time's not quite the charm."

Anne pushes her. "I like her," she says. "She's not as worn as you. Is that because she hasn't fucked as many dudes?"

I purse my lips to keep from snarking back. Anne's hurt. Even as we say goodbye, I'm itching for Meredith's soft lips, for that leer that means I'm in for it. For those vulnerable nights when Meredith tells me, back turned, about depression. How it's a thin word that will break if you push it too hard.

I call Meredith as soon as Anne leaves.

"I'm moving to Colorado in November," Meredith whispers one night. That means we have four months, and it makes it sweeter, that end-date staring at us from the future. Meredith holds both of me. We imagine the day she'll go. We feel comfortable with permanence as long as it's temporary. We imagine ourselves kissing her as she loads herself into her car, our face wet and our voices strained at goodbye. We write a poem and call it "November."

A month into our relationship, I pull Meredith into the kitchen and tell her that I love her because I know she wants to hear it and I can't stop thinking about her. She flirts with other people and I don't care because they're just words and looks and it doesn't impede what we have. She accuses me at every turn of loving other people.

But it's her and her only. It's her because she pulled me from a dangerous loop.

Then it's still one month until our scheduled end, her move to Colorado, and I catch her with Cathryn. Meredith admits to it straightaway as we stand in the rain outside my house, hoodies up. The other me stands beside me. I tell Meredith to go.

"I mean, look at how you got together," the other me says as we watch Meredith walk away down the sidewalk of our backyard.

"It's not her leaving that gets to me," I say.

"Then what is it?"

I shrug. "I'm hurt," I say, "but it's because she ruined what would have been a beautiful ending. She's just a confused girl. She's so young."

"Not much younger than you."

I shake my head. "No, she is," I say. "She'll grow up. But right now she's young and scared, and I wouldn't have known how to help her. It's good that she's going. I only wish she would have taken a different route."

But down my back yard there is only one sidewalk. She pauses at the fence and looks back at me, her hoodie obscuring her red cheeks.

"Did we really love her?" The other me presses her hands against her chest, as though to warm her heart. "I can't tell."

"It's hard," I say. "I still don't know."

I grab hold of the other me's hand. There's only one path, and we've already traveled it.

Next thing, we're in a garage apartment on Halloween. Across from us sits a butch woman in a Chick Magnet costume. We kiss her. We fade. Short and sweet.

"This next thing," I say to the other me, "is something you may not understand."

We're in a room lit by the orange string of lights strung around its ceiling. Anne's old roommate, Dana, stands naked at the foot of the mattress on the floor. She slaps a ruler against her open palm: Do you measure up? the ruler reads.

"Kiss her," Dana says, motioning to Cathryn, Anne's ex, the woman Meredith fucked. I kiss Cathryn. The other me furrows her eyebrow, pulls me away. Cathryn kisses Dana, the timid woman turned dominatrix-lite while I follow myself into the bathroom.

"What the fuck is this?" the other me says.

"I don't know," I say. "It's revenge. It's everything coming full circle."

"It's ugly," she says. "It's wrong."

"No, there's something beautiful in this," I say. "It's not immediate on the surface, but it's a method of forgiveness."

"Maybe sex shouldn't be a vessel for forgiveness."

"Sex can be whatever it needs to be. Sex can be whatever you want it to be. Sex can be nothing, even, if you play it right."

I jerk away from myself. "You can't judge things when you haven't seen the whole story. You'll see. You'll know eventually. Sex isn't about love all the time every time."

She lets go and crosses her arms. "Shouldn't it be?" she says, and I can't tell if she's telling or asking.

I shrug. "We're not exactly the same people," I say. "I can't answer that for you."

"Is this fun for you?" she says.

I think back, to the first time, the second time, the third time I slept with these two. A mess of memories. I thought, for a moment, I might find a routine with them both. But then the painful truth crept in: I wanted to forge my own path. If monogamy wasn't for me, I wanted to find that on my own terms.

I never once thought monogamy wasn't for me with Dover.

The truth of those threesomes with Cathryn and Dana: I wanted Dana, the woman who had never fucked me over, who had never slept with two of my exes, but in order to have sex with her, I had to have sex with Cathryn too. They were a matched pair even if Cathryn cheated on her. I was acutely aware that Cathryn was both superior and inferior to me simultaneously. That women chose to be with me in the light and her in the dark. That women got from her what they couldn't get from me.

"It's not particularly fun," I say to myself. "But you never know if you don't try."

One thing I was always proud of: I knew what I really needed, and maybe I tried to need something different, maybe I tried many things, but I was always honest, in the end, with myself.

"I guess," she says. "I'm so tired. Doesn't this get tiring?"

She's still the relationship one. The one who wants a promise before the naked glimpse.

I remember not-sleeping. I remember crying until my cheeks burned. I remember lying on my wood floor and playing the same song over and over. Heartbreak is terrible and wonderful and numbing, and I missed it when I was stable.

"It's hard," I say.

"Then why not stop?"

"Because it's all hard. Not just this. Everything. Being alive," I say. "It's hard, but it's what you know and so you go with it. Go with it."

"I'll go with it," she says. "If it seems like something worth going with."

I peek out the door. She's right; I didn't enjoy this night, or the night after, or the night after. I wanted complicated and I got complicated.

I grab her hand. "You're right," I say.

My muscles ache. My mind's numb, not just my body.

"I need a break," I say. "This is the part where I need to be by myself."

"Let's do that then," she says. "Let's be by ourselves."

We spend the week we would have been with Cathryn and Dana writing, reading. We don't go to class; what's the point, when we'll only have to leave again and forget all we learned about Physical Anthropology and Statistics. We spend evenings with friends who will later move away.

One night I buy a gram of weed and place it into a metal tin. FOR DOVER, I write on it. FROM YOUR SECRET ADMIRER. We drive by her house and leave it on her doorstep.

She might think it's creepy. She'll probably think it's a prank being played by her friends. But she'll smoke it nonetheless.

I try to see her through the front window, but there's no one home.

At home I show the other me her picture on Facebook. "This is it," I say. "This is her. Maybe you can do it different, when you get there. Maybe you can keep from fucking it up."

She tries to smile. "If I'm you,' she says, "doesn't that mean we'll make the same mistakes?"

This is where I said I would leave her. But I don't want to let her go. I stay a little longer.

We go to the astronomy center for their monthly star party. We lay on a blanket and name the constellations. She remembers many that I can no longer name. I know only a few she hasn't yet learned.

"What do we do, in the future?" she asks.

"It's a surprise," I say. I can't tell her about the numerous shitty desk jobs, the two years of cleaning houses, writing essays on the side, in stolen hours, losing friends to make time, trimming the fat to make time. No more painting. No more running. Until we catch a break: one book deal, then two, then a third. Dover's celebratory dances. Then the stress. Then the disappointment that success did not fill the void. Then a man who came along and made me feel desired again. Then the need for a wreckage that would move the rock blocking me from more, from new ideas. A stalemate of a house. Another advance, this one enough to pay for the procedure but no more than the one trip through.

At the end of our week, myself and I are watching a movie on my old beat-up couch, and I get a phone call from a guy who was in one of my classes, someone I used to buy weed from and flirt with when there wasn't anyone else in the picture. The tattooed misfit. Jeremiah asks me over. I look over at the woman who is both me and not-me. She won't like this one: no-emotions, hardly even a kiss between us.

I try to hold on, but I feel us slipping into his apartment. And if we don't, if I let us keep ourselves from going there, we won't get to our final destination.

Because I don't want to shield her from the ugliness that is sex with the wrong people—because I want to instill in her that regrets will not ruin us—I keep us there long enough that she can see our mistake, long enough that she can look him in his face, then go. Go again. Go again. Go again. Jeremiah and Michael and Grayson and Eliot.

"What are you doing?" she asks. "Who are these people?"

"They're the low before the high," I say.

When we wake up in Eliot's strange bed, our memories wiped by too much booze, I look over at my own wounded and confused face.

Eliot drives us home. He jokes about herpes.

"This guy's a real asshole," the other me says.

I sit with her on our couch. "He is," I say. "But Dover is next."

"As long as you know." She crosses her arms. "I don't trust your taste at all. What if I don't like Dover?"

I shrug. "You won't," I say, "at first." I grab her hand. "Are you ready?"

She looks so scared and so rundown that I hardly recognize her. I think of the past few years: years of rundown and scared, scared of everything. How Dover must have seen that in me day after day and still loved me. How Dover loved me even after I fucked someone else. How she insisted we stay together, work it out. How I couldn't look at her anymore. How it was me who walked out the door and made her realize that she could live without me.

"Let's go," I say, and then we're off. We're in Dover's bedroom. We're kissing. As innocent as fools. Dover's lips are beautiful and terrible, a reminder I wanted nothing more than to have. Her glasses hit mine and her violinist hands tangle themselves in my hair and she is a different person. I am a different person. The other me watches, her hand at her chest. I imagine the other me is stricken with a feeling like remembering something you never knew.

I push my finger against Dover's lips. She gives me a goofy grin. It doesn't suit her, too drunken, her weed-eyes half-closed.

Dover doesn't love me yet. I don't love her yet. When we first meet someone, we cannot love them. As we remain in one another's company, we absorb pieces of the other: a party trick. Only once we are part of this other person, only once they are part us, can we love them. Narcissism at its best. It will take us six months to amalgamate.

I look over at the other me. I step out of the bed. Dover's room is a mess of dirt and dirty clothes: failed gardening experiments and the slovenliness that comes from college living. She's cute like a child is cute. So is the other me. I miss the Dover who loved me, the one who stood by me through disappointment, the one I held when she needed it. But that Dover isn't mine to kiss anymore. I've spent a long time trying to get back someone who isn't here. I wrap my arms around my other self. Her heart hammers.

"Don't leave," she says. But I let go and jump before she can stop me.

"No thanks," I say to the next man, unwrapping myself from him. I'm alone, the other me still in that world-before-the-fall. "I've got to get home." I climb out of his bed. I fall into the dark. This time it catches me.

The doctor waits with me until I wake. She hands me a box of juice and a cracker. It has been less than six hours since I went in. She checks her watch as I drag the juice box straw across my lips.

"Was it worth it?" she asks as I sit up in her chair. She hands me the paperwork to take to the front desk, sign. There's no price on it, as though numbers don't exist, as though to trick me into forgetting what I've done until I emerge from the fog. There will be a number later: delivered to my mailbox.

"Is it ever?" I say.

I walk home, too drowsy to drive. I pick up my phone and

dial Dover's number. Her voicemail picks up, as it always does when I call these days.

"I'd be lying if I said I didn't want anything from you," I say. "I want you to hear this and come running back. But I'm not going to ask it. I'll do what you requested. I'll leave you alone now. I only needed to say, because I don't think I ever did, not really, not without bending it in the hopes that it would pull you back. I'm sorry I cheated on you. That mistake was on me. I hope you're happy where you are. I hope you're safe. I hope you can forget the good parts enough to move on. I hope—"

The voicemail cuts me off. I stand in the desolate street and stare at the bright screen.

Press 2 to start over, the phone says.

I press 2. I hang up. I walk home.

PART FOUR
NOVELLA

FINNA

BY NINO CIPRI

PUBLISHED BY TOR.COM

Chapter One

The bus abandoned Ava on the outskirts of LitenVärld's vast parking lot, nearly three-quarters of a mile from the doors. The box store stuck out like a giant square pimple on the landscape, which had been scraped into gently undulating drifts of snow by February's wind. Ava marched grimly toward the exterior, painted a cheery sky-blue and sunflower-yellow. The parking lot was mostly empty; it was a Tuesday and the weather was shit. Who would want to go shopping today?

"Fucking Derek," she muttered into the wind, cursing the coworker who'd called in sick. If the world were even the slightest bit fair, she'd be home in bed, alternating Netflix binges with long intermissions to listen to Florence and the Machine and actively feel like shit. That's what she wanted from her days off: equal time to nourish her heartbreak and distract from it. That's all she'd been doing since she broke up with Jules, three days before.

LitenVärld was the bastard offspring of more popular big box stores, hanging in the margins between home goods giants and minimalist furniture mavens. It compromised between clean

Scandinavian design and bougie Americana by selling furnishings that displayed neither virtue. Instead of sections, the store ushered shoppers through an upsetting and uncoordinated procession of themed showrooms, which bounced from baroque to postmodern design. The showrooms sat next to each other uneasily, like habitats in a hyper-condensed zoo. Here was the habitat for the Pan-Asian Appropriating White Yoga Instructor, complete with tatami mats and a statue of Shiva; next to it huddled the Edgelord Rockabilly Dorm Room, with black leather futon and Quentin Tarantino posters.

Ava made her way to Her Majesty's Romper Room, a princess-themed play area, which had a doorway to the break room and time clock. It gave Ava a headache if she paid too much attention as she walked through the store, even using the shortcuts only staff knew about. The best she could do was to shut off her peripheral vision and focus only on her goal.

Maybe Jules won't show up today, Ava thought as she squeezed past the gaudy miniature throne. Ava had told Jules that she needed space, and had changed her schedule so that she wouldn't have to see them at work. Jules had listened grimly, then shrugged and said, "I'm not going to fight over territory I don't want to be in anyway. I hate that place."

Ava wasn't quite willing to hope that they'd gotten fired, but a generalized wish that Jules wouldn't be at the store? That felt okay. They were already on their last excused absence for the quarter; maybe they'd just quit.

Ava clung to that thought—that Jules might not be at Liten-Värld today—hating that it brought her so much comfort. She clocked in, dumped her stuff in her locker, and got ready to go out onto the floor. She would have had to come back here anyway on Tuesday. She could do this.

As she turned the corner out of the break room, Ava collided with her ex.

"Crap, sorry," Jules said, sounding distracted. Then Jules caught sight of who they were talking to, and froze. "Ava? What are you doing here?"

Jules had brought the cold in with them, ice clinging to their jacket and the thin ends of their twists, melted snow coursing down their brown skin. They smelled like wet wool and Old Spice, which had always been improbably attractive. Ava backed out of the danger zone, back into the smell of stale coffee and ancient crusts of food splatter from the microwave that emanated from all break rooms.

"I got called in," Ava said. "Fucking Derek is sick." Jules looked panicked. Ava felt bad for them; she'd been prepared for this to happen, and they hadn't. "It's just for today," she added.

"Okay," Jules said. They were visibly pulling themself back together. "I'm just gonna—"

The two of them did that annoying dance forced on any two people who wanted to get past each other in a narrow space. Finally, Ava backed all the way against the wall, waving Jules past her.

"Look, just go," she snapped.

Jules opened their mouth to snap back, then shut it and moved past her. As they did, Ava caught sight of the scarf around Jules's neck; light green dotted with blue, brown, and gray, crocheted with thick yarn. She'd made it for Jules for Christmas. In retrospect, the project had sprung from a desperate hope that the two of them might come together again, stitch fragile connections over the yawning holes opening up between them.

"Is that. . . ?" she asked, gesturing.

Jules looked puzzled, then glanced down with a tense grimace. Jules's emotions were always written clear on their face, and they looked like they'd found a snake wrapped around their neck.

"Never mind," Ava said, and fled down the hallway, onto the shop floor.

Ava volunteered for shifts at the customer service desk with

Tricia, their manager, to keep far away from Jules in stocking and assembly. Heartache felt like a persistent hangover: lethargy, a headache, an unshakeable belief in the cruelty of the world, drifting outside of time. It was hard to keep up the bullshit facade of industriousness when she felt entirely dead inside. The minutes dragged by as Ava attempted to look busy while Tricia hovered behind her.

A young woman with olive skin and thick, black- brown hair approached the desk, and Ava turned toward her desperately. "Good morning," she said, trying to inject some cheerfulness into her voice—mostly for Tricia's benefit. Ava thought she sounded strangled.

"Hi," the woman said. "I'm sorry to bother you, but I think I lost my grandmother."

"Lost her?" asked Ava.

"She was right behind me in the showrooms? I turned around to get her opinion, and she was gone. I've been looking for her for ten minutes and. . . " She trailed off, shrugging help-lessly. Ava turned to find Tricia, then flinched back when she saw the manager already looming behind her. She hadn't even heard Tricia approach.

"I'm so sorry to hear that," Tricia said gravely. She had donned one of her Managerial Faces that Jules had reportedly seen her practicing alone in her office: Calm And In Charge. She tilted her head, the blond highlights in her midwestern manager-class haircut catching the light. "Let me make an announcement over the PA system. What's her name?"

"Ursula," the young woman replied. "Ursula Nouri."

Tricia nodded, her face serious as she picked up the phone and pressed a button. Her voice came squawking out of the over-head speakers. "Good morning, shoppers. Would Ursula Nouri please meet her party at the customer service desk? Ursula Nouri to the customer service desk, please."

Ava tried to smile reassuringly at the young woman. Tricia treated everything with the gravity usually reserved for state funerals and hostage negotiations.

Tricia set the phone back down in the cradle. "Can you tell me what your grandmother was wearing?"

The girl nodded. "She had on a red coat and some purple fleece gloves. Oh, and a leather purse. I've got a picture of her, if that helps?"

Tricia and Ava dutifully looked at the picture the girl pulled up on her phone. Ursula looked like a fairly average grandmother: white hair pulled into a low bun at the back of her neck, a billowy shirt hanging over a plump frame. The picture was obviously a selfie of Ursula and her granddaughter, the two of them smiling identically up at the camera.

"She seems nice," Ava ventured.

"She is. I mean, she'll tell you when your cleavage is hanging out or your boyfriend is trash, but. . . " The woman trailed off, staring harder at the small screen. After a moment, more words spilled out: "She doesn't normally wander off like this? She knows I get really worried about her, because we're like, the only family we have. It's this whole, stupid, tragic story that I *super* don't want to get into right now, so if you could just. . . "

Ava shot a helpless look at Tricia, who thankfully took charge.

"Ava, go through the showrooms and see if you can find her. I'll send a couple of other people up there to look with you. Miss, why don't you wait with me?"

Ava nodded. As she walked past the young woman, she hesitated. "I'm sure she's fine," she said.

The woman's face cracked into an uncertain smile. "Thanks."

The showrooms were eerily empty. The customer service desk was located at the central hub of the store, and even on slow days, it tended to bustle. The rest of the store felt abandoned, besides a few desultory shoppers and a pair of teenagers alternately making out and taking selfies in the Pastel Goth Hideaway. Then again, it was the downseason, a stark contrast to the roiling hell that had been six weeks prior to Christmas. And sure, it was hard to leave the house in February. Ava had suffered enough coming to LitenVärld today, and she was paid to be here. Still, it was odd to see all the fake apartments vacant; it reminded Ava of the haunting feeling of being the last one out of the store. Each showroom was like an empty home, waiting for its ghostly inhabitants to return.

Or maybe the inhabitants had never left, but were just hiding out, watching the interlopers pass through their abodes.

"Get it together," Ava told herself. Could she blame her paranoia and morbid thoughts on the heartache? Or maybe she should blame it on February. The shortest month, and objectively the worst.

LitenVärld was laid out like a twisting vine, with showrooms branching off a central walkway that wound through the store, curving back on itself before dumping people out into the food court and registers. Ava made her way quietly down the path, peering into the cubes for Ursula Nouri. Each room was alien and strange relative to the one before it. Strung together, they resembled an ugly necklace designed by a child, picking out the most garish beads to thread.

That familiar sense of disorientation came over Ava, that slight queasiness at seeing all these clashing rooms squeezed together. It mixed with her dread and made her stomach churn. She turned a corner, saw a tall figure in the middle of the Nihilist Bachelor Cube, and let out a shriek before she realized it was Jules.

"Fuck!" Jules shouted, colliding with modular shelves stacked with Camus and Palahniuk novels. "What the hell! Why are you screaming at me?"

"Sorry!" Ava said. Her fright was quickly transmuting to irritation, as all her feelings seemed to do when Jules was concerned. "You startled me."

"I startled you?" they asked incredulously. "I'm not the one sneaking up behind people and screaming like a Nazgûl. God, I almost pissed myself."

They had a fist pressed to their chest, like enough pressure would slow down their pulse.

"Sorry," Ava said again, the word sour in her mouth. Seemed like too many of her conversations with Jules had required apologies. "Did Tricia send you to look for the missing grandmother?"

"I volunteered. A soccer mom enlisted me to help harangue her husband into shelling out money for a new bathroom vanity. She managed to misgender me four times in two minutes," Jules said. They bent down to pick up the books they'd knocked off the shelf. "Two different pronouns, completely ignored my nametag, eventually settled on calling me 'the kid.'"

"Have you seen the old woman?" Ava asked, cutting off Jules's nervous rambling. "The granddaughter says she disappeared around here."

Jules shook their head. "I've been through all the rooms back there," they said, waving their hand the opposite way Ava had come. "Didn't see anything."

"Shit," Ava said. Where could an old woman escape to in a furniture store? She leaned against a showroom wall to think.

"I still think this is the most depressing showroom," Jules said conversationally. "It reeks of misogyny and sadness."

The Nihilist Bachelor's room was one of the smallest show apartments. Tiny kitchenette, a fold-out desk beneath a loft bed, fake exposed brick along the walls. A single brown leather chair in front of a flatscreen TV. Ava thought briefly of Jules's studio, which wasn't much bigger, but was infinitely more comfortable. Jules had refused to buy anything except a set of plates from LitenVärld, and had furnished it from estate sales and Goodwill trips instead. *Everything at work is part of a set with everything else,* they'd explained. *I don't fit into any of those sets.*

Ava realized that they'd been standing and staring at each other. She turned on her heel and said, "Maybe she wandered into housewares."

"Am I that awful to be around?" Jules asked. There was something raw in their question; something flushed and bruised, radiating hurt. "You can't even stand being in the same room as me. I thought you wanted to be friends."

Had she said that? Probably. That's what you were supposed to say when you ended a relationship with someone you couldn't hate, but didn't know how to love, either.

"Please don't be so dramatic about this," Ava said, trying to keep her voice cool.

"Me?" Jules said. "You switched your entire schedule around so you'd never have to see me again. And you're calling me dramatic?"

"I think it's reasonable to want some space!" If it was so reasonable, some distant, detached part of her wondered, why was she so defensive?

"You're acting like a stranger, or like I don't exist, like we never—"

"So what, you think I'm just *overreacting*?" Ava spat. It was one of the accusations that had stung her the most. She was emotionally volatile. She made mountains out of molehills. She couldn't control her feelings. She'd never claimed otherwise, she'd just stopped being able to fake it around Jules.

Jules opened their mouth to answer, then snapped it shut. "I'm not gonna do this with you in this stupid room," they said, and turned to go.

"*This* is why I changed my schedule," Ava hissed at their back.

Jules suddenly stopped, and Ava felt her hackles rise. Was this it? A rehash of the fight, their last fight, which was just the same as every fight?

"Ava," they said instead. And there was something in their voice that cut through the fight-or-flight haze: something low, confused, vulnerable. They said her name like they were reaching for a life jacket.

"What?" she replied. Still on guard, but putting away her guns.

"Weren't we in the Bachelor Cube?"

What kind of question was that? But Jules's uncertainty

infected her. She glanced to the right; *Fight Club* and *The Stranger* were still on the bookshelf. "Yeah?" she said. "So?"

Jules slowly turned around. "Doesn't it look kind of. . . big?"

The Nihilist Bachelor Cube—like its cousins Coked- out Divorcée, Parental Basement Dweller, and Massage Therapist Who Lived in Their Studio—were all two hundred square feet or smaller, with an open floor plan to make each feel less claustrophobic. Jules had stomped into a separate room that shouldn't have existed, a room Ava hadn't seen from the walkway. Its design was radically different: bright, colorful, filled with floral prints and fake plants, posters of fantastic places on the wall. It resembled the Midlife Crisis Mom room, but that was on the other side of the store, and had been painted a warm peach color. This one was done in sand and cerulean.

Past the edges of the cube, Ava could see a whole other walkway, one that shouldn't exist. Her gaze traveled up, and she gasped as she saw a seam connecting the two rooms. It was a dark purple, the color of a fresh bruise, and wriggled and squirmed as if it were alive.

"This is weird, right?" Jules said from the other side of the seam. Their voice was normal. Ava had expected it to be warped by passing through the seam.

"This is *really fucking* weird," agreed Ava. She couldn't seem to tear her eyes from that writhing border. It took a moment to hear Jules calling her name.

"What?" she asked.

They held up a pair of purple fleece gloves. "The old woman was wearing purple gloves, right?"

"Shit," Ava sighed. She pulled out the phone on her hip.

"This is amazing," Jules said. "It's a creepy Scandinavian Narnia. I can't believe we found something like this." "Tricia," Ava said into the phone, and Jules whipped their head around. "We've got a situation up in the showrooms."

"I'll be right there," Tricia replied, and hung up. "Seriously?" Jules said. They sighed with melodramatic disappointment. "We find a wrinkle in time and you tell the manager?"

"What did you expect me to do?" Ava said. "Will you get out of the. . . whatever that is?

You don't know what's in there." That seam between the rooms twitched unpleasantly, and Ava took a step back.

"It can't be much worse than what's back there," Jules said, waving vaguely at Ava, LitenVärld, who knew what. Jules always wanted to run away. For a long time they'd talked about the two of them leaving together, moving or traveling. The destination changed, but the wanderlust remained the same. The last few weeks, they had more often talked about disappearing on their own. No destination in particular, just. . . away.

"Jules," Ava said urgently, but couldn't think of anything to follow it with. What could she possibly say to bring them back?

Jules sighed, looked down at the gloves in their hand, and then trudged over the threshold. "Ursula had the right idea," they muttered as they passed Ava.

Chapter Two

Tricia called an emergency meeting, and everyone who wasn't working a register crammed into the break room.

It always surprised Ava how many people worked at Liten-Värld. She only saw most of them crammed in here during the pre-Black Friday war meeting, or for their exquisitely painful "sensitivity training." She'd only gotten through the latter by focusing on her and Jules's plans to get obliteratingly drunk afterward.

They hadn't even been dating at that point. They'd woken up the next day in Ava's apartment; Jules's shoes had been in the bathtub, while Ava was wearing their shirt. It had smelled like blunts and Old Spice, unexpectedly comforting. Jules was sleeping on the couch, wearing an oversized sweater and a pair of boxers, using Ava's bathrobe as a blanket. She'd stared at them for nearly a minute, trying to piece together the events that had led to her cute new coworker sleeping half-naked on the couch. Eventually, she shook herself out of her daze, told herself to stop being a creep, and went into the kitchen to make coffee. Jules had stumbled in twenty minutes later, wearing the bathrobe they'd slept under, curls flattened on one side. "I will trade you my soul for coffee," they'd said solemnly. Then, when they saw that all Ava had were Nifty! brand beans from PriceLow, they cringed and said, "Those only get part of my soul."

They hadn't hooked up that night, or even that week, but infatuation was already sinking its claws into Ava, catching her bleary and unprepared.

Ava went to the far side of the room, opposite to where Jules was standing. She caught a few whispered conversations between her coworkers, a couple of raised eyebrows, but kept her eyes down. This was the other reason she hadn't wanted to be scheduled with Jules. She hated being gossip fodder. Jules, of course, was impervious to gossip, willfully oblivious. They'd never understood why it irked Ava so much. *People are going to talk,* they always said. *No matter what you do.* Ava had admired their courage at first, but she eventually recognized it as yet another way of shutting people out before they could hurt you.

Tricia finally came in, wheeling a boxy television that looked like it predated LitenVärld itself, or at least this particular store. She plugged it into the wall, then turned to address everyone.

"Can I have some quiet, please?" she called into the already quiet room. After a few seconds, she said, "Thank you. So for anyone that hasn't already heard, we've got a maskhål."

There was a swell of dismayed groans and whispers. Ava, almost unwillingly, found herself seeking out Jules. They had done the same, and mouthed, *A what?*

"Quiet, please," Tricia said again. "And please hold all of your questions until the end. For the benefit of those who've joined us since our last maskhål, I'm going to play a short instructional video."

Another groan, this one softer and more hushed. Tricia didn't even bother to shush anyone, just bent over and pressed play on. . . was that a VHS player?

The video began with a click and a whir. Static flickered in lines across the screen, then cleared, but the color was still slightly off, oversaturated and alien.

Yellow letters traveled across the screen, marquee style: *Maskhål och du.* Below it, in subtitles, "WORMHOLES AND YOU."

The LitenVärld logo appeared at the bottom of the screen as a man and woman walked into the shot. Judging by their hair and fashion, this video had been made before Ava was born. They both wore polo shirts in LitenVärld's signature sky-blue, with yellow and crimson accents, tucked into unflattering khakis with pleats where no pleats should ever be. Their hair didn't seem to move, stuck in helmet-like structures to their scalps, which

made the rest of their faces look weirdly mobile.

Their voices were overdubbed. Badly.

"What's up, amigos?" said the pallid white man. His voice was a cross between Wolf of Wall Street and California beach bum. "I'm Mark!"

"And I'm Dana," warbled the blonde.

"Is Dana drunk?" Ava whispered to one of her coworkers. The coworker rolled his eyes and didn't say anything. (God, they were all so *boring*. She'd forgotten how this store sucked the life from people.)

Mark spoke again. "We're here to tell you what to do if a wormhole opens up on your shift!"

Mark spoke in exclamation points. His voice was far more energetic than the actor, who was wan, bland in that vaguely Scandinavian way, an off-brand Mads Mikkelsen with all the interesting bits filed off.

"First, we should get our disclaimer out of the way," Dana said, in her wobbly, nasal whine. She had an affected mid-Atlantic accent, like she was auditioning for a minor role in *Breakfast at Tiffany's*. The original actress moved with the confidence and poise of a piece of seaweed washed ashore. "LitenVärld accepts no responsibility or liability for any losses or injuries that wormholes incur, since they fall under the Act of God clauses on our employee insurance. This training video does not replace the longer and more in- depth training for our FINNA division—"

Tricia bent over and skipped ahead on the video, speeding through what looked like several more minutes of banter and/or legalese. "The FINNA divisions were made redundant during the Recession. Each store handles the maskhål in-house now."

She restarted the video on a close-up of Mark. "—that's out of the way, it's time for a short physics lesson. In physics, the term *quantum entanglement* refers to particles that are linked in strange ways that we don't entirely understand, but that we can measure."

Mark's pallid face with its receding hairline faded into a cheesy animation. Two blobs appeared on the screen: one a dusky pink, the other a sky-blue. Ava could guess what was coming next, but that didn't stop the physical pain of watching it happen. The pink blob grew eyes with heavy lashes, two spots of reddish purple appearing on what could generously be called its cheeks. The blue blob also grew eyes, along with a heavy brow and—god save them all—a handlebar mustache.

Then the two blobs began *flirting*—cooing and blowing kisses at each other. It was the most obnoxiously heterosexual thing Ava had seen since the last St. Patrick's Day parade.

"Even across vast distances of space and time. . . " Dana said in a dreamy voiceover.

The two blobs were torn away from each other, flung to opposite sides of the screen with a crude galaxy projected between them. *Good,* Ava thought savagely, as the blobs squeaked in distress.

". . . entangled particles find ways of reconnecting," intoned Dana, and the two blobs snaked out long, ghostly limbs toward each other, joining hands across the galaxy. The two blobs burbled happily, and Ava rolled her eyes.

"This video is making me gayer out of spite," Jules muttered, clear even from the other side of the room.

Ava snorted. She couldn't help it. Jules turned toward her in surprise, and she cleared her throat and turned away.

"Quiet, please!" Tricia said.

On the screen, the obnoxiously heterosexual blobs had been replaced with the vapidly heterosexual actors. They relaxed in a retro LitenVärld showroom—Newly Retired Swinger, Ava would call it. It was done up in beige and mauve tones, with some palm tree and flamingo accents to keep it from being too bland.

"You may be wondering what this has to do with the wormhole in your store," Mark said. The actors' mouths always kept on moving for seconds after the end of the dub, which was giving Ava a headache.

Dana addressed the camera head-on. "Some scientists believe in the *many worlds theory.*" She pronounced it as if it were something strange and exotic, not three words that could come up by themselves in any conversation.

The blue-and-crimson logo on-screen shivered and split into two parts. Mark spread his arms, fingertips ex- tended, augmenting the physics lesson with jazz hands. It was embarrassing to watch him try to emote.

"This means that there are an infinite number of universes," Mark said. "Endless varieties of them. That means that there are endless varieties of LitenVärlds!"

Dana and Mark snapped their fingers. Suddenly, they were sitting in two entirely different rooms; hers was a lavish, baroque French drawing room, and she wore the gown and powdered wig to match. Mark sat in a room that might have been considered "futuristic" when the video was made: lots of neon, inflatable furniture, and one of the largest and ugliest desktop computers Ava had ever seen. He was wearing wraparound sunglasses, a puffy orange vest, and fingerless gloves.

Mark took off the sunglasses and continued. "The unique layout of LitenVärld encourages wormholes to form between universes. These wormholes connect our stores to LitenVärlds in parallel worlds."

Mark and Dana looked at each other, then snapped their fingers again. Now Mark stood in a rustic log cabin, wearing lederhosen and carrying an ax. Dana relaxed in a beach house, wearing a sarong over a bathing suit and holding a daiquiri in her hand.

"That is *not* how physics works," Jules muttered. Why was it so easy to always catch their voice?

Tricia bent over to fast-forward the video again. "It goes on for a while," she said. "You all get the idea."

They watched Mark and Dana flicker through a series of settings and costumes, some of them benign or bizarre, others straight-up racist. Dana in a teahouse and an exaggerated geisha getup got a couple of disgusted sighs, but Mark in a hut and with fake black dreadlocks and a bone through his nose earned widespread groans, and someone (probably Jules) threw a wadded-up paper at the screen. Not even Tricia could say anything about that.

The bizarre zoetrope of Marks and Danas ended with the two actors in foam dinosaur costumes. They attempted to snap their fingers again, fumbling with their thick, rubbery claws, but the sound effect was apparently enough to bring them back to their original world, original bodies. They both heaved affected sighs of relief.

"Now," Mark said, putting his hands on his hips. "Be- fore you decide that traveling to other universes is all fun and games, we should warn you that not all LitenVärlds are as nice as the one *you* work in."

Dana added, "Here's some footage taken by one of our FINNA divisions during recoveries."

Ava's eyes grew wide at the shaky, grainy footage that blasted across the screen. It was hard to make out the details, but Ava caught glimpses of something enormous, something with far more legs than a sane universe could ask for. There were shouts and screams in what a distant, shocked part of Ava's mind guessed was Swedish. A spray of blood hit the camera, and the footage cut out.

Back to Mark and Dana in the bland Retired Swinger living room. Ava broke out into goosebumps when she saw their smiles again.

"Now that you understand what wormholes are, and what might lay on the other side of them, we're going to tell you what to do in case one opens up in your store," Dana said.

Mark leaned forward. "After alerting your manager to the presence of a wormhole, the first and best thing to do is rope off the affected area. Make sure that no customers or associates enter it. They'll usually collapse on their own within a couple hours."

"The only time you need to worry is if someone accidentally wanders into the wormhole. Since 1989, all LitenVärld stores have been equipped with the FINNA, a patented piece of equipment that can locate lost people using quantum entanglement. It helps the FINNA division in your store navigate the series of wormholes that the lost person may have wandered through. In our experience, wormholes tend to travel in packs."

A piece of technology popped up on the screen. To Ava, it looked vaguely like the brick phones that bankers talked on in movies set in the '80s. It faded into an exploded view, familiar to anyone who had had to put together a piece of furniture from a LitenVärld instruction booklet.

Tricia paused the movie, then shut off the TV. It went black with a quiet pop. "As I mentioned, the company closed its FINNA divisions back in 2009, as a cost-saving measure. Instead, I'll need two volunteers who are willing to take the store's FINNA and go after the missing woman."

The room went silent, as every employee became in- tent on disappearing. Ava shrunk down in her seat and avoided Tricia's eyes. She felt a momentary pang of guilt, thinking of the young woman who'd reported her grandmother missing. But Ava had no interest in death by. . . by whatever those things had been.

"Are we getting overtime for this?" someone else asked.

Ava glanced up long enough to see Tricia shake her head. "Not unless you remain in the other worlds past eighty hours in a single pay period. But! I do have a couple of Pasta and Friends gift cards for the brave volunteers."

Ava scrunched down in her chair even further. Nobody in their right mind would volunteer for—

"Jules!" Tricia said, and Ava felt the name go through her like an electric shock. "Thank you for stepping up."

Ava looked over to see Jules with their hand raised. Everyone else in the room was staring too. Jules shrank under the attention, and awkwardly waved before slumping back down in their plastic chair.

"I don't really need the gift card," they told Tricia.

Tricia shrugged. "Well, that just doubles the incentive for the next volunteer. Any takers? Two gift cards would make for a pretty good date night."

If it had been possible to crawl underneath her chair, transform into a literal puddle, Ava would have done it. She hadn't thought she could sit through a worse work meeting than the sensitivity training.

"Well, if nobody volunteers, corporate policy is to have the people with the least seniority go. That's Jules, but since—since Jules has already volunteered, we need someone else to join Jules on this mission."

Ava winced as she listened to Tricia contort her speech in an effort to avoid using they or them. *I just can't do it!* Tricia had cheerfully told Ava once, completely unprompted. *I guess I'm too much of a grammar nazi!* Since then, she went out of her way to avoid using any pronouns at all when talking about Jules, warping her sentences around her refusal. Ava wondered, not for the first time, why anyone would so proudly declare themselves to be any kind of nazi. She was so distracted by her irritation that she missed the last bit of Tricia's speech, and it took her a few seconds to realize everyone was staring at her.

Rewind: The policy was to send the person with the least seniority. That was Jules. Jules had been hired on two months after Ava. Was there anybody else in between them?

Derek. Fucking Derek, who was the entire reason that Ava was here on a day she'd explicitly asked not to work.

"Oh, *hell* no," Ava said.

"Why don't the three of us talk in my office?" Tricia said sweetly.

Tricia's office was a purgatory of fallen LitenVärld fashions, a claustrophobic island of misfit furniture. Chairs with denim upholstery, a glass-top desk with chrome accents, and a gag novelty lamp in the shape of a hairy, muscular leg, complete with sock garters. The look was completed by a couple of soulless art prints that re- minded Ava of waiting rooms in urgent care clinics.

Ava decided to take a reasonable approach, since it was that or run screaming out of the store. "Tricia," she said.

"This is really unfair. I know I don't have the seniority—"

"You do have the right to refuse the assignment," Tricia said.

Relief flooded through Ava. "Okay, in that case—"

"But it would be grounds for termination."

All the relief flooded right back out of her, replaced by a vision of her current checking account balance. "What?!"

"Listen, Tricia," Jules said, leaning forward. "I'm happy to do this by myself. I don't need—"

"Jules, I appreciate your willingness to go above and beyond. It's a nice change from your usual MO." Tricia laughed like the soulless bitch she was. "But we do have to stick to policy, which says that nobody goes through a maskhål alone." Tricia turned her blank gaze back to Ava. "Furthermore, I'd like you both to keep in mind that there's a young woman sitting in the cafeteria who's scared for her grandmother. Customers always come first."

Ava was, possibly for the first time in her life, too angry to speak. If she lived through this, she decided, she was going to track Derek down and kill him.

"Let's get you the FINNA," Tricia said. "Oh! And don't forget these!"

She slid the two gift cards across the table.

Chapter Three

"Okay, so, listen," Jules said.

Ava dropped the box carrying the FINNA on the ground and squatted next to it. Behind them, in the Nihilist Bachelor Cube, the maskhål squirmed in the air. The seam between their world and *another universe* twitched restlessly. Ava turned her back to it, so she wouldn't have to look.

"I'm listening," Ava said, opening the box. The FINNA looked like some of the equipment she'd seen on Ghost Hunters reruns, with a massive gray case, a black-and- green console, and two antennae on the side. It was lighter than it looked, at least.

Jules peered over her shoulder. "The instructions should be in here," they said, plucking the booklet out. "In Swedish, French, and Japanese, great. I can muddle through the French— Or yank them out of my hands, that works too."

"You don't need written instructions, the diagrams are made to be universally understandable," Ava said, flipping to the pictures.

She knew she was acting like a royal bitch, but she was still so angry at Tricia, at her corporate overlords, and at the universe— sorry, the *multiverse*—in general. She tried to rein her irritation in as she said, "What were you going to say before?"

Jules took a deep breath and let it out slow. They'd gotten good at not rising to her bullshit, not taking the bait she waved in front of them. Their discretion hadn't helped; Jules's calm demeanor while Ava lost her shit had just made her feel even angrier. The heart was a stupid, hurting animal, and her heart was stupider than most.

"I know that you don't want to do this," Jules said. "And that I'm the last person you want to do it with. So here's my proposal."

Ava stopped flipping through the diagrams, enough to signal that she was listening.

Jules took a breath. "Go through the maskhål far enough to be out of sight, and chill. I'll find Ursula on my own, and then meet you back there."

The worst part is that she was tempted. Sorely tempted. For a few seconds anyway, before the ever-present anger seeped back in.

"I'm not going to make you wander through a bunch of creepy worlds by yourself," Ava said grumpily. "You can't even follow foolproof diagrams."

"That's why there are instructions."

"It's supposed to be intuitive!"

"It's not intuitive for me!" Jules said. They always lost their patience with Ava eventually, because she could never keep herself from pushing them past their limit. "My brain isn't wired like that, and I don't want it to be!" Why couldn't Ava keep herself—keep both of them—from getting stuck in these same stupid arguments? "That's why I'm not going to make you explore some weird alternate universe all alone. I don't want you running into whatever the hell those things were in that video," she said, crossing her arms.

"I'd rather face down a whatever-the-hell than constantly hear I'm a screw-up who can't do obvious, simple tasks," Jules said. Their tone was quiet but vehement, full of a subdued anger that cut through Ava's defenses.

"That's not what I think." Had she ever said that? She and Jules had said a lot—a *lot*—of things to each other when they'd broken up, but she'd never. . .

"It's what everyone thinks," Jules said. Their face—normally open, armed with joy and humor—was stony and closed off. "Like doing things my own way is the most ridiculous shit they've ever heard of, even though it's the only way I've ever been happy. Nobody says it to my face, but everyone here treats me like it's a miracle I've gotten this far on my own. I'm on my last warning before I get fired. Tricia would probably be thrilled if I didn't come back."

Ava wanted to deny it, but remembered how often she'd told Jules *this is why we can't have nice things,* in every tone from accusatory to laughing, but most often with that underlying frustration. Jules was so unpredictable, so messy, forever losing or misplacing things, seeming to move in a personal chaos field. It had been thrilling, until it wasn't, until it felt like an extra weight on her own shaky mental health. But she'd never meant to make it seem like Jules should change for her, or for anyone. Especially this stupid job.

"Tricia is garbage anyway," Ava said. "So it's not like her opinion counts for shit."

Jules looked askance at her. "Let's just figure out how this thing works."

Ava spread out the instructions enough for Jules to peer over her shoulder, then tapped one of the diagrams. The diagram pointed to a large bubble on the bottom of the FINNA, like the plastic capsules for vending machine toys. "I'm assuming 'insérez un objet personnel' means insert a personal object?"

Jules wrinkled their nose at Ava's pronunciation. They used to tease her for only knowing English, when they'd grown up speaking English and French, Creole to their Guianan parents and cousins, and knew enough Spanish to crack jokes with the Honduran and Mexican dudes working down in assembly. "You're not wrong," they said begrudgingly. "Just mildly offensive. Here."

They handed over one of the purple gloves they'd found on the other side of the maskhål. Ava pressed a button, and the bubble cracked in half to open. She stuffed the fleece glove into the hollow space, which stretched to accommodate it like hard plastic never could.

"Cool, just gonna not think about how weird that is," she said.

"There should be a switch on the side," said Jules. "Turn it to. . . I guess that's a compass?"

When she did, there was a momentary whine, high-pitched as a mosquito. The glove dissolved into a gently glowing purple haze, trapped underneath the plastic. There was a pleasant ding, like an oven timer, and the console lit up.

"That's so cool," Jules said.

Ava looked back at the diagrams. "I guess we just point it at the maskhål, and it should. . . "

The FINNA beeped cheerfully, and a neon-green arrow appeared on the screen, juddering and moving as she swept the device from side to side. Some of the gauges on the console jumped as she pointed it toward that puckered seam where the two worlds joined.

"I guess that's it," Ava said. The dread that she'd successfully tamped down with anger bloomed in her stomach again.

"I guess so," Jules agreed. They picked up the instructions, put them in their back pocket, then held a hand out to Ava. She wanted to roll her eyes, but she wasn't sure she'd be able to force her leaden legs to move without any assistance.

She let Jules pull her up, and they walked toward the maskhål together.

THE FOUR PROFOUND WEAVES

BY R.B. LEMBERG

PUBLISHED BY TACHYON

<u>EXCERPT</u>

I: Change

The Snake-Surun' Encampment

Uiziya e Lali

I sat alone in my old goatskin tent. Waiting, like I had for the last forty years, for Aunt Benesret to come back. Waiting to inherit her loom and her craft, the mastery of the Four Profound Weaves. I wasn't sure how long I'd been sitting like this, and it was dark in the tent; I no longer knew day from night.

When the faded red woven tapestry at the entrance shifted aside, I drew my breath sharply, waiting for my aunt's thin, almost skeletal hand—but it was not Benesret. Of course not. Instead, one of my grand-nieces stepped in, plump and full of life, bedecked in embroideries and circlets hammered with snakes. Her eyes shone like stars in the gloom.

"Aunt Uiziya, don't sit here alone. Aunt Uiziya, you should come to the trading tent. Aunt Uiziya, bring some of these weaves—" The girl's bejeweled hand motioned at the weavings that hung, heavy and lifeless, around my tent. "You might sell something, and if not, just show your craft, yes?" And just like a flutter of wind, she was gone.

I kept sitting. But something had changed, as if some sliver of song entered my dead domain and withdrew. I had woven so much in those decades of waiting for my aunt to come back, but I wouldn't show them. None of them sang and yearned like hers did, none of them called the goddess Bird down from the merciless heat of the sky. My weaves hung lifeless, like bodies. Who would want them? Did I want them? I had not thought about that, just sat among them, the guardian of all the unwanted, forgotten things. I turned sixty-three this year; I would sit like this, until I sat among bones. My aunt could weave even from bones, but she never finished teaching me.

The flap of my tent had not been fully closed, and now the riot of light and of sounds trickled in, only half-real to my senses after a day spent in gloom. It was the commotion of trading—the rustling of cloth, the heavy sound of carpets unrolled for display, the bleating of goats. So much excitement in the encampment—the traders must be foreign. Show my craft? What craft? My life had stopped, like a wind trapped in a fist.

I'll make a weaver out of you yet, my aunt Benesret had said to me. *I'll teach you—I'll teach you, just wait. I'll teach you the Four Profound Weaves so that you will inherit my loom.*

Where was she, then? Where was she? The guardian snakes that circumnavigated the encampment all knew her, and I doubted she would be allowed to enter, but she could have tried, at least. She could have sent me a letter. She could have sent an assassin, one of those she worked with, to kill the snakes and find me and bring me to her.

The girl should have left me alone, but now I was angry and hot and I wanted. . . I wanted something that wasn't this endless wait. Show my craft, like it once was, all the promise of the desert and its secret weaves, endless future that never came to be.

I was too large and too old for rash movements, but I dragged myself up, stiff in my joints from being still for so long.

Hesitantly, I unlatched a large chest of leather in which I kept especially precious things. My late husband's wedding shirt, embroidered by my own hands before they wrinkled. A small ball of spidersilk spun by my daughter when she was a little girl. A note from the nameless man before he became nameless, given to me forty years ago. Beneath the precious debris of my life, a rustle of sand.

At last I pulled the thin, rolled-up carpet, hidden away these forty years. Shook it out. It was as long as I was tall, and slightly shorter in width. Sand grains made its threads, yellow and dun and shadow-warmth; thread-bones peeked out of their hiding places in the weave. If I called on my magical deepnames, I could make the carpet of sand float and fly, all the way up to the guardian poles of the tent.

Show your craft. You might even sell it.

"I have a carpet for sale," I said to no one in particular. "A carpet woven from sand, the second of the Four Profound Weaves that Aunt Benesret taught me before she was exiled." This carpet, that I had never shown anyone else but her. I would sell it, give it away, even—and then my yearning and my waiting would be done. And I would be done.

---

the nameless man

Everybody seemed to have gone to the trading tents, and so I made my way there as well. I was hoping to see my grandchildren, always too busy those days to spend time with me. It was true that I did not want to be trading, but if someone was trading, Aviya for sure would be there.

The trading tents were open to the air, supported with carved poles to which the lightweight cloths of the roof attached festive woven ribbons. People milled under these awnings, mostly women—Surun' weavers of all ages, each with a carpet or carpets for sale; and a few of their beloved snakes. The crowd parted as I entered, and in that moment my fears came true.

Three men stood in the middle of the trading tent. They had the gold rods of trade, and gold coins sewn onto the trim of their red felt hats. The men's eyes shone; their dark beards were groomed and oiled, and adorned with the tiniest bells that shook and jingled as they bent over the wares. I sensed powerful magic from all three of them. Their magic—multiple short deepnames—shone in their minds, each deepname like a flaring, spiky star. I was powerful myself, but the strangers' power was that of capturing, of imprisonment, of destruction, held tightly at bay. The vision made me recoil. These men— and it was always men—belonged to the Ruler of Iyar. The Collector.

I had been living here for three months with my grandchildren, among our friends the snake-Surun'. Almost three months after my transformation, my ceremony of change. I thought I had finally broken free from Iyar. But now Iyar came here.

My Surun' friends did not seem to feel any danger. They brought forth carpet after carpet, traditional indigo weaves embroidered with lions, with snakes, with birds, and more modern designs of dyed madder and bold geometric shapes. The Iyari traders examined the offerings one by one yet chose nothing, their faces still with masked disgust.

I wanted to shout at my friends to stop this trade. I wanted to run away, to escape unseen. I wanted to fight, to strike at these men, to demand recompense for all the wrongs the Collector inflicted upon me and mine forty years ago.

But then I saw my granddaughter.

Aviya-nai-Bashri was dressed in her trading best—a matching shirt and voluminous pants of green and pink cloth that contrasted so beautifully with her smooth brown skin. Her fish earrings, fashioned of hammered silver, chimed in tune with her words. Her Surun' friends, all girls of nineteen and twenty, milled around, giggling with excitement.

"We offer a carpet of wind," Aviya nai-Bashri all but sang, "A cloth woven of purest wind caught wandering over the desert—a treasure like this you will never see. . . "

The carpet she offered was small and exquisite, made from the tiniest movements of air that come awake, breath after breath, as the dawn tints the desert pink and silver. The threads that made the carpet were delicate flurries of blue not so much woven but whispered into cloth, convinced to come together by the magic of deepnames and laughter.

I'd never seen this weave, but knew who made it. My youngest grandchild. Something like tears welled in my eyes, but I would not allow myself that emotion. I looked around instead, and yes, I saw Kimi, a child of twelve, dancing between two guardian snakes. Kimi laughed, and a flurry of pink butterflies shook themselves loose from the carpet of wind. They sparkled in the air for a moment, then winked out of sight, delicate like my grandchild's magic.

I remembered Uiziya's words, spoken to me before my ceremony. *The first of the Four Profound Weaves is woven from wind. It signifies change.*

One of the emissaries leaned forward over Kimi's carpet. He pressed a finger to the carpet, and a butterfly rose from it, its wings so delicate I could barely discern the movement of pink against the Iyari man's palm. "What price for this?"

Why did Aviya deal with these men? What was the need, the necessity? We were well supplied from our previous trades, we were doing well and could refuse any trade, especially such a troubling one—what was she doing?

I spoke in my native Khana. "This carpet is not for sale."

"Yes, it is," Aviya said stubbornly.

I grabbed her by the arm, dragged her out from under the awning, carpet and all. She glared at me, defiant, and I did my best to ignore it. "What are you doing?"

"Trading. I'm trading, grandfather, that thing I trained for all my life. You trained me. Before you went through your change."

I grimaced. "This is for the Collector. We did not leave Iyar to trade with him, we left Iyar to never see him again—"

"This is Kimi's first carpet they wove completely alone," Aviya said. "Their first trade. Don't spoil it, grandfather. Please."

"First trade?" I shouldn't have gotten so angry, so bitter. "The Collector imprisoned your grandmother. Killed her. You want Kimi's first trade to be to this man?"

She propped her fists at her waist and glared at me, half-angry, half-exasperated. "And yours wasn't? Your first trade, your second, your third? The weave of song, the greatest carpet ever woven—you sold it to the Collector!"

"Yes, but there was a reason. . . "

"We are traders, grandfather. Khana women trade. Shouldn't you go sit with the men?"

It would have been better if she'd slapped me.

I turned away. She ran after me, perhaps not wanting to wound me after the spear of her words had already made its way through my chest. "I am sorry, grandfather. I did not mean. . . "

I waited, for a brief moment, for her to say what she meant, but she looked confused—not because she couldn't find a way to speak her mind, I thought, but because my existence, the change, had confused her—had confused and hurt every Khana person who loved me, or so I thought to myself. I had thought about it for forty years before I finally changed my body. I thought how my people judged me, how my lovers Bashri had judged me, how my grandchildren judged me, except perhaps Kimi, who did not know how to judge. Forty years. Even in a woman's body I wanted so desperately to be a man, I was a man—and now, a month after my change, in a man's body at last, I did not know how to stop flinching from their judgment. At best, their confusion. Aviya loved me, I knew, but her tongue kept slipping.

"It's fine." It wasn't, but I did not want to talk anymore. It hurt too much to talk, again and again, about the same thing. So I walked away.

Something made me look back. Aviya remained standing by the trading tent, the cloth of winds tucked clumsily under her arm. A stray butterfly followed me, pink and translucent; I reached out to it, but it slipped through my fingers, into the air.

Uiziya e Lali

Everybody seemed to be in the trading tents, but I dragged my feet—and not just because of the pain from sitting still for so long. The encampment felt empty. The carpet of sand on my shoulder whispered into my ear of the wide-open spaces where I wanted and dreaded to go. It was thin, almost weightless, as if it wanted to fly away from my shoulder. I tried to imagine what I would do next, after I traded the carpet away. Sell my tent and my weavings and move to some other encampment, where nobody knew me and nobody gossiped? Walk out into the desert without any water, and wait for the goddess Bird to come for my soul? Go look for that thing that I dreaded? Go back to my tent and sit once again?

I stepped closer and closer, my resolve liquefying like sweat, when I saw my old acquaintance, the nameless man. He was all but running away from the tents, his lighter brown face a grimace of anger-pain-anger I'd come to recognize in him.

Seeing me, he stopped, and averted his gaze.

"What's going on?" I asked.

"Nothing."

A thin green snake slithered in the dusk between us, as if drawing a boundary I should not cross. I stepped right over it.

"So what is going on?" I had a habit of repeating a question until it was answered.

"Go see for yourself," he said. "Trading is a woman's business, I'm told."

"Is it Aviya again? Telling you to go sit with the men?"

"Yes. But there's more—they are selling Kimi's weave." He spoke bitterly. "Like the one you'd all woven for my transformation, but Kimi made it alone, out of joy and wind and—and these butterflies. . . "

I had woven a carpet of change for myself, at the dawn of my life.

"I will teach you to weave from wind," my aunt had said to me then, *"the first mystery of the ever-changing desert. A weave of change: the first of the Four Profound Weaves I will teach you until you are ready to put together my loom."*

The nameless man spoke on, his voice shaking with the speed and vehemence of his feeling. "My grandchild's first carpet, first trade, to be traded to the Collector, to be held by the Collector's hands, and they all think it's nothing. Joyful even. Joyful!" He took a deep breath. Spoke a bit slower. "What joy is there in trading the cloth of change to a man who will never change? The Collector will lock this cloth in his coffers, away from all eyes but his, away from the people who would use it, who need it, themselves, to change."

I sighed. "Kimi doesn't want to change yet."

"Then she should—he should—they should—" The nameless man waved his hand in exasperation. "Kimi should keep the cloth and transform already!"

"Your grandchild hasn't chosen whether to transform," I said patiently, as I had many times before. "It may never matter to them to go through the change in the body. It is enough that they would weave." I was a good listener, if nothing else; but this I had listened to over and over. The nameless man's people, the Khana, did not recognize in-betweeners. The nameless man's people did not recognize people like him, either; instead, they insisted that the shape of one's body determined one's fate. "The Khana are not the only people in the world who make up these rules and these freedoms."

The nameless man waved his hand in the air again, as if to shoo a stray butterfly. Then he eyed me with a bit more attentiveness. "You, too, bring a carpet to the tent?"

"As you see." I wanted him to ask me about the carpet. I wanted him to ask me why. I wanted to tell him then of my endless waiting, and how I wanted it to be over. I was a good listener, but now I wanted him to listen as I told him about Aunt Benesret. After he came back to us after forty years away, he kept asking about Benesret, and everybody shushed him, because in our encampment we did not say her name.

But he asked me nothing. Just squinted at my carpet and said, "You shouldn't sell it, either."

"How like a man, to tell me what I should and shouldn't do." Half-exasperation, half-compliment in acknowledgment of his change, the words flew out of my mouth before I knew it.

He grimaced bitterly. "That's right. I'll just go sit with the men, then."

Then he walked past me, head drawn into his shoulders.

---

the nameless man

I walked where my feet took me, to the outskirts of the encampment. I thought Uiziya might follow me, but she didn't. I was on my own, and perhaps that was best.

After my transformation, I tried sitting with the Surun' men. They had showed me how to speak Surun' like a man and how to move, how to shave my face Surun'-style. They were friends and good people, but I did not want to go much deeper into their ways. I was no warrior. I could fight when I needed, but that was not what being a man meant to me. I wasn't Surun'. I was Khana.

Our people lived in Iyar, but we weren't Iyari. Behind the walls of our quarter, walled off from the rest of the city by royal decrees, the Khana lived separate lives, and in the Khana quarter, women and men lived separate lives yet again, divided from each other by an inner wall.

Our men were scholars, not warriors. Scholars and makers of magical automata for the utter glory of Bird and her hidden brother, the singer Kimri. As a child I would wake up in darkness to stand under the white walls of the men's inner quarter, where I wasn't allowed—waiting—waiting for our men to sing the dawn-song to bring the sibling gods closer, and with them, the dawn.

But now I was here, far east and away from Iyar, in the great Burri desert. It was here, at this very place, in this dust, on the outskirts of the snake-Surun' encampment, I had stood in my cloth made of winds, the weave of transformation my friends and my grandchildren had woven for me out of love. I'd lifted my arms to the sky and the sandbirds had come to me, sent to me by the goddess Bird and summoned by the cloth of winds. They were birds of bright fire that fell from the sky and cocooned me, until I could see and hear nothing except the warmth and the feathers enveloping me and the threads of the wind singing each to each until my whole skin was ignited by the sun, my body changing and changed by the malleable flame. And when it was done, I sang.

I sang as the wind and the feathers dissolved into sand under my feet; I sang because my transformation was complete. I sang the dawnsong—the sacred melody that the men of my people sing, standing on the roof of the men's quarter every morning.

Since then, I had not sung again. As it had for the decades before, the sacred melody sat like a lump in my throat, and I could neither voice it nor swallow it.

I did not know how much time passed, but when I lifted my gaze from the sand where I knelt, I saw Uiziya, the dun-colored carpet still over her shoulder.

Uiziya was a friend from earlier days, when I was young and full of hope still, but now I did not know her that well. She was always at gatherings, weaving with the others—weaving even my own cloth of winds preparing for my transformation, but she did not say much. She was Benesret's niece, and I asked about Benesret, but the others were wary of Uiziya speaking. Every time she opened her mouth to speak of her aunt, she was shushed.

Now she came closer. Her shadow, broad and round, fell over me, sheltering me from the glare of the sky. The carpet she carried over her shoulder stirred, whispering in a language I did not understand.

"Why did you come back here?" she asked.

I looked away. "You would not understand."

Uiziya shrugged. "I think I do. It is not hard to be a changer among my people. I know that it is not true everywhere, but in the great Burri desert, changing your body to match your heart is not a thing to bleed your eyes over."

"It is for me." Of course, she would say this. She grew up here, the vast Burri desert ruled by the Old Royal, who was a changer themself, and welcomed all changers. I was from Iyar.

"I know it is hard for you, heart." Uiziya stretched out a hand, but I made no motion or word to welcome her touch, and she pulled back.

"If I was from the desert," I said, "Benesret would weave my cloth of transformation then and there, when I saw her first when I was twenty-four and she was forty and wise and splendid under the ancient discolored weavings in her tent."

"If you were from the desert," echoed Uiziya, "you would not need Benesret. You would have the cloth woven for you by family, if any were gifted enough. Or you would travel southeast to the Old Royal's capital, and transform at the Sandbird Festival. You would make the transformation as a youth, and go sit with the men and go speak with the men and go guard with the men, and sire children as a man, and raise children as a man, and think no more these noisy, agitated thoughts of yours."

I did not want to think my noisy, agitated thoughts, but they sat better with me than the matter-of-fact, "everything is perfectly commonplace about a swarm of sandbirds cocooning your body and helping you transform, and then you just go sit with the men" conversation I'd had with so many Surun' people. I was not Surun'. I was not from the desert at all. As a Khana person from Iyar, I did not fit, among women, among men. Even far away from home, with only myself for company, I did not fit.

I did not want to wound her, but I did not know how to talk to anyone anymore.

"Forgive me. I think you would understand better if you were a changer."

She lowered herself down slowly, as if the movements pained her, until she sat by my side. "I, too, am a changer."

"Oh?" I frowned, uncomfortable. I had always assumed—I shouldn't have assumed—how could I have assumed? "Forgive me."

Uiziya shrugged. "I made my own cloth of transformation when I was a child."

I did not know that she was a changer, like me. I never thought anyone was. I had never met others who went through the change in Iyar. They were banished or imprisoned or hiding or dead. But here, in the desert, changing one's shape was a matter of ritual, of love, not of desperate secrets.

Uiziya kept speaking. "The first weave is the weave of change, the first mystery of the everchanging desert, the first of the Four Profound Weaves that Aunt Benesret taught me. I wove my cloth of winds, and sandbirds came to me, like they did to you. They cocooned me and burned without burning, and when they were done, I was myself in my body."

"I did not know," I said again. "I'm sorry."

"Nobody remembers anymore. I do not think about it too much. It was a relief. I'd always been a little girl."

We were face to face, Uiziya crouching, me kneeling, and between us the finest threads of sand whispered each to each in a language I did not understand. No longer dun, the carpet of sand undulated with every shade of yellow and brown and gold, and between these strands I saw glimpses of sunset and shadow, and bones—always bones—bones of strange, beguiled animals that had once roamed the desert before the goddess Bird brought our people here, and our stars.

"Why did you return to this place?" Uiziya asked again. She had a habit of asking the same question over and over until she was satisfied.

Because I was running away. No, that wasn't it. "Looking for something."

"Yes?"

My song. I had it for the brief moment after my transformation, but now it felt farther away from me than ever before. *My people.* Except they were far, in Iyar, behind layers of walls, and I did not want to go back.

"My name," I said at last. "I always thought Benesret would give it to me when I came back here, came back to her, ready at last to transform. But when I came back, she was gone."

"They exiled her," said Uiziya.

"Why?" I asked. "Why did they exile her?"

"Because they were afraid."

Uiziya e Lali

The nameless man swallowed. Remembering, no doubt, the first time he came here with his lover Bashri-nai-Leylit, looking for the greatest carpet ever woven, to bring back to the Collector.

How Benesret greeted them, helped them. How she wove for them.

"Are you afraid of Benesret?" he asked at last.

I shrugged. "I am not afraid of death. I think I will welcome it. I would give my death to her willingly if only she would teach me." Such raw yearning was in my voice that it scalded me, scared me. In response, the nameless man's magical deepnames glittered for a moment in his mind, like warm stars flaring, then settled before I had a chance to see them clearly.

"I do not want you to die," he blurted out, his eyes on the ground.

"You do not want me to die or to sell my carpet," I said, frustration knotted with amusement in my voice. "What would you want me do, nameless man?"

"Nen-sasaïr." The rustle of it was so soft on his lips I almost missed it. "It is just a way-name, until I am given one that is mine."

"Nen-sasaïr," I echoed. "Sandbirds, and. . . ?" I did not know the other word.

"The son of sandbirds. Nen: a son. I would be called my father's son, if I was a Khana man."

"You are a Khana man," I said, but saying this, I knew that I would be rebuked.

"I do not fit anywhere," he said. "Except that I fit with the sandbirds for a brief moment, when I put on the cloth of winds and the sandbirds came to me; when everything sang and swirled and I sang, too, I sang the dawnsong which had been forbidden to me all my life, a religious rite for the glory of Bird's hidden brother, the singer god, Kimri."

I remembered the melody from his ritual, yes, devastating and joyous, a promise, a cresting of dawn on his lips, in that moment when a dream was becoming, and the fragility of becoming was not yet revealed in nen-sasaïr's heart. "Will you sing the dawnsong again?"

"No. Maybe. I don't know. Sometimes I feel the god—Kimri —just there, behind me, waiting for my song where I cannot see. But I am silent. Khana women are forbidden to sing. I am a man —so I am allowed to sing, but I cannot. My body feels mine like never before; I am whole in my body, but my people will never accept my changing. The thought of it stoppers my throat."

"You should talk to your people," I said. "Talk to them before you decide whether or not they would accept you."

His face flooded with a feeling I could not name. "I can't, Uiziya. And I won't. I want to talk to Benesret."

His hand stirred the dry, hard ground by the carpet of sand, as if he wanted to touch the fringed knots and did not dare. He did not look up when he spoke. "We should find her. Perhaps she will teach you. Perhaps she will give me my name."

I laughed so bitterly the strands of the carpet of sand shook and moved. "If she wanted to teach me, she would return, exiled or no—with all her power of death, with all her knowledge she would teach me. She weaves the white clothes for the Orphan's assassins—do you think mere mortals would stop her? She came to my tent once. . . " I stopped. I did not want him to know my secret.

To master the weave of death you must embrace death. Are you ready?

I thought I was ready then, but I wasn't. Afraid for my children. Myself. Perhaps I was ready now. But nen-sasaïr would reject me like all the others did when I told them. "You will not like me when you learn my secret. You will not want to journey with me."

"Try me," he said, his eyes still firmly on the ground. "If nothing else, I am brave." In his mind, his magic flared again. He did not shroud his mind, so I could see it clearly: three deepnames of different lengths, a single-syllable, a two-syllable, and a three-syllable. A rare and powerful configuration that could not be easily defeated; the Builder's Triangle, as it was called in his land.

My carpet stirred in response to this magic, the eddies and whirls of sand around slivers of bone that transformed for a moment into bejeweled lizards and snakes, then smoothed out again.

I did not want this moment to end.

It would end when he knew me better.

Everything ends. What would happen if he disdained me? I could just sell my carpet as I wanted. "Then I will show you. My secret. And then you'll decide."

"Yes," nen-sasaïr said.

"If you'll watch my carpet, I'll go get provisions. And then we should travel south from here, travel in cool hours and rest when the sun is hottest."

"Yes," nen-sasaïr said again. Not questioning anything.

"How will you travel?" I asked him.

"On sand-skis. I'll show you when you return."

I saw no sand-skis. I wondered if he'd simply take my carpet and leave; but when I made my way back, my breath short from carrying supplies in the heat, my carpet was still there. And nen-sasaïr was still there, his slim, tall frame shifting on two longish, wide planes of bent wood.

In his mind, nen-sasaïr's deepnames flared one by one: first the weakest, the three-syllable, like a thin line of light; then the two-syllable, a short, strong line; and finally, the single-syllable, bright like a star—the strongest of them. His deepnames connected to each other, light running between them until they formed a triangle, then spilled their power onto the sand-skis.

"The blades will float just above ground. It's as if I am gliding on air."

"Me too. On my carpet." I wanted to smile at him, but I had forgotten how. The motion of my lips stretched my face in odd ways.

The Four Profound Weaves. A carpet of wind, a carpet of sand, a carpet of song, and a carpet of bones. Change, wanderlust, hope, and death.

Nen-sasaïr watched me intently as I breathed my deepnames into the carpet of sand. It floated, lifting me above ground, carrying me out of the encampment, where the tents of my people swayed in the wind, empty. They all were trading, but I had not even tried to sell my carpet, and I did not look back. My weave of wanderlust floated over the boundary spirals drawn in the dust, over the guardian snakes that lifted their heads in recognition and farewell, then settled.

My past lay ahead, and its secrets. The wind and the sand to all sides. Behind me, nen-sasaïr followed.

I had woven the carpets of air and sand. Benesret's great carpet had been made of song. Only death was missing now.

II: Wanderlust
The Great Burri Desert
nen-sasaïr

We traveled in silence through the cooler hours—I on my sand-skis, Uiziya floating ahead of me, only slightly above ground. I had known her for forty years—no, I had only known her briefly, forty years ago. When we were both young. When I traveled with my lover Bashri-nai-Leylit on a desperate trading venture to find the greatest treasure ever woven, to buy our other lover's life from the Collector.

It was strange to travel with someone again. Uiziya and I, we were not lovers. Friends, perhaps. Two people making a journey together. I did not know where we were going, but I followed Uiziya. Closer to the encampment, I saw the dun grasses and shrubs that clung to patches of ground; then, deeper into that domain, the vegetation became even scarcer and drier, and the sandhills began to waver in my sight. I waited for the wind to shift the layers of sand, revealing to me its secrets like years before, but I saw no miracles this time. Just the sand and the dust in the wake of Uiziya's carpet, the sun—even in cooler hours—forever following me.

I had left my grandchildren behind without even saying goodbye.

Aviya—Aviya-nai-Bashri—my granddaughter was an adult now, and a fine trader, traveling with an oreg of her own. The newly formed Aviya oreg consisted of my granddaughter and her lover, Aviya-nai-Lur—and they would be all right. The two had already made a journey of their own, from Iyar to the desert. And they had taken good care of Kimi.

Kimi, a child of eleven summers, a child we named after the men's god Kimri, a child who was neither a boy nor a girl, who back in Iyar could not be recognized, but here, in the desert, could thrive with an ease that required no discussion. A child who did not talk, a child who wove butterflies from wind, a child whose first-woven carpet was sold to my tormentor.

I did not recall having stopped or closing my eyes, but I must have. I stood there, not willing to look or think of anything, until the rough, grainy threads of a carpet brushed over my face, and I smelled the old threads and dust of Uiziya's carpet. I opened my eyes into sand-cloud in which dim shapes moved and trans-formed into others, then closed them, my fists in my sand-scrubbed eyes. I coughed and rubbed my eyes and swayed, and Uiziya waited, but not very long.

"What troubles you?" she asked.

That I left my grandchildren to fend for themselves among your people.

I was glad I did not speak this. The Surun' people were our friends, not adversaries. My grandchildren wanted to travel without me, had traveled on their own before. They would continue to be safe. Perhaps. Probably. Likely.

My problem was different.

I said, "All my life, I was a man. And yet I kept that a secret. Not because I wanted to keep such a secret, but because other people told me that I must, that it was shameful and wrong to reveal it, that it was selfish to be who I was. I had to remain—a lover, a trader, a grandmother. I was a reluctant grandmother, but now that I'm free, now that I am a grandfather, am I supposed just not to care for them anymore?"

"Why is there a difference?" Uiziya shrugged. "You can choose to care or not, as all people do."

But in my culture, we never even saw the grandfathers. They were behind the inner white wall. As a part of a traditional family-trading group, called an oreg, a small group of women lovers made trading journeys together, returning to the outer quarter of Iyar. There they met with their husbands only for rituals, in the special rooms tucked in-between the outer and inner parts of the Khana quarter. Grandmothers raised the children while the young women traveled and traded.

And I did not fit. I never fit.

"You make it sound so simple, nen-sasaïr. What your people do, what your people don't do. What they told you to do. What they did not tell you to do, but you think they told you to do. What you think your lovers thought. What you think they think now that they died. Always you lived in the shadow of these people and their rules. Even forty years ago. But nobody's world is clear and simple, much as we want it to be."

"You did not live my life," I said. "And yet you judge me."

She laughed, bitterly. "Judge you? Me? Who am I to judge anyone?"

"You lived your life openly. . . "

She cut me short. "You do not know me. And if you knew, you would surely judge me."

"I wouldn't—"

"No? How can you know?" She seemed angrier now, her

carpet swirling with visions of bones and jewels. I took a step back, not from her, from the dust and the threads that once again threatened my face. "I am not afraid."

She looked me up and down. "Then let me show you."

She turned away and I followed. The sand was different here, as if freer, wilder, stirring about the visions of bones and wind. I remembered moments like these from before, when I traveled with Bashri-nai-Leylit, so full of desperate hope for our venture. I was twenty-four then, but now I was sixty-four, and Bashri-nai-Leylit was dead, and Bashri-nai-Divrah was dead, and the world was very short on hope. But even my bones sang the need to wander.

Uiziya e Lali

My carpet shifted as I shifted my weight. It was slightly too large for just one person sitting; another person would balance it out, but I worried my weight made it sag. Benesret had been thin, almost skeletal always, but I was a woman of size. I'd woven this carpet at sixteen. I was big then, too, but I wanted back then to be slim like Benesret, to be lithe and limber like the snakes in our encampment. I wanted to cast a long, elegant shadow. I had always been big, but at sixteen, I had not yet embraced it, so I'd woven my carpet for a thinner person. It carried me well, even now, but it wasn't well-balanced; the tasseled edges rose up as it moved.

"I will teach you to weave from sand," my aunt had said to me back then, "the second mystery of the ever-changing desert. A weave of wanderlust: the second of the Four Profound Weaves I will teach you until you are ready to put together my loom."

I had never been ready to put together a loom. The one I continued to use was the training loom that I'd made at sixteen. Others in the encampment gossiped at first, then they stopped, thinking perhaps that I had persisted with such a simple, small frame as a boast about my skills. But my craft, like the frame, had not grown much after I wove this very carpet of sand that carried me now. It whispered of wanderings, and of bones, always bones, for I had woven bones into it —sparsely, as decoration, peeking out of the sand-weaves in glimpses of white. The true weave of bones I had not mastered, for that was the last of the four—the weave of death Aunt Benesret said she would teach me when I was ready. I'd have learned it perhaps, if I hadn't drawn away—from her, from this place.

Oh, this place.

I made my carpet stop. Nen-sasaïr, also deep, perhaps, in his thoughts, kept moving until we were level. We stood side by side on a small outcropping. Below us, we saw collapsed tents, their weavings half-gnawed by time and transformations that happen in the desert when nobody looks. Ghost snakes slithered in the dust, their skeletons glimmering white from their long, limber bodies of smoke.

Nen-sasaïr turned to me. "What is it that I'm seeing, Uiziya? Are these things dangerous?"

"Only if you are afraid to die." I was beyond such things. My life was over.

"What is there?" He was pointing out at a tent that still stood proud. Or so it seemed. It was smaller, white and embroidered blue—but it wasn't embroidery we saw. It was covered in insects. Brilliant, sparkling, winking in and out of sight.

"My husband. This is why we came here. Look."

---

nen-sasaïr

The brilliant insects shifted about. I saw a young woman, brown-skinned and beautifully large, her face so full of yearning and hope. Uiziya in her youth, as I met her all those years ago, perhaps just a little bit older. She opened the fold of her tent and peeked out tentatively as the stars shone, but these were just pinpricks and slivers of light from the flies.

The flesh-and-blood Uiziya said, "You see other lives as easy because you don't see them. You see your story as complex and hard because you know it best."

"I am sorry," I said. "I didn't mean to imply that you had no hardship."

"I was so full of hope after I saw your great carpet of song being woven. Again and again I pleaded with my aunt to teach me the remaining weave. The weave of death."

"Did she? Benesret?" Out of the corner of my eye, I saw something white flash, a motion, around the tent.

"She said to me, 'Do you know what it means? What it means to weave from the people you care for, from sisters, from lovers, from kin? What it means to weave out of your body, your flesh, to weave your own death as if you saw it for the first time?' Her eyes were hungry but still I said, teach me. *Please, teach me.* So she tried."

"What happened?" I whispered.

"Let us go down."

"Something is there," I said, in a warning, but Uiziya shrugged.

"Something is always there."

We trekked down, until we stood in front of the brilliant buzzing tent. Uiziya drew open the flap, and then suddenly there was movement. Too quick for my eyes to follow at first. A youth, his eyes wide and startled, clutching a handful of white cloth in his right hand. His left held a knife, and he lunged. I breathed, and my names flared to life, but not quickly enough. The youth pushed past Uiziya, the knife making a long, thin graze on her arm as he past her, Uiziya's blood spraying him and the white cloth he held. The youth ran. I formed my Builder's Triangle as fast as I could, but my magic was not that of offense.

Uiziya called after me, "Don't pursue!" as the youth's lean, wavering shadow ran up and out of the ghost encampment. Out of sight.

IFE-IYOKU, THE TALE OF IMADEYUNUAGBON

BY OGHENECHOVWE DONALD EKPEKI

PUBLISHED BY AURELIA LEO

EXCERPT

Hunters

Morako stayed quiet. He was a lero – or feeler – and oversaw the hunt. On his signal the rest would move. For now, he lay waiting, careful not to alert the beast lest the intended prey became the hunter. Here, the roles of the prey and the hunter could switch in a flash, leaving the hunter to scurry for survival. But he knew that father Obatala himself had chosen them and imbued them with sacred gifts which, though not making them immune, offered them a measure of protection.

The Nlaagama – an enormous, lizard-like beast – slithered forward. At almost twelve feet tall, it towered over banana trees. Its forked tongue of about eight inches swung pendulously and tasted the air. It bent to rip into the horned antelope which the Umzingeli, hunters had butchered and left as bait. The antelope was like a horse, tall and possessing thick, strong legs and a horn like the mythical creatures of the old world. The Nlaagama ripped into the antelope with the savagery that made Morako swallow.

This was Igbo Igboya, the forest of fears.

With the beast distracted, Morako gave the signal. The Umzingeli, four coal black forms, detached themselves from the trees around. The beast only stirred before resuming its feeding. The Umzingeli merged, activating the power of anjayiyan-okan, the chameleon mind. They became part of what they merged with and assumed their properties to remain hidden and unde-tectable until they detached themselves. The beast would sense them soon. Morako signalled them again. They ran towards the beast with their wooden spears extended. It stood still, trying to detect them, sensing that something was wrong.

Morako shot a spike of placidity at the beast. It struggled to cast off the artificial lethargy. The warriors were closing on it. They needed to be close enough to access the gaps between its scales. Without their skill of merging, the beast would detect them before they got close enough to use their weapons. This was not a static merging which shielded them completely from detec-tion. It was a minute merger of their feet with the ground and the leaves and twigs and droplets of water as they ran. It was activated as they stepped, but deactivated when their feet left the ground, so that they had to consciously reactivate with each step. It was more difficult and required a delicate touch and a contin-uous synchronization with the environment. It was a skill that only the best of the Umzingeli could use. Properly timed, it enabled them to mask their movement as when they used static merger in complete stillness.

They were almost on the beast. This was the tricky part: attacking while maintaining the chameleon mind, the delicate merger that allowed them to move silently and remain invisible. They were close enough, within striking distance…

One of them lost it. Not totally, for he still managed to remain silent and unseen, but he failed to include his weapon in the merger. From where Morako watched, he saw it.

Though he could sense their presence with his own skill as a lero, to his eyes, they were invisible and silent to his ears. He only saw a spear coming out of thin air while the body of the hunter remained unseen. The beast's long tail swivelled with a snap, almost faster than his eyes could follow. Its tail slapped the spear away and turned to curl around something that became visible in its grasp as the hunter lost hold of the merger. It flung the hunter at another shape that just became visible and both went down on contact.

The beast reared suddenly and howled, shaking its neck violently and throwing something off. The last hunter materialised some yards away and Morako noticed the broken half of the spear protruding from the back of the beast. It was wounded but far from defeated. He stared at it. The hunter pulled out another spear and twirled it, preparing to attack. The beast pawed the earth and roared, belching liquid flames at the hunter. From his vantage position where he watched, Morako saw the hunter roll out of the path of the lava like substance the monster spat and vanish, re-merging and blending into the environment. The beast howled again as a spear found a way into one of the gaps between its scales. It bathed the clearing with lava, turning to search if the burnt body of a hunter would appear. None did.

The beast screeched at the unseen enemy. Two large wings unfurled from its body. With its enormous wings, the beast fanned the air. In a swift movement, it lifted itself off the ground. Morako nudged the Climbers. It was time for their role. As the beast soared upwards, the Climbers dropped a net from the trees and entangled its wings, dropping it to the ground. Flames cackled around, and the climbers, armed with clubs and spears, attacked it. Most of their attacks snapped on the beast's thick scales as it ripped the net with its claws and fangs. The reinforcements would be in trouble if it managed to free itself. The remaining hunter materialised as from thin air and buried his spear in the neck of the beast, through an opening in its armour. As he pulled it off, hot blood came gushing out, scalding the climbers who scurried away. The hunter backed off to join the other hunters who had been knocked off. The beast belched its liquid fire amidst its dying throes.

Yet it panted, refusing to die. A figure walked in, dragging a tree trunk. It was Oni, the elephant man. The climbers and hunters made way for him. He hefted the trunk and walloped the dying beast in the head. He didn't need to do it twice.

Weaver

It was night in the village of Ife-Iyoku. Everywhere was alight and alive with merriment. Children danced and laughed at the pursuit of masquerades. Palm wine and ogogoro flowed freely for the quaffing of Amala and Ewedu. A group of children gathered in front of a wrinkled but firm-looking old woman, Ologbon the Weaver. She enraptured them with the tales she spun for them. They were content to sit and listen while the other children ran around eating and playing games of Ite and Suwe.

Tonight, she spun the history of Ife-Iyoku to her attentive audience.

"This is how the people of Ife-Iyoku came to be. Long before you were born, the world was not like this. It was much bigger and encompassed different countries and cultures. Then there was a war, and all was lost. The contenders attempted the destruction of one another and ended up almost destroying us. It was a fight between two elephants in which the ground suffers."

The gravity of her voice moistened the eyes of the children. "I see you don't know what an elephant is, as none of you have ever seen one. So much of our culture was lost in the catastrophe, and with them, life itself. But we thank the Orishas father Olorun and his son Obatala for sending us some things to replace what we lost." Her voice, initially grand and majestic, became dry and ordinary as one passing commentary on distant object. The children followed the expressions on her face.

She lifted her hand and the lights dimmed to almost quenching. The illumination was replaced by glowing lines in the air. The weaver Ologbon spun with her hands as she had with her mouth. The children watched in wonder. The light took the shape of two elephants. The elephants trumpeted and stamped on the ground, then rushed at each other. They tussled. The children felt the vibration of the earth and clutched each other's hands tightly. The weaver raised both hands and the images of the two battling elephants dissipated and faded. The ground was muddied up.

"That," she said, pointing, "is the ground after two elephants fought. Oni the brawny is named after them. In any night but this, I would go on weaving you tales of wonder and valour. But tonight, is a special night, the night of the Onye Lana Riri festival. Tonight, marks the night many years ago when the war came upon us. You must know your history if you are to seize for yourself a future. All of you are Onye Lana Riri, the ones that survive. I believe there is more in store for you than just existence. I believe that you will thrive. For those of you who do not remember or have not heard this tale, I shall tell it again. It is the story of our death and rebirth to what we are today."

As she spoke, she raised her hand to weave again. The light from the fire dimmed once more and strands of light rose into various forms in line with the tale she wove.

"Once we were a vast group of peoples called Afrika, peoples of special and diverse cultures and breeding. They lived in peace and unity before the war of the nations around them. These nations had developed nuclear weapons but entered into a pact not to use them against one another. Why someone would make something they never intended to use I never got. Like the wicked senior wife that obtained poisonous charms claiming never to have intended it for the newest wife's soup. So, one side broke the pact, as pacts are wont to be broken in wars by the desperate or losing parties."

As she spoke, the images she conjured intensified and were matched by sound. Factions launched missiles and the children watched them travel towards the raised outlines of other cities.

"Everyone launched their warheads. The pact of mutually assured destruction was broken. But the disaster did not happen now."

As she spoke, she flicked her hand. The images continued

projecting. The missiles hit an invisible dome above the city and were rendered defective. Some of them jerked in the air, spiralling sporadically before ricocheting and returning the way they had come.

"America, the greatest nation in the war at the time, had prepared for this day. She had missile defence systems in place. She also had systems to seize the missiles in the air and redirect them whence they came."

She gestured to the returning missiles.

"America had the power to quash the missiles. But instead, she wanted to show her power. She wanted to punish the offenders, the Middle Easterners from a continent called Asia who she felt had bred trouble for countless centuries. That was how the seed of destruction that is fully grown today was sown. Hundreds of nuclear warheads were sent sailing back to the shores of Iraq and Afghanistan and their Moslem brethren. Unbeknownst to the West and its allies, their foes had obtained some of the missile redirecting technology from their allies, the Chinese and the Russians.

"But having technology is not mastery of it. They could not manage what they were given. Their control of the technology was not strong enough to allow them to send the weapons all the way back. Their range was small and they had friends and allies around them. So, they redirected the weapons to the closest place they could, where their friends would not suffer them and there would be no retribution: Afrika."

She whispered this last word with sharp, dramatic emphasis. The missiles in her images of light paused in the air. There was total quietude as she continued her tale.

"Afrika was a place of culture and learning. We had no implements of war and destruction, or of defence against them. We stayed out of international disputes. Our brothers to the South of Africa developed such armaments, but they disarmed them, wise enough to see that they would do nothing but destroy us and the rest of the world. However, being right didn't stop us from paying the price of the wrong parties. When wise ones are surrounded by fools, they often end up suffering as the fools. Sometimes they suffer more than the fools."

She flicked her hand and the missiles landed all at once. A blinding yellow light rose from where they landed, followed by fire and smoke which billowed out and spread till it covered the whole area. The children gasped. Some were weeping. The Weaver continued her story.

"Nearly all of Afrika was destroyed by the missiles of the combatants. Nothing would have been left of Afrika but for the fact that we are a special people. Our land, Ife, is a sacred ground where all life originated. We have always been deeply spiritual and in tune with the gods, with heaven and with the earth. We called on Obatala who interceded on our behalf as he had done when his sister Olokun threatened the world with water in a period they called the age of global warming. He pleaded with Olorun, the sky father, to save us. Olorun urinated in a gourd and told Obatala to sprinkle the water on the affected area and all the destruction and left-over radiation would dissipate.

"The urine was not sufficient to sprinkle in all the affected parts of Afrika. Obatala could only use the urine in the healing of the land of his own people. Despite Obatala's intercession, Olorun did not care about the rest of the world. The smoke from the bombs covered the sun and temperatures dropped. All life was threatened, not just the lives in Afrika. Obatala in his infinite love and mercy decided to share the cure with rest of the world even though they were responsible for the disaster. With the sacred urine, he was able to wash away the radiation and nuclear waste. However, what was left was insufficient to totally reverse the effect of the bombs in Afrika.

"Obatala cut himself and let some drops of his blood mix with the urine in the gourd to increase its potency. With the mixture he saved Ife. Nothing was left to save the rest of Afrika. Only this small circle around Ife is clean. We are trapped and all around us is the lingering destruction from the folly of man. The first rain that fell after the destruction affected the land and people around Ife. The sacred land rejects and repels the radiation and waste. Our blood and bodies are stronger. We adapted abilities to make up for what we lost and to enable us to survive in this new world. We became Ndi Lana Riri, the ones who survived. And what is more, Obatala left us a lasting gift. Each time one of us dies, our blood thickens, and the remaining ones evolve further to make up for the numbers lost with strength. His blood keeps us and strengthens us further to ensure that his people endure. It is said that in the hour of our greatest need, he will return to restore us and Afrika fully.

"The rest of the world learned and moved on from their folly. We were the lesson. They believed that either we had all been wiped out or the corruption around us is so thick they could not reach through. Perhaps, they refused to attempt saving us for fear of contaminating the rest of the world. They created one of their barriers to keep us away, until they discover how to undo their error and cleanse the environment. But that may not be a long time coming because it's easier to destroy than to rebuild.

"Some may wonder why he saved the world. It is because despite all that happened, survival is collective. If man would survive, we must do so together, as one. We must think of all and not of individuals."

"If we don't die out before that day comes," a gruff male voice said.

The Weaver looked up to note the presence of three people who had just joined the campfire. One was an old man who had a wrapper tied around his chest in the manner of Igbo chiefs. The other two, a man and a woman, were much younger. The man was sturdy but lean. He bore the traditional marks of a hunter: crossed slashes on his chest and claw tattoos. The woman followed him closely. She was lean too but not as hard looking. Her softer features followed him in concern before she turned to look at the seated children with a smile. They smiled back.

The Weaver rose to greet the old Chief. "Welcome, husband."

"Thank you, wife," he said affectionately.

The children all rose to squat and greet him in the traditional manner.

"Ekaro sir."

"Ekaro my children," he responded with a fatherly smile.

"At least all is not lost. Even if gold and land are lost, our culture and blood which are our greatest assets still endure."

The Weaver sniffed. He gave her a curt and slightly annoyed look. She responded with an affectionate one. The children returned to their seats.

The Chief said, "The fell beast has been slain. Imade has healed the hunters and drained their bodies of the corruption they contacted in Igbo Igboya. The beast lies ready for the final phase of the ceremony and I came personally to inform you. As Chief Priestess, you must be there to consecrate the sacrifice to Obatala."

The Weaver nodded. He turned to the children to dismiss the campfire session, but she raised a finger to forestall him. He cut off with a slight frown.

She said, "The night's session is not done. The Chiefs' Council may be your domain, but this is mine. Obatala entrusted this sacred task on me and my successor. My time is nigh, and I must do as much of my duty as I can before it comes."

Morako who accompanied the Chief stood in rigid observance of the exchange between the Chief and his wife. But Imade caught his eye with a sly smirk on her face.

Ologbon the wise, weaver of tales said, "We shall give the Nlaagama in sacrifice to Obatala in this festival. Every day before this festival, our best warriors must go to hunt these creatures which have been twisted by the corruption filtering from the outside. They are for sacrifices to Obatala. We do this to show that we are strong enough to play our part in guarding and preserving the sacred life he gave us with his blood."

Morako thumped his chest and said, "We are strong and must remain so till Obatala returns again to lead us to our destiny."

The Chief squatted to address the gathering. His wife shifted uncomfortably but he ignored her. "I speak in my authority as Ooni, head Chief. Obatala may return, or he may not. Whether Obatala comes or not, we will be strong and lead ourselves to our own destinies. Ife thins every day. The corruption keeps creeping in and the creatures in Igbo Igboya grow more twisted. We have been given the sacred gifts already. We carry the power of our salvation in our blood. In our moment of near destruction, we were mutated and thus acquired resistance to things that would have killed us. Perhaps it was Obatala who had done this for us; perhaps it was not him. Whatever the cause or reason, we have become stronger than we were before. We have acquired the ability to heal and manipulate the elements. Every time one of us dies, our powers wax stronger. Let us use these gifts to counteract our possible extinction. Our powers were less when we were more. With the reduction in our population, our gifts are strengthened. The gifts call on us to use them. We must take our destiny in our own hand, whether Obatala returns or not."

The Weaver clicked her tongue and asked: "Is this another exhortation for migration? You know, beloved, that we have tried that before and many were lost. There is no way through the corruption surrounding Ife. The outside world does not even know we exist. This issue has been raised before the council and voted down."

The Chief raised a placatory hand. "This isn't the council indeed, peace woman. I merely informed them of what they must face someday."

He turned to the children. "Tomorrow is your first day in the house of learning. You will be tested. All who are old enough will begin training on how to use the sacred gifts you are imbued with and how to take on your sacred duty of survival so that someday you may face and take on your destiny. You are no longer children. You will be great men and woman of Ife-Iyoku." He thumped his chest and all the people did the same.

He continued. "With the permission of the Weaver of tales and teacher of the sacred lore of Obatala, we go to offer the beast as saifice to Obatala in honour of our sacred charge to survive."

The Weaver pulled out a clay cup and one of the children came forward. He took the cup from her, took in his breath and dragged with his fingers as if pulling something, his focus on the cup. There was a rushing sound. He handed the cup to the weaver and resumed his seat. She put the cup to her mouth and took a pull. Water leaked out and ran down her mouth. The Chief looked at the child and nodded in approval. The child beamed with pleasure.

The Weaver set the cup down and explained. "This is our ritual. Talking is thirsty work and Ake here keeps me hydrated. He is a puller and can pull the elements. He helps me with water after our sessions."

"That is very good, but we will need more than a cup of water to survive," the Chief muttered.

"I heard that," the Weaver said.

"Well, the festival awaits."

"One more thing," the Weaver said as she manipulated her light weaving gifts in complex patterns. A trail of light followed her fingers. The light glowed brighter until it became a full ball of light. She released it and it shot into the night. It exploded in a brilliant rainbow of colours and illuminated everywhere. The hitherto solemn children jumped up squealing and screaming in joy and wonder, running, laughing and clutching each other. The Chief shook his head in amusement as the four adults went walking after them towards the festival grounds.

The Chief asked, "The substance manipulation that Ake pulled off couldn't have conjured up palm wine, could it?"

The Weaver sniffed, "You know very well that at his age, the wonder is that he could do anything at all. Besides, from what palm trees could he have pulled the moisture? He could only pull water from the moisture in the environment. It was even a bit salty, and I think there must have been some sweat mixed in it."

"What a shame," the Chief said. "If he could conjure palm wine, that would have been something."

Feeler

Later that night, Morako and Imade lay cuddled up on a mat listening to the drumming and singing from the festival and watching the stars. The corrupted beast had been given in fires to Obatala. Kolanut and palm wine flowed freely, but only amongst the chiefs. Kolanut was the food of the gods and only meant for elders and those closest to the gods. The rest enjoyed the general merriment. Children danced and played and ran from masquerades.

But Morako and Imade lay watching the stars, enjoying the festival in their own corner. She ran a teasing finger up his arm, her breath warm against his cheek. He trembled at her touch.

She whispered in his ear, "Why does a warrior of your calibre quake so?"

"Ah," he said, "my skill as a feeler makes me more susceptible to your wiles. With it I feel this... overwhelming, enveloping warmth seeping from you, yet each time I ask you to be joined to me as a full-grown woman who has passed all the rites of womanhood, you refuse. Why do you refuse me so?"

"Not so, my strong one. I am only not sure of joining with you and bringing a child into this uncertain world."

"But it's our sacred duty to survive and that involves..."

She looked at him reproachfully. "Sacred duty, is it? You're all about duty, my dear brave hunter and feeler."

He chuckled. "I do confess my desire to be more than just for fulfilment of duty."

She nibbled on his ear lobe and clutched him tightly. "I, too, my brave hunter. Maybe someday when something changes we will get our desire. I assure you that my refusal is not about you but about other things. I find you quite sufficient and can desire nothing more for a mate, my brave hunter." She snuggled tighter by his side.

"That enveloping, overwhelming warmth is a fire now," he

said. "I am quite assured of your affections. But let us try not to burn down Ife-Iyoku."

"As a healer, I do have ways of sensing and affecting you as well. Healing is control and manipulation. When I nudge the body in certain ways, I can dampen pain receptors, and enhance and inflame other parts like your immune system. Supposing I do this…"

She ran a finger down his belly and drew on her gift, sending a line of energy into him.

His eyes widened.

"Do not wake the beast," he said, "unless you are ready to do battle."

"The beast was already awake. I was merely teasing it a bit. And who said I am not ready for battle?"

She drew his mouth to hers and kissed him thoroughly. They pulled the covers over their head and let the sounds of merriment pass over them as they created theirs.

RING SHOUT

NEBULA WINNER: BEST NOVELLA

BY P. DJÈLÍ CLARK, PUBLISHED
BY TOR.COM

EXCERPT

ONE

You ever seen a Klan march?

We don't have them as grand in Macon, like you might see in Atlanta. But there's Klans enough in this city of fifty-odd thousand to put on a fool march when they get to feeling to.

This one on a Tuesday, the Fourth of July, which is today. There's a bunch parading down Third Street, wearing white robes and pointed hoods. Not a one got their face covered. I hear them first Klans after the Civil War hid behind pillowcases and flour sacks to do their mischief, even blackened up to play like they colored. But this Klan we gotin 1922 not concerned with hiding.

All of them—men, women, even little baby Klans— down there grinning like picnic on a Sunday. Got all kinds of fireworks —sparklers, Chinese crackers, sky rockets, and things that sound like cannons. A brass band competing with that racket, though everybody down there I swear clapping on the one and the three. With all the flag-waving and cavorting, you might forget they was monsters.

But I hunt monsters. And I know them when I see them.

"One little Ku Klux deaaaad," a voice hums near my ear. "Two little Kluxes deaaaad, Three little Kluxes, Four little Kluxes, Five little Kluxes deaaaad."

I glance to Sadie crouched beside me, hair pulled into a long brown braid dangling off a shoulder. She got one eye cocked, staring down the sights on her rifle at the crowd below as she finishes her ditty, pretending to pull the trigger.

Click, click, click, click, click!

"Stop that now." I push away the rifle barrel with a beaten-up book. "That thing go off and you liable to make me deaf. Besides, somebody might catch sight of us."

Sadie rolls big brown eyes at me, twisting her lips and lobbing a spitty mess of tobacco onto the rooftop. I grimace. Girl got some disgusting habits.

"I swear Maryse Boudreaux." She slings her rifle across blue overalls too big for her skinny self and puts hands to her hips to give me the full Sadie treatment, looking like some irate yella gal sharecropper. "The way you always worrying. Is you twenty-five or eighty-five? Sometimes I forget. Ain't nobody seeing us way up here but birds."

She gestures out at buildings rising higher than the telegraph lines of downtown Macon. We up on one of the old cotton warehouses off Poplar Street. Way back, this whole area housed cotton coming in from countryside plantations to send down the Ocmulgee by steamboat. That fluffy white soaked in slave sweat and blood what made this city. Nowadays Macon warehouses still hold cotton, but for local factory mills and railroads. Watching these Klans shamble down the street, I'm reminded of bales of white, still soaked in colored folk sweat and blood, moving for the river.

"Not too sure about that," Chef puts in. She sits with her back against the rooftop wall, dark lips curled around the butt of a Chesterfield in a familiar easy smirk. "Back in the war, we always watched for snipers. 'Keep one eye on the mud, one in front, and both up top,' Sergeant used to say. Somebody yell, 'Sniper!' and we scampered quick!"

Beneath a narrow mustard-brown army cap her eyes tighten and the smirk wavers. She pulls out the cigarette, exhaling a white stream. "Hated fucking snipers."

"This ain't no war," Sadie retorts. We both look at her funny. "I mean, it ain't *that* kind of war. Nobody down there watching for snipers. Besides, only time you see Winnie is before she put one right between the eyes." She taps her forehead and smiles crookedly, a wad of tobacco bulging one cheek.

Sadie's no sniper. But she ain't lying. Girl can shoot the wings off a fly. Never one day in Uncle Sam's army neither— just hunting with her grandpappy in Alabama. "Winnie" is her Winchester 1895, with a walnut stock, an engraved slate-gray receiver, and a twenty-four-inch barrel. I'm not big on guns, but got to admit—that's one damn pretty killer. "All this waiting making me fidgety," she huffs, pulling at the red-and-black-check-ered shirt under her overalls. "And I can't pass time reading fairy tales like Maryse."

"Folktales." I hold up my book. "Say so right on the cover."

"Whichever. Stories 'bout Bruh Fox and Bruh Bear sound like fairy tales to me."

"Better than those trashy tabloids you like," I retort. "Been told y'all there's truth in there. Just you watch.

Anyway, when we gon' kill something? This taking too long!" Can't argue there. Been three-quarters of an hour now we out here and this Macon sun ain't playing at midday. My nice plaited and pinned-up hair gone damp beneath my tan newsboy cap. Perspira-tion sticking my striped white shirt to my back. And these gray wool knickers ain't much better. Prefer a summer dress loose on my hips I can breathe in. Don't know how men stay all confined like this. Chef stands, dusting off and taking a last savoring drag on the Chesterfield before stamping it beneath a faded Pershing boot. I'm always impressed by her height—taller than me certainly, and some men for that matter. She lean too, all dark long legs and arms fitted into a tan combat tunic and breeches. Imagine the kaiser's men musta choked on their sauerkraut seeing her and the Black Rattlers charging in the Meuse-Argonne.

"In the trenches only thing living besides us was lice and rats. Lice was damn useless. Rats you could eat. Just had to know the proper bait and trap."

Sadie gags like she swallowed her tobacco. "Cordelia Lawrence, of all the nasty stories you done told about that nasty war, that is by far the *nastiest*!"

"Cordy, you ate rats?"

Chef just chuckles before walking off. Sadie looks to me, mimicking throwing up. I tighten the laces on my green gaiters before standing and stuff my book into a back pocket. When I reach Chef she at the other end of the roof, peering off the edge.

"Like I say," she picks up again. "You want to catch a rat, get the right bait and trap. Then, you just wait him out."

Sadie and I follow her gaze to the alley tucked behind the building, away from the parade and where nobody likely to come. On the ground is our bait. A dog carcass. It's been cut to pieces, the innards spilled out bloody and pink on the paving stones amid charred black fur. The stink of it carries even up here.

"You have to chop it up like that?" I ask, my belly unsettled.

Chef shrugs. "You want to catch bees, you gotta put out enough honey."

Like how Bruh Fox catch Bruh Rabbit, I imagine my brother saying.

"Look like all we catching is flies," Sadie mutters. She leans over the ledge to spit tobacco at the carcass, missing wide.

I cut my eyes to her. "Could you be more respectful?"

Sadie scrunches up her face, chewing harder. "Dog dead. Spit won't hurt it none."

"Still, we can try not to be vulgar."

She snorts. "Carrying on over a dog when we put down worse."

I open my mouth, then decide answering ain't worth the bother.

"Macon not missing another stray," Chef says. "If it helps, ol' girl never saw her end coming." She pats the German trench knife at her waist—her prize souvenir. It don't help. We take to staring at the dog, the hurly-burly of the parade at our backs in our ears.

"I wonder why Ku Kluxes like dog?" Sadie asks, breaking our quiet.

"Seared but bloody," Chef adds. "Roasted that one on a spit."

"That's what I'm saying. Why dog and not, say, chicken? Or hogs?"

"Maybe they ain't got chickens where they from, or hogs— just got dogs."

"Or something that *taste* like dog."

My belly could do without this particular conversation, but when Sadie on a rant, best just ride it out.

"Maybe I shoulda put some pepper and spices on it," Chef jokes.

Sadie waves her off. "White folk don't care 'bout pepper and spices. Like they food bland as water."

Chef squints over her high cheekbones as loud sky rockets go off, followed by the booms of gas bottle bombs. "I dunno. When we was in France, them Frenchies could put they foot on up in some food."

Sadie's eyes narrow. "You talking rats again, Cordy?" "Not in the trenches. In Paris, where we was after the armistice. Frenchie gals loved cooking for colored soldiers. Liked doing a heap more than cooking too." She flashes the wink and smile of a rogue. "Had us some steak tartare and cassoulet, duck confit, ratatouille —Sadie, fix your face, ratatouille not made from rats."

Sadie don't look convinced. "Well, don't know what type of white folk they got in France. But the ones here don't put no proper seasoning in they food unless they got Niggers to do so for 'em." Her eyes widen. "I wonder what Niggers smell like to Ku Kluxes? You think Niggers smell like burnt dog to their noses, and that's why they come after us so? I wonder if there's even Niggers where they from? And if—"

"Sadie!" I snap, losing what little patience I got. "Heaven knows I asked you more than once to stop using that word. At least in my presence?"

That yella gal rolls her eyes so hard at me it's a wonder she don't fall asleep. "Why you frettin', Maryse? Always says my Niggers with a big *N*."

I glare at her. "And that make a difference how?"

She has the gall to frown like I'm simple. "Why with a big *N*, it's respectful like."

Seeing me at a loss, Chef intervenes. "And how can we tell if you using a big *N* or a common *n*?"

Now Sadie takes to staring at both of us, like we don't understand two plus two is four. "Why would I use a small *n* nigger? That's insulting!"

I can see Chef's stumped now too. They could get all the scientists the world over to try and figure out how Sadie's mind works—wouldn't do no good. Chef soldiers on anyway. "So can white folk ever use a big *N* Nigger?"

Sadie shakes her head, as if this is all settled scripture written down between Leviticus and Deuteronomy. "Never! White folk always mean the small *n*! And if they try to say it with the big *N*, you should put they front teeth in the back of they mouth. Honestly, you two! What kind of Niggers even need to ask me that?"

I purse my lips up into their full rounded glory, set to tell her exactly *what kind*, but Chef holds up a fist and we drop to peer over the rooftop wall. There's three Ku Kluxes entering the alley.

They dressed in white robes, with the hoods pulled up. The first one is tall and lanky, with an Adam's apple I can spot from here. His eyes dart around the alley, while a nose like a beak sniffs the air. When he spots the dog carcass he slinks over, still sniffing. The two other Ku Kluxes— one short and portly, the other a broad-chested block of muscle—soon join him.

I can tell right off there's something's peculiar about them.

Not just those silly costumes neither. Or because they sniffing at a chopped-up, half-burnt dog like regular folk sniff a meal. They don't walk right—all jerky and stiff. And they breathing too fast. Those things anybody can notice, if they paying attention. But what only a few can see—people like me, Sadie, and Chef—is the way the faces on these men move. And I mean *move*. They don't stay still for nothing—wobbling and twisting about, like reflections in those funny mirrors at carnivals.

The first Ku Klux goes down on all fours, palms flat and back legs bent so he's raised up on his toes. He sticks out a tongue to take a long lick at the dog carcass, smearing his lips and chin bloody. A growl in the back of his throat sends a tickle up my spine. Then with a quickness, he opens his mouth full and plunges teeth-first into the carcass, tearing out and swallowing chunks of dogmeat. The other two scramble over on all fours, all of them feeding at once. It makes my stomach do somersaults.

My eyes flick to Sadie. She already crouched into position, Winnie aimed, eyes fixed, and her breathing steady. There's no more chewing tobacco or any talk. When she ready to shoot, she can be calm as a spring rain.

"Think you can hit it from here?" Chef whispers. "They all so close together!"

Sadie don't answer, gone still as a statue. Then, as a fierce thunder of firecrackers goes off at the parade, she pulls the trigger. That bullet flies right between the open crook of a Ku Klux's bent elbow, hitting the dog carcass, and striking what Chef buried inside.

Back in the war, Cordy picked up the nickname Chef. Not for cooking—at least not food. Frenchie soldiers learned her to make things for blowing up Germans and collapsing trenches—like what she stuffed in that carcass. Soon as Sadie's bullet punches through dog flesh, the whole thing explodes! The blast louder than those bottle bombs, and I duck, covering my ears. When I dare to peek back down, there's nothing left of the dog but a red smear. The Ku Kluxes all laid out. The lanky one got half his face blowed off. Another missing an arm, while the big one's chest look caved in.

"Lord, Cordy!" I gasp. "How big a bomb you put in there?"

She stands there grinning, marveling at her handiwork. "Big enough, I think."

Wasn't just blasting powder that took down the Ku Kluxes. That dog was filled with silver pellets and iron slags. Best way to put down one of these haints. I fish a sidewinder pocket watch from my knickers, glancing at the open-face front.

"You and Sadie bring the truck." I nod at the Ku Kluxes. "I'll get them ready for hauling. Hurry now. We ain't got much time."

"Why I got to go get the truck?" Sadie whines. "Because we need to get a yella gal with a big ol' gun off the streets," Chef retorts, throwing a rope over the warehouse edge.

I don't wait to argue Sadie's complaints; she got lots of those. Grabbing hold of the rope, I start making my way down. Tried our best to mask what we been doing. But anybody come looking and find three dead Ku Kluxes and three colored women—well, that's for sure trouble.

I'm about halfway to the ground when Sadie calls out, "I think they moving."

"What?" Chef asks, just above me. "Get on down the rope, gal, and let's go—"

Sadie again: "I'm telling y'all, them Ku Kluxes is moving!"

What she going on about now? I twist about on the rope, holding to the thick cord with my legs locked onto the bottom. My heart catches. The Ku Kluxes *are* moving! The big one sitting up, feeling at his caved-in chest. The portly one's stirring too, looking to his missing arm. But it's the lanky one that jumps up first, face half gone so that you can see bone showing. His good eye rolls around till it lands on me and he opens his mouth to let out a screech that ain't no ways human. That's when I know, things about to get bad.

The sickening sound of bone cracking, of muscle and flesh stretching and pulling, fills the alley. The lanky man's body grows impossibly large, tearing out his skin as easy as it shreds away his white robes. The thing standing in his place now can't rightly be called a man. It's easily nine feet tall, with legs that bend back like the hindquarters of a beast, joined to a long torso twice as wide as most men. Arms of thick bone and muscle jut from its shoulders, stretching to the ground. But it's the head that stands out—long and curved to end in a sharp bony point.

This is a Ku Klux. A *real* Ku Klux. Every bit of the thing is a pale bone white, down to claws like carved blades of ivory. The only part not white are the eyes. Should be six in all: beads of red on black in rows of threes on either side of that curving head. But just like the lanky man, half its face been ripped away by Chef's bomb. The eyes that's left are all locked on me now, though. And what passes for lips on a long muzzle peel back, revealing a nest of teeth like spiky icicles—before it lunges.

Watching a Ku Klux raging at me while dangling off the side of a building is one sight I could do with forgetting. There's the crack of a rifle and a bullet takes it in the shoulder. Another crack and a second bullet punches its chest. I glance up to find Sadie, looking like a photo I once seen of Stagecoach Mary, shells flying as she works the lever. She hits the Ku Klux two more times before stopping to reload. That don't kill it, though—just sends it reeling back, bleeding, in pain, and mad as hell.

Still, Sadie's bought me precious seconds. Above, Chef is calling with an arm extended. But I won't make that climb— not before the Ku Klux is on me. Searching frantic for a way out, my eyes land on a window. I slide down the rope, palms burning on the coarse fibers. Please let it be open! Not open, but I almost shout, "Hallelujah!" when I see it's missing glass on one side. I grab the upper edge with a hand while planting a brown Oxford on the bottom. Above I hear shouts, and from the corner of my eye catch the Ku Klux running for me and leaping, claws extended and mouth wide.

I push through that open slot and practically fall inside, just before the Ku Klux hits the wall. A long snout breaks through the remaining glass, snapping at air. Sadie's rifle goes off again, and the monster roars in pain. Turning its gaze up, it digs bony claws into the brick and starts to climb. I watch all this lying on a bale of cotton. Lucky, because I'd be a sight more tore up landing on the wood floor. Still, that fall hurt something awful. It takes a moment to roll off my back and stumble to my feet, feeling bruised all over. Except for sunlight streaking through windows, it's dark in here. Stifling hot too. I shake my head to clear it. Don't hear no more rifle shots, but I know there must be a fight on the roof. Need to get back up there to help Chef and Sadie. Need to—

Something heavy rams the warehouse doors, making me jump. Did somebody finally hear all the noise we making behind the fireworks and whatnot and come looking? But when the doors get hit again, strong enough to almost buckle them, I know that's not people. Only thing big enough to do that is—the doors are ripped near off their hinges before I can finish the thought, spilling in daylight and monsters. The two other Ku Kluxes. My luck done run out.

They easy enough to recognize. One missing an arm. The other, possibly the biggest Ku Klux I ever seen, got a dent in its pale white chest. The two sniff at the air, searching. Ku Kluxes don't have good eyesight, even though they got six. But they can smell better than the best hound. It takes two heartbeats for them fix on me. Then they're galloping on all fours, snarling and marking me as prey.

But like I said already, I hunt monsters. And I got a sword that sings.

It comes to me at a thought and a half-whispered prayer, pulled from nothingness into my waiting grip—a silver hilt joined to smoke that moves like black oil before dripping away. The flat, leaf-shaped blade it leaves behind is almost half my height, with designs cut into the dark iron. Visions dance in my head as they always do when the sword comes: a man pounding out silver with raw, cut-up feet in a mine in Peru; a woman screaming and pushing out birth blood in the bowels of a slave ship; a boy, wading to his chest in a rice field in the Carolinas.

And then there's the girl. Always her. Sitting in a dark place, shaking all over, wide eyes staring up at me with fright. That fear is powerful strong—like a black lake threatening to anoint me in a terrible baptism.

Go away! I whisper. And she do.

Except for the girl, the visions always different. People dead now for Lord knows how long. Their spirits are drawn to the sword, and I can hear them chanting—different tongues mixing into a harmony that washes over me, settling onto my skin. It's them that compel the ones bound to the blade—the chiefs and kings who sold them away—to call on old African gods to rise up, and dance in time to the song.

All this happens in a few blinks. My sword is up and gripped two-fisted to meet the Ku Kluxes bearing down on me. Big as it is, the blade is always the same easy balanced weight—like it was made just for me. In a sudden burst the black iron explodes with light like one of them African gods cracked open a brilliant eye.

The first Ku Klux is blinded by the glare. It stops short, reaching its remaining arm to put out the small star. I dance back, moving to chants thrumming in my head, their rhythm my guide, and swing. The blade cuts flesh and bone like tough meat. The Ku Klux shrieks at losing a second arm. I follow through with a slash at its exposed neck, and the monster crashes down, gurgling on dark spurting blood. The bigger Ku Klux lumbers right atop it to reach me and there's a sharp crack I think is the wounded monster's spine.

One down.

But that big Ku Klux not giving me time to rest. It launches at me, and I jump out the way before I get crushed. I give a good biting slash as I do and it howls, but lunges again, snapping jaws almost catching my arm. I duck, moving deeper into the maze of bundled cotton, zigzagging before squeezing into a space and going still.

I can hear the Ku Klux, raking claws through cotton bales, searching for me. My sword has thankfully gone dark. But I won't stay hidden long. I have to become the hunter again. End this.

C'mon, Bruh Rabbit, my brother urges. Think up a trick to fool ol' Bruh Bear!

Pulling out my pocket watch, I kiss it once. Quick as I can, I rise up and hurl it clattering across the wood floor. The Ku Klux whips about, tearing after the noise. As it does I climb onto the bales, running and hopping from one to the other, until I get to where it's hunched over, sniffing the pocket watch—before smashing it under a clawed foot.

That makes me madder than all else.

With a cry I hurl myself at it, the chants in my head rising to a fever pitch.

I land on the monster's back, the blade sinking through flesh into the base of its neck. Before it can throw me off I clutch at ridges on its pointed head and with my whole body push the blade up and deep. The Ku Klux jerks once before collapsing facedown, like its bones turned to jelly. I fall with it, careful not to get rolled under, still gripping the silver hilt of my sword. Regaining my breath, I do a quick check to make sure nothing's broken. Then, pushing to my feet, I press a boot onto the dead thing's back and pull the blade free. Dark blood sizzles off the black iron like water on a hot skillet.

Catching movement out the corner of my eye I spin about. But it's Chef and Sadie. Relief forces my muscles to relax and the chanting in my head lowers to a murmur. Chef lets out a low whistle seeing the two dead Ku Kluxes. Sadie just grunts—closest she comes to a compliment. I must look a sight. Somewhere along the way I lost my cap, and my undone hair is framing my coffee-brown face in a tangled black cloud.

"Called up your little pig sticker?" Sadie asks, eyeing my sword.

"The one up top?" I ask, ignoring her and breathing hard. Sadie pats Winnie in answer. "Took a mess of bullets too." "And this knife when things got close," Chef adds, patting her war souvenir.

Outside the parade's moved on. But I can still hear the brass band and fireworks. As if a whole lot of monster battling ain't happened just some streets over. Still, somebody over there bound to know the difference between firecrackers and a rifle.

"Let's get moving," I say. "Last thing we need is police." Macon's constables and the Klan not on good terms. Surprising, ain't it? Seems the police don't take well to them threatening to run one of their own for sheriff. That don't mean the police friendly with colored folk, though.

So we try not to cross them.

When Bruh Bear and Bruh Lion get to fighting, I remember my brother saying, *Bruh Rabbit best steer clear!*

Chef nods. "C'mon, yella gal—say, what you doing there?"

I turn to find Sadie poking at a cotton bale with her rifle. "Y'all ain't ever worked a field," she's muttering, "so don't expect you to know better. But July is when the harvest just starting. Warehouse like this should be empty." "So?" I glance nervous at the alley. Don't got time for this. "So," she throws back at me, reaching inside a bale. "I want to see what they hiding." Her arm comes back, holding a dark glass bottle. Grinning, she pulls out the cork and takes a swig that sets her shivering.

"Tennessee whiskey!" she hoots.

Chef dives for another bale, digging with her knife to pull out two more bottles.

I give Sadie my own grunt. Tennessee whiskey worth a pretty penny, what with the Prohibition still on. And this little monster-hunting operation costs money.

"We'll take what we can, but we need to hurry!"

I look down at the dead Ku Klux. The monster's bone-white skin is already turned gray, scraps peeling and floating into the air like ashes of paper, turning to dust before our eyes. That's what happens to a Ku Klux when it's killed. Body just crumbles away, as if it don't belong here—which I assure you it *does not*. In about twenty minutes won't be no blood or bones or nothing— just dust. Make it feel like you fighting shadows.

"You need help with—?" Chef gestures at the dead Ku Klux.

I shake my head, hefting my sword. "Y'all bring the truck. Nana Jean been expecting us. I got this."

Sadie huffs. "All that fuss over a dog, and this don't make you blink."

I watch them go before fixing my eyes back to the dead Ku Klux. Sadie should know better. That dog didn't hurt nobody. These haints evil and need putting down. I ain't got a bit of compunction about that. Lifting my sword, I bring it down with a firm swing, severing the Ku Klux's forearm at the elbow. Blood and gore splatters me, turning at once to motes of dust. In my head the chanting of longdead slaves and bound-up chiefs starts up again. I find myself humming along, lost to the rhythm of my singing blade, as I set about my grisly work.

RIOT BABY

BY TOCHI ONYEBUCHI
PUBLISHED BY TOR.COM

EXCERPT

"You ain't gonna ask who did this?" Kev doesn't need to point to the laceration at his temple and the bandage that struggles to cover the length of slice and can't.

Ella leans back in her chair across the table from Kev while loved ones or family or friends or old classmates or people settling a grudge or people burying a hatchet do this visit thing. She has her arms crossed, posture all defiant. Anger, unfamiliar and slow, swirls at the bottom of her gut, creeps into the back of her brain. "Nope," she says.

Kev leans forward and already has that conspiratorial convict hunch that cons have on TV or in movies. "You gonna read my mind or something? Scan one of the CO's brains or something? I bet you could just put your hand to the floor and get all the stories that ever passed through this place."

He's not wrong. Ella's mind had wandered into one of the female COs who stood by a wall with her baton cradled under her crossed arms. There's one inmate, a black guy with tight cornrows meeting with another dude, probably a brother or cousin who repped the same set, that she has made it her duty not to look at, and Ella knows, can probably tell without Diving, that they're fucking. Memories run like shards across her line of sight: the two of them on the outside, he with his crew when he was younger and she with her older cousin, both her and her cousin sporting big hoop earrings with their names in gold, walking back from the movies and passing the boy with his crew and the boy hollering at her and the big cousin telling the boy off in sharp, smooth, knife-blade Spanish. Then furtive sneaking from one's house or the other's to fuck after the girl'd gotten out of school, and the boy not doing well in class and his mother not around because she was working three jobs, and he couldn't bear to see an eviction notice slide under their door like it did to the people one floor up, so he starts slanging, and when he hollers at the girl with his new kicks and his chain (that will be snatched in a week or so and that he'll have to stomp someone out to get back), she smirks, and the cousin fights even harder to keep the girl away from that sweat-sheened, Carhartt-clothed, muscled, bejeweled embodiment of Trouble. More fucking, then the girl goes to college, and the guy goes to jail for dope and a parole violation from a prior, and there's a guard shift and as he's lined up with the other inmates on his block, he looks out the corner of his eye and sees homegirl walking down the line tapping her baton against thighs he remembers she used to wrap around his back when they got the springs in her bedframe to squeak and groan.

"It wasn't her," Kev says, and Ella realizes she's been staring.

"I know." But Ella can barely concentrate because an inmate three tables ahead has a shank wrapped up and shoved into his rectum and Ella feels herself boofing. And in that inmate's mind's eye and now Ella's eye is an image, a flash, of tissue he stuck in the door's locking mechanism so that he could jiggle it open even though it showed up as closed on the guard's boards. Then a jagged, slow-motion clip of the inmate's plan to pop his cell after lights out and join two others who'd done the same to knife an Aryan whose son, on the outside, put that guy's son in the hospital at a Confederate flag rally.

"But that's the thing about the hospital, you know? You get

your little bit of freedom. That's how you get it. That's how you get the attention you been dying to get. Gets to be a bit like home after a while."

"I ain't been around much." Ella dislikes that it feels like an apology. She hasn't gotten to hate yet. "But you know how the fam is."

When Kev finally looks up from his folded hands, there's fear in his eyes. For the first time since Ella started visiting. In his brain are capsules, pills. Seroquel. Benadryl, drugs the medical staff give him, sometimes saved up so that he can just lie there and take a bunch at once and just wait for them to hit, only to wake up the next day and realize "Fuck, I can't do this." It's all in Kev's eyes, and Ella sees it, though her ephemeral fingers only touch the con- tours of that thought. And Kev asking her without opening his mouth: *you could burn it down; you could just burn this motherfucker down, all of it; please, just burn it down.*

She looks down, then up again and past her brother. There's an inmate talking to his baby's mother, and the inmate's leg is bobbing up and down because earlier in the day, he splashed a CO, threw urine all over the guy's face and soaked the front of his uniform, practically popped a balloon on him, then put his arms behind his head so that the cameras would see that he wasn't resisting or striking the CO. He knew that guy and a bunch of his buddies would be waiting for him, maybe right outside the showers in the cameras' blind spot, to put him in the hospital or maybe even kill him, and this might be the last time he sees his baby's face ever again.

The metal table dips where Ella's fingers press into it, and she realizes what she's doing and takes her hand off and puts it in her lap.

An older man tells his grandson, brought in by his daughter, about how he's learning chess so that when he gets out he can play his grandson, who's getting really good, apparently. He says this, knowing he will not get out, that he will die either here or somewhere upstate where, he hears, the prisons are starting to turn more into hospices than anything else. But he still tells his grandson about how he's learning to play in solitary, because that makes his situation seem less scary, though his daughter knows exactly what a stay in the Bing entails. And the older man's words are brightly colored, even as Ella sees the man's imagination, sees the man and the inmate in the cell next door both drawing the board on pieces of paper and screaming their moves out to each other, and the loneliness washes purple over the image and reminds the older man about how dirty his cell was when he first moved in and how the only way to get Sanitation to come in and clean it was to stuff the toilet with books he was sent and flood the cell or to break the toilet so that the cell became unusable.

Ella wants to tell Kev to just survive, as though that would be enough. Just survive. But, in her chest, it becomes a cruel thing to ask him to do.

She doesn't want to reduce this entire compound—its ten jail facilities with approximately sixty beds in each, its eight-by-ten solitary confinement chambers, its hallways and the cameras placed so that there were blind spots where the bleeding happened, and its railings and its bars and its slatted windows and its shitty air- conditioning—all to dust. She wants to be able to go port back in time, reach her hand in and put it to Kev's chest the night of that attempted armed robbery. Or to go back even further and stay closer to Kev for longer to keep him in that bubble of protection so that cops would leave him alone more often. Or to go back even further and keep him from becoming friends with Freddie, who would one day get picked up by cops for looking at one for too long and in the police van on the way to the station would get his spine severed. Because maybe if Kev didn't know him as a friend, as a brother, almost, in Ella's absence while Ella went to discover her powers where she couldn't hurt people, maybe Kev might not be here. Or maybe reach back even further and nudge Mama to bring the family somewhere else where the land didn't burn underneath them and catch fire, where they could settle and where white people were maybe a little less thirsty for his blood.

I'd stop time for you, Kev, she almost says.

The fear dampens in Kev's eyes, and Ella realizes Kev heard her anyway.

Brother and sister smile across the table at each other.

Later, as Ella gets up to leave and walks back to the gate, she brushes past a young woman and pain spikes through her spine, and she sees it: sees the Latina with the dark, wavy hair and the little Dominican boy at her knee and sees them at home and sees the Latina woman in the kitchen on the phone screaming upon hearing that her child's father has died and sees the Latina woman and the dead man's mother and their lawyer poring over the autopsy reports saying he'd had ulcers and reports and memos that indicated that, when they'd ruptured, the other prisoners had called for help while the guard on duty sipped coffee at his desk down the hall and watched. Ella sees the woman and her son return to the jail to pick up the decedent's things: a red Champ hoodie, his wallet, and a gray-red-and-black Bulls hat. The woman outside hugging herself against the cold and giving the sweater to her son, who is shivering.

TOWER OF MUD AND STRAW

BY YAROSLAV BARSUKOV
PUBLISHED BY METAPHOROSIS

EXCERPT

"**A** chance at the crown means nothing to you, does it? Then consider this: if the tower doesn't get finished within the next two years, Duma will attempt an incursion."

Shea couldn't contain a hiss. "Come on, are you one of those idiots who believe Duma has the densest population of megalomaniacs in the world?"

"I don't *believe* anything." Aidan skewed his mouth, from the looks of it probing his teeth in search of a wayward piece of food. "I *know*. Duma is my motherland, I spent the first thirteen years of my life there; I know how they think, their opinion of other countries, of *you*."

"Well, it's not like we have a lot to do, so why don't you convince me that they're the furnace of the world's evil?"

"I'll tell you a story, Shea." Aidan slouched in his chair a bit, but one of the black gloves squeezed into a fist, crumpling the napkin. "It was my father who'd decided, single-handedly, that we needed to leave the country. He decided it when the crown prince, only fifteen then, only three years older than me, assumed command of the royal cavalry battalion.

"People went crazy. You know how it happens: everybody

ecstatic, everybody talking of a new emerging leader. Father, he saw the writing on the wall. One morning at the end of summer I woke up and saw him through the window, in the sun, exchanging papers with a man I didn't recognize.

"They shook hands, and the man left. Father turned and walked, too. I couldn't see him past the window's edge, but I knew the front door would bang in a few seconds, and that moment was for me—I realize it sounds trite, but still—it was a loss of innocence. My sisters, Maria and Isabel..." He paused. "Maria and Isabel slept in another room. I remember a toy, a bear, perched on the table in mine.

"The door banged and he walked in, or rather, darted through the anteroom. I heard him say something to Mother in a loud voice—normally, he was all quiet in the mornings, afraid of disturbing our sleep.

"When I tiptoed over the ice-cold floor, into the living room, Mother was collecting things, some silly stuff—pictures from the walls, porcelain cats from the shelves. Father told her to stop, pack the clothes, and wake us up.

"The carriage already waited outside. Our cook flapped her apron at her face, and the stable-hand, Michael, ran after us, waving his hands. Michael had first put me on a horse and taught me to ride."

Aidan slid away his plate. "Past the city gates, I remember, Father relaxed. He even smiled at me. Isabel asked for her doll. That was when the bomb exploded."

He traced with his fingers a pattern on the table.

"Something hit me on the head, and I flew out through the carriage's door like a sack. I sat on the pavement, bawling, snot all over my face. My hearing was gone. And you know what the worst thing is? I don't even remember the corpses. I remember a wheel rolling past me, people running toward us, but not the corpses.

"Mother and Father survived—Isabel and Maria didn't. It was Michael who'd planted the bomb, of course. They'd found out Father wanted to leave the country, and they bribed our stable hand to blow us up."

"I'm sorry, Aidan," Shea said.

"You don't have to be. It was twenty-five years ago; I healed. Which brings me to another point…" He pinched the rim of his glove. "You're afraid that people at the tower will never learn to work with the Drakiri devices? Well, you can live with these things for your entire life."

In one motion, he pulled the glove off. The old lady at the neighboring table gasped, and her fork rang like a little bell.

Aidan's arm ended at the wrist; what came after branched off in metal and purple veins, glowed in sparks, roughly following the contours of a human hand—but only roughly. Knotted 'fingers' rolled in the air as though strumming a chord.

Carefully, Aidan put the glove back on and smiled at the old lady who sat there with huge, frozen eyes.

Shea exhaled. "Gosh. I never knew."

"Now you do. The bomb maimed me, and I had this thing fitted instead by a wandering Drakiri craftsman when I was twenty-one."

"You said you found out it was Michael who'd planted the bomb. What did you do to him?"

Aidan didn't say anything, but his smile sharpened while the eyes went to ice.

Isabel, Maria. Lena. Shea exhaled, struck by an analogy. *I could've been Aidan. If it were a* person *that had taken Lena from me, I quite possibly would've been him.*

And then they passed the next hill, and, sure enough, there were the ripples on water, and the white sails, and the valley's saddle onto which a palette knife had scrawled the contours of a city.

Somehow, the magic of it appeared dull; all he could think about was a boy looking at dead bodies, an image that held, in itself, a similar picture from his own past, like a Dumian stacking doll.

In the past

Upon entering the workshop, Shea ducked in a nick of time to avoid getting smashed against the wall by a gliding wardrobe.

"Sorry, brother!"

He scanned the room but couldn't understand where Lena's voice was coming from.

On the far side of the hall, Danny and another worker caught the wardrobe and stabilized it in the air. It hung there, spinning lazily, surreal in the purple light that oozed from the 'tulip' fastened to its back. Danny stared at it, mouth open. Other pieces of furniture floated across the workshop, too—a mahogany dining table, a padded sofa for four, an oak-and-leather chair: a scene from someone's dream.

"Grand, isn't it?" Lena descended to the floor, sitting with legs crossed atop a Drakiri device.

"This is dangerous, sis. You could fall."

"Why don't you give it a ride yourself?" She smiled, rose, and tapped the inky surface. "Come on."

"No thank you."

The moment the tulip had touched down, the purple light inside began to die.

"Look." She waved around the hall. "No more hauling things. No more accidents when something falls on someone. We can have twice as much space, we can get rid of all the workbenches —people will work on the furniture while it's suspended in the air. Hey, they can even work outside if they wish."

"Why didn't you wait for me, sis? I thought we wanted to try those things out together."

"I thought so, too." She thumped her fist playfully on his arm. "But today, you seemed more interested in that new maid— what's her name? Muriel? Did you take her out to the vineyards?"

Shea felt red rising to his cheeks. "No. Listen, I had a talk with that Drakiri, you know, the one who works in the town hall."

"Mmm?"

"He told me those things—tulips, eggs, whatever you call them—they're dangerous. So dangerous, in fact, that I asked him to come here and take a look at them, and he wouldn't even consider it."

"Brother."

"He said they're volatile and difficult to operate."

"There's a valve, and there's a lever. You saw how I operated them—did it seem difficult to you?"

"I saw you working with them, sis, yes. What about the others here?"

"I can turn the tulips on and off. Once they're in the air, you don't need to do anything else, just push them here and there. I can take care of everything."

"Perhaps," Shea said. "But what if you get sick? What if something happens at home, and you have to leave in the middle of the day?"

"Hopefully nothing happens at home."

"Yes, but what if…?"

"Then we'll deal with it when we get there. Oh, and by the way…" She turned and ran her fingers across the tulip's surface, now completely dark. "I've ordered another thirty devices from the Drakiri settlement in Owenbeg. They'll arrive in a few days."

"What? No! This is my workshop as well as yours, and I forbid it. Even those six…" He glanced at the people trying to get hold of the rotating mahogany table. "…they may've been a mistake."

Something sparkled in her eyes. "Let's make a bet."

"A bet?"

"A bet. Like we did when we were children. Give me till tomorrow evening, and I bet you I'll change your mind about the tulips."

Shea chuckled. "What do you…?"

She smiled dreamily. "I have an idea." Without warning, she stepped forward and squeezed him in an embrace. "Everything will be beautiful. You'll see, brother."

———

In the present

The carriage took them from the port's breeze into Oakville's narrow, sand-colored streets.

In no particular order: sunlight-watered shadows under the house bridges; a barber on the corner catching the clouds with his mirror; a bigger dog chasing a smaller one; a woman, her hand on her hip, talking to a man with bald temples.

Inconceivable how something could carry the sugary-powder flavor of childhood and, at the same time, a much more bitter, corroding taste.

"I never wanted to return," he said.

Aidan didn't respond.

Sun Plaza. Memory lane zigzagged around striped market stands, past doors the color of green bottle-glass. Summer always managed to prolong its stay here: yellow leaves on the cherry trees seemed simply an extension of daylight.

The driver half-turned to them. "Where to now?"

"Ashcr..." *Damn it.* Something made him swallow the word— whether it was the sun that stung his eyes, or all the things rising up his chest. "Ashcroft family workshop."

"What's that?"

"The furniture shop a few streets away."

"Oh." The man pursed his lips. "Oh. You mean Imogen's."

"I mean that street, right ahead. I'll show you the way from there."

What had he expected? After a decade—dead windows, still criss-crossed by wooden boards? Of course the place had a new owner, and he could only hope they hadn't discovered the rose-wood trapdoor.

"You've mentioned the proprietor's name," he said.

"A gal called Imogen." The driver smacked his lips. "That shop, after what had happened, folks were afraid it was cursed or something. All those people who died—"

"What *did* happen there?" Aidan said.

The man shrugged. "People died. You know. Anyway, no one

wanted to buy the place until Imogen came along and made it into a clothing store."

The carriage drove into a small square in front of a building which still reminded Shea—even though his young, romantic self had long faded—of a yacht: the dark wood of the first floor and the white sail of the second.

The sign read 'Flying Tulip Dresses.' Imogen hadn't simply bought the workshop—she'd bought its history, too.

Leaving the black gloves to meter out the coins, Shea hopped off the carriage.

"What do you have in mind?" Aidan called out to him.

"To talk."

The doorbell silver-chimed.

The main hall wasn't the way he remembered it: no more wheels under the ceiling—or ropes—no scent of resin and finished wood. No laughter; no clinking, somewhere in the corner, of beer mugs. People in white stood at equal distances from one another, each hunched over their own small table. Neat, clean, an invisible checkerboard.

A tall woman sailed up to him. "May I help you?"

"Good afternoon." Shea looked around, remembering. "I…"

"Are you here to order a dress?"

"No… Maybe. I would be interested in a guided tour."

"We don't offer tours, I'm afraid. But if you're looking to buy a dress, I can show you our fabrics."

"Sure," he said. "Thank you." *That door, across the hall. Still there. Here's hoping they hadn't tried to change the floorboards—*

"This is cotton with lozenges, and here's some striped linen. It's particularly beautiful with…"

There was zero chance they would get to the trapdoor with all those people around.

"When do you close?" Shea asked.

"…purple velvet. I beg your pardon?"

"When do you close the workshop?"

"At six. But it's still plenty of time to take your measurements if—"

"Listen, I've some money with me. I know it sounds very strange, but I assure you, there's no malicious intent involved."

"I don't understand."

"You just need to let me in after your close. I'll pay you whatever you ask."

"Let you in?"

Shea lowered his voice. "I won't take anything from the workshop. I'm not trying to rob you. I only require ten minutes …I'll pay you, okay? I promise I won't get you into trouble."

She nodded slowly, staring at him. "Please give me a second."

A guy at one of the tables cursed loudly and puffed at his fingers—for a moment, that distracted Shea, and then the woman wasn't there anymore. When he caught sight of her again, she stood at the other side of the hall next to a bulky fellow with hands that, from the looks of them, could bend small trees.

Shea saw her say something and point at him.

Fuck.

The bell chimed again as he tumbled out into the street.

"Find out anything?" Aidan said.

"Found out we need to scramble, fast."

Rushing toward a back alley, déjà vu gripped him that he first couldn't place; then he remembered—*catch it, Danny, catch it.* The sudden influx of memory was so painful that he doubled over, palms on his knees.

Aidan interpreted this in his own way. "You should exercise more, my friend."

From the shadows, they watched the 'bouncer' step out through the front door, scan the street, disappear back into the shop.

Catch it, Danny.

"Let's forget the entire thing," Shea said. "Do you hear me, Aidan? Let's forget it and return to Owenbeg."

Aidan slowly turned his head and chuckled in disbelief. "What the hell is wrong with you?"

"Coming here was a mistake."

"Do you realize—damn it, I'm repeating myself—do you realize what's at stake? This is our future, combined. *And* the country's future—"

"No, this is your *belief.*" Shea pressed his back against the wall and slid down into a crouch. "Or Daelyn's belief. Against someone else's. You believe Duma would instigate a world war. The queen believes her legacy is a two thousand foot monstrosity. Drakiri believe that same monstrosity will bring about the apocalypse. One belief against the other."

"Except some beliefs have foundation in reality and some are pure superstition. What's the deal with the Drakiri, you said?"

"They're convinced..." Shea sighed. "They're convinced that once the tower is finished, another will materialize. They even have a name for it—the Mimic Tower. It's supposed to be a portal to hell."

"Surely you realize how crazy this sounds."

"Crazy, Aidan?" Shea glanced at him. "Same crazy as in 'devices we don't understand that can fly'?"

"That's different. That's technology, as opposed to superstition."

It was Shea's turn to chuckle.

"Look," Aidan said, "you have some weaknesses that would make it difficult for you to run the court, should all of this..." He raised his hands, palms up. "Should our plans work. You need to get rid of those weaknesses. Focus on the goal at hand."

Take the next step in the golden dance.

"I'm afraid we're out of options anyway—we can't get to the tulips," Shea said.

"Have you at least found out when they close?"

"At six."

"Then we're in luck, cause some of those bloody places stay open through midnight."

Aidan turned around. "Let's meet here at ten."

"Where are you going?"

"You said thirty devices. We'll need help to transport them."

"How would we even get them?"

"Well, that one's pretty obvious," Aidan said. "We break in."

The past / the present

"Shea, wake up. Shea."

Hands shook him, disembodied hands, with no person behind them. He tried to free himself when things came into focus, arms appeared, then the face framed by strands of red hair.

Muriel.

"I had a nightmare," he said.

"Forget it. Look out the window."

"Let me just lie here for a few minutes."

"Wake up, something's wrong. I think something's happened in the city."

He sat on the bed, and a sickening feeling tapped on his abdomen. "Am I still sleeping?"

"What's the matter with you? Look out the window."

He did. It must've been seven or eight in the evening—he'd dozed for an hour, no more, and the void in his body left by the lovemaking had yet to close. In front of him, vineyards stretched down the hill's slope. A road snaked in the distance, and between it and the sunset orange of the river lay Oakville.

Against the darkening rim of the sky, a cone of purple light expanded from behind the roofs.

Give me time till tomorrow evening, she'd told him yesterday.

"What the hell is that?" said Muriel. "And what are you doing?"

He didn't answer, frantically trying to push his right foot into his pants.

The purple light boiled.

Heartbeat.

"I still think we should've simply smashed one of the windows," Aidan said. "Where did you learn to pick locks?"

"My sister taught me. She used to do it for fun when we were kids."

No questions followed: no *I didn't know you had a sister,* no *where is she now.* And anyway, in a few seconds, with a click, the front door opened into the transparent dark of 'Flying Tulips'.

"Shall we wait for your people, Aidan?"

"No, let's go in. They'll arrive in ten minutes or so."

Tables with fabrics heaped on them, clothing stretchers. A child's suit hanging from a coat hook. Shea had to remind himself why he wasn't a thief, why it was all warranted.

The door at the end of the hall drew closer, and with it, a vomit-inducing, ether-inhaling vertigo. There used to be a work-bench here; Danny and himself had drunk beer over there. *You're fine, Danny, you're fine. Don't worry. You'll fit in.*

Voices in the street, Aidan's whisper: *Duck.*

Shea crouched behind a table, praying that the pile of cloth on it would be enough to conceal the top of his head. When the voices gained in force, he peeked over the linen waves.

A group of young people passed outside the windows. One of them, a girl, got close to the glass, either trying to look inside or examining her own reflection. A man laughed.

"Let's go…" Something loud and unintelligible. "Come on."

The girl leaned against the window with her palms. Darkness erased all features from her face, and moonlight went right through the hair. Shea imagined her lips moving.

The next moment, tiny purple garlands stretched among the shadows: Aidan pulled off one of his gloves.

More laughter. "…Let's go."

"Aidan," Shea whispered. "It's okay, they're leaving."

The girl pushed herself away from the window—but the garlands continued to shimmer until the voices outside became an echo.

Heartbeat.

The purple light boiled.

"Lena!"

In the square before the workshop—hands, more hands, tugging at his biceps, at the lapels of his suit.

"Get the fuck off of me." Shea slapped the palms and fingers away, shouldering his way through the crowd. "Lena! *Lena!*"

Of course she couldn't hear him. If she were even inside the workshop—he still clung to the hope that the mammoth vortex boiling purply toward the sky had nothing to do with her.

Maybe she'd gone to the vineyards. Maybe she'd gone for a drink.

The building loomed ahead, a shadow stretching over the centipede of the crowd.

He broke out into the free part of the square suddenly and unexpectedly, stumbling and almost falling. There was no transition, not a single onlooker left; ten feet before the front door, a dead zone started.

He noticed the details, the way the roof arched, as though crumpled by a giant hand, the way the windows curved inward.

Someone yelled, *Stop him*—and yet nobody did.

A second's hesitation was all he could afford. He raised his head. Somewhere above, invisible to him now, the purple cone swirled.

Shea stepped into the workshop.

Wheels and ropes, tangled into a nightmarish spiderweb. The wall opposite the entrance, grinning, and the wardrobe, no longer flying, squeezed into the hole.

It looked like something had tried to *suck the building in from the inside,* and from the ripples frozen into the ceiling, he gauged where this something was.

The epicenter lay behind the door at the other side of the hall.

Or rather, a door frame, a twisted and crippled one.

Heartbeat.

———————

Aidan pushed on the doorknob.

It was a small room, twenty by twenty feet. Some shelves, brooms huddled together in thick shadow. Moonlight seeped in through the single window by the ceiling, reflecting off the lacquered floor.

"Okay, we're here, apparently." Aidan said. "So where are the devices?"

Shea tapped the floorboards with the tip of his boot. "We'll need a hammer and a crowbar."

"Or anything to tear apart wood. It doesn't have to be clean, you know. You go through those shelves, I'll look in the adjacent rooms."

Aidan's steps staccatoed through the main hall, and Shea swallowed the lump in his throat, wishing he could do the same with the fit of claustrophobia.

Forgive me, sis. I never wanted to return. But I need to see the dance to its end.

"I think this would do," Aidan said from the door frame, holding up an oil lamp and something that resembled a pair of goat's legs.

They worked in the jittering light like two coal miners, taking a pause each time Shea lost the grip or hit his finger—he could no longer feel his hands, heartbeat having occupied the entirety of his body.

One by one, the floorboards came off and the rosewood trap-door emerged.

Aidan slid the crowbar between its edge and the floor.

"A hand here?" he said. "The damn thing's heavy."

Together, they lifted the door into an upright position. Underneath, a black rectangle gaped at them, all stale air and the reek of mildew. Shea put his foot on the first stair and thought, *help me, sis, help me save face, help me not to faint.*

"I can't see a thing." Aidan swung the lamp behind him.

"You will."

At this point, Shea didn't need light. He descended the staircase and took a few blind steps forward.

His hands found a lever and a valve.

Forgive me, Lena.

Then it occurred to him he no longer knew which Lena he was apologizing to.

The tulip hummed, rising into the air, painting the cellar in purple, rows upon rows of the Drakiri devices stacked on top of each other like wine barrels.

Aidan whistled. "Well, I'd be damned."

Heartbeat.

———————

A twisted, crippled door frame. Past it, a small room, twenty by twenty feet. Good for keeping brooms in, good for indoor picnics.

The ceiling and the top of the walls had been torn off—a sculptor's mold of a closet, started, but not finished. At head height, a black egg hovered, wobbling and spewing purple light into the sky in a circular pattern.

Lower, soot covered the plaster where the two oil lamps had smashed into it.

Even lower lay the chairs with twisted legs—and the bodies.

Danny was dead, mouth agape in childlike wonder, skin on the right side of his face one big burn—he'd probably held a lamp when everything happened.

Lena's chest was still going up and down.

The only sound Shea could produce was a cawk. He fell on his knees, crawled up to her.

"Lena, Lena, Lena."

He stretched out his hand, then pulled it back, not knowing what to do with that broken flower of a body, whether to try and hold it.

She opened her left eye. "Shea. Danny… Where's… Where is he?"

"Sis, sis, lie still."

"Where's... Danny..."

"Danny's dead, Lena. Please, please." He touched her hair with his fingertips.

"Wanted... to teach him... show you how easy... that even he could use..." She coughed and spat blood.

Anyone but my brother, he remembered—and realized she could choke any moment. He gently wrapped his arm around her shoulders and pressed her face into his chest.

"You have to stop it," she mumbled. "Switch off... the device."

"Everything will be all right," Shea said. "We'll sit here for a while. For a little while. Everything will be okay."

"You have... to stop it."

"I have to, yes."

He never realized tears could flow uninterrupted, without beginning or end, the body simply fulfilling one of its biological functions.

"I love you, sis."

"Love you... too... brother."

With his boot, he pulled the remnants of the nearest chair under the tulip. Keeping balance atop that heap of wood proved difficult, but somehow he managed—maybe because he wasn't thinking anymore.

He screamed and fell when the black surface burned his hands. The device was red-hot.

"Damn you." He slammed his fist into the floor. "I don't have time for this. I don't have time for this."

When his palms lay on the lever and the valve again, he clenched his teeth and tried to forget about his skin melting away, turning and pulling through the pain's curtain, turning and pulling the way Lena did it.

The device shook one last time, spewed the last of its phlegm, and lowered itself onto the floor.

He smiled briefly. Chuckled. "I did it, sis. I did it."

There was no answer.

The people who found him—the ones who'd mustered enough courage to venture into the crippled building once the vortex had died—said he sat beside her body like a praying monk. He hadn't said a word, allowing himself to be brought to his feet, bandaged, and led out.

He didn't speak the next day either, or the day after. Only listened.

Heartbeat.

Heartbeat.

Silence.

PART FIVE
NOVEL

NETWORK EFFECT

NEBULA WINNER: BEST NOVEL
BY MARTHA WELLS, PUBLISHED
BY TOR.COM

EXCERPT

HelpMe.file Excerpt 1

(File detached from main narrative.)

Since I'd decided to stay (temporarily) on Preservation Station, Dr. Mensah had asked me to go places with her seven times. Six of those times were just relatively short boring meetings on ships in orbit or in dock. The seventh was when she had asked me to go down to the local planet's surface with her. I don't like planets but she lured me there by explaining that it was for an Art Festival/Conference/Religious Observation that would include "a lot of" live performances. After checking to find out the definition of "a lot of" was eighty-seven plus, I agreed to go.

Some of the live performances were demonstrations or seminars I wasn't interested in, but I managed to fit in thirty-two plays and musicals while Mensah was at meetings or doing things with her family members. (I used drones to record the performances that were overlapping or scheduled against each other. They were all being recorded for the local planetary entertainment feed, and the popular ones would be re-configured as video productions, but I wanted to see all the versions.) One evening a play was interrupted when Mensah tapped my feed and asked me to please come get her.

The request was so abrupt and out of character I replied with the code phrase we had come up with in case she was being held against her will. She said she was just tired. That was even more out of character. I mean, I could see she got tired, she just hated to admit it.

I left a drone to record the rest of the play and slipped out of the theater. It was night and the crowd in the street was beginning to thin out, but the big open pavilion across the plaza where the party was being held was still bright and noisy.

If you had to be in a crowd of humans, the crowds at this festival weren't bad, since they were the distracted kind where all the humans and augmented humans are talking to each other or on comm or feed or hurrying to get places. The downside was a lot of humans were waving sticks with lighted objects or spark-emitting toys, or tossing colored powders that popped and emitted light. (I have no idea.) But whatever, with all that going on, nobody noticed me.

Plus, it was Preservation and there were no scanning drones, no armed human security, just some on-call human medics with bot assistants and "rangers" who mainly enforced environmental regulations and yelled at humans and augmented humans to get out of the way of the ground vehicles.

In the pavilion, I located Mensah near the edge of the crowd talking to Thiago and Farai, who was one of her marital partners. I stopped next to Mensah and she grabbed my hand.

Right, it's usually a good idea to warn bot/human constructs who call themselves Murderbot before making grabby hands, except during a security incident when you would expect/need the human you're trying to extract from lethal circumstances to grab you and hold on. And this read as the latter; like Mensah needed me to save her. So I didn't react except to shift closer to her. Thiago was saying, "I don't know why you can't just talk to us."

I heard him clearly, since I was looping my ambient audio to lower the level of the music from blaring down to a pleasant background soundtrack level. The glance Thiago threw at me was annoyed, like I had interrupted their conversation. Hey, she called me. I have a job here, I get paid in hard currency cards and everything.

"I told you why," Mensah said, and she sounded normal, calm and firm. Except that was also how she sounded when humans were trying to kill us, so. I had the whole pavilion covered by my drones, and weapons scan was negative. (Weapons weren't even permitted on the planet except in designated wilderness areas where hostile fauna was a problem.) Voices were loud, but my filters showed they were still well within the range of happy-intoxicated-interested emotional tones. But Mensah's grip on my hand told me how tense her arm muscles were. Situation assessment: I have no idea.

Farai said, "Thiago, no. She asks for space, you need to give that to her." She smiled at me politely. I never know how to react to that. She leaned in to Mensah to kiss her, and said, "We'll see you at the house."

Mensah nodded and turned, and I let her tow me out of the pavilion.

We made it outside to the pedestrian plaza and I asked her, "Do you need a medic?" I thought she might be sick. If I was a human and I'd had to be in the pavilion with all those other humans for the past two and a half hours, I'd be sick.

"No," she told me, still sounding calm and normal. "I'm just tired."

I sent a feed request to the ground vehicle (which on Preservation was called a "go-cart" for some reason) (some stupid reason) to meet us at the nearest transportation area.

The plaza and streets were lit with little floating balloon-lights, and the dirt and temporary paving painted with elaborate designs in light-up paint (fortunately it wasn't the marker paint that broadcasts on the feed, which would have been a nightmare). As we walked through the crowd, people recognized Mensah and smiled and waved. Mensah smiled and waved back, but didn't let go of my hand. On the fringe near the transport area, an intoxicated human wandered toward us with a handful of glitter dust but veered off when I made deliberate eye contact.

Our vehicle was waiting for us and I handed her in, and climbed into the other seat. I told it to head for the family camp house, which had been erected in a habitation area on the outskirts of the festival site. The vehicle had a limited bot-driver, which would take humans all over the campground and festival site but knew not to go into the designated no-vehicle sections.

It hummed out of the court and into the dark, along the path that led through high grass and scrub trees. Mensah sighed and opened the window. The breeze was still warm and smelled like vegetation, and the guide-lights along the way were low enough not to obscure the starfield. All the humans and augmented humans staying here for the festival made it a heavily populated area, but we were traveling through the section reserved for humans who actually wanted to sleep. The temporary housing (pop-up shelters of all shapes and sizes, camping vehicles, tents and collapsible structures that looked more like art installations) were all mostly dark and quiet. The camp area for humans who had to be loud was on the far side of the grounds with a sound baffle field to deflect the music and crowd noise.

She said, "Thank you. I'm sorry I interrupted your evening."

I recalled my drones except for the one that was recording the play and the detachment I had designated to keep tabs on the family still at the party. (Another detachment was at the camp house, maintaining a perimeter and keeping watch on the two adults and seven children who had gone back earlier.) I wasn't sure how to react. Mensah wasn't acting like I had rescued her from certain death, but she wasn't acting like we were heading back to the habitat after a boring but successful day collecting samples, either. I said, "I recorded the plays. Do you want to see them?"

She perked up. "I never get to see the performances at this thing. Did you get the one— Oh, what was it called? The new historical by Glaw and Ji-min?"

The difference between "calm and normal" and actual normal was measurable enough that I could have made a chart. I just said, "Yes. It's pretty good."

Something was bothering her, and it wasn't just that her family was clearly as weirded out by me as I was by them. They had assumed I would stay in the camp house, which, no. Mensah had told them I didn't need any help or supervision and could find my own way around. (Quote: "If it can infiltrate high security corporate installations while people are shooting at it, it can certainly handle a domestic festival.")

It wasn't that her family was phobic about the scary rogue SecUnits the entertainment media and the newsfeeds were so fond of, or that they didn't like bots. (There were "free" bots wandering around on Preservation, though they had guardians who were technically supposed to keep track of them.) It was just me-the-SecUnit they didn't like.

(That didn't apply to the seven kids. I was illicitly trading downloads via the feed with three of them.)

I think if I had been a normal bot, or even like a normal SecUnit, just off inventory, naive and not knowing anything about how to get along in the human world or whatever, like the way humans would write it for the media, basically, it would have been okay. But I wasn't like that. I was me, Murderbot.

So instead of Mensah having a pet bot like poor Miki, or a sad bot/human construct that needed someone to help it, she had me.

(I told this to Dr. Bharadwaj later, because we talked about a lot of things while she was doing research about bot/human relations for her documentary. After thinking about it, she said, "I wish I thought you were wrong.")

(Farai was a possible exception. Up on the station, when Mensah had first introduced me to her family, she'd had a conversation with me. Or a conversation at me, you could say.

Farai: "You know we're grateful for how you returned her to us."

I did know, I guess. What do humans say in this situation? A quick archive search came up with some variation on "okay, um" and even I knew that wasn't going to cut it.

(Just a heads-up, when a murderbot stands there looking to the left of your head to avoid eye contact, it's probably not thinking about killing you, it's probably frantically trying to come up with a reply to whatever you just said to it.)

She added, "I wanted to ask what your relationship to her is."

Uh. In the Corporation Rim, Mensah was my owner. On Preservation, she was my guardian. (That's like an owner, but Preservation law requires they be nice to you.) But Mensah and Pin-Lee were trying to get my status listed as "refugee working as employee/security consultant."

But I knew Farai knew all that, and I knew she was asking for an answer that was closer to objective reality. And wow, I did not have that answer. I said, "I'm her SecUnit." (Yes, that's still in the buffer.)

She lifted her brows. "And that means?"

Backed into yet another conversational corner, I fell back on honesty. "I don't know. I wish I knew."

She smiled. "Thank you."

(And that was that.)

Mensah's family were also weirded out by the idea that I would be providing security, and were afraid I would be, I don't know, scaring legitimate visitors and killing people, I guess.

And granted, while I have been a key factor in certain clusterfucks of gigantic proportions and my risk assessment module has serious issues, my threat assessment record is pretty great, like 93 percent. (Most of the negative points came from that time I didn't know that Wilken and Gerth were hired killers until Wilken tried to shoot Don Abene in the head, but that was an outlier.)

Mensah's family also thought they didn't need security, which, maybe before GrayCris, that had been true. But as it was, during the festival I only had to deal with five incursions, four by outsystem newsfeed journalists with recording drones. I took control of the drones (I can always use a few more) and notified the local Rangers who drove off the human journalists.

The fifth incursion was the one that got me in trouble with Amena, Mensah's oldest offspring.

Since the festival had started, I had been taking note of a potential hostile that Amena had been associating with. Evidence was mounting up and my threat assessment was nearing critical. Things like: 1) he had informed her that his age was comparable to hers, which was just below the local standard for legal adult, but my physical scan and public record search indicated that he was approximately twelve Preservation standard calendar years older, 2) he never approached her when any family members or verified friends were with her, 3) he stared at her secondary sexual characteristics when her attention was elsewhere, 4) he encouraged her to take intoxicants that he wasn't ingesting himself, 5) her parental and other related humans all assumed she was with her friends when she was seeing him and her friends all assumed she was with family and she hadn't told either group about him, 6) I just had a bad feeling about the little shit.

You might think the obvious thing to do was to notify Mensah or Farai or Tano, the third marital partner. I didn't.

If there was one thing I understood, it was the difference between proprietary and non-proprietary data.

So, on the night when Potential Target invited Amena to come back to his semi-isolated camp house with him to "meet some friends," I decided to come along.

He led her into the darkened house, and she stumbled on a low table. She giggled and he laughed. Sounding way more intoxicated than he actually was, he said, "Wait, I got it," and tapped the house's feed to turn on the lights.

And I was standing in the middle of the room.

He screamed. (Yes, it was hilarious.)

Amena clapped a hand over her mouth, startled, then recognized me. She said, "What the hell? What are you doing here?"

Potential Target gasped, "What—Who—?"

Amena was furious. "That's my second mother's. . . friend," she said through gritted teeth. "And her security. . . person."

"What?" He was confused, then the word "security" penetrated. He stepped away from her. "Uh. . . I guess. . . You'd better go."

Amena looked at him, and then glared at me, then turned and stamped out the door and down the steps to the path. I followed her, and he backed away as I passed him. Yeah, you better.

On the dirt path, lit by the low floating guide-lights, I caught up with her. (Not so much intentionally, but my legs were longer and she was putting more energy into stamping her feet than gaining distance.)

She said, "How did you know where I was? What were you doing, hiding under the porch?"

She thought I wouldn't get the domestic animal reference. I said, "Wow, that was rude. Especially considering that I'm your second mother's—" I made ironic quote marks. " 'Friend.' Is that how you talk to your bot-servants?"

My drone cam showed her expression turn startled and then a combination of sulky and guilty. "No. I don't have bot-servants! I didn't know—I never heard you talk."

"You didn't ask." Had I not been talking? I had been talking to the kids on the feed, and to Mensah. Maybe with the rest of the family it had been easier to pretend to be a robot again. I added, "No one else approached that house. He lied about meeting other humans there."

She stamped along in silence for twelve point five seconds. "Look, I'm sorry, but I'm not some kind of idiot, and I don't fuck around. If he'd done anything I didn't like, I was going to leave. And if he wouldn't let me leave, I have the feed, I can call for help whenever I want." She was scornful, and way overconfident. "I wasn't going to let him hurt me."

I said, "If I thought he was going to hurt you, I'd be disposing of his body. I don't fuck around, either."

She stopped and stared up at me. I stopped but kept my gaze on the path ahead. I said, "Mensah is a planetary leader of a minor political entity that has managed to get the angry attention of major corporates. Her situation has changed. Your situation has changed. You need to grow up and deal with it."

She took a breath to say something, stopped, then shook her head. "He wasn't a corporate spy. He was just someone. . . "

"Someone you don't know who showed up out of nowhere at a massive public festival attended by half the continent and whatever offworld humans happen to be wandering through." I knew he wasn't a corporate spy (see above, disposing of bodies) but she sure didn't.

She was quiet for sixteen seconds. "Are you going to tell my parents about this?"

Is that what she was worried about? I was insulted and exasperated. "I don't know. I guess you'll find out."

She stamped away.

So, in retrospect, I could see that hadn't gone so well.

Our vehicle rumbled through the dark, up the low hill to the camp house, which was a pop-up two-story structure with broad covered balconies off both levels. It had been placed near a couple of large trees with frilly leaves that curved over the roof. It had been built by Mensah's grandfather, while her grandmothers and other assorted family members had been working on the original planetary survey and terraforming. The colonists who hadn't been living in orbit on their ship had all stayed in temporary structures at that point, that were moved seasonally to avoid destructive weather patterns in the parts of the planet that had been habitable at that time.

There were other pop-ups, large and small, planted all over the hills around us, the nearest twenty-seven meters away. Lights were on inside the house and one light floated above the beacon spot for the vehicles. I would have worried about the lack of lighting if I hadn't had thirty-seven drones on patrol in the immediate area.

(Drones had picked up previously identified humans and augmented humans returning to the other houses or passing through the area, and I'd conducted safety checks on unidentified humans encountered for the first time. I was cataloguing power signatures on some small mobility devices used by non-augmented humans for medical reasons; I hadn't seen these anywhere in the Corporation Rim, though maybe that was because I hadn't spent much time hanging out on planets with human populations not exclusively engaged in corporate slave labor. (The entertainment media showed planets that weren't all corporate slave labor, I had just never been on one.)) (The drones had also tracked the five younger kids on a completely illicit expedition to a nearby creek where they had performed some kind of ritual that involved jumping out at each other from behind bushes and rocks. They returned to the house without being caught by the adult humans or older siblings and were now collapsed in their upstairs bunk room, watching media.)

(The house actually had secure sealable window and door hatches, WHICH NO ONE USED, but at least this made it easy for my patrol drones.)

As the vehicle settled into its spot, Mensah said, "I'm just going to sit outside for a bit. Why don't you go on back to the festival? There's a few more plays tonight, aren't there?"

I try to avoid asking humans if there's anything wrong with them. (Mostly because I don't care.) (On the rare occasions where I did care, it would have meant starting a conversation not directly related to security protocol, and that was just a slippery slope waiting to happen, for a variety of reasons.) But humans asked each other about their current status all the time, so how hard could it be? It was a request for information, that was all. I did a quick search and pulled up a few examples from my media collection. None of the samples seemed like anything I'd ever voluntarily say, so before I could change my mind I went with, "What's wrong?"

She was surprised, then gave me a sideways look. "Don't you start."

So there was something wrong and even the other humans had noticed. I said, "I have to know about any potential problems for an accurate threat assessment."

She lifted a brow and opened the vehicle door. "You never mentioned that on our survey contract."

I got out of the vehicle and followed her toward a group of chairs next to the house, scattered around in the grass under the trees. The shadow was deep so I had to switch to a dark filter to see her. "That was because I was half-assing my job."

She took a seat. "If that was you half-assing your job, I don't want to see what you're like when. . . " The smile faded and she trailed off, then added, "But I suppose I did see you when you were doing your best."

I sat down, too. (Sitting down with a human like this would never not feel strange.) Her expression wasn't upset, but it wasn't not upset, either. But I could tell my smartass comment had taken us down an awkward conversational avenue where I hadn't wanted to go. I wished I was ART, who was good at this kind of thing. (The thing being getting you to talk about what it wanted you to talk about but also making you think about what it wanted you to talk about in different ways.) (I wasn't kidding when I said ART was an asshole.) "You didn't answer the question."

She settled back in her chair. "You sound worried."

"I am worried." I could feel my face making the expression whether I wanted it to or not.

She let her breath out. "It's nothing. I've been having night-mares. About being held prisoner on TranRollinHyfa, and. . . you know." She made an impatient gesture. "It's completely normal. It would be odd if I wasn't having nightmares."

I hadn't seen much of the recovery phase of trauma (my job was to get the client to the MedSystem before they died; it took care of all the messy aftermath, including the retrieved client protocol) but in the shows I watched, recovery was featured a lot. There was a trauma recovery program that Bharadwaj had used in the Station Medical Center, and the big hospital in the port city had one, too.

I wasn't the only one who thought Mensah should go get the trauma treatment. I was probably the only one who knew she hadn't. (She hadn't exactly lied; it was more a way of letting the other humans assume she had.) But the treatment wasn't like a one-time thing with a MedSystem; it took multiple long visits, and I knew she had never made time for it in her schedule. I said, "Is that why you're afraid to go off-station without me?"

So there were two positions on whether the Preservation Planetary leader needed security. The first was the one 99 percent of the population shared, that she did not unless she went on a formal visit to somewhere like the Corporation Rim. And to a large extent, they were right.

The crime stats on Preservation Station and the planet were pitifully low, and usually involved intoxication-related property damage or disturbances and/or minor infractions of station cargo handling or planetary environmental regulations. Mensah had never needed on-station or on-planet security before this, except for the young Preservation Council-trainee humans who followed her around and kept track of her appointments and handed her things occasionally. (And they did not count as security.)

The other 1 percent was composed of me, Mensah's survey team, all the humans working in Station Security, and the members of the Preservation Council who had seen the Gray-Cris assassins try to kill her. But that incident had been kept out of the newsfeeds, so hardly anyone thought Mensah needed a security consultant let alone a SecUnit.

But GrayCris was not doing so hot now due to their hired security service Palisade making an extremely bad decision to punch my ex-owner bond company in the operating funds by attacking one of its gunships. (The company is paranoid and greedy and cheap but also ruthless, methodical, and intensely violent when it thinks it's being threatened.) Relations between the two corporates had deteriorated since what we call The Gunship Incident, with GrayCris assets getting mysteriously destroyed a lot in supposedly random accidents and its executives and employees getting blown up or found stuffed in containers way too small for intact adult humans and so on.

And once GrayCris had started to cease to exist, even my threat assessment had dropped drastically, but Mensah had still wanted me to continue to provide security. I thought she was humoring me, and taking the opportunity to pay me in hard currency cards which I would need if/when I left Preservation, and giving me practice in being around humans in a setting where I was not categorized as a tool and/or deadly weapon. (Yeah, I assumed it was about me, but humans assume everything is about them, too. It's not an uncommon problem, okay?)

But for a while now I had been thinking it was about something else.

Her mouth twisted a little and she looked away, over the dark hills and fields toward the lighted windows of the other camp houses and tents. She said, "I suppose it was obvious."

I said, "Not obvious." Not to most of the humans, anyway. I had a feeling that Farai and Tano knew, but weren't sure what to do about it.

She shrugged a little. "It's hardly surprising that I feel safer with you. It's also easier to be around people who understand what happened, what it's like to be in that situation. That's you and the rest of the survey team." She hesitated. "Farai and Tano understand, but I haven't explained to my brother and sister and Thiago and the others why I can't just rely on them for emotional support about this, as usual." Her face turned grim. "They don't understand what it's like to be under corporate authority."

That I got. Humans in the Preservation Alliance didn't have to sign up for contract labor and get shipped off to mines or whatever for 80 to 90 percent of their lifespans. There was some strange system where they all got their food and shelter and education and medical for free, no matter what job they did. It had something to do with the giant colony ship that had brought them here, and a promise by the original crew to take care of everyone in perpetuity if they would just get on the damn thing and not die in the old colony. (It was complicated and when I watched their historical dramas, I tended to fast forward through the economics parts.) Whatever, the humans seemed to like it.

But she was right, these humans had no concept of what it was like to live under corporate authority. And they really didn't know what it was like to be the target of a corporate entity that wanted to kill you.

I replayed my recording of Mensah talking to Thiago and Farai at the party. Mensah had been abducted from Port Free-Commerce at a meeting for the relatives of the murdered survey members. Maybe the noisy party, where the other humans who would normally help her had been distracted, had just started to feel too similar.

I said, "You need to get the trauma treatment."

Her voice sharpened. "I will. But I have some things to finish first." She turned toward me. "And I want you to go on that survey mission with Arada. They need you. And it's a wonderful opportunity for you."

It was too dark for her to see my expression. I'm not sure what it was but you could probably describe it as "skeptical." (Ratthi says that's how I look most of the time.)

With that confident planetary leader I am totally convincing you of this tone, she added, "And you know Amena and Thiago are going, too. I'll feel better if you're there to keep an eye on them."

Uh-huh. "What about you?"

She took a breath to say she'd be fine. I knew her well enough to know those exact words were about to come out. But then she hesitated. The drone I had watching her face increased magnification, its low-light filter rendering her features in black and white. Her expression was intense and fierce and she was biting her lower lip. She said, "I hate feeling so weak. I just need to stop.

And I need to stop leaning on you. It's not fair to you. We need to be apart so I can. . . stand on my own feet again."

I didn't think she was wrong, but I still wasn't used to things that were unfair to me being a major point of consideration for humans. It also sounded vaguely like the break-up part of the romance scenes on the shows I watched, most of which I usually skimmed over. I said, "It's not me, it's you."

She huffed a laugh.

And then I sort of blackmailed her.

end HelpMe.file Excerpt 1

PART SIX
MIDDLE GRADE AND YOUNG ADULT FICTION

A WIZARD'S GUIDE TO DEFENSIVE BAKING

ANDRE NORTON NEBULA AWARD WINNER FOR MIDDLE GRADE & YOUNG ADULT FICTION

BY T. KINGFISHER, PUBLISHED BY ARGYLL

<u>EXCERPT</u>

Chapter One

There was a dead girl in my aunt's bakery.

I let out an undignified yelp and backed up a step, then another, until I ran into the bakery door. We keep the door open most of the time because the big ovens get swelteringly hot otherwise, but it was four in the morning and nothing was warmed up yet.

I could tell right away that she was dead. I haven't seen a lot of dead bodies in my life—I'm only fourteen, and baking's not exactly a high-mortality profession—but the red stuff oozing out from under her head definitely wasn't raspberry filling. And she was lying at an awkward angle that nobody would choose to sleep in, even assuming they'd break into a bakery to take a nap in the first place.

My stomach made an awful clenching, like somebody had grabbed it and squeezed hard, and I clapped both hands over my mouth to keep from getting sick. There was already enough of a mess to clean up without adding my secondhand breakfast to it.

The worst thing I've ever seen in the kitchen was the occasional rat—don't judge us, you can't keep rats out in this city, and we're as clean an establishment as you'll ever find—and the zombie frog that crawled out of the canals. Poor thing had been downstream of the cathedral, and sometimes they dump the holy water a little recklessly, and you get a plague of undead frogs and newts and whatnot. (The crawfish are the worst. You can get the frogs with a broom, but you have to call a priest in for a zombie crawfish.)

But I would have preferred any number of zombie frogs to a corpse.

I have to get Aunt Tabitha. She'll know what to do. Not that Aunt Tabitha had bodies in her bakery on a regular basis, but she's one of those competent people who always know what to do. If a herd of ravenous centaurs descended on the city and went galloping through the streets, devouring small children and cats, Aunt Tabitha would calmly go about setting up barricades and manning crossbows as if she did it twice a week.

Unfortunately, to get to the hallway that led to the stairs up to Aunt Tabitha's bedroom, I would have to walk the length of the kitchen, and that meant walking past the corpse. Stepping over it, in fact.

Okay. Okay. Feet, are you with me? Knees? Can we do this?

The feet and knees reported their willingness. The stomach was not so happy with this plan. I wrapped one hand around my waist and clamped the other firmly over my mouth in case it decided to rebel.

Okay. Okay, here we go…

I inched into the kitchen. I spent six days a week here, sometimes seven, running back and forth across the tile, flinging dough onto counters and pans into ovens. I crossed the kitchen floor hundreds of times a day, without even thinking about it. Now it seemed to be about a mile long, an unfamiliar and hostile landscape.

I had a dilemma. I didn't want to look at the body, but if I didn't, I might step on it—on her—and that just didn't bear thinking about.

No help for it. I looked down.

The dead girl's legs were splayed across the floor. She was wearing grimy boots with mismatched socks. That seemed very sad. I mean, it was sad that she was dead anyway—probably, unless she'd been a horrible person—but dying with mismatched socks seemed especially sad somehow.

I imagined her throwing the socks on, never thinking that a few hours later, an apprentice baker and half-baked wizard of dough would be tiptoeing past her and thinking about the condition of her footwear.

There was probably a moral lesson there somewhere, but I'm not a priest. I thought about becoming one once, but they don't really like wizards, even minor wizards whose only talents are making bread rise and keeping the pastry dough from sticking together. Right about the time I gave up on hopes of joining the priesthood, Aunt Tabitha had taken me on in the bakery, and the siren song of flour and shortening pretty much sealed my fate.

I wondered what had sealed this poor girl's fate. Her hair was mostly over her face, so it was hard to tell how old she was—and I wasn't looking very closely—but I got the feeling she was young, maybe not much older than me. How did she wind up dead in our bakery? Somebody who was cold or hungry might conceivably creep into the bakery—it's warm, even at night, since we bank the big stoves but we don't put them out, and there's always food around, even just the day-old stuff in the case. But that didn't explain why she was dead.

I could see one of her eyes. It was open. I looked away again.

Maybe she slipped and hit her head. Aunt Tabitha always swears I'll break my neck one of these days, the way I race around the kitchen like a flour-crazed greyhound, but it seems weird that you'd break into a bakery and then run around inside it.

Maybe she was murdered, whispered a traitorous little voice in my brain.

Shut up, shut up! That's just stupid! I told it. People hold murders in back alleys and things, not in my aunt's kitchen. And it'd be stupid to leave a body in a bakery. The whole city is built on canals, there are fifty bridges to a street, and the basements flood every spring. Who'd dump a body in a bakery when you could dump it in a perfectly good canal not twenty feet from the door?

I held my breath and stepped over the dead girl's ankles.

Nothing happened. I wasn't expecting anything to happen, but I was still relieved.

I looked straight ahead, took two more careful steps, then broke into a run. I knocked the door open with my shoulder and tore up the stairs, yelling *"Aunt Tabithaaaaa! Come quick!"*

———

It was four in the morning, but bakers are used to getting up at four in the morning, and the only reason that Aunt Tabitha was sleeping until the decadent hour of six-thirty was because her niece had finally been trusted to open the bakery in the last few months. (That's me, in case you aren't following along.) She'd been nervous about letting me take over, and I'd been really proud that nothing had gone wrong when I was opening. This made me feel twice as guilty that a dead body had turned up on my watch, even though it wasn't my fault. I mean, it's not like I had killed her.

Don't be stupid, nobody *killed her. She just slipped. Probably.*

"Aunt Tabithaaaa!"

"Gracious, Mona…" muttered my aunt from behind the door. "Is the building on fire?"

"No, Aunt Tabitha, I have discovered a dead body in our kitchen!" was what I meant to say. What came out was something more along the lines of "Aunt Body! There's a Tabitha—the kitchen—dead, she's dead—I—come quick—she's *dead!*"

The door at the top of the stairs was flung open, and my aunt emerged, shouldering into her housedress. Her housedress is large and pink and has winged croissants embroidered across it. It's quite hideous. Aunt Tabitha herself is large and pink but doesn't have winged croissants flying across her except when wearing the housedress.

"Dead?" She narrowed her eyes down at me. "Who's dead?"

"The body in the kitchen!"

"In my kitchen!?"Aunt Tabitha came barreling down the stairs at top speed, and not wanting to be trampled, I retreated in front of her. She brushed me aside, not unkindly, and went sideways through the door to the bakery. I followed, poking my head timidly around the doorframe and waiting for the explosion.

"Huh."Aunt Tabitha put a fist on each generous hip. "That's a dead body, all right. Lord save us. *Huh.*"

There was a long silence, while I stared at her back and she stared at the dead girl and the dead girl stared at the ceiling.

"Err...Aunt Tabitha...what should we do?"I finally asked.

Aunt Tabitha shook herself. "Well. I'll go wake your uncle up and send him around to the constables. You start lighting the fires and put a tray of sweet buns on."

"*Sweet buns?* We're going to *bake?*"

"We're a bakery, girl!"my aunt snapped. "Besides, never knew a copper who didn't love a sweet bun, and we'll be swarming with 'em before long. Better put on two trays, there's a dear."

"Err..."I drew myself together. "Should I start the rest of the baking then?"

My aunt frowned and tugged at her lower lip. "N-o-o-o...no, I don't think so. They'll be in and out and making a mess of things for a few hours at least. We'll just have to open late, I suppose."

She turned and stalked heavily away to roust my uncle.

I was left alone with the dead girl and the ovens.

I could get to one of the ovens easily enough, and I poked up the fire underneath and threw another log on. There's a trick to keeping the ovens heated evenly, and it's the first thing you learn. If you have spots that are too hot or too cool, your bread gets fallen spots and comes out looking lumpy and sort of squashed in places.

I couldn't reach the other oven without stepping over her.

After a moment's thought, I threw one of our dishtowels over her face. It was easier somehow if I couldn't see that one eye staring upward at nothing. I fired up the other oven.

Sweet buns are easy. I could make sweet buns in my sleep, and occasionally, at four in the morning, I pretty much do. I threw the dry ingredients together in a bowl and started whisking them together. I gazed up at the rafters so that I didn't have any chance of seeing the body. There was a brief shine of eyes as a mouse looked down at me, then scurried across the rafters on his way back to his mousehole. (Having mice is actually a good thing, since it means we don't have rats any more. Rats think mice are yummy.)

There were eggs on the counter and a big crockery jar of shortening in the corner. I cracked the eggs and separated out the yolks—perfectly, I might add—and dumped all the ingredients into a bigger bowl and started beating.

I heard the front door open and close, as Uncle Albert went out to get the constable. Aunt Tabitha was bustling around the front of the shop, probably getting ready to turn the first wave of customers away.

I wondered how many constables we'd get. A couple, right, for a murder? Murders are important. Would the body wagon come? Well, it'd have to, wouldn't it? We couldn't very well just set the body out with the garbage. The wagon would come, and then all the neighbors would think my uncle had died—nobody'd think Tabitha had died, of course, she was a force of nature—and they'd come around gossiping, and they'd find out there had been a murder—

Wait, when did I decide it was a murder? She just slipped, right?

I discovered that between not-looking at the dead girl and wondering about the constables that I'd been kneading the sweet bun dough for much too long. You don't want to knead them too much, or it makes them tough. I stuck a floury hand in the dough and suggested that maybe it didn't want to be tough. There was a sort of fizziness around my fingers and the dough went a little stickier. Dough is very amicable to persuasion if you know how to ask it right. Sometimes I forget that other people can't do it.

I separated out a dozen evenly sized lumps of raw dough and set them on the wooden baking paddle, then shoved them into the oven with strict orders that they didn't want to burn. They wouldn't. Not burning is one of the few magics I'm really good at. Once, when I was having a really awful day, I did it too hard, and half the bread wouldn't bake at all.

That was the sweet buns done. I wiped my hands on my apron and dipped a cup of flour out of one of the bins. There was one other task that had to be done, no matter what, whether there was one body in the kitchen or a dozen.

The steps down to the basement are slippery, because everybody's basements leak. It's amazing we still have basements. My father, who was a builder before he died, used to say that it was because there was another city down there, and people just kept on building upwards as the canals rose, so the basement floors were really the roofs and ceilings of old houses.

In the darkest, warmest corner of the basement, a bucket bubbled slowly. Every now and then one of the bubbles would pop, and exhale a damp, yeasty aroma.

"C'mon, Bob…" I said, using the sugary tones you'd use to approach an unpredictable animal. "C'mon. I've got some nice flour for you…"

Bob popped several bubbles, which is his version of an enthusiastic greeting. Bob is my sourdough starter. He's the first big magic I ever really did, and I didn't know what I was doing, so I overdid it.

A sourdough starter is kind of a gloppy mess of all the yeast and weird little growing things that you need to make bread rise. The taste of the bread can change a lot depending on the starter. Most of them live for a couple of weeks, but in the right hands, they can stay alive for years. There's one in Constantine that's supposed to be over a century old.

When I first started working in my aunt's bakery, I was just ten, and really scared that I'd screw something up. My magic tended to do weird things to recipes sometimes. So I was put in charge of tending her sourdough starter, which she'd been using since she started the bakery, and which was really important, because Aunt Tabitha's bread was famous.

And…I don't know if I gave it too much flour or too much water or not enough of either, but it dried up and nearly died. When I found that out, I was so scared that I stuck both hands into it (and it was pretty icky, let me tell you) and ordered it not to die. *Live!* I told it. *C'mon, don't die on me, live! Grow! Eat! Don't dry up!*

Well, I was ten, and I was really scared, and sometimes being scared does weird things to the magic. Supercharges it, for one thing. The starter didn't die, and it grew. A *lot.* It foamed out of the jar and over my hands and I started yelling for Aunt Tabitha, but by the time she got there, the starter had reached the sack of flour I'd been using to feed it and ate the whole thing. I started crying but Aunt Tabitha just put her hands on her hips and said, "It's still alive, it'll be fine,"and scraped it into a much bigger jar and that was the beginning of Bob.

I'm not actually sure if we could kill him any more. One time the city froze so hard that nobody could go anywhere, and Aunt Tabitha was stuck across town for three days and I couldn't get down the block, and nobody fed Bob. I expected to come back and find him frozen or starved or something.

Instead, the bucket had moved across the basement, and there were the remains of a couple of rats scattered around. He hadn't eaten the bones. That was how we figured out that Bob could feed himself. I'm still not sure how he moves—like a slime-mold maybe. I'm not going to pick the bucket up and find out. I doubt there's a bottom on it any more, but I don't want to risk annoying Bob.

He likes me best, maybe because I feed him the most often. He tolerates Aunt Tabitha. My uncle won't go into the basement any more, he claims Bob actually hissed at him once. It would have been a belching sort of hiss, I imagine.

I dumped the flour in on top of Bob, and he glubbed happily in his bucket and extended a sort of mushy tentacle. I pulled it off, and the starter settled back and began digesting the flour. He doesn't seem to mind me taking bits to make bread, and it's still the best sourdough in town.

We just don't tell anybody about the eating-rats thing.

Chapter Two

Constable Alphonse was tall and broad and red-faced. He came into the kitchen, stopped, and said, sounding surprised "There's a dead body in here!"

"That's what I *told* you," said Uncle Albert behind him, sounding aggrieved.

"Well, yes, but…" The Constable trailed off, but still made it abundantly clear that he'd expected a hysterical member of the public to be getting upset about nothing, not that there would be a genuine dead body in a respectable bakery.

Aunt Tabitha took charge. "It's a dead body all right. Mona found it this morning when she came in. Have a sweet bun."

Constable Alphonse took a sweet bun, chewed it thoughtfully, and decided to go for a second opinion.

Constable Montgomery was also tall, also broad, but instead of being red-faced was rather sallow. He ate three sweet buns, confirmed that yes, indeed, it was a dead body, and then he and Alphonse stood in the kitchen in silence until Aunt Tabitha testily suggested that maybe they should call for the body-wagon.

"We'll need the coroner," said Montgomery, and helped himself to another sweet bun.

"The coroner, yep," agreed Alphonse.

They went out.

"Better put in another tray of sweet buns," said Aunt Tabitha heavily. "And a pot of tea, I think. Looks like we'll be all morning about this."

The coroner, when he arrived, was a short man, bald and slabby, like a half-melted candle. He ate most of a tray of sweet buns by himself, but I didn't get to hear what he said, because once they started moving the body, Aunt Tabitha shooed me out to the front of the store to take care of customers.

Most of the customers are regulars (with their regular orders) and while they were disappointed that their muffins and bread and scones weren't available, they were more worried that something was wrong. I repeated over and over again that everything was fine, somebody'd just broken into the kitchen and the police were looking at it, but nothing seemed to have been stolen, and we hoped to be open for business later today.

"Nobody's safe anymore," said old Miss McGrammar (one lemon scone, no icing) with a sniff. She rapped her cane against the counter for emphasis. "Imagine, someone breaking into a bakery! We'll all be murdered in our beds soon and no mistake!"

"Some of us sooner than others," muttered Master Elwidge the carpenter, (two cinnamon rolls, one loaf of cheese bread) winking at me.

"Hmmph!" Miss McGrammar shook her cane at him. "You can laugh! Little Sidney, the boy of Mrs. Weatherfort who does the washing, he went missing just last week, and have they seen hide nor hair of him since?"

"No?" I ventured.

"They have not!" She smacked her cane down like a judge's gavel.

"Probably ran away to sea," offered Brutus the chandler (one of whatever looks good today, m'dear, and a loaf of the day-old for the pigeons if you have it).

"Run away to *sea?*" asked Miss McGrammar, scandalized. Elwidge put a hand over his mouth to stifle a smile. "Sidney? Nothing doing! He was a good boy, he was!"

"Even good boys will be boys," said Brutus mildly, rubbing his forearms. He had several faded tattoos, and I suspect he was speaking from personal experience.

"Sidney Weatherfort wouldn't run away to sea," piped up the tiny Widow Holloway (one blackberry muffin, two ginger cookies, and thank you so much, dear Mona, you're getting to look more like your poor dear mother every day, you know...) "He was a magicker, and you know how superstitious sailors are about taking on wizard-folk. They think the winds will fail if you're carrying wizard-folk aboard."

"A magicker?" Elwidge looked surprised. "I didn't know that."

"He was a mender," said the Widow Holloway. "Little things. He fixed my glasses for me once when the lens cracked, and I thought I'd have to send away to Constantine to have a new one ground." She smiled at me. "Small things, though. Nothing like as good as our Mona, here."

I flushed. As wizards go, I'm pretty much the bottom of the barrel. Even Master Elwidge, who's got just enough magic to take knots out of wooden boards, is better than me. Dough and pastries are about all I can do. The great wizards, the magi that serve the Duchess, they can throw fireballs around or rip mountains out of the earth, heal the dying, turn lead into gold.

Me, I can turn flour and yeast into tasty bread, on a good day. And occasionally make carnivorous sourdough starters.

Still, they were all looking at me expectantly, and I didn't have any food for them, so I felt like I ought to do something. I reached into the case and pulled out one of the day-old gingerbread men. It's early spring, and much too late to still be carrying gingerbread men, but we're the one bakery that stocks a few all year 'round, just for this purpose.

I set the gingerbread man up on the counter and focused my attention on it. *Live. Move. Up, up, up!*

The cookie woke up. It stretched its arms and pushed itself up onto its gingerbread feet. Then it bowed to the Widow Holloway, and to Miss McGrammar, threw a salute to Elwidge and Brutus, and walked along the counter until it came to a clear space.

Dance, I ordered it.

The gingerbread man began to dance a very respectable hornpipe. Don't ask me where the cookies get the dances they do —this batch had been doing hornpipes. The last batch did waltzes, and the one before that had performed a decidedly lewd little number that had even made Aunt Tabitha blush. A little too much spice in those, I think. We had to add a lot of vanilla to settle them down.

I don't know how I learned to make cookies dance. Apparently I used to do it when I was very, very young. Aunt Tabitha still loves to tell the story of the time I was three and threw a tantrum in the bakery, and the entire case of gingerbread men came alive, even the ones that were still in the oven. Those started hammering on the door to be let out, and the already-baked ones ran through the store, giggling like little maniacs. "They got into the mouseholes," she always says, "and it took us months to see the end of the little devils! That's when I knew our Mona was meant to be a baker."(Depending on how much she's gotten into the kitchen sherry at that point, I get either an affectionate glance or a floury pat on the back. During rum-cake season, there is hugging.)

Being a wizard is almost all like that—you don't know what you can do until you actually do it, and then sometimes you aren't sure what you just did. There aren't teachers who can help you, either. Everybody's different, and there's usually only a couple dozen magic folk in any given city anyway. A few hundred if it's a really big city. Maybe in the army the war-wizards get special training, but down here, it's all trial and error and a lot of wasted bread dough.

Anyway, the cookies. For me, it works best with cookies that are mostly people or animal shaped. Something to do with sympathetic magic, the parish priest said (six loaves of plain bread and—oh, all right, one berry scone, but don't tell the abbot!) And it has to be something made of dough. The puppeteers who put on the Punch and Judy shows in the park can make wooden puppets dance, but I could focus on wood until I got a splitting headache and it'd just lie there. Dough is all I can do. It's not a very useful skill.

Still, it's occasionally handy. If I can't get something at the back of a shelf, I can usually get a gingerbread man to climb up there and push it forward until I can grab it. We bake up a new batch once a week. Aunt Tabitha says that if nothing else, it's good advertising.

I've heard—well, overheard, I wasn't *supposed* to hear it—that there's some people who won't come into the bakery now that I'm here. I don't know if dancing gingerbread bothers them, or if it's the notion of a magicker baking their bread. I think Aunt Tabitha lost a couple of regulars when I started working, but she's never said anything about it. I figure if they'll let a little thing like that bother them, they deserve to miss out on the best sourdough in the city.

The gingerbread man finished his hornpipe and bowed to his audience, who applauded. Even Miss McGrammar unbent enough to smile, and she's one of those people who watches magic-folk like they're about to run mad or explode into a shower of frogs. The cookie blew a kiss to the Widow Holloway, who giggled as if she were a much younger woman, and then marched back to his bin.

Thank you, I told it. *That's enough for now.* It saluted me—this batch was rather military, now that I think of it, maybe we went heavy on the cardamom—and went back to being an ordinary cookie.

"Very nice," said Master Elwidge.

"It's not much," I said, embarrassed.

"Better than I can do," he said, and winked at me. I know he's another magicker, but I've never seen him do anything but straighten bent wood. Still, that's got to be more useful than making cookies dance.

When everyone had been shooed out of the shop—which took a while, in the case of Miss McGrammar—I went back into the kitchen, just in time to be accused of murder.

Chapter Three

"Wh-what?"

There was a new man in the bakery, and he didn't look like he was interested in tea or sweet buns. He was wearing dark purple robes past his ankles, and the hems weren't dusty at all. The street sweepers do a good job, once the snow's melted, but not *that* good. He definitely hadn't walked here.

"This is Inquisitor Oberon, Mona," said Aunt Tabitha, in the very careful voice she uses for customers that are being difficult. I looked at her, and she made a very tiny shake of her head. A warning, obviously, but against what?

"You, girl," said Inquisitor Oberon, folding his arms. "You claim to have found the body, do you not?"

"Uh..." That was a sneaky sort of question. "I found the body this morning when I came to work, yes."

"At *four in the morning?*" He looked at me over his glasses. They had tiny, fussy metal frames, the sort of glasses that a bird of prey would wear if its eyesight was starting to go.

"I'm a baker," I said. "I always come to work at four in the morning..." My voice sounded weak and scared, which was no good at all. I sounded like I was apologizing for the hours that bakers keep.

"That's true, *Your Lordship*," rumbled Constable Alphonse, also sounding apologetic for having the temerity to confirm my story.

From the Your Lordship, I knew that Inquisitor Oberon worked for the Duchess (if he'd been a member of the priesthood, he would have been *Your Holiness*, or *Your Worship*) but what a servant of the royal house was doing in our bakery—I mean, even if it was a murder, unless the victim was somebody really important, there was no reason for the royals to be involved. And if she was that important, why was she in our bakery, and why was she wearing mismatched socks?

"You're a *wizard*, are you not?" Oberon growled.

"I...sort of...I guess..." I looked helplessly at Aunt Tabitha. "I mean, I can make bread rise..."

"She's a fine baker," put in Aunt Tabitha firmly, as if this put to rest any question of guilt or innocence.

"There is a taint of magic around this girl's death," said Inquisitor Oberon, with such authority that it didn't occur to any of us until much later to ask how he knew, or what exactly that *meant.* "She was murdered here, in a bakery known to employ a wizard. A wizard who *conveniently* was the one to find the body."

The way he said "conveniently" made it sound like I'd been found standing over the body with a bloody baguette.

"But—" I started laughing. I couldn't help it. This was too stupid. "I don't even know who she is! Why would I want to kill her?"

"A question that we will aim to answer," said Inquisitor Oberon, pushing his glasses back up and straightening his shoulders. "Coroner, remove the body. Constables, bring the girl to the palace."

I stopped laughing. This didn't seem funny anymore. The horrible clenching in my stomach was coming back again.

"The palace?" asked Constable Montgomery—not questioning, I could tell, but simply surprised. You didn't bring prisoners to the palace. You took them to jail.

Inquisitor Oberon sniffed, exactly like Miss McGrammar does when we run out of lemon scones. "Her Grace, the Duchess, is concerned with what she perceives as the rash of murders by wizards. She insists on overseeing these cases herself. Constables, if you please!"

"But..." I said.

"Now wait just a minute—" Aunt Tabitha said.

"Oh, dear..." Uncle Alfred said.

And despite what any of us said, I found myself pushed into a coach, and driven away to the palace.

CONTRIBUTOR BIOGRAPHIES

Yaroslav Barsukov is a writer of fantasy, science fiction, and everything in between. His work has been nominated for the Nebula Award and the SCKA Award. A graduate of both the Moscow Engineering Physics Institute and the Vienna University of Technology, he's left one empire only to settle in another. After leaving his ball and chain at the workplace, Yaroslav goes on to write stories that deal with things he himself, thankfully, doesn't have to deal with. His short fiction appeared in *Galaxy's Edge* (edited by the great, late Mike Resnick), *Nature*, and *StarShipSofa*, among others. Bibliography, interviews, guest blog posts, and other goodies can be found at https://www.barsukov.com/

Rae Carson is a Hugo and Nebula finalist, and the *New York Times* best-selling author of numerous novels and short stories published by HarperCollins, Del Rey Star Wars, and Disney-Lucasfilm Press. Literary honors include the Spur Award, Morris Award finalist, Indie Next List, National Book Award longlist, and ALA Best Fiction for Young Adults, among others. Rae lives in Ohio with editor C.C. Finlay and their five rescue cats.

Nino Cipri is a queer and trans/nonbinary writer, editor, and educator. A graduate of the Clarion Writers' Workshop, and University of Kansas's MFA, Nino's fiction has been nominated for the Shirley Jackson, World Fantasy, Lambda, Nebula, and Hugo Awards. A multidisciplinary artist, Nino has also written plays, screenplays, and radio features; performed as a dancer, actor, and puppeteer; and worked as a stagehand, bookseller, bike mechanic, and labor organizer. Once upon a time, an angry person on the internet called Nino a verbal terrorist, which was pretty funny. Nino's 2019 story collection *Homesick* won the Dzanc Short Fiction Collection Prize and was chosen as one of the top ten books on the ALA's Over the Rainbow Reading List. Their novel *Finna* — about queer heartbreak, working retail, and wormholes — was published by Tor.com in 2020, and its sequel *Defekt* was released in 2021. Nino's YA horror debut, *Dead Girls Don't Dream*, will be published by Holt Young Readers in 2024.

Phenderson Djéli Clark is the award-winning and Hugo, Nebula, World Fantasy, and Sturgeon nominated author of the novel *A Master of Djinn*, and the novellas *Ring Shout*, *The Black God's Drums*, and *The Haunting of Tram Car 015*. His short stories have appeared in online venues such as Tor.com and in print anthologies including, *Hidden Youth* and *Black Boy Joy*. His upcoming middle grade novel, *Abeni's Song*, will be out in July 2023 from Starscape/Tor.

Leah Cypess is the author of the middle grade *Sisters Ever After* series, which retells fairy tales from the points of view of forgotten younger sisters. The first three books in the series, *Thornwood*, *Glass Slippers*, and *The Piper's Promise*, are out now. Leah has also written four young adult fantasy novels and numerous works of short fiction. She is a three-time Nebula Award finalist and a World Fantasy Award finalist. You can learn more about her and her books at www.leahcypess.com.

Meg Elison is a Hugo, Philip K. Dick and Locus award winning author, as well as a Nebula, Sturgeon, and Otherwise awards finalist. A prolific short story writer and essayist, Elison has been published in *Scientific American*, *McSweeney's*, *Fantasy & Science Fiction*, *Fangoria*, and *Best American Science Fiction and Fantasy*. Elison is a high school dropout and a graduate of UC Berkeley. She lives in Brooklyn. Visit her at megelison.com.

Oghenechovwe Donald Ekpeki is an African speculative fiction writer, editor & publisher from Nigeria. He has won the Nebula, Otherwise, Nommo, British & World Fantasy awards and been a finalist in the Hugo, Locus, Sturgeon, British Science Fiction and NAACP Image awards. His works have appeared in *Asimov's, F&SF, Uncanny Magazine, Tordotcom, Galaxy's Edge,* and others. He edited the *Bridging Worlds, Year's Best African Speculative Fiction* anthology and co-edited the *Dominion* and *Africa Risen* anthologies. He was a CanCon GOH and a guest of honour at the Afrofuturism themed ICFA 44 where he coined a new term/genre label: Afropantheology.

A. T. Greenblatt is a Nebula Award winning writer and mechanical engineer. She lives in New York City where she's known to frequently subject her friends to various cooking and home brewing experiments. Her work has been nominated for a Hugo, Locus, and Sturgeon Award, has been in multiple *Year's Best* anthologies, and has appeared in *Tor.com, Beneath Ceaseless Skies, Lightspeed,* and *Clarkesworld,* as well as other fine publications. You can find her online at atgreenblatt.com and on Bluesky at @AtGreenblatt.

Greg Kasavin is writer and creative director at Supergiant Games, the small independent studio that created 2020's highly acclaimed *Hades,* which earned more than 70 Game of the Year Awards as well as the Nebula award for Best Game Writing.

Ursula Vernon, aka T. Kingfisher, is the author of more than forty books, most recently *Thornhedge* and *A House With Good Bones.* Her work has won multiple Hugo, Nebula, Locus, and Dragon Awards, and on a good day she can be found in the garden, trying to photograph interesting bugs.

R.B. Lemberg is a queer, bigender immigrant originally from L'viv, Ukraine. Many of R.B.'s stories and poems are set in Bird-verse, an LGBTQIA+-focused secondary world. R.B.'s Birdverse novella *The Four Profound Weaves* has been a finalist for the Nebula, Ignyte, World Fantasy, and Locus awards; the book was also an Otherwise Award honoree. Their first novel *The Unbalancing* and short story collection *Geometries of Belonging*, both set in Birdverse, came out in 2022. You can find R.B. on Twitter at @rb_lemberg, on Mastodon at rblemberg@wandering.shop, on Patreon at http://patreon.com/rblemberg, and at rblemberg.net.

Tochi Onyebuchi is the author of *Goliath*, finalist for the Hurston/Wright Legacy Award, and *Riot Baby*, a finalist for the Hugo, Nebula, and NAACP Image Awards and winner of the New England Book Award for Fiction and the World Fantasy Award. His short fiction has appeared in *The Best American Science Fiction and Fantasy* and elsewhere. His non-fiction includes the book *(S)kinfolk* and has appeared in *The New York Times* and NPR, among other places. He has earned degrees from Yale University, New York University's Tisch School of the Arts, Columbia Law School, and the Paris Institute of Political Studies.

Aimee Picchi is a journalist by day and Nebula-nominated science fiction and fantasy writer by night. Her short fiction has been published in *Apex, Podcastle, Fireside Magazine*, and *Flash Fiction Online*, among other fine publications. She's a former classical musician (viola) who graduated from Juilliard Pre-College and the Eastman School of Music. She lives in Burlington, Vermont with her family. You can find her online at aimeepicchi.com or on Twitter @aimeepicchi.

Sarah Pinsker is the Hugo and Nebula winning author of *A Song For A New Day, We Are Satellites, Sooner or Later Everything Falls Into the Sea*, and over fifty works of short fiction. Her second collection, *Lost Places*, was published by Small Beer Press in 2023. She is also a singer/songwriter and toured nationally behind three albums on various independent labels. A fourth, *Something to Hold*, came out in 2021. She lives in Baltimore, Maryland with her wife and two weird dogs.

Vina Jie-Min Prasad is a Singaporean writer working against the world-machine. She has been a finalist for the Nebula, Hugo, Astounding, Sturgeon and Locus Awards. Her short fiction has appeared in places such as *Clarkesworld, Uncanny Magazine,* and *Fireside Fiction.* You can find links to her work at vinaprasad.com.

Cat Rambo's 300+ fiction publications include stories in *Asimov's, Clarkesworld Magazine,* and *The Magazine of Fantasy and Science Fiction.* In 2020 they won the Nebula Award for their fantasy novelette *Carpe Glitter.* They are a former two-term President of the Science Fiction and Fantasy Writers Association (SFWA). Their most recent works are the space opera *Devil's Gun* (Tor Macmillan, 2023) and anthology *The Reinvented Detective* (Arc Manor, 2023), co-edited with Jennifer Brozek. For more about Cat, as well as links to fiction and their popular online school, The Rambo Academy for Wayward Writers, see catrambo.com.

Kelly Robson is a Canadian short fiction writer. Her novelette "A Human Stain" won the 2018 Nebula Award, and her short fiction won the 2022, 2019, and 2016 Aurora Awards. She has been a finalist for the Hugo, Nebula, World Fantasy, Theodore Sturgeon, Locus, and Astounding awards. Her short fiction collection *Alias Space and Other Stories* was published by Subterranean Press in 2022.

Jason Sanford is an award-winning science fiction and fantasy writer who's also a passionate advocate for fellow authors, creators, and fans, in particular through reporting in his Genre Grapevine column (for which he is a three-time finalist for the Hugo Award for Best Fan Writer). He's also published dozens of stories in magazines such as *Apex Magazine, Asimov's Science Fiction, Interzone,* and *Beneath Ceaseless Skies* along with appearances in a number of *Year's Best* anthologies and *The New Voices of Science Fiction.* His first novel *Plague Birds* was a finalist for both the 2022 Nebula Award and the 2022 Philip K. Dick Award. Born and raised in the American South, Jason's previous experience includes work as an archaeologist and as a Peace Corps Volunteer. His website is www.jasonsanford.com.

Bonnie Jo Stufflebeam is the author of *Grim Root* and *Where You Linger & Other Stories*. Her fiction has appeared in over 90 publications such as *LeVar Burton Reads* and *Popular Science*, as well as in six languages. She has been a Nebula nominee twice. By day, she works as a Narrative Designer writing games. She lives with her partner and two cats, Wednesday and Ichabod.

Eugenia Triantafyllou is a Greek author and artist with a flair for dark things. Her work has been nominated for the Ignyte, Nebula, and World Fantasy Awards, and she is a graduate of Clarion West Writers Workshop. You can find her stories in *Reactor* (formerly *Tor.com*), *Uncanny*, *Strange Horizons*, and other venues. She currently lives in Athens with a boy and a dog. Find her on Twitter or Bluesky @foxesandroses, her IG @eugeniatriantafyllou, or her website https://eugeniatriantafyllou.wordpress.com.

Martha Wells has been a science fiction and fantasy author since her first fantasy novel was published in 1993. Her *New York Times* Bestselling series *The Murderbot Diaries* has won Nebula Awards, Hugo Awards, Locus Awards, and an American Library Association/YALSA Alex Award. Her work also includes *The Books of the Raksura* series, the Ile-Rien series, and several other fantasy novels, most recently *Witch King* (Tordotcom, 2023), as well as short fiction, non-fiction, and media tie-ins for *Star Wars*, *Stargate: Atlantis*, and *Magic: The Gathering*. Her work has also appeared on the Philip K. Dick Award ballot, the British Science Fiction Association Award ballot, the *USA Today* Bestseller List, the *Sunday Times* Bestseller List, and has been translated into twenty-six languages.

John Wiswell is a disabled writer who lives where New York keeps all its trees. His fiction has been translated into ten languages, and he has won both the Nebula Award for Best Short Story for "Open House on Haunted Hill" and the Locus Award for Best Novelette for "That Story Isn't The Story." His debut novel, *Someone You Can Build A Nest In,* will be out from DAW Books in the U.S. and Jo Fletcher Books in the U.K. in April of 2024. You can find him around the internet via his Linktree: https://linktr.ee/johnwiswell

Caroline M. Yoachim is a three-time Hugo and six-time Nebula Award finalist. Her short stories have been translated into several languages and reprinted in multiple best-of anthologies, including four times in *Best American Science Fiction and Fantasy.* Yoachim's short story collection *Seven Wonders of a Once and Future World & Other Stories* and the print chapbook of her novelette *The Archronology of Love* are available from Fairwood Press. For more, check out her website at carolineyoachim.com.

COPYRIGHT INFORMATION

Printed in Great Britain
by Amazon